THE CITY & THE CITY

CHINA MIÉVILLE is the award-winning author of several books, including *The City & The City* and *Embassytown*. He lives and works in London.

By *China Miéville*

King Rat

Perdido Street Station

The Scar

Iron Council

Looking for Jake and Other Stories

Un Lun Dun

The City & The City

Kraken

Embassytown

Railsea

Three Moments of an Explosion: Stories

CHINA MIÉVILLE

THE CITY & THE CITY

PAN BOOKS

First published in Great Britain 2009 by Macmillan

This edition published 2011 by Pan Books
an imprint of Pan Macmillan
The Smithson, 6 Briset Street, London EC1M 5NR
EU representative: Macmillan Publishers Ireland Ltd, 1st Floor,
The Liffey Trust Centre, 117–126 Sheriff Street Upper,
Dublin 1, D01 YC43
Associated companies throughout the world
www.panmacmillan.com

ISBN 978-0-330-53419-2

26

A CIP catalogue record for this book is available from
the British Library.

Typeset by Ellipsis Books Ltd, Glasgow
Printed in the UK by CPI Group (UK) Ltd, Croydon, CR0 4YY

Visit www.panmacmillan.com to read more about all our books
and to buy them. You will also find features, author interviews and
news of any author events, and you can sign up for e-newsletters
so that you're always first to hear about our new releases.

In loving memory of my mother,

Claudia Lightfoot

ACKNOWLEDGEMENTS

For all their help with this book I'm extremely grateful to Stefanie Bierwerth, Mark Bould, Christine Cabello, Mic Cheetham, Julie Crisp, Simon Kavanagh, Penny Haynes, Chloe Healy, Deanna Hoak, Peter Lavery, Farah Mendlesohn, Jemima Miéville, David Moench, Sue Moe, Sandy Rankin, Maria Rejt, Rebecca Saunders, Max Schaefer, Jane Soodalter, Jesse Soodalter, Dave Stevenson, Paul Taunton, and to my editors Chris Schluep and Jeremy Trevathan. My sincere thanks to all at Del Rey and Macmillan. Thanks to John Curran Davis for his wonderful translations of Bruno Schulz.

Among the countless writers to whom I'm indebted, those I'm particularly aware of and grateful to with regard to this book include Raymond Chandler, Franz Kafka, Alfred Kubin, Jan Morris, and Bruno Schulz.

'Deep inside the town there open up, so to speak, double streets, doppelganger streets, mendacious and delusive streets.'

—Bruno Schulz,
The Cinnamon Shops and Other Stories

PART ONE

BESŹEL

CHAPTER ONE

I COULD NOT SEE THE STREET or much of the estate. We were enclosed by dirt-coloured blocks, from windows out of which leaned vested men and women with morning hair and mugs of drink, eating breakfast and watching us. This open ground between the buildings had once been sculpted. It pitched like a golf course – a child's mimicking of geography. Maybe they had been going to wood it and put in a pond. There was a copse but the saplings were dead.

The grass was weedy, threaded with paths footwalked between rubbish, rutted by wheel tracks. There were police at various tasks. I wasn't the first detective there – I saw Bardo Naustin and a couple of others – but I was the most senior. I followed the sergeant to where most of my colleagues clustered, between a low derelict tower and a skateboard park ringed by big drum-shaped trash bins. Just beyond it we could hear the docks. A bunch of kids sat on a wall before standing officers. The gulls coiled over the gathering.

'Inspector.' I nodded at whomever that was. Someone offered a coffee but I shook my head and looked at the woman I had come to see.

She lay near the skate ramps. Nothing is still like the dead are still. The wind moves their hair, as it moved hers, and they don't respond at all. She was in an ugly pose, with legs crooked as if about to get up, her arms in a strange bend. Her face was to the ground.

A young woman, brown hair pulled into pigtails poking up like plants. She was almost naked, and it was sad to see her skin smooth that cold morning, unbroken by gooseflesh. She wore only laddered stockings, one high heel on. Seeing me look for it, a sergeant waved at me from a way off, from where she guarded the dropped shoe.

It was a couple of hours since the body had been discovered. I looked her over. I held my breath and bent down toward the dirt, to look at her face, but I could only see one open eye.

'Where's Shukman?'

'Not here yet, Inspector . . .'

'Someone call him, tell him to get a move on.' I smacked my watch. I was in charge of what we called the *mise-en-crime*. No one would move her until Shukman the patho had come, but there were other things to do. I checked sightlines. We were out of the way and the garbage containers obscured us, but I could feel attention on us like insects, from all over the estate. We milled.

There was a wet mattress on its edge between two of the bins, by a spread of rusting iron pieces interwoven with discarded chains. 'That was on her.' The constable who spoke was Lizbyet Corwi, a smart young woman I'd worked with a couple of times. 'Couldn't exactly say she was well hidden, but it sort of made her look like a pile of rubbish, I guess.' I could see a rough rectangle of darker earth surrounding the dead woman – the remains of the mattress-sheltered dew. Naustin was squatting by it, staring at the earth.

'The kids who found her tipped it half off,' Corwi said.

4

'How did they find her?'

Corwi pointed at the earth, at little scuffs of animal paws.

'Stopped her getting mauled. Ran like hell when they saw what it was, made the call. Our lot, when they arrived . . .' She glanced at two patrolmen I didn't know.

'They moved it?'

She nodded. 'See if she was still alive, they said.'

'What are their names?'

'Shushkil and Briamiv.'

'And these are the finders?' I nodded at the guarded kids. There were two girls, two guys. Midteens, cold, looking down.

'Yeah. Chewers.'

'Early morning pick-you-up?'

'That's dedication, hm?' she said. 'Maybe they're up for junkies of the month or some shit. They got here a bit before seven. The skate pit's organised that way, apparently. It's only been built a couple of years, used to be nothing, but the locals've got their shift patterns down. Midnight to nine a.m., chewers only; nine to eleven, local gang plans the day; eleven to midnight, skateboards and rollerblades.'

'They carrying?'

'One of the boys has a little shiv, but really little. Couldn't mug a milkrat with it – it's a toy. And a chew each. That's it.' She shrugged. 'The dope wasn't on them; we found it by the wall, but' – shrug – 'they were the only ones around.'

She motioned over one of our colleagues and opened the bag he carried. Little bundles of resin-slathered grass. *Feld* is its street name – a tough crossbreed *of Catha edulis* spiked with tobacco and caffeine and stronger stuff, and fibreglass threads or similar to abrade the gums and get it into the blood. Its name is a trilingual pun: it's *khat* where it's grown, and the animal called 'cat' in English is *feld* in our own language. I sniffed it and it was pretty low-grade stuff. I walked over to where the four teenagers shivered in their puffy jackets.

"*Sup, policeman?*' said one boy in a Besź-accented approximation of hip-hop English. He looked up and met my eye, but he was pale. Neither he nor any of his companions looked well. From where they sat they could not have seen the dead woman, but they did not even look in her direction.

They must have known we'd find the *feld*, and that we'd know it was theirs. They could have said nothing, just run.

'I'm Inspector Borlú,' I said. 'Extreme Crime Squad.'

I did not say *I'm Tyador*. A difficult age to question, this – too old for first names, euphemisms and toys, not yet old enough to be straightforward opponents in interviews, when at least the rules were clear. 'What's your name?' The boy hesitated, considered using whatever slang handle he'd granted himself, did not.

'Vilyem Barichi.'

'You found her?' He nodded, and his friends nodded after him. 'Tell me.'

'We come here because, 'cause, and . . .' Vilyem waited, but I said nothing about his drugs. He looked down. 'And we seen something under that mattress and we pulled it off.

'There was some . . .' His friends looked up as Vilyem hesitated, obviously superstitious.

'Wolves?' I said. They glanced at each other.

'Yeah man, some scabby little pack was nosing around there and . . .

'So we thought it . . .'

'How long after you got here?' I said.

Vilyem shrugged. 'Don't know. Couple hours?'

6

'Anyone else around?'

'Saw some guys over there a while back.'

'Dealers?' A shrug.

'And there was a van came up on the grass and come over here and went off again after a bit. We didn't speak to no one.'

'When was the van?'

'Don't know.'

'It was still dark.' That was one of the girls.

'Okay. Vilyem, you guys, we're going to get you some breakfast, something to drink, if you want.' I motioned to their guards. 'Have we spoken to the parents?' I asked.

'On their way, boss; except hers' – pointing to one of the girls – 'we can't reach.'

'So keep trying. Get them to the centre now.'

The four teens looked at each other. 'This is bullshit, man,' the boy who was not Vilyem said, uncertainly. He knew that according to some politics he should oppose my instruction, but he wanted to go with my subordinate. Black tea and bread and paperwork, the boredom and striplights, all so much not like the peeling back of that wet-heavy, cumbersome mattress, in the yard, in the dark.

STEPEN SHUKMAN AND HIS ASSISTANT Hamd Hamzinic had arrived. I looked at my watch. Shukman ignored me. When he bent to the body he wheezed. He certified death. He made observations that Hamzinic wrote down.

'Time?' I said.

'Twelve hours-ish,' Shukman said. He pressed down on one of the woman's limbs. She rocked. In rigor, and unstable on the ground as she was, she probably assumed the position of her death lying on other contours. 'She wasn't killed here.' I

7

had heard it said many times he was good at his job but had seen no evidence that he was anything but competent.

'Done?' he said to one of the scene techs. She took two more shots from different angles and nodded. Shukman rolled the woman over with Hamzinic's help. She seemed to fight him with her cramped motionlessness. Turned, she was absurd, like someone playing at dead insect, her limbs crooked, rocking on her spine.

She looked up at us from below a fluttering fringe. Her face was set in a startled strain: she was endlessly surprised by herself. She was young. She was heavily made up, and it was smeared across a badly battered face. It was impossible to say what she looked like, what face those who knew her would see if they heard her name. We might know better later, when she relaxed into her death. Blood marked her front, dark as dirt. Flash flash of cameras.

'Well, hello cause of death,' Shukman said to the wounds in her chest.

On her left cheek, curving under the jaw, a long red split. She had been cut half the length of her face.

The wound was smooth for several centimetres, tracking precisely along her flesh like the sweep of a paintbrush. Where it went below her jaw, under the overhang of her mouth, it jagged ugly and ended or began with a deep torn hole in the soft tissue behind her bone. She looked unseeingly at me.

'Take some without the flash, too,' I said.

Like several others I looked away while Shukman murmured – it felt prurient to watch. Uniformed *mise-en-crime* technical investigators, *mectecs* in our slang, searched in an expanding circle. They overturned rubbish and foraged among the grooves

8

where vehicles had driven. They lay down reference marks, and photographed.

'Alright then.' Shukman rose. 'Let's get her out of here.' A couple of the men hauled her onto a stretcher.

'Jesus Christ,' I said, 'cover her.' Someone found a blanket I don't know from where, and they started again towards Shukman's vehicle.

'I'll get going this afternoon,' he said. 'Will I see you?' I wagged my head noncommittally. I walked towards Corwi.

'Naustin,' I called, when I was positioned so that Corwi would be at the edge of our conversation. She glanced up and came slightly closer.

'Inspector,' said Naustin.

'Go through it.'

He sipped his coffee and looked at me nervously.

'Hooker?' he said. 'First impressions, Inspector. This area, beat-up, naked? And . . .' He pointed at his face, her exaggerated makeup. 'Hooker.'

'Fight with a client?'

'Yeah but . . . If it was just the body wounds, you know, you'd, then you're looking at, maybe she won't do what he wants, whatever. He lashes out. But this.' He touched his cheek again uneasily. 'That's different.'

'A sicko?'

He shrugged. 'Maybe. He cuts her, kills her, dumps her. Cocky bastard too, doesn't give a shit that we're going to find her.'

'Cocky or stupid.'

'Or cocky *and* stupid.'

'So a cocky, stupid sadist,' I said. He raised his eyes, *Maybe*.

'Alright,' I said. 'Could be. Do the rounds of the local girls.

9

Ask a uniform who knows the area. Ask if they've had trouble with anyone recently. Let's get a photo circulated, put a name to Fulana Detail.' I used the generic name for woman-unknown. 'First off I want you to question Barichi and his mates, there. Be nice, Bardo, they didn't have to call this in. I mean that. And get Yaszek in with you.' Ramira Yaszek was an excellent questioner. 'Call me this afternoon?' When he was out of earshot I said to Corwi, 'A few years ago we'd not have had half as many guys on the murder of a working girl.'

'We've come a long way,' she said. She wasn't much older than the dead woman.

'I doubt Naustin's delighted to be on streetwalker duty, but you'll notice he's not complaining,' I said.

'We've come a long way,' she said.

'So?' I raised an eyebrow. Glanced in Naustin's direction. I waited. I remembered Corwi's work on the Shulban disappearance, a case considerably more Byzantine than it had initially appeared.

'It's just, I guess, you know, we should keep in mind other possibilities,' she said.

'Tell me.'

'Her makeup,' she said. 'It's all, you know, earths and browns. It's been put on thick, but it's not—' She vamp-pouted. 'And did you notice her hair?' I had. 'Not dyed. Take a drive with me up GunterStrász, around by the arena, any of the girls' hangouts. Two-thirds blonde, I reckon. And the rest are black or bloodred or some shit. And . . .' She fingered the air as if it were hair. 'It's dirty, but it's a lot better than mine.' She ran her hand through her own split ends.

For many of the streetwalkers in Besźel, especially in areas like this, food and clothes for their kids came first; *feld* or crack

10

for themselves; food for themselves; then sundries, in which list conditioner would come low. I glanced at the rest of the officers, at Naustin gathering himself to go.

'Okay,' I said. 'Do you know this area?'

'Well,' she said, 'it's a bit off the track, you know? This is hardly even Besźel, really. My beat's Lestov. They called a few of us in when they got the bell. But I did a tour here a couple years ago – I know it a bit.'

Lestov itself was already almost a suburb, six or so k out of the city centre, and we were south of that, over the Yovic Bridge on a bit of land between Bulkya Sound and, nearly, the mouth where the river joined the sea. Technically an island, though so close and conjoined to the mainland by ruins of industry you would never think of it as such, Kordvenna was estates, warehouses, low-rent bodegas scribble-linked by endless graffiti. It was far enough from Besźel's heart that it was easy to forget, unlike more inner-city slums.

'How long were you here?' I said.

'Six months, standard. What you'd expect: street theft, high kids smacking shit out of each other, drugs, hooking.'

'Murder?'

'Two or three in my time. Drugs stuff. Mostly stops short of that, though: the gangs are pretty smart at punishing each other without bringing in ECS.'

'Someone's fucked up then.'

'Yeah. Or doesn't care.'

'Okay,' I said. 'I want you on this. What are you doing at the moment?'

'Nothing that can't wait.'

'I want you to relocate for a bit. Got any contacts here still?' She pursed her lips. 'Track them down if you can; if not, have

11

a word with some of the local guys, see who their singers are. I want you on the ground. Listen out, go round the estate – what's this place called again?'

'Pocost Village.' She laughed without humour; I raised an eyebrow.

'It takes a village,' I said. 'See what you can turn up.'

'My commissar won't like it.'

'I'll deal with him. It's Bashazin, right?'

'You'll square it? So am I being seconded?'

'Let's not call it anything right now. Right now I'm just asking you to focus on this. And report directly to me.' I gave her the numbers of my cell phone and my office. 'You can show me around the delights of Kordvenna later. And . . .' I glanced up at Naustin, and she saw me do it. 'Just keep an eye on things.'

'He's probably right. Probably a cocky sadist trick, boss.'

'Probably. Let's find out why she keeps her hair so clean.'

There was a league-table of instinct. We all knew that in his street-beating days, Commissar Kerevan broke several cases following leads that made no logical sense; and that Chief Inspector Marcoberg was devoid of any such breaks, and that his decent record was the result, rather, of slog. We would never call inexplicable little insights 'hunches,' for fear of drawing the universe's attention. But they happened, and you knew you had been in the proximity of one that had come through if you saw a detective kiss his or her fingers and touch his or her chest where a pendant to Warsha, patron saint of inexplicable inspirations, would, theoretically, hang.

Officers Shushkil and Briamiv were surprised, then defensive, finally sulky when I asked them what they were doing

12

moving the mattress. I put them on report. If they had apologised I would have let it go. It was depressingly common to see police boots tracked through blood residue, fingerprints smeared and spoiled, samples corrupted or lost.

A little group of journalists was gathering at the edges of the open land. Petrus Something-or-other, Valdir Mohli, a young guy called Rackhaus, a few others.

'Inspector!'

'Inspector Borlú!' Even: 'Tyador!'

Most of the press had always been polite, and amenable to my suggestions about what they withhold. In the last few years, new, more salacious and aggressive papers had started, inspired and in some cases controlled by British or North American owners. It had been inevitable, and in truth our established local outlets were staid to dull. What was troubling was less the trend to sensation, nor even the irritating behaviour of the new press's young writers, but more their tendency to dutifully follow a script written before they were born. Rackhaus, who wrote for a weekly called *Rejal!*, for example. Surely when he bothered me for facts he knew I would not give him, surely when he attempted to bribe junior officers, and sometimes succeeded, he did not have to say, as he tended to: 'The public has a right to know!'

I did not even understand him the first time he said it. In Besź the word 'right' is polysemic enough to evade the peremptory meaning he intended. I had to mentally translate into English, in which I am passably fluent, to make sense of the phrase. His fidelity to the cliché transcended the necessity to communicate. Perhaps he would not be content until I snarled and called him a vulture, a ghoul.

'You know what I'm going to say,' I told them. The stretched tape separated us. 'There'll be a press conference this afternoon, at ECS Centre.'

'What time?' My photograph was being taken.

'You'll be informed, Petrus.'

Rackhaus said something that I ignored. As I turned, I saw past the edges of the estate to the end of GunterStrász, between the dirty brick buildings. Trash moved in the wind. It might be anywhere. An elderly woman was walking slowly away from me in a shambling sway. She turned her head and looked at me. I was struck by her motion, and I met her eyes. I wondered if she wanted to tell me something. In my glance I took in her clothes, her way of walking, of holding herself, and looking.

With a hard start, I realised that she was not on GunterStrász at all, and that I should not have seen her.

Immediately and flustered I looked away, and she did the same, with the same speed. I raised my head, towards an aircraft on its final descent. When after some seconds I looked back up, unnoticing the old woman stepping heavily away, I looked carefully instead of at her in her foreign street at the facades of the nearby and local GunterStrász, that depressed zone.

CHAPTER TWO

I HAD A CONSTABLE DROP ME north of Lestov, near the bridge. I did not know the area well. I'd been to the island, of course, visited the ruins, when I was a schoolboy and occasionally since, but my rat-runs were elsewhere. Signs showing directions to local destinations were bolted to the outsides of pastry bakers and little workshops, and I followed them to a tram stop in a pretty square. I waited between a care-home marked with an hourglass logo, and a spice shop, the air around it cinnamon scented.

When the tram came, tinnily belling, shaking in its ruts, I did not sit, though the carriage was half-empty. I knew we would pick up passengers as we went north to Besźel centre. I stood close to the window and saw right out into the city, into these unfamiliar streets.

The woman, her ungainly huddle below that old mattress, sniffed by scavengers. I phoned Naustin on my cell.

'Is the mattress being tested for trace?'

'Should be, sir.'

'Check. If the techs are on it we're fine, but Briamiv and his buddy could fuck up a full stop at the end of a sentence.' Perhaps she was new to the life. Maybe if we'd found her a week later her hair would have been electric blonde.

These regions by the river are intricate, many buildings a century or several centuries old. The tram took its tracks through byways where Besźel, at least half of everything we passed, seemed to lean in and loom over us. We wobbled and slowed, behind local cars and those elsewhere, came to a cross-hatching where the Besź buildings were antique shops. That trade had been doing well, as well as anything did in the city for some years, hand-downs polished and spruced as people emptied their apartments of heirlooms for a few Besźmarques.

Some editorialists were optimists. While their leaders roared as relentlessly at each other as they ever had in the Cityhouse, many of the new breed of all parties were working together to put Besźel first. Each drip of foreign investment – and to everyone's surprise there were drips – brought forth encomia. Even a couple of high-tech companies had recently moved in, though it was hard to believe it was in response to Besźel's fatuous recent self-description as 'Silicon Estuary.'

I got off by the statue of King Val. Downtown was busy: I stop-started, excusing myself to citizens and local tourists, unseeing others with care, till I reached the blocky concrete of ECS Centre. Two groups of tourists were being shepherded by Besź guides. I stood on the steps and looked down Uropa-Strász. It took me several tries to get a signal.

'Corwi?'

'Boss?'

'You know that area: is there any chance we're looking at breach?'

There were seconds of silence.

'Doesn't seem likely. That area's mostly pretty total. And Pocost Village, that whole project, certainly is.'

'Some of GunterStrász, though . . .'

16

'Yeah but. The closest crosshatching is hundreds of metres away. They couldn't have . . .' It would have been an extraordinary risk on the part of the murderer or murderers. 'I reckon we can assume,' she said.

'Alright. Let me know how you get on. I'll check in soon.'

I HAD PAPERWORK ON OTHER CASES that I opened, establishing them a while in holding patterns like circling aircraft. A woman beaten to death by her boyfriend, who had managed to evade us so far, despite tracers on his name and his prints at the airport. Styelim was an old man who had surprised an addict breaking and entering, been hit once, fatally, with the spanner he himself had been wielding. That case would not close. A young man called Avid Avid, left bleeding from the head after taking a kerb-kiss from a racist, 'Ébru Filth' written on the wall above him. For that I was coordinating with a colleague from Special Division, Shenvoi, who had, since some time before Avid's murder, been undercover in Besźel's far right.

Ramira Yaszek called while I ate lunch at my desk. 'Just done questioning those kids, sir.'

'And?'

'You should be glad they don't know their rights better, because if they did Naustin'd be facing charges now.' I rubbed my eyes and swallowed my mouthful.

'What did he do?'

'Barichi's mate Sergev was lippy, so Naustin asked him the bareknuckle question across the mouth, said he was the prime suspect.' I swore. 'It wasn't that hard, and at least it made it easier for me to *gudcop*.' We had stolen *gudcop* and *badcop* from English, verbed them. Naustin was one of those who'd switch to hard questioning too easily. There are some suspects that methodology works on, who need to fall down stairs during an interrogation, but a sulky teenage chewer is not one.

'Anyway, no harm done,' Yaszek said. 'Their stories tally. They're out, the four of them, in that bunch of trees. Bit of naughty naughty probably. They were there for a couple of hours at least. At some point during that time – and don't ask for anything more exact because you aren't going to get it beyond 'still dark' – one of the girls sees that van come up onto the grass to the skate park. She doesn't think much of it because people do come up there all times of day and night to do business, to dump stuff, what have you. It drives around, up past the skate park, comes back. After a while it speeds off.'

'Speeds?'

I scribbled in my notebook, trying one-handedly to pull up my email on my PC. The connection broke more than once. Big attachments on an inadequate system.

'Yeah. It was in a hurry and buggering its suspension. That's how she noticed it was going.'

'Description?'

'"Grey." She doesn't know from vans.'

'Get her looking at some pictures, see if we can ID the make.'

'On it, sir. I'll let you know. Later at least two other cars or vans come up for whatever reason, for business, according to Barichi.'

'That could complicate tyre tracks.'

'After an hour or whatever of groping, this girl mentions the van to the others and they go check it out, in case it was dumping. Says sometimes you get old stereos, shoes, books, all kinds of shit chucked out.'

18

'And they find her.' Some of my messages had come through. There was one from one of the mectec photographers, and I opened it and began to scroll through his images.

'They find her.'

COMMISSAR GADLEM CALLED ME IN. His soft-spoken theatricality, his mannered gentleness, was unsubtle, but he had always let me do my thing. I sat while he tapped at his keyboard and swore. I could see what must be database passwords stuck on scraps of paper to the side of his screen.

'So?' he said. 'The housing estate?' Yes.

'Where is it?'

'South, suburbs. Young woman, stab wounds. Shukman's got her.'

'Prostitute?'

'Could be.'

'Could be,' he said, cupped his ear, 'and yet. I can hear it. Well, onward, follow your nose. Tell if you ever feel like sharing the whys of that "and yet," won't you? Who's your sub?'

'Naustin. And I've got a beat cop helping out. Corwi. Grade-one constable. Knows the area.'

'That's her beat?' I nodded. Close enough.

'What else is open?'

'On my desk?' I told him. The commissar nodded. Even with the others, he granted me the leeway to follow Fulana Detail.

'SO DID YOU SEE the whole business?'

It was close to ten o'clock in the evening, more than forty hours since we had found the victim. Corwi drove – she made no effort to disguise her uniform, despite that we had an unmarked car – through the streets around GunterStrász. I had not been home until very late the previous night, and after a morning on my own in these same streets now I was there again.

There were places of crosshatch in the larger streets and a few elsewhere, but that far out the bulk of the area was total. Few antique Besź stylings, few steep roofs or many-paned windows: these were hobbled factories and warehouses. A handful of decades old, often broken-glassed, at half capacity if open. Boarded facades. Grocery shops fronted with wire. Older fronts in tumbledown of classical Besź style. Some houses colonised and made chapels and drug houses: some burnt out and left as crude carbon renditions of themselves.

The area was not crowded, but it was far from empty. Those who were out looked like landscape, like they were always there. There had been fewer that morning but not very markedly.

'Did you see Shukman working on the body?'

'No.' I was looking at what we passed, referring to my map. 'I got there after he was done.'

'Squeamish?' she said.

'No.'

'Well . . .' She smiled and turned the car. 'You'd have to say that even if you were.'

'True,' I said, though it was not.

She pointed out what passed for landmarks. I did not tell her I had been in Kordvenna early in the day, sounding these places. Corwi did not try to disguise her police clothes because that way those who saw us, who might otherwise think we were there to entrap them, would know that was not our intent; and the fact that we were not in a bruise, as we called the black-

20

and-blue police cars, told them that neither were we there to harass them. Intricate contracts!

Most of those around us were in Besźel so we saw them. Poverty deshaped the already staid, drab cuts and colours that enduringly characterise Besź clothes – what has been called the city's fashionless fashion. Of the exceptions, some we realised when we glanced were elsewhere, so unsaw, but the younger Besź were also more colourful, their clothes more pictured, than their parents.

The majority of the Besź men and women (does this need saying?) were doing nothing but walking from one place to another, from late-shift work, from homes to other homes or shops. Still, though, the way we watched what we passed made it a threatening geography, and there were sufficient furtive actions occurring that did not feel like the rankest paranoia.

'This morning I found a few of the locals I used to talk to,' Corwi said. 'Asked if they'd heard anything.' She took us through a darkened place where the balance of crosshatch shifted, and we were silent until the streetlamps around us became again taller and familiarly deco-angled. Under those lights – the street we were on visible in a perspective curve away from us – women stood by the walls selling sex. They watched our approach guardedly. 'I didn't have much luck,' Corwi said.

She had not even had a photograph on that earlier expedition. That early it had been aboveboard contacts: it had been liquor-store clerks; the priests of squat local churches, some the last of the worker-priests, brave old men tattooed with the sickle-and-rood on their biceps and forearms, on the shelves behind them Besź translations of Gutiérrez, Rauschenbusch,

Canaan Banana. It had been stoop-sitters. All Corwi had been able to do was ask what they could tell her about events in Pocost Village. They had heard about the murder but knew nothing.

Now we had a picture. Shukman had given it to me. I brandished it as we emerged from the car: literally I brandished it, so the women would see that I brought something to them, that that was the purpose of our visit, not to make arrests.

Corwi knew some of them. They smoked and watched us. It was cold, and like everyone who saw them I wondered at their stockinged legs. We were affecting their business of course – plenty of locals passing by looked up at us and looked away again. I saw a bruise slow down the traffic as it passed us – they must have seen an easy arrest – but the driver and his passenger saw Corwi's uniform and sped again with a salute. I waved back to their rear lights.

'What do you want?' a woman asked. Her boots were high and cheap. I showed her the picture.

They had cleaned up Fulana Detail's face. There were marks left – scrapes were visible below the makeup. They could have eradicated them completely from the picture, but the shock those wounds occasioned were useful in questioning. They had taken the picture before they shaved her head. She did not look peaceful. She looked impatient.

'I don't know her.'

'I don't know her.' I did not see recognition quickly disguised. They gathered in the grey light of the lamp, to the consternation of punters hovering at the edge of the local darkness, passed the picture among themselves and whether or not they made sympathy noises, did not know Fulana.

22

'What happened?' I gave the woman who asked my card. She was dark, Semitic or Turkish somewhere back. Her Besź was unaccented.

'We're trying to find out.'

'Do we need to worry?'

'I . . .'

After I paused Corwi said, 'We'll tell you if we think you do, Sayra.'

We stopped by a group of young men drinking strong wine outside a pool hall. Corwi took a little of their ribaldry then passed the photograph round.

'Why are we here?' My question was quiet. 'They're entry-level gangsters, boss,' she told me. 'Watch how they react.' But they gave little away if they did know anything. They returned the photograph and took my card impassively.

We repeated this at other gatherings, and afterwards each time we waited several minutes in our car, far enough away that a troubled member of any of the groups might excuse himself or herself and come find us, tell us some dissident scrap that might push us by whatever byways towards the details and family of our dead woman. No one did. I gave my card to many people and wrote down in my notebook the names and descriptions of those few that Corwi told me mattered.

'That's pretty much everyone I used to know,' she said. Some of the men and women had recognised her, but it had not seemed to make much difference to how she was received. When we agreed that we had finished it was after two in the morning. The half-moon was washed out: after a last inter-vention we had come to a stop, were standing in a street depleted of even its latest-night frequenters.

'She's still a question mark.' Corwi was surprised.

'I'll arrange to have the posters put around the area.'

'Really, boss? Commissar'll go for that?' We spoke quietly. I wove my fingers into the wire mesh of a fence around a lot filled only with concrete and scrub.

'Yeah,' I said. 'He'll roll over. It's not that much.'

'It's a few uniforms for a few hours, and he's not going to . . . not for a . . .'

'We have to shoot for an ID. Fuck it, I'll put them up myself.' I would arrange for them to be sent out to each of the city's divisions. When we turned up a name, if Fulana's story was as we had tentatively intuited, what few resources we had would vanish. We were milking leeway that would eradicate itself.

'You're the boss, boss.'

'Not really, but I'm the boss of this for a little bit.'

'Shall we?' She indicated the car.

'I'll walk it to a tram.'

'Serious? Come on, you'll be hours.' But I waved her off. I walked away to the sounds only of my own steps and some frenzied backstreet dog, towards where the grey glare of our lamps was effaced and I was lit by foreign orange light.

SHUKMAN WAS MORE SUBDUED in his lab than out in the world. I had been on the phone to Yaszek asking for the video of the kids' interrogation, the previous day, when Shukman contacted me and told me to come. It was cold, of course, and fuggy with chemicals. There was as much dark and many-stained wood as steel in the huge windowless room. There were notice boards on the walls, from each of which grew thickets of papers.

Dirt seemed to lurk in the room's corners, on the edges of

its workstations: but once I had run a finger along a grubby-looking groove by the raised spill-stopper, and it had come back clean. The stains were old. Shukman stood at the head of a steel dissecting table on which, covered with a slightly stained sheet, the contours of her face plain, was our Fulana, staring as we discussed her.

I looked at Hamzinic. He was only slightly older, I suspected, than the dead woman. He stood respectfully close by, his hands folded. By chance or not he stood next to a pinboard to which was attached among the postcards and memos a small gaudy *shahada*. Hamd Hamzinic was what the murderers of Avid Avid would also term an *ébru*. These days the term was used mainly by the old-fashioned, the racist, or in a turnabout provocation by the epithet's targets: one of the best-known Besź hip-hop groups was named Ébru W.A.

Technically of course the word was ludicrously inexact for at least half of those to whom it was applied. But for at least two hundred years, since refugees from the Balkans had come hunting sanctuary, quickly expanding the city's Muslim population, *ébru*, the antique Besź word for 'Jew,' had been press-ganged into service to include the new immigrants, become a collective term for both populations. It was in Besźel's previously Jewish ghettos that the Muslim newcomers settled.

Even before the refugees' arrival, indigents of the two minority communities in Besźel had traditionally allied, with jocularity or fear, depending on the politics at the time. Few citizens realise that our tradition of jokes about the foolishness of the middle child derives from a centuries-old humourous dialogue between Besźel's head rabbi and its chief imam about the intemperance of the Besźel Orthodox Church. It had, they

25

agreed, neither the wisdom of the oldest Abrahamic faith, nor the vigour of its youngest.

A common form of establishment, for much of Beszel's history, had been the *DöplirCaffé*: one Muslim and one Jewish coffeehouse, rented side by side, each with its own counter and kitchen, halal and kosher, sharing a single name, sign, and sprawl of tables, the dividing wall removed. Mixed groups would come, greet the two proprietors, sit together, separating on communitarian lines only long enough to order their permitted food from the relevant side, or ostentatiously from either and both in the case of freethinkers. Whether the *DöplirCaffé* was one establishment or two depended on who was asking: to a property tax collector, it was always one.

The Beszel ghetto was only architecture now, not formal political boundary, tumbledown old houses with newly gentrified chic, clustered between very different foreign alter spaces. Still, that was just the city; it wasn't an allegory, and Hamd Hamzinic would have faced unpleasantnesses in his studies. I thought slightly better of Shukman: a man of his age and temperament, I was perhaps surprised that Hamzinic felt free to display his statement of faith.

Shukman did not uncover Fulana. She lay between us. They had done something so she lay as if at rest.

'I've emailed you the report,' Shukman said. 'Twenty-four-, -five-year-old woman. Decent overall health, apart from being dead. Time of death, midnightish the night before last, give or take, of course. Cause of death, puncture wounds to the chest. Four in total, of which one pierced her heart. Some spike or stiletto or something, not a blade. She also has a nasty head wound, and a lot of odd abrasions.' I looked up. 'Some under

26

her hair. She was whacked round the side of the head.' He swung his arm in slow-motion mimicry. 'Hit her on the left of her skull. I'd say it knocked her out, or at least down and groggy, then the stab wounds were the coup de grace.'

'What was she hit with? In the head?'

'Something heavy and blunt. Could be a fist, if it was big, I suppose, but I seriously doubt it.' He tugged the corner of the sheet away, expertly uncovered the side of her head. The skin was the ugly colour of a dead bruise. 'And voilà.' He motioned me closer to her skinheaded scalp.

I got near the smell of preservative. In among the brunette stubble were several little scabbed puncture marks.

'What are they?'

'I don't know,' he said. 'They're not deep. Something she landed on, I think.' The abrasions were about the size of pencil-points pushed into skin. They covered an area roughly my hand-breadth, irregularly breaking the surface. In places there were lines of them a few millimetres long, deeper in the centre than at either end, where they disappeared.

'Signs of intercourse?'

'Not recently. So if she's a working girl maybe it was a refusal to do something that got her in this mess.' I nodded. He waited. 'We've washed her down now,' he said eventually. 'But she was covered in dirt, dust, grass stains, all the stuff you'd expect from where she was lying. And rust.'

'Rust?'

'All over. Lots of abrasions, cuts, scrapes, postmortem mostly, and lots of rust.'

I nodded again. I frowned.

'Defensive wounds?'

'No. Came quick and unexpected, or her back was turned.

There's a bunch more scrapes and whatnot on the body.' Shukman pointed to tear marks on her skin. 'Consistent with dragging her along. The wear and tear of murder.'

Hamzinic opened his mouth, closed it again. I glanced up at him. He sadly shook his head: *No nothing.*

CHAPTER THREE

THE POSTERS WERE UP. Mostly around the area our Fulana was found but some in the main streets, in the shopping streets, in Kyezov and Topisza and areas like that. I even saw one when I left my flat.

It wasn't even very close to the centre. I lived east and south a bit of the Old Town, the top-but-one flat in a six-storey towerlet on VulkovStrász. It is a heavily crosshatched street – clutch by clutch of architecture broken by alterity, even in a few spots house by house. The local buildings are taller by a floor or three than the others, so Besź juts up semiregularly and the roofscape is almost a machicolation.

Laced by the shadows of girdered towers that would loom over it if they were there, Ascension Church is at the end of VulkovStrász, its windows protected by wire grilles, but some of its stained panes broken. A fish market is there every few days. Regularly I would eat my breakfast to the shouts of vendors by their ice buckets and racks of live molluscs. Even the young women who worked there dressed like their grand-mothers while behind their stalls, nostalgically photogenic, their hair tied up in dishcloth-coloured scarves, their filleting aprons in patterns of grey and red to minimise the stains of gutting. The men looked, misleadingly or not, straight off their boats, as if they had not put their catches down since they emerged from the sea, until they reached the cobbles below me. The punters in Beszél lingered and smelled and prodded the goods.

In the morning trains ran on a raised line metres from my window. They were not in my city. I did not of course, but I could have stared into the carriages – they were quite that close – and caught the eyes of foreign travellers.

They would have seen only a thin man in early middle age in a dressing gown at his morning yoghurt and coffee, shake-folding a copy of a paper – *Inkyistor* or *Iy Déurnem* or a smudgy *Beszél Journal* to keep my English practiced. Usually alone – once in a while one or other of two women about his age might be there. (An economic historian at Beszél University; a writer for an art magazine. They did not know of each other but would not have minded.)

There when I left, a short distance from my front door on a poster stand, Fulana's face watched me. Though her eyes were closed, they had cropped and tinkered with the picture so that she did not look dead but stupefied. *Do you know this woman?* it said. It was printed in black and white, on matte paper. *Call Extreme Crime Squad*, our number. The presence of the poster might be evidence that the local cops were particularly efficient. Maybe they were all over the borough. It might be that, knowing where I lived, they wanted to keep me off their back with one or two strategic placements, especially for my eyes.

It was a couple of kilometres to ECS base. I walked. I walked by the brick arches: at the top, where the lines were, they were elsewhere, but not all of them were foreign at their bases. The ones I could see contained little shops and squats decorated in art graffiti. In Besźel it was a quiet area, but the streets were crowded with those elsewhere. I unsaw them, but it took time to pick past them all. Before I had reached my turning on Via Camir, Yaszek called my mobile.

'We've found the van.'

I PICKED UP A CAB, which sped-stalled repeatedly through the traffic. The Pont Mahest was crowded, locally and elsewhere. I had minutes to look into the dirty river as we edged toward the western bank, the smoke and the grimy dockyard ships in the reflected light of mirrored buildings on a foreign waterfront – an enviable finance zone. Besź tugs bobbed in the wakes of ignored water taxis. The van was skew-whiff between buildings. It was not a lot that it was in, but a channel between the premises of an import-exporters and an office block, a stub of space full of trash and wolf shit, linking two larger streets. Crime-scene tape secured both ends – a slight impropriety, as the alley was really crosshatch, but rarely used, so the tape was a common rule-bend in such circumstances. My colleagues were faddling around the vehicle.

'Boss.' It was Yaszek.

'Is Corwi on her way?'

'Yeah, I gave her the info.' Yaszek said nothing about my commandeering of the junior officer. She walked me over. It was an old, beat-up VW, in very bad condition. It was more off-white than grey, but it was darkened with dirt.

'Are you done dusting?' I said. I put on rubber gloves. The mectecs nodded and worked around me.

'It was unlocked,' Yaszek said.

I opened the door. I prodded the split upholstery. A trinket on the dashboard – a hula-dancing plastic saint. I pulled open the glove compartment onto a battered road atlas and dirt. I splayed the pages of the book but there was nothing inside: it was the classic Besź driver's aid, though an edition old enough to be black and white.

'So how do we know this is it?' Yaszek led me to the rear and pulled it open. I looked in on more dirt, a dank though not sick-making smell at least as much rust as mould, nylon cord, piled-up junk. 'What is all this?'

I poked it. A few bits. A little motor from something, rocking; a broken television; remnants of unidentifiable bits and pieces, corkscrewed detritus, on a layer of cloth and dust. Layers of rust and scabs of oxide.

'See that?' Yaszek pointed at stains on the floor. Had I not been looking carefully I might have said it was oil. 'A couple of people in the office call it in, a deserted van. The uniforms see its doors are open. I don't know whether they listen to their alerts or if they're just thorough when they check through out-standings, but either way we're lucky.' One of the messages that would have been read to all Besź patrols the previous morning would have requested they investigate and report any grey vehicles, and refer to ECS. We were fortunate these of-ficers had not just called in the impounders. 'Anyway they saw some muck on the floor, had it tested. We're verifying, but it looks like it's Fulana's blood type, and we'll have a definite match soon.'

Lying like a mole below heavy refuse, I leaned down to look under the debris. I moved it gently, tilting the junk. My hand came away red. I looked piece by piece, touched each to gauge their heft. The engine thing might be swung by a pipe that was part of it: the bulk of its base was heavy and would break what it was swung into. It did not look scuffed, though, nor bloodied nor specked with hair. As a murder weapon it did not convince me.

'You've not taken anything out?'

'No, no paperwork, no nothing. There was nothing in here. Nothing here except this stuff. We'll get results in a day or two.'

'There's so much crap,' I said. Corwi had arrived. A few passersby were hesitating at either end of the alleyway, watching the mectecs working. 'It's not going to be a problem of not enough trace; it's going to be too much.

'So. Let's assume for a minute. That junk in there's got rust all over her. She's been lying around in there.' The smears had been on her face as well as her body, not concentrated on her hands: she had not tried to push the rubbish away from her, or protect her head. She was unconscious or dead when she was in the van while the rubbish knocked against her.

'Why were they driving around with all this shit?' said Corwi. By that afternoon we had the name and address of the van's owner, and by the next morning we had verification that the blood was our Fulana's.

THE MAN'S NAME was Mikyael Khurusch. He was the van's third owner, officially at least. He had a record, had done time for two assault charges, for theft, the last time four years previously. And – 'Look,' said Corwi – he had been done for Sex Buying, had approached a policewoman undercover in a prostitution blackspot. 'So we know he's a John.' He had been off radar since, but was, according to hurried intel, a tradesman selling bits and pieces in the city's many markets, as well as three days a week from a shop in Mashlin, in western Besźel.

We could connect him and the van, and the van and Fulana – a direct link was what we wanted. I went to my office and

33

checked my messages. Some make-work on the Styelim case, an update from our switchboard on the posters and two hang-ups. Our exchange had promised for two years to upgrade to allow Caller ID.

There had been, of course, many people calling to tell us they recognised Fulana, but only a few – the staff who took those calls knew how to filter the deluded and the malicious and to a startling degree were accurate in their judgements – only a few so far that looked worth chasing. The body was a legal assistant in a small practice in Gyedar borough, who had not been seen for days; or she was, an anonymous voice insisted, 'a tart called Rosyn "The Pout," and that's all you get from me.' Uniforms were checking.

I told Commissar Gadlem I wanted to go in and talk to Khurusch in his house, get him to volunteer fingerprints, saliva, to cooperate. See how he reacted. If he said no, we could subpoena it and keep him under watch.

'Alright,' Gadlem said. 'But let's not waste time. If he doesn't play along put him in *seqyestre*, bring him in.'

I would try not to do that, though Besź law gave us the right. *Seqyestre*, 'half-arrest,' meant we could hold a nonwilling witness or 'connected party' for six hours, for preliminary interrogation. We could not take physical evidence, nor, offi-cially, draw conclusions from noncooperation or silence. The traditional use was to get confessions from suspects against whom there was not sufficient evidence to arrest. It was also, occasionally, a useful stalling technique against those we thought might be a flight risk. But juries and lawyers were turning against the technique, and a half-arrestee who did not confess usually had a stronger case later, because we looked too eager. Gadlem, old-fashioned, did not care, and I had my orders. Khurusch worked out of one of a line of semiactive businesses, in an economically lacklustre zone. We arrived in a hurried operation. Local officers on cooked-up subterfuge had ascertained that Khurusch was there.

We pulled him out of the office, a too-warm dusty room above the shop, industrial calendars and faded patches on the walls between filing cabinets. His assistant stared stupidly and picked up and put down stuff from her desk as we led Khurusch away.

He knew who I was before Corwi or the other uniforms were visible in his doorway. He was enough of a pro, or had been, that he knew he was not being arrested, despite our manner, and that therefore he could have refused to come and I would have had to obey Gadlem. After a moment when he first saw us – during which he stiffened as if considering running, though where? – he came with us down the wobbling iron staircase on the building's wall, the only entrance. I muttered into a radio and had the armed officers we had had waiting stand down. He never saw them.

Khurusch was a fatly muscular man in a checked shirt as faded and dusty looking as his office walls. He watched me from across the table in our interview room. Yaszek sat; Corwi stood under instructions not to speak, only watch. I walked. We weren't recording. This wasn't an interrogation, not technically.

'Do you know why you're here, Mikyael?'

'No clue.'

'Do you know where your van is?'

He looked up hard and stared at me. His voice changed – suddenly hopeful.

'Is that what this is about?' he said eventually. 'The van?'

He said a *ha* and sat a little back. Still guarded but relaxing. 'Did you *find it? Is that—*'

'Find it?'

'It was stolen. Three days ago. Did you? Find it? Jesus. What was . . . Have you got it? Can I have it back? What happened?'

I looked at Yaszek. She stood and whispered to me, sat again, and watched Khurusch.

'Yes, that's what this is about, Mikyael,' I said. 'What did you think it was about? Actually no, don't point at me, Mikyael, and shut your mouth until I tell you; I don't want to know. Here's the thing, Mikyael. A man like yourself, a delivery man, needs a van. You haven't reported yours as missing.' I looked down briefly at Yaszek, *Are we sure?* She nodded. 'You've not reported it stolen. Now I can see that the loss of that piece of shit and I do stress piece of shit wouldn't cut you up too badly, not on a human level. Nonetheless, I'm wondering, if it was stolen, I can't see what would stop you alerting us and indeed your insurance. How can you do your job without it?'

Khurusch shrugged.

'I didn't get it together. I was going to. I was busy . . .'

'We know how busy you are, Mik, and still I ask, why didn't you report it gone?'

'I didn't get it together. Really there's nothing fucking dubious—'

'For three days?'

'Have you got it? What happened? It was used for something, wasn't it? What was it used for?'

'Do you know this woman? Where were you on Tuesday night, Mik?' He stared at the picture.

'Jesus.' He went pale, he did. 'Someone was killed? Jesus.

36

Was she hit? Hit and run? Jesus.' He pulled out a dented PDA, then looked up without turning it on. 'Tuesday? I was at a meeting. Tuesday night? Christ's sake I was at a *meeting*.' He gave a nervous noise. 'That was the night the goddamn van got stolen. I was at a meeting, and there's twenty people can tell you the same.'

'What meeting? Where?'

'In Vyevus.'

'How'd you get there, with no van?'

'In my fucking car! No one's stolen that. I was at Gamblers Anonymous.' I stared. 'Fuck's sake I go every week. Last four years.'

'Since you were last in prison.'

'*Yes* since I was in fucking prison, Jesus, what do you think put me there?'

'Assault.'

'Yeah, I broke my fucking bookie's nose because I was behind and he was threatening me. What do you care? I was in a room full of fucking people on Tuesday night.'

'That's, what, two hours at the most . . .'

'Yeah and then afterwards at nine we went to the bar – it's GA not AA – and I was there till after midnight, and I didn't go home alone. There's a woman in my group . . . They'll all tell you.'

He was wrong about that. Of the GA group of eighteen, eleven wouldn't compromise their anonymity. The convenor, a wiry pony-tailed man who went by Zyet, 'Bean,' would not give us their names. He was right not to do so. We could have forced him, but why? The seven who would come forward all verified Khurusch's story.

None was the woman he claimed to have gone home with,

but several of them agreed that she existed. We could have found out, but again what would the point have been? The mectecs got excited when we found Khurusch's DNA on Fulana, but it was a tiny number of his arm hairs on her skin: given how often he hauled things in and out of the vehicle, it proved nothing.

'So why didn't he tell anyone it was missing?'

'He did,' Yaszek told me. 'He just didn't tell us. But I spoke to the secretary, Ljela Kitsov. He's been pissing and moaning about it for the last couple of days.'

'He just never got it together to tell us? What does he even do without it?'

'Kitsov says he just piddles stuff up and down across the river. The occasional import, on a very small scale. Pops abroad and picks up stuff to resell: cheap clothes, dodgy CDs.'

'Abroad where?'

'Varna. Bucharest. Turkey sometimes. Ul Qoma, of course.'

'So he's just too dithery to report the theft?'

'It does happen, boss.'

Of course, and to his rage – despite having not reported it stolen, he was now suddenly eager to have it returned – we wouldn't give him his van back. We did take him to the pound to verify it was his.

'Yes, it's mine.' I waited for him to complain about how ill it had been used, but that was obviously its usual colour. 'Why can't I have it? I need it.'

'As I keep saying, it's a crime scene. You'll get it when I'm ready. What's all this for?' He was huffing and grumping, looked into the back of the van. I held him back from touching anything.

'This shit? I don't fucking know.'

'This, I'm talking about.' The ripped-up cord, the pieces of junk.

'Yeah. I don't know what it is. I didn't put it here. Don't look at me like that – why would I carry garbage like this?'

I said to Corwi in my office afterwards: 'Please, do please stop me if you have any ideas, Lizbyet. Because I'm seeing a may-or-may-not-be working girl, who no one recognises, dumped in plain sight, in a stolen van, into which was carefully placed a load of crap, for no reason. And none of it's the murder weapon, you know – that's pretty certain.' I prodded the paper on my desk that told me.

'There's rubbish all over that estate,' she said. 'There's rubbish all over Besźel; he could've picked it up anywhere. "He" . . . They, maybe.'

'Picked it up, stashed it, dumped it, and the van with it.'

Corwi sat rather stiff, waiting for me to say something. All the rubbish had done was roll into the dead woman and rust her as if she, too, were old iron.

CHAPTER FOUR

BOTH OF THE LEADS WERE BOGUS. The office assistant had resigned and not bothered to tell them. We found her in Byatsialic, in the east of Beszel. She was mortified to have caused us trouble. 'I never hand in notice,' she kept saying. 'Not when they're employers like that. And this has never happened, nothing like this.' Corwi found Rosyn 'The Pout' without any difficulty. She was working her usual pitch.

'She doesn't look anything like Fulana, boss.' Corwi showed me a jpeg Rosyn had been happy to pose for. We couldn't trace the source of that spurious information, delivered with such convincing authority, nor work out why anyone would have mistaken the two women. Other information came in that I sent people to chase. I found messages and blank messages on my work phone.

It rained. On the kiosk outside my front door the printout of Fulana softened and streaked. Someone put up a glossy flyer for an evening of Balkan techno so it covered the top half of her face. The club night emerged from her lips and chin. I unpinned the new poster. I did not throw it away – only moved it so Fulana was visible again, her closed eyes next to it. DJ Radic and the Tiger Kru. Hard Beats. I did not see any other pictures of Fulana though Corwi assured me they were there, in the city.

Khurusch was all over the van, of course, but with the exception of those few hairs Fulana was clean of him. As if all those recovering gamblers would lie, anyway. We tried to take the names of any contacts to whom he had ever lent the van. He mentioned a few but insisted it had been stolen by a stranger. On the Monday after we found the body I took a call.

'Borlú.' I said my name again after a long pause, and it was repeated back to me.

'Inspector Borlú.'

'Help you?'

'I don't know. I was hoping you could help me days ago. I've been trying to reach you. I can help you more like.' The man spoke with a foreign accent.

'What? I'm sorry, I need you to speak up – it's a really bad line.'

It was staticking, and the man sounded as if he was a recording on an antique machine. I could not tell if the lag was on the line, or if he was taking a long time to respond to me each time I said anything. He spoke a good but odd Besź, punctuated with archaisms. I said, 'Who is this? What do you want?'

'I have information for you.'

'Have you spoken to our info-line?'

'I can't.' He was calling from abroad. The feedback from Besźel's outdated exchanges was distinctive. 'That's kind of the point.'

'How did you get my number?'

'Borlú, shut up.' I wished again for logging telephones. I sat up. 'Google. Your name's in the papers. You're in charge of the investigation into the girl. It's not hard to get past assistants. Do you want me to help you or not?'

41

I actually looked around but there was no one with me. 'Where are you calling from?' I parted the blinds in my window as if I might see someone watching me from the street. Of course I did not.

'Come on Borlú. You know where I'm calling from.'

I was making notes. I knew the accent.

He was calling from Ul Qoma.

'You know where I'm calling from and that is why please don't bother asking my name.'

'You're not doing anything illegal talking to me.'

'You don't know what I'm going to tell you. *You don't know what I'm going to tell you.* It is—' He broke off, and I heard him mutter something with his hand over the phone, for a moment. 'Look Borlú, I don't know where you stand on things like this but I think it is lunatic, an insult, that I *am* speaking to you from another country.'

'I'm not a political man. Listen, if you'd rather . . .' I started the last sentence in Illitan, the language of Ul Qoma.

'This is fine.' He interrupted in his old-fashioned Illitan-inflected Besź. 'It's the same damn-faced language anyway.' I wrote that he said that. 'Now shut up. Do you want to hear my information?'

'Of course.' I was standing, reaching, trying to work out a way to trace this. My line was not equipped, and it would take hours to go backwards, through BesźTel, even if I could get hold of them while he was speaking to me.

'The woman who you're . . . She's dead. Isn't she? She is. I knew her.'

'I'm sorry to . . .' I only said this after he was silent many seconds.

'I've known her . . . I met her a time ago. I want to help

42

you, Borlú, but not because you're a *cop*. Holy Light. I don't recognise your authority. But if Marya was . . . if she was killed, then some people I care about may not be safe. Including the one I care about most, my very own self. And she deserves . . . So – this is all I know.

'Her name's Marya. That's what she went by. I met her here. Ul Qoma-here. I'm telling you what I can, but I never knew much. Not my business. She was a foreigner. I knew her from politics. She was serious – committed, you know? Just not to what I thought at first. She knew a lot; she was no time-waster.'

'Look,' I said.

'That's all I can tell you. She lived here.'

'She was in Besźel.'

'Come on.' He was angry. 'Come on. Not officially. She couldn't. Even if she was, she was here. Go look at the cells, the radicals. Someone'll know who she is. She went every-where. All the underground. Both sides, must have done. She wanted to go everywhere because she needed to know every-thing. And she did. That's all.'

'How did you find out that she'd been killed?' I heard his hiss of breath.

'Borlú, if you really mean that you're stupid and I'm wasting my time. I recognised her picture, Borlú. Do you think I'd be helping you if I didn't think I had to? If I didn't think this was important? How do you think I found out? *I saw your fucking poster.*'

He put the phone down. I held my receiver to my ear a while as if he might return.

I saw your poster. When I looked down at my notepad, I had written on it, beside the details he had given me, *shit/ shit/shit.*

43

I DID NOT STAY in the office much longer. 'Are you alright, Tyador?' Gadlem said. 'You look . . .' I'm sure I did. At a pavement stall I had a strong coffee *aj Tyrko* – Turkish style – a mistake. I was even more antsy.

It was, not surprisingly that day perhaps, hard to observe borders, to see and unsee only what I should, on my way home. I was hemmed in by people not in my city, walking slowly through areas crowded but not crowded in Besźel. I focused on the stones really around me – cathedrals, bars, the brick flourishes of what had been a school – that I had grown up with. I ignored the rest or tried.

I dialled the number of Sariska, the historian, that evening. Sex would have been good, but also sometimes she liked to talk over cases that I was working on, and she was smart. I dialled her number twice but disconnected twice before she could respond. I would not involve her in this. A disguised-as-hypothesis infraction of the confidentiality clause on ongoing investigations was one thing. Making her accessory to breach was another.

I kept coming back to that *shit/shit/shit*. In the end I got home with two bottles of wine and set out slowly – cushioning them in my stomach with a pick-pick supper of olives, cheese, sausage – to finish them. I made more useless notes, some in arcane diagram form as if I might draw a way out, but the situation – the conundrum – was clear. I might be the victim of a pointless and laboured hoax, but it did not seem likely. More probable was that the man on the telephone had been telling the truth.

In which case I had been given a major lead, close information about Fulana-Marya. I had been told where to go and who to chase to find out more. Which it was my job to do. But if it came out that I acted on the information no conviction would ever stand. And much more serious, it would be far worse than illegal for me to pursue it, not only illegal according to Besź codes – I would be in breach.

My informant should not have seen the posters. They were not in his country. He should never have told me. He made me accessory. The information was an allergen in Besźel – the mere fact of it in my head was a kind of trauma. I was complicit. It was done. (Perhaps because I was drunk it did not occur to me then that it had not been necessary for him to tell me how he had come by the information, and that he had to have had reasons for doing so.)

I WOULD NOT, but who would not be tempted to burn or shred the notes of that conversation? Of course I would not, but. I sat up late at my kitchen table with them spread out in front of me, idly writing *shit/shit* on them crosswise from time to time. I put on music: *Little Miss Train*, a collaboration, Van Morrison duetting with Coirsa Yakov, the Besź Umm Kalsoum as she was called, on his 1987 tour. I drank more and put the picture of Marya Fulana Unknown Foreign Detail Breacher next to the notes.

No one knew her. Perhaps, God help us, she had not been properly here in Besźel at all, though Pocost was a total area. She could have been dragged there. The kids finding her body, the whole investigation, might be breach too. I should not incriminate myself by pushing this. I should perhaps just walk away from the investigation and let her moulder. It was escapism for a moment to pretend I might do so. In the end I would do my job, though doing it meant breaking a code, an existential protocol more basic by a long way than any I was paid to enforce.

As kids we used to play Breach. It was never a game I much enjoyed, but I would take my turn creeping over chalked lines and chased by my friends, their faces in ghastly expressions, their hands crooked as claws. I would do the chasing too, if it was my turn to be invoked. That, along with pulling sticks and pebbles out of the ground and claiming them the magic Besź mother lode, and the tag/hide-and-seek crossbreed called Insile Hunt, were regular games.

There is no theology so desperate that you can't find it. There is a sect in Besźel that worships Breach. It's scandalous but not completely surprising given the powers involved. There is no law against the congregation, though the nature of their religion makes everyone twitchy. They have been the subject of prurient TV programs.

At three in the morning I was drunk and very awake, looking over the streets of Besźel (and more – the crosshatch). I could hear the barking of dogs and a call or two of some scrawny, wormy street wolf. The papers – both sides of the argument still as if it were that, an argument – were all over the table. Fulana-Marya's face was wineglass-ringed, as were the illegal *shit/shit/shit* notes.

It is not uncommon for me to fail to sleep. Sariska and Biszaya were used to sleepily walking from the bedroom to the bathroom to find me reading at the kitchen table, chewing so much gum that I would get sugar blisters (I would not take up smoking again). Or looking over the night city and (inevitably, unseeing but touched by its light) the other city.

Sariska laughed at me once. 'Look at you,' she said, not without affection. 'Sitting there like an owl. Melancholy

46

bloody gargoyle. You mawkish bugger. You don't get any insight, you know, just because it's night. Just because some buildings have their lights on.' She was not there to tease me though just then and I wanted whatever insight I could get, even spurious, so I looked on out.

Planes went over the clouds. Cathedral spires were lit by glass skyscrapers. Recurved and crescent neoned architecture across the border. I tried to hook up my computer to look some stuff up, but the only connection I had was dial-up and it was all very frustrating so I stopped.

'Details later.' I think I actually said it aloud. I made more notes. Eventually, at last, I called the direct line to Corwi's desk.

'Lizbyet. I've had a thought.' My instinct as always when I lie was to say too much, too quickly. I made myself speak as if idly. She was not stupid though. 'It's late. I'm just leaving this for you because I'm probably not going to be in tomorrow. We're not getting anywhere with the street-beat, so it's pretty obvious it's not what we thought – someone would've recognised her. We've got the picture out to all the precincts, so if she's a street girl off her patch maybe we'll get lucky. But meanwhile I'd like to look in a couple of other directions while we can keep this running.

'I'm thinking, look, she's not in her area, it's a weird situation, we can't get any beep. I was talking to a guy I know in Dissident Unit, and he was saying how secretive the people he's watching are. It's all Nazis and reds and unifs and so on. Anyway it got me thinking about what kind of people hide their identities, and while we've still got any time I'd like to chase that a bit. What I'm thinking is – hold on I'm just looking at some notes . . . Okay, might as well start with unifs.

'Talk to the Kook Squad. See what you can get by way of addresses, chapters – I don't know much about it. Ask for Shenvoi's office. Tell him you're on a job for me. Go by the ones you can, take the pictures, see if anyone recognises her. I don't need to tell you they're going to be weird with you – they're not going to want you around. But see what you can do. Keep in touch, I'll be on the mobile. Like I say, I won't be in. Okay. Talk tomorrow. Okay, bye.'

'That was terrible.' I think I said that aloud, too.

When I had done that I called the number of Taskin Cerush in our admin pool. I had been careful to take a note of her direct line when she had helped me through bureaucracy three or four cases ago. I had kept in touch. She was excellent at her job.

'Taskin, this is Tyador Borlú. Can you please call me on my mobile tomorrow or when you get the chance and let me know what I might have to do if I wanted to put a case to the Oversight Committee? If I wanted to push a case to Breach. Hypothetically.' I winced and laughed. 'Keep this to yourself, okay? Thanks, Task. Just let me know what I need to do and if you've got any handy insider suggestions. Thanks.'

There had not been much question about what my terrible informant had been telling me. The phrases I had copied and underlined.

same language
recognise authority – not
both sides of the city

It made sense of why he would call me, why the crime of it, of what he'd seen, or that he'd seen it, would not detain him as it would most. Mostly he had done it because he was afraid, of whatever Marya-Fulana's death implied for him.

48

What he had told me was that his coconspirators in Besźel might very possibly have seen Marya, that she would not have respected borders. And if any group of troublemakers in Besźel would be complicit in that particular kind of crime and taboo, it would be my informer and his comrades. They were obviously unificationists.

SARISKA MOCKED ME in my mind as I turned back to that night-lit city, and this time I looked and saw its neighbour. Illicit, but I did. Who hasn't done that at times? There were gasrooms I shouldn't see, chambers dangling ads, tethered by skeletal metal frames. On the street at least one of the passersby – I could tell by the clothes, the colours, the walk – was not in Besźel, and I watched him anyway.

I turned to the railway lines a few metres by my window and waited until, as I knew it would eventually, a late train came. I looked into its rapidly passing, illuminated windows, and into the eyes of the few passengers, a very few of whom even saw me back, and were startled. But they were gone fast, over the conjoined sets of roofs: it was a brief crime, and not their faults. They probably did not feel guilty for long. They probably did not remember that stare. I always wanted to live where I could watch foreign trains.

CHAPTER FIVE

IF YOU DO NOT KNOW much about them, Illitan and Besź sound very different. They are written, of course, in distinct alphabets. Besź is in Besź: thirty-four letters, left to right, all sounds rendered clear and phonetic, consonants, vowels and demivowels decorated with diacritics – it looks, one often hears, like Cyrillic (though that is a comparison likely to annoy a citizen of Besźel, true or not). Illitan uses Roman script. That is recent.

Read the travelogues of the last-but-one century and those older, and the strange and beautiful right-to-left Illitan calligraphy – and its jarring phonetics – is constantly remarked on. At some point everyone has heard Sterne, from his travelogue: 'In the Land of Alphabets *Arabic* caught *Dame Sanskrit's* eye (drunk he was despite Muhamed's injunctions, else her age would have dissuaded). Nine months later a *disowned child* was put out. The feral babe is *Illitan*, Hermes-Aphrodite not without beauty. He has something of both his parents in his form, but the voice of those who raised him – the birds.'

The script was lost in 1923, overnight, a culmination of Ya Ilsa's reforms: it was Atatürk who imitated him, not, as is usually claimed, the other way around. Even in Ul Qoma, no one can read Illitan script now but archivists and activists.

Anyway whether in its original or later written form, Illitan bears no resemblance to Besź. Nor does it sound similar. But these distinctions are not as deep as they appear. Despite careful cultural differentiation, in the shape of their grammars and the relations of their phonemes (if not the base sounds themselves), the languages are closely related – they share a common ancestor, after all. It feels almost seditious to say so. Still.

Besźel's dark ages are very dark. Sometime between two thousand and seventeen hundred years ago the city was founded, here in this curl of coastline. There are still remains from those times in the heart of the town, when it was a port hiding a few kilometres up the river to shelter from the pirates of the shore. The city's founding came at the same time as another's, of course. The ruins are surrounded now or in some places incorporated, antique foundations, into the substance of the city. There are older ruins too, like the mosaic remnants in Yozhef Park. These Romanesque remains predate Besźel, we think. We built Besźel on their bones, perhaps.

It may or may not have been Besźel, that we built, back then, while others may have been building Ul Qoma on the same bones. Perhaps there was one thing back then that later schismed on the ruins, or perhaps our ancestral Besźel had not yet met and stand-offishly entwined with its neighbour. I am not a student of the Cleavage, but if I were I still would not know.

'BOSS.' Lizbyet Corwi called me. 'Boss you are on fire. How did you know? Meet me at sixty-eight BudapestStrász.'

I had not yet dressed in day clothes though it was after noon. My kitchen table was a landscape of papers. The books I had

51

on politics and history were propped in a Babel-tower by the milk. I should keep my laptop from the mess, but I never bothered. I brushed cocoa away from my notes. The blackface character on my French drinking chocolate smiled at me. 'What are you talking about? What's that address?'

'It's in Bundalia,' she said. An industrial presuburb north-west of Funicular Park, by the river. 'And are you kidding me what is it? I did what you said – I asked around, got the basic gist of which groups there are, who thinks what of each other, blah blah. I spent the morning going round, asking questions. Putting the fear in. Can't say you get much respect from these bastards with the uniform on, you know? And I can't say I had much hopes for this, but I figured what the hell else did we have to do? Anyway I'm going around trying to get a sense of the politics and whatnot, and one of the guys at one of the – I guess you'd say lodges maybe – he starts to give me some-thing. Wasn't going to admit it at first, but I could tell. You're a fucking genius, sir. Sixty-eight BudapestStrász is a unifica-tionist HQ.'

Her awe was already close to suspicion. She would have looked at me even harder if she had seen the documents on my table, that I had negotiated with my hands when she phoned me. Several books were open to their indices, propped to show what references they had to unificationism. I really had not come across the BudapestStrász address.

In typical political cliché, unificationists were split on many axes. Some groups were illegal, sister-organisations in both Beszel and Ul Qoma. The banned had at various points in their history advocated the use of violence to bring the cities to their God-, destiny-, history-, or people-intended unity. Some had, mostly cack-handedly, targeted nationalist intellectuals – bricks through windows and shit through doors. They had been accused of furtively propagandising among refugees and new immigrants with limited expertise at seeing and unseeing, at being in one particular city. The activists wanted to weaponise such urban uncertainty.

These extremists were vocally criticised by others keen to retain freedom of movement and assembly, whatever their secret thoughts and whatever threads connected them all out of view. There were other divisions, between different visions of what the united city would be like, what would be its language, what would be its name. Even these legal grouplets would be watched without ceasing, and checked up on regularly by the authorities in whichever their city. 'Swiss cheese,' Shenvoi said when I spoke to him that morning. 'Probably more informers and moles in the unifs even than in the True Citizens or Nazis or other nutters. I wouldn't worry about them – they're not going to do dick without the say-so of someone in security.'

Also, the unifs must know, though they would hope never to see proof of it, that nothing they did would be unknown to Breach. That meant I would be under Breach's purview too, during my visit, if I was not already.

Always the question of how to get through the city. I should have taxied as Corwi was waiting, but no, two trams, a change at Vencelas Square. Swaying under the carved and clockwork figures of Besź burghers on the town facades, ignoring, unseeing, the shinier fronts of the elsewhere, the alter parts.

The length of BudapestStrász, patches of winter buddleia frothed out from old buildings. It's a traditional urban weed in Besźel, but not in Ul Qoma, where they trim it as it intrudes, so BudapestStrász being the Besźel part of a crosshatched area, each bush, unflowered at that time, emerged unkempt for one or two or three local buildings, then would end in a sharp vertical plane at the edge of Beszel.

The buildings in Beszel were brick and plaster, each surmounted with one of the household *Lares* staring at me, a little manlike grotesque, and bearded with that weed. A few decades before these places would not have been so tumbling down; they would have emitted more noise and the street would have been filled with young clerks in dark suits and visiting foremen. Behind the northern buildings were industrial yards, and beyond them a curl in the river, where docks used to bustle and where their iron skeletons still graveyard lay.

Back then the region of Ul Qoma that shared the space had been quiet. It had grown more noisy: the neighbours had moved in economic antiphase. As the river industry of Beszel had slowed, Ul Qoma's business picked up, and now there were more foreigners walking on the worn-down crosshatched cobbles than Besz locals. The once-collapsing Ul Qoma rookeries, crenellated and lumpen-baroque (not that I saw them – I unsaw carefully, but they still registered a little, illicitly, and I remembered the styles from photographs), were renovated, the sites of galleries and .uq startups.

I watched the local buildings' numbers. They rose in stutters, interspersed with foreign alter spaces. In Beszel the area was pretty unpeopled, but not elsewhere across the border, and I had to unseeing dodge many smart young businessmen and -women. Their voices were muted to me, random noise. That aural fade comes from years of Besz care. When I reached the tar-painted front where Corwi waited with an unhappy-looking man, we stood together in a near-deserted part of Beszel city, surrounded by a busy unheard throng.

54

'Boss. This is Pall Drodin.'

Drodin was a tall and thin man in his late thirties. He wore several rings in his ears, a leather jacket with obscure and unmerited membership insignia of various military and other organisations on it, anomalously smart though dirty trousers. He eyed me unhappily, smoking.

He was not arrested. Corwi had not taken him in. I nodded a greeting to her, then turned around slowly 180 degrees and looked at the buildings around us. I focused only the Besź ones, of course.

'Breach?' I said. Drodin looked startled. So in truth did Corwi, though she covered it. When Drodin said nothing I said, 'Don't you think we're watched by powers?'

'Yeah, no, we are.' He sounded resentful. I am sure he was. 'Sure. Sure. You asking me where they are?' It is a more or less meaningless question but one that no Besź nor Ul Qoman can banish. Drodin did not look anywhere other than in my eyes. 'You see the building over the road? The one that used to be a match factory?' A mural's remains in scabs of paint almost a century old, a salamander smiling through its corona of flames. 'You see stuff moving, in there. Stuff you know, like, comes and goes, like it shouldn't.'

'So you can see them appear?' He looked uneasy again. 'You think that's where they manifest?'

'No no, but process of elimination.'

'Drodin, get in. We'll be in in a second,' Corwi said. Nodded him in and he went. 'What the fuck, boss?'

'Problem?'

'All this Breach shit.' She lowered her voice on *Breach*. 'What are you doing?' I did not say anything. 'I'm trying to establish a power dynamic here and *I'm* at the end of it, not

Breach, boss. I don't want that shit in the picture. Where the fuck you getting this spooky shit from?' When I still said nothing she shook her head and led me inside.

The Besźqoma Solidarity Front did not make much of an effort with their decor. There were two rooms, two and a half at generous count, full of cabinets and shelves stacked with files and books. In one corner wall space had been cleared and cleaned, it looked like, for backdrop, and a webcam pointed at it and an empty chair.

'Broadcasts,' Drodin said. He saw where I was looking. 'Online.' He started to tell me a web address until I shook my head.

'Everyone else left when I came in,' Corwi told me.

Drodin sat down behind his desk in the back room. There were two other chairs in there. He did not offer them, but Corwi and I sat anyway. More mess of books, a dirty computer. On a wall a large-scale map of Besźel and Ul Qoma. To avoid prosecution the lines and shades of division were there – total, alter, and crosshatched – but ostentatiously subtle, distinctions of greyscale. We sat looking at each other a while.

'Look,' Drodin said. 'I know . . . you understand I'm not used to . . . You guys don't like me, and that's fine, that's understood.' We said nothing. He played with some of the things on his desktop. 'And I'm no snitch either.'

'Jesus, Drodin,' Corwi said, 'if it's absolution you're after, get a priest.' But he continued.

'It's just . . . If this has something to do with what she was into, then you're all going to think it has something to do with us and maybe it even might *have* something to do with us and I'm giving no one any excuses to come down on us. You know? You know?'

'Alright enough,' Corwi said. 'Cut the shit.' She looked around the room. 'I know you think you're clever, but seriously, how many misdemeanours do you think I'm looking at right now? Your map, for a start – You reckon it's careful, but it wouldn't take a particularly patriotic prosecutor to interpret it in a way that'll leave you inside. What else? You want me to go through your books? How many are on the proscribed list? Want me to go through your papers? This place has Insulting Besź Sovereignty in the Second Degree flashing over it like neon.'

'Like the Ul Qoma club districts,' I said. 'Ul Qoma neon. Would you like that, Drodin? Prefer it to the local variety?'

'So while we appreciate your help, Mr. Drodin, let's not kid ourselves as to why you're doing it.'

'You don't understand.' He muttered it. 'I have to protect my people. There's weird shit out there. There's weird shit going on.'

'Alright,' Corwi said. 'Whatever. What's the story, Drodin?' She took the photograph of Fulana and put it in front of him. 'Tell my boss what you started telling me.'

'Yeah,' he said. 'That's her.' Corwi and I leaned forward. Perfect synchronised timing.

I said, 'What's her name?'

'What she said, she said her name was Byela Mar.' Drodin shrugged. 'It's what she said. I know, but what can I tell you?'

It was an obvious, and elegantly punning, pseudonym. Byela is a unisex Besź name; Mar is at least plausible as a surname. Together their phonemes approximate the phrase *byé lai mar*, literally 'only the baitfish,' a fishing phrase to say 'nothing worth noting.'

'It isn't unusual. Lots of our contacts and members go by handles.'

'*Noms*,' I said, '*de unification.*' I could not tell if he understood. 'Tell us about Byela.' Byela, Fulana, Marya was accruing names.

'She was here I don't know, three years ago or so? Bit less? I hadn't seen her since then. She was obviously foreign.'

'From Ul Qoma?'

'No. Spoke okay Illitan but not fluent. She'd talk in Besź or Illitan – or, well, the root. I never heard her talk anything else – she wouldn't tell me where she came from. From her accent I'd say American or English maybe. I don't know what she was doing. It's not . . . it's kind of rude to ask too much about people in this line.'

'So, what, she came to meetings? She was an organiser?' Corwi turned to me and said without lowering her voice, 'I don't even know what it is these fuckers do, boss. I don't even know what to ask.' Drodin watched her, no more sour than he had been since we arrived.

'She turned up like I said a couple of years ago. She wanted to use our library. We've got pamphlets and old books on . . . well on the cities, a lot of stuff they don't stock in other places.'

'We should take a look, boss,' Corwi said. 'See there's nothing inappropriate.'

'Fuck's sake, I'm helping, aren't I? You want to get me on banned books? There's nothing Class One, and the Class Twos we got are mostly available on-fucking-line anyway.'

'Alright alright,' I said. Pointed for him to continue.

'So she came and we talked a lot. She wasn't here long. Like a couple of weeks. Don't ask me about what she did otherwise and stuff like that because I don't know. All I know is every day she'd come by at odd times and look at books, or talk to me about our history, the history of the cities, about what was going on, about our campaigns, that kind of thing.'

'What campaigns?'

'Our brothers and sisters in prison. Here *and* in Ul Qoma. For nothing but their beliefs. Amnesty International's on our side there, you know. Talking to contacts. Education. Helping new immigrants. Demos.' In Besźel, unificationist demonstrations were fractious, small, dangerous things. Obviously the local nationalists would come out to break them up, screaming at the marchers as traitors, and in general the most apolitical local wouldn't have much sympathy for them. It was almost as bad in Ul Qoma, except it was more unlikely they would be allowed to gather in the first place. That must have been a source of anger, though it certainly saved the Ul Qoman unifs from beatings.

'How did she look? Did she dress well? What was she like?'

'Yeah she did. Smart. Almost chic, you know? Stood out here.' He even laughed at himself. 'And she was clever. I really liked her at first, you know? I was really excited. At first.'

His pauses were requests for us to chivvy him, so that none of this discussion was at his behest. 'But?' I said. 'What happened?'

'We had an argument. Actually I only had an argument with her because she was giving some of the other comrades shit, you know? I'd walk into the library or downstairs or whatever and someone or other would be shouting at her. She was never shouting at them, but she'd be talking quietly and driving them mad, and in the end I had to tell her to go. She was . . . she was dangerous.' Another silence. Corwi and I looked at each

59

other. 'No I ain't exaggerating,' he said. 'She brought you here, didn't she? I told you she was dangerous.'

He picked up the photograph and studied it. Across his face went pity, anger, dislike, fear. Fear, certainly. He got up, walked in a circle around his desk – ridiculous, too small a room to pace, but he tried.

'See the problem was . . .' He went to his small window and looked out, turned back to us. He was silhouetted against the skyline, of Besźel or Ul Qoma or both I could not tell.

'She was asking all this stuff about some of the kookiest underground bollocks. Old wives' tales, rumours, urban myths, craziness. I didn't think much of it because we get a lot of that shit, and she was obviously smarter than the loons into it, so I figured she was just feeling her way around, getting to know stuff.'

'Weren't you curious?'

'Sure. Young foreign girl, clever, mysterious? *Intense?*' He mocked himself with how he said that. He nodded. 'Sure I was. I'm curious about all the people who come here. Some of them tell me shit, some of them don't. But I wouldn't be leader of this chapter if I went around pumping them. There's a woman here, a lot older than me . . . I been meeting her on and off for fifteen years. Don't know her real name, or anything about her. Okay, bad example because I'm pretty sure she's one of your lot, an agent, but you get the point. I don't ask.'

'What was she into, then? Byela Mar. Why did you kick her out?'

'Look, here's the thing. You're into this stuff . . .' I felt Corwi stiffen as if she would interrupt him, needle him to get on with it, and I touched her *no, wait,* to give him his head on this.

60

He was not looking at us but at his provocative map of the cities. 'You're into this stuff you know you're skirting with . . . well, you know you step out of line you're going to get serious trouble. Like having you lot here, for a start. Or make the wrong phone call we can put our brothers in shit, in Ul Qoma, with the cops there. Or – or there's worse.' He looked at us then. 'She couldn't stay, she was going to bring Breach down on us. Or something.

'She was into . . . No, she wasn't *into* anything, she was *obsessed*. With Orciny.'

He was looking at me carefully, so I did nothing but narrow my eyes. I was surprised, though.

By how she did not move it was clear that Corwi did not know what Orciny was. It might undermine her to go into it here, but as I hesitated he was explaining. It was a fairy tale. That was what he said.

'Orciny's the third city. It's between the other two. It's in the *dissensi*, disputed zones, places that Besźel thinks are Ul Qoma's and Ul Qoma Besźel's. When the old commune split, it didn't split into two, it split into three. Orciny's the secret city. It runs things.'

If split there was. That beginning was a shadow in history, an unknown – records effaced and vanished for a century either side. Anything could have happened. From that historically brief quite opaque moment came the chaos of our material history, an anarchy of chronology, of mismatched remnants that delighted and horrified investigators. All we know is nomads on the steppes, then those black-box centuries of urban instigation – certain events, and there have been films and stories and games based on speculation (all making the censor at least a little twitchy) about that dual birth – then history comes back and there are Beszel and Ul Qoma. Was it schism or conjoining?

As if that were not mystery enough and as if two crosshatched countries were insufficient, bards invented that third, the pretend-existing Orciny. On top floors, in ignorable Roman-style town-houses, in the first wattle-and-daub dwellings, taking up the intricately conjoined and disjointed spaces allotted it in the split or coagulation of the tribes, the tiny third city Orciny ensconced, secreted between the two brasher city-states. A community of imaginary overlords, exiles perhaps, in most stories machinating and making things so, ruling with a subtle and absolute grip. Orciny was where the Illuminati lived. That sort of thing. Some decades previously there would have been no need for explanations – Orciny stories had been children's standards, alongside the tribulations of 'King Shavil and the Sea-Monster That Came to Harbour.' Harry Potter and Power Rangers are more popular now, and fewer children know those older fables. That's alright.

'Are you saying – what?' I interrupted him. 'You're saying that Byela was a folklorist? She was into old stories?' He shrugged. He would not look at me. I tried again to make him out and say what he was implying. He would only shrug. 'Why would she be talking to you about this?' I said. 'Why was she even here?'

'I don't know. We have stuff on it. It comes up. You know? They have them in Ul Qoma, too, you know, Orciny stories. We don't just keep documents on, you know, just *just* what we're into. You know? We know our history, we keep all kinds of . . .' He trailed off. 'I realised it wasn't us she was interested in, you know?'

Like any dissidents they were neurotic archivists. Agree, disagree, show no interest in or obsess over their narrative of history, you couldn't say they didn't shore it up with footnotes and research. Their library must have defensively complete holdings of anything that even implied a blurring of urban boundaries. She had come – you could see it – seeking information not on some ur-unity but on Orciny. What an annoyance when they realised her odd researches weren't quirks of investigation but the very point. When they realised that she did not much care about their project.

'So she was a time-waster?'

'No, man, she was dangerous, like I said. For real. She'd cause trouble for us. She said she wasn't sticking around anyway.' He shrugged his shoulders vaguely.

'Why was she dangerous?' I leaned in. 'Drodin, was she breaching?'

'Jesus, I don't think so. If she did I don't know shit about it.' He put up his hands. 'Fuck's sake, you know how watched we are?' He jerked his hand in the direction of the street. 'We've got you lot on a semipermanent patrol in the area. Ul Qoman cops can't watch us, obviously, but they're on our brothers and sisters. And more to the goddamned point, watching us out there is . . . you know. Breach.'

We were all silent a moment then. We all felt watched.

'You've seen it?'

'Course not. What do I look like? Who *sees* it? But we know it's there. Watching. Any excuse . . . we're gone. Do you . . .' He shook his head, and when he looked back at me it was with anger and perhaps hate. 'Do you know how many of my friends have been taken? That I've never seen again? We're *more* careful than anyone.'

It was true. A political irony. Those most dedicated to the

perforation of the boundary between Besźel and Ul Qoma had to observe it most carefully. If I or one of my friends were to have a moment's failure of unseeing (and who did not do that? who failed to fail to see, sometimes?), so long as it was not flaunted or indulged in, we should not be in danger. If I were to glance a second or two on some attractive passerby in Ul Qoma, if I were to silently enjoy the skyline of the two cities together, be irritated by the noise of an Ul Qoman train, I would not be taken.

Here, though, at this building not just my colleagues but the powers of Breach were always wrathful and as Old Testament as they had the powers and right to be. That terrible presence might appear and disappear a unificationist for even a somatic breach, a startled jump at a misfiring Ul Qoma car. If Byela, Fulana, had been breaching, she would have brought that in. So it was likely not suspicion of that specifically that had made Drodin afraid.

'There was just something.' He looked up out of the window at the two cities. 'Maybe she would, she would have brought Breach on us, eventually. Or something.'

'Hang on,' Corwi said. 'You said she was leaving . . .'

'She said she was going over. To Ul Qoma. Officially.' I paused from scribbling notes. I looked at Corwi and she at me. 'Didn't see her again. Someone heard she'd gone and they wouldn't let her back here.' He shrugged. 'I don't know if that's true, and if it is I don't know why. It was just a matter of time . . . She was poking around in dangerous shit, it gave me a bad feeling.'

'That's not all, though, is it?' I said. 'What else?' He stared at me.

'I don't *know*, man. She was trouble, she was scary, there

was too much ... there was just something. When she was going on and on about all the stuff she was into, it started to give you the creeps. Made you nervous.' He looked out of the window again. He shook his head.

'I'm sorry she died,' he said. 'I'm sorry someone killed her. But I'm not that surprised.'

THAT STINK OF INSINUATION and mystery – however cynical or uninterested you thought yourself it stuck to you. I saw Corwi look up and around at the shabby fronts of the warehouses when we left. Perhaps seeing a little long in the direction of a shop she must realise was in Ul Qoma. She felt watched. We both did, and we were right, and fidgety.

When we drove out, I took Corwi – a provocation I admit though not aimed at her but at the universe in some way – for lunch in Beszel's little Ul Qomatown. It was south of the park. With the particular colours and script of its shop fronts, the shape of its facades, visitors to Beszel who saw it would always think they were looking at Ul Qoma, and hurriedly and ostentatiously look away (as close as foreigners could generally get to unseeing). But with a more careful eye, experience, you note the sort of cramped kitsch to the buildings' designs, a squat self-parody. You can see the trimmings in the shade called Beszel Blue, one of the colours illegal in Ul Qoma. These properties are local.

These few streets – mongrel names, Illitan nouns and a Besz suffix, YulSainStrász, LiligiStrász, and so on – were the centre of the cultural world for the small community of Ul Qoman expatriates living in Beszel. They had come for various reasons – political persecution, economic self-betterment (and how the patriarchs who had gone through the considerable difficulties of emigrating for that reason must be rueing it now), whim, romance. Most of those aged forty and below are second and now third generation, speaking Illitan at home but Besź without an accent in the streets. There is maybe an Ul Qoman influence to their clothes. At various times local bullies and worse break their windows and beat them in the streets.

This is where pining Ul Qoman exiles come for their pastries, their sugar-fried peas, their incense. The scents of Besźel Ul Qomatown are a confusion. The instinct is to unsmell them, to think of them as drift across the boundaries, as disrespectful as rain ('Rain and woodsmoke live in both cities,' the proverb has it. In Ul Qoma they have the same saw, but one of the subjects is 'fog.' You may occasionally also hear it of other weather conditions, or even rubbish, sewage, and, spoken by the daring, pigeons or wolves). But those smells are in Besźel.

Very occasionally a young Ul Qoman who does not know the area of their city that Ul Qomatown crosshatches will blunder up to ask directions of an ethnically Ul Qoman Besźel-dweller, thinking them his or her compatriots. The mistake is quickly detected – there is nothing like being ostentatiously unseen to alarm – and Breach are normally merciful.

'Boss,' Corwi said. We sat at a corner café, Con ul Cai, that I frequented. I had made a great show of greeting the proprietor by name, like doubtless many of his Besź clientele. Probably he despised me. 'Why the fuck are we here?'

'Come on,' I said. 'Ul Qoman food. Come on. You know you want it.' I offered her cinnamon lentils, thick sweet tea. She declined. 'We're here,' I said, 'because I'm trying to soak up the atmosphere. I'm trying to get into the spirit of Ul Qoma. Shit. You're smart, Corwi, I'm not telling you anything you don't know here. Help me with this.' I counted off on my fingers. 'She was here, this girl. This Fulana, Byela.' I almost said Marya. 'She was here – what? – three years ago. She was around dodgy local politicos, but she was looking for something else, which they couldn't help her with. Something even *they* thought was dodgy. She leaves.' I waited. 'She was going to Ul Qoma.' I swore, Corwi swore.

'She's been researching stuff,' I said. 'She goes over.'

'We think.'

'We think. Then suddenly she's back here.'

'Dead.'

'Dead.'

'Fuck.' Corwi leaned in, took and began thoughtfully to eat one of my pastries, stopped mouth full. For a long time neither of us said anything.

'It is. It's fucking breach, isn't it?' Corwi said eventually.

'. . . It looks like it might be breach, I think – yes I think it does.'

'If not to get over, to come back. Where she gets done. Or postmortem. Gets dumped.'

'Or something. Or something,' I said.

'Unless she crossed legit, or she's been here the whole time. Just because Drodin's not seen her . . .'

I recalled the phone call. I made a sceptical *maybe* face. 'Could be. He seemed pretty sure. It's sus, whatever.'

'Well . . .'

'Alright. So say it's breach: that's alright.'

'Bullshit it is.'

'No, listen,' I said. 'That means it wouldn't be our problem. Or at least . . . if we can persuade the Oversight Committee. Maybe I'll get that started.'

67

She glowered. 'They'll give you shit. I heard they were getting—'

'We'll have to present our evidence. It's circumstantial so far but *might* be enough to get it passed over.'

'Not from what I heard.' She looked away and back. 'Are you sure you'd want to, boss?'

'Shit yes. Shit yes. Listen. I get it. It's a credit to you that you want to keep it, but listen. If there's a chance we're right . . . you can't investigate breach. This Byela Fulana Foreigner Murdered Girl needs someone to look after her.' I made Corwi look at me by waiting. 'We're not the best people, Corwi. She deserves better than we can do. No one's going to be able to look out for her like Breach. Christ, who gets Breach on their behalf? Sniffing out a murderer?'

'Not many.'

'Yeah. So if we can we need to hand it over. The committee knows that everyone would try to pass off everything; that's why they make you jump through hoops.' She looked at me dubiously and I kept on. 'We don't have proof and we don't know the details, so let's take the next couple of days putting a cherry on top. Or proving ourselves wrong. Look at the profile we've got of her now. We've got enough at bloody last. She disappears from Beszel two, three years ago, turns up dead now. Maybe Drodin's right she was in Ul Qoma. Aboveboard. I want you to hit the phone, make some contacts here *and* over there. You know what we've got: foreigner, researcher, et cetera. Find out who she is. Anyone fobs you off, hint this is a Breach issue.'

On my return I went by Taskin's desk.

'Borlú. Got my call?'

'Ms. Cerush, your laboured excuses for seeking my company are becoming unconvincing.'

'I got your message and I've got it in motion. No, don't commit to eloping with me yet, Borlú, you're bound to be disappointed. You may have to wait a while to talk to the committee.'

'How's it going to work?'

'When did you last do this? Years ago, right? Listen, I'm sure you think you've got a slam dunk – Don't look at me like that, what's your sport? Boxing? I know you think they'll have to invoke' – her voice grew serious – 'instantly I mean, but they won't. You'll have to wait your turn, and it could be a few days.'

'I thought—'

'Once, yes. They'd have dropped what they were doing. But it's a tricky time, and it's more us than them. Neither set of reps relish this, but honestly Ul Qoma's not your issue at the moment. Since Syedr's lot came into the coalition screaming about national weakness the government's fretting about seeming too eager to invoke, so they're not going to rush. They've got public enquiries about the refugee camps, and there's no way they're not going to milk those.'

'Christ, you're kidding. They're still freaking out about those few poor sods?' Some must make it through and into one city or the other, but if they did it would be almost impossible for them not to breach, without immigration training. Our borders were tight. Where the desperate newcomers hit crosshatched patches of shore the unwritten agreement was that they were in the city of whichever border control met them, and thus incarcerated them in the coastal camps, first. How crestfallen were those who, hunting the hopes of Ul Qoma, landed in Besź.

'Whatever,' Taskin said. 'And other stuff. Glad-handing.

They're not going to shunt off business meetings and whatnot like they would've done once.'

'Whoring it for the Yankee dollar.'

'Don't knock it. If they're getting the Yankee dollar here that'll do me. But they're not going to rush for you, no matter who's died. Did someone die?'

IT DID NOT TAKE CORWI LONG to find what I had sent her to find. Late the next day she came into my office with a file.

'I just got it faxed over from Ul Qoma,' she said. 'I been trail-chasing. It wasn't even so hard, when you knew where to start. We were right.'

There she was, our victim – her file, her picture, our death mask, and suddenly and rather breathtakingly photographs of her in life, monochrome and fax-smudged but there, our dead woman smiling and smoking a cigarette and midword, her mouth open. Our scribbled notes, her details, estimated and now others in red, no question marks hesitating them, the facts of her; below her various invented names, there her real one.

CHAPTER SIX

'MAHALIA GEARY.'

There were forty-two people around the table (antique, would there ever be question?), and me. The forty-two were seated, with folders in front of them. I stood. Two minutes-takers transcribed at their stations in the room's corners. I could see microphones on the table, and translators sat nearby.

'Mahalia Geary. She was twenty-four. American. This is all my constable's doing, Constable Corwi, all this information, ladies and gentlemen. All the information's in the papers I sent.' They were not all reading them. Some did not have them open.

'American?' someone said.

I did not recognise all of the twenty-one Besź representatives. Some. A woman in her middle ages, severe skunk-stripe hair like a film-studies academic, Shura Katrinya, minister without portfolio, respected but past her moment. Mikhel Buric of the Social Democrats, official opposition, young, capable, ambitious enough to be on more than one committee (security, commerce, arts). Major Yorj Syedr, a leader of the National Bloc, the rightist grouping with whom Prime Minister Gayardicz controversially worked in coalition, despite Syedr's reputation not only as a bully but a less than competent one. Yavid Nyisemu, Gayardicz's under-minister for Culture and committee chair. Other faces were familiar, and with effort more names would come. I recognised none of the Ul Qoma counterparts. I did not pay close attention to foreign politics.

Most of the Ul Qomans flicked through the packets I had prepared. Three wore headphones, but most were fluent enough in Besź at least to understand me. It was strange not to unsee these people in formal Ul Qoma dress – men in collarless shirts and dark lapel-less jackets, the few women in spiral semiwraps in colours that would be contraband in Besźel. But then I was not in Besźel.

The Oversight Committee meets in the giant, baroque, concrete-patched coliseum in the centre of Besźel Old Town, and of Ul Qoma Old Town. It is one of very few places that has the same name in both cities – Copula Hall. That is because it is not a crosshatched building, precisely, nor one of staccato totality-alterity, one floor or room in Besźel and the next in Ul Qoma: externally it is in both cities; internally, much of it is in both or neither. All of us – twenty-one lawmakers from each state, their assistants, and I – were meeting at a juncture, an interstice, one sort-of border built above another.

To me it was as if another presence were there: the reason for the meeting. Perhaps several of us in the room felt watched.

As they fussed with their papers, those who did so, I thanked them again for seeing me. A little political gush. These meetings of the Oversight Committee were regular, but I had had to wait days to see them. I had despite Taskin's warning tried to convene an extraordinary meeting to pass over responsibility for Mahalia Geary as quickly as possible (who wanted to think of her murderer free? There was one best chance of sorting

72

that), but short of epochal crisis, civil war or catastrophe, this was impossible to arrange.

What about a diminished meeting? A few people missing surely wouldn't . . . But no, I was quickly informed, that would be quite unacceptable. She had warned me and she had been right, and I had grown more impatient with each day. Taskin had given me her best contact, a confidential secretary to one of the ministers on the committee, who had explained that the Beszel Chamber of Commerce had one of its increasingly regular trade fairs with foreign businesses, and that counted out Buric, who had had some success overseeing such events, Nyisemu, and even Syedr. These of course were sacrosanct occurrences. That Katrinya had meetings with diplomats. That Hurian, commissioner of the Ul Qoma Exchange, an impossible-to-reschedule meeting with the Ul Qoman health minister, and very et cetera, and there would be no special meeting. The young dead woman would have to remain inadequately investigated a few more days, until the gathering, at which time, between the indispensable business of adjudication on any *dissensus*, of the management of shared resources – a few of the larger grid power lines, drains and sewage, the most intricately crosshatched buildings – I would be given my twenty-minute slot to make my case.

Perhaps some people knew the details of these strictures, but the specifics of the Oversight Committee's machinations had never been of interest. I had presented to them twice before, long before. The committee's makeup had been different then, of course. Both times, the Besź and Ul Qoman sides almost bristled at each other: relations had been worse. Even when we had been noncombatant supporters of opposing sides in conflicts, such as during the Second World War – not

Ul Qoma's finest hour – the Oversight Committee had had to convene. What uncomfortable occasions those must have been. It had not met, however, as I recalled from my lessons, during our two brief and disastrous open wars against each other. In any case, now our two nations were, in rather a stilted fashion, supposed to be effecting some sort of rapprochement.

Neither of these previous cases I had presented had been so urgent. The first time was a contraband breach, as most such referrals are. A gang in western Beszel had started selling drugs purified from Ul Qoman medicines. They were picking up boxes near the city's outskirts, from near the end of the east-west axis of the crossroad railway lines that split Ul Qoma into four quadrants. An Ul Qoman contact was dumping the boxes from the trains. There is a short stretch in the north of Beszel where the tracks themselves cross-hatch with and serve also as Ul Qoman tracks; and the miles of north-seeking railroads leading out of both city-states, joining us to our northern neighbours through the mountain gash, are also shared, to our borders, where they become a single line in existential legality as well as mere metal fact: up to those national edges, the track was two juridical railroads. In various of those places the boxes of medical supplies were dropped in Ul Qoma, and stayed there, abandoned trackside in Ul Qoman scrub: but they were picked up in Beszel, and that was breach.

We never observed our criminals taking them, but when we presented our evidence that that was the only possible source, the committee agreed and invoked Breach. That drug trade ended: the suppliers disappeared from the streets.

The second case was a man who had killed his wife and when we closed in on him, in stupid terror he breached – stepped into a shop in Beszel, changed his clothes, and

74

emerged into Ul Qoma. He was by chance not apprehended in that instance, but we quickly realised what had happened. In his frantic liminality neither we nor our Ul Qoman colleagues would touch him, though we and they knew where he went, hiding in Ul Qoman lodgings. Breach took him and he was gone too.

This was the first time in a long time I had made this request. I put my evidence. I addressed myself as much, politely, to the Ul Qoman members as to the Besź. Also to the observing power that must, surely, invisibly have watched.

'She's resident in Ul Qoma, not Besźel. Once we knew that we found her. Corwi did, I mean. She'd been there for more than two years. She's a PhD student.'

'What's she studying?' Buric said.

'She's an archaeologist. Early history. She's attached to one of the digs. It's all in your folders.' A little ripple, differently iterated among the Besź and the Ul Qomans. 'That's how she got in, even with the blockade.' There were some loopholes and exceptions for educational and cultural links.

Digs are constant in Ul Qoma, research projects incessant, its soil so much richer than our own in the extraordinary artefacts of pre-Cleavage ages. Books and conferences bicker over whether that preponderance is coincidence of scattering or evidence of some Ul Qoman specific thing (the Ul Qoman nationalists of course insist the latter). Mahalia Geary was affiliated with a long-term dig at Bol Ye'an, in western Ul Qoma, a site as important as Tenochtitlan and Sutton Hoo, which had been active since its discovery almost a century ago.

It would have been nice for my compatriot historians had it cross-hatched, but though the park on the edge of which it was located did, just a little, the crosshatch coming quite close

75

to the carefully ploughed-up earth full of treasures, a thin strip of total Besźel even separating sections of Ul Qoma within the grounds, the dig itself did not. There are those Besź who will say that lopsidedness is a good thing, that had we had half as rich a seam of historic rubble as Ul Qoma – anything like as many mixed-up sheila-na-gigs, clockwork remnants, mosaic shards, axe heads, and cryptic parchment scraps hallowed with rumours of physical misbehaviour and unlikely effects – we would simply have sold it off. Ul Qoma, at least, with its mawkish sanctimoniousness about history (obvious guilty compensation for the pace of change, for the vulgar vigour of much of its recent development), its state archivists and export restrictions, kept its past somewhat protected.

'Bol Ye'an's run by a bunch of archaeologists from Prince of Wales University in Canada, which is where Geary was enrolled. Her supervisor's lived on and off in Ul Qoma for years – Isabelle Nancy. There's a bunch of them who live there. They organise conferences sometimes. Even have them in Besźel one year in every few.' Some consolation prize for our remnant-barren ground. 'The last big one was a while ago, when they found that last cache of artefacts. I'm sure you all remember.' It had made the international press. The collection had quickly been given some name, but I could not remember it. It included an astrolabe and a geared thing, some intricate complexity as madly specific and untimed as the Antikythera mechanism, to which as many dreams and speculations had attached, and the purpose of which, similarly, no one had been able to reconstruct.

'So what is the story with this girl?' It was one of the Ul Qomans who spoke, a fat man in his fifties with a shirt in shades that would have made it questionably legal in Besźel.

'She's been based there, Ul Qoma, for months, for her research,' I said. 'She came to Besźel first, before she'd been to Ul Qoma, for a conference about three years ago. You might remember, there was the big exhibition of artefacts and stuff borrowed from Ul Qoma, and there was a whole week or two of meetings and so on. Loads of people came over from all over the place, academics from Europe, North America, from Ul Qoma and everything.'

'Certainly we remember,' Nyisemu said. 'Plenty of us were involved.' Of course. Various state committees and quangos had had stands; government and opposition ministers had attended. The prime minister had started the proceedings, Nyisemu had formally opened the exhibition at the museum, and it had been required attendance for all serious politicians.

'Well she was there. You might even have noticed her – she caused a bit of a stink, apparently, was accused of Disrespect, made some terrible speech about Orciny at a presentation. Almost got chucked out.' A couple of faces – Buric and Katrinya certainly, Nyisemu perhaps – looked as if that sparked something. At least one person on the Ul Qoman side of things looked reminiscent too.

'So she calms down, it seems, finishes her MA, starts a PhD, gets entry into Ul Qoma, this time, to be part of this dig, do her studies – she'd never have got back in here, I don't think, not after that intervention, and frankly I'm surprised she got in there – and she'd been there since except for holidays for a while. There's student accommodation near the dig. She disappeared a couple of weeks ago and turned up in Besźel. In Pocost Village, in the estate, which is, you will recall, total in Besźel, so alter for Ul Qoma, and she was dead. It's all in the folder, Congressman.'

'You haven't shown breach, have you? Not really.' Yorj Syedr spoke more softly than I would expect from a military man. Opposite him several of the Ul Qoman congressmen and -women whispered in Illitan, his interjection spurring them to confer. I looked at him. Near him Buric rolled his eyes, saw me see him doing so.

'You have to forgive me, Councillor,' I said eventually. 'I don't know what to say to that. This young woman lived in Ul Qoma. Officially, I mean, we have the records. She disappears. She turns up dead in Besźel.' I frowned. 'I'm not really sure . . . What else would you suggest was evidence?'

'Circumstantial, though. I mean, have you checked the Foreign Office? Have you found out, for example, whether perhaps Miss Geary left Ul Qoma for some event in Budapest or something? Maybe she did that, then came to Besźel? There's almost two weeks unaccounted for, Inspector Borlú.'

I stared. 'As I say, she wouldn't have got back into Besźel after her little performance . . .'

He made an almost regretful face and interrupted me. 'Breach is . . . an alien power.' Several of the Besź and some of the Ul Qoman members of the committee looked shocked. 'We all know it's the case,' Syedr said, 'whether it is polite to acknowledge it or not.

'Breach is and I say it again *alien power*, and we hand over our sovereignty to it at our peril. We've simply washed our hands of any difficult situations and handed them to a – apologies if I offend, but – a shadow over which we have no control. Simply to make our lives easier.'

'Are you joking, Councillor?' someone said.

'I've had enough of this,' Buric began.

'We don't all cosy up to enemies,' Syedr said.

78

'Chair,' Buric shouted. 'Will you allow this slander? This is outrageous . . .' I watched the new nonpartisan spirit I had read about.

'Of course where its intervention's necessary I fully support invocation,' Syedr said. 'But my party's been arguing for some time that we need to stop . . . rubber-stamping the ceding to the Breach of considerable authority. How much research have you actually done, Inspector? Have you spoken to her parents? Her friends? What do we actually *know* about this poor young woman?'

I should have been more prepared for this. I had not expected it.

I had seen Breach before, in a brief moment. Who hadn't? I had seen it take control. The great majority of breaches are acute and immediate. Breach *intervenes*. I was not used to seeking permissions, invoking, this arcane way. Trust to Breach, we grow up hearing, unsee and don't mention the Ul Qoman pickpockets or muggers at work even if you notice, which you shouldn't, from where you stand in Besźel, because breach is a worse transgression than theirs.

When I was fourteen I saw the Breach for the first time. The cause was the most common of all such – a traffic accident. A boxy little Ul Qoman van – this was more than thirty years ago, the vehicles on Ul Qoma's roads were much less impressive than they are now – had skidded. It had been travelling a crosshatched road, and a good third of the cars in that area were Besź.

Had the van righted, the Besź drivers would have responded traditionally to such an intrusive foreign obstacle, one of the inevitable difficulties of living in crosshatched cities. When an Ul Qoman stumbles into a Besź, each in their own city; if an

79

Ul Qoman's dog runs up and sniffs a Besź passerby; a window broken in Ul Qoma that leaves glass in the path of Besź pedestrians – in all cases the Besź (or Ul Qomans, in the converse circumstances) avoid the foreign difficulty as best they can without acknowledging it. Touch if they must, though not is better. Such polite stoic unsensing is the form for dealing with protubs – that is the Besź for those protuberances from the other city. There is an Illitan term too, but I do not know it. (Only rubbish is an exception, when it is old enough. Lying across crosshatched pavement or gusted into an alter area from where it was dropped, it starts as protub, but after a long enough time for it to fade and the Illitan or Besź script to be obscured by filth and bleached by light, and when it coagulates with other rubbish, including rubbish from the other city, it's just rubbish, and it drifts across borders, like fog, rain and smoke.)

The van driver I saw did not recover. He ground diagonally across the tarmac – I do not know what the street is in Ul Qoma, it was KünigStrász in Besźel – and thudded into the wall of a Besź boutique and the pedestrian window-shopping there. The Besź man died; the Ul Qoman driver was badly hurt. People in both cities were screaming. I did not see the impact, but my mother did, and grabbed my hand so hard I shouted in pain before I even registered the noise.

The early years of a Besź (and presumably an Ul Qoman) child are intense learnings of cues. We pick up styles of clothing, permissible colours, ways of walking and holding oneself, very fast. Before we were eight or so most of us could be trusted not to breach embarrassingly and illegally, though licence of course is granted children every moment they are in the street.

80

I was older than that when I looked up to see the bloody result of that breaching accident, and remember remembering those arcana, and that they were bullshit. In that moment when my mother and I and all of us there could not but see the Ul Qoman wreck, all that careful unseeing I had recently learned was thrown.

In seconds, the Breach came. Shapes, figures, some of whom perhaps had been there but who nonetheless seemed to coalesce from spaces between smoke from the accident, moving too fast it seemed to be clearly seen, moving with authority and power so absolute that within seconds they had controlled, contained, the area of the intrusion. The powers were almost impossible, seemed almost impossible, to make out. At the edges of the crisis zone the Besź and, I could still not fail to see, Ul Qoman police were pushing away the curious in their own cities, taping off the area, closing out outsiders, sealing off a zone inside of which, their quick actions still visible though child-me so afraid to see them, Breach, organising, cauterising, restoring.

These kind of rare situations were when one might glimpse Breach, performing what they did. Accidents and border-perforating catastrophes. The 1926 Earthquake, a grand fire. (There had once been a fire grosstopically close to my apartment. It had been contained in one house, but a house not in Besźel, that I had unseen. So I had watched footage of it piped in from Ul Qoma, on my local TV, while my living-room windows had been lit by the fluttering red glow of it.) The death of an Ul Qoman bystander from a stray Besź bullet in a stickup. It was hard to associate those crises with this bureaucracy.

I shifted and looked about the room at nothing. Breach has

to account for its actions to those specialists who invoke it, but that does not feel like a limitation to many of us.

'Have you spoken to her colleagues?' Syedr said. 'How far have you taken this?'

'No. I haven't spoken to them. My constable has, of course, to verify our information.'

'Have you spoken to her parents? You seem very keen to divest yourself of this investigation.' I waited a few more seconds before speaking over the muttering on both sides of the table.

'Corwi's got word to them. They're flying in. Major, I'm not sure you understand the position we're in. Yes I *am* keen. Don't you want to see the murderer of Mahalia Geary found?'

'Alright, enough.' Yavid Nyisemu. He galloped his fingers on the table. 'Inspector, you might not take that tone. There's a concern, both reasonable and growing, among representatives that we're too quick to cede to Breach in situations where we might actually choose not to, and that doing so's dangerous and potentially even a betrayal.' He waited until eventually his requirement was clear and I made a noise that could be thought apology. 'However,' he continued. 'Major, you might also consider being less argumentative and ridiculous. For goodness' sake, the young woman's in Ul Qoma, disappears, turns up dead in Besźel. I can hardly think of a more clear-cut case. Of course we'll be endorsing the surrender of this to Breach.' He cut the air with his hands as Syedr began to complain.

Katrinya nodded. 'A voice of sense,' Buric said. The Ul Qomans had obviously seen these internal fights before. The splendours of our democracy. Doubtless they conducted their own squabbles.

'I think that'll be all, Inspector,' he said, over the major's raised voice. 'We've got your submission. Thank you. The usher'll show you out. You'll be hearing from us shortly.'

THE CORRIDORS OF COPULA HALL are in a determined style that must have evolved over the many centuries of the building's existence and centrality to Besź and Ul Qoman life and politics: they are antique and haute, but somehow vague, definitionless. The oil paintings are well executed but as if without antecedent, bloodlessly general. The staff, Besź and Ul Qoman, come and go in those in-between corridors. The hall feels not collaborative but empty.

The few Precursor artefacts in alarmed and guarded bell jars that punctuate the passages are different. They are specific, but opaque. I glanced at some as I left: a sag-breasted Venus with a ridge where gears or a lever might sit; a crude metal wasp discoloured by centuries; a basalt die. Below each one a caption offered guesses.

Syedr's intervention was unconvincing – he gave the impression that he had decided to make his stand on the next petition that crossed the desk, and had the misfortune for it to be mine, a case with which it was hard to argue – and his motivations questionable. If I were political I would not in any circumstances follow his lead. But there was a reason to his caution.

The powers of the Breach are almost limitless. Frightening. What does limit Breach is solely that those powers are highly circumstantially specific. The insistence that those circumstances be rigorously policed is a necessary precaution for the cities.

That is why these arcane checks and balances between Besźel, Ul Qoma, and the Breach. In circumstances other than

83

the various acute and unarguable breaches – of crime, accident or disaster (chemical spill, gas explosion, a mentally ill attacker attacking across the municipal boundary) – the committee vetted all potential invocations – which were, after all, all circumstances in which Beszel and Ul Qoma would denude themselves of any powers.

Even after the acute events, with which no one sane could argue, the representatives of the two cities on the committee would carefully examine ex post facto justifications they commissioned for Breach's interventions. They might, technically, question any of these: it would be absurd to do so, but the committee would not undermine their authority by not going through important motions.

The two cities need the Breach. And without the cities' integrities, what is Breach?

Corwi was waiting for me. 'So?' She handed me coffee. 'What did they say?'

'Well, it's going to be handed over. But they made me jump through hoops.' We walked towards the police car. All the streets around Copula Hall were crosshatched, and we made our way unseeing through a group of Ul Qoman friends to where Corwi had parked. 'You know Syedr?'

'That fascist prick? Sure.'

'He was trying to make out as if he wouldn't let the case go to Breach. It was weird.'

'They hate Breach, don't they, the NatBloc?'

'Weird to hate it. Like hating air or something. And he's a nat, and if there's no Breach, there's no Beszel. No homeland.'

'It's complicated, isn't it,' she said, 'because even though we need them, it's a sign of dependence that we do. Nats are divided, anyway, between balance-of-power people and triumphalists. Maybe he's a triumphalist. They reckon Breach are protecting Ul Qoma, the only thing stopping Besźel taking over.'

'They want to take it over? They're living in a dreamworld if they think Besźel would win.' Corwi glanced at me. We both knew it was true. 'Anyway, it's moot. He was posturing, I think.'

'He's a fucking idiot. I mean, as well as being a fascist he's just not very clever. When are we going to get the nod?'

'A day or two, I think. They'll vote on all the motions put in front of them today. I think.' I did not know how it was organised, in fact.

'So in the meantime, what?' She was terse.

'Well, you've got plenty of other stuff to be getting on with, I take it? This isn't your only case.' I looked at her as we drove.

We drove past Copula Hall, its huge entrance like a made, secular cave. The building is much larger than a cathedral, larger than a Roman circus. It's open at its eastern and western sides. At ground level and for the first vaulted fifty feet or so above it is a semienclosed thoroughfare, punctuated with pillars, traffic streams separated by walls, stop-started with checkpoints.

Pedestrians and vehicles came and went. Cars and vans drove into it near us, to wait at the easternmost point, where passports and papers were checked and motorists were given permission – or sometimes refused it – to leave Besźel. A steady current. More metres, through the inter-checkpoint interstice under the hall's arc, another wait at the buildings' western gates, for entry into Ul Qoma. A reversed process in the other lanes.

Then the vehicles with their stamped permissions-to-cross emerged at the opposite end from where they entered, and drove into a foreign city. Often they doubled back, on the cross-hatched streets in the Old Town or the Old Town, to the same space they had minutes earlier occupied, though in a new juridic realm.

If someone needed to go to a house physically next door to their own but in the neighbouring city, it was in a different road in an unfriendly power. That is what foreigners rarely understand. A Besź dweller cannot walk a few paces next door into an alter house without breach.

But pass through Copula Hall and she or he might leave Besźel, and at the end of the hall come back to exactly (corporeally) where they had just been, but in another country, a tourist, a marvelling visitor, to a street that shared the latitude-longitude of their own address, a street they had never visited before, whose architecture they had always unseen, to the Ul Qoman house sitting next to and a whole city away from their own building, unvisible there now they had come through, all the way across the Breach, back home.

Copula Hall like the waist of an hourglass, the point of ingress and egress, the navel between the cities. The whole edifice a funnel, letting visitors from one city into the other, and the other into the one.

There are places not crosshatched but where Besźel is interrupted by a thin part of Ul Qoma. As kids we would assiduously unsee Ul Qoma, as our parents and teachers had relentlessly trained us (the ostentation with which we and our Ul Qoman contemporaries used to unnotice each other when we were grosstopically close was impressive). We used to throw stones across the alterity, walk the long way around in Besźel and pick them up again, debate whether we had done wrong. Breach never manifested, of course. We did the same with the

86

local lizards. They were always dead when we picked them up, and we said the little airborne trip through Ul Qoma had killed them, though it might just as well have been the landing.

'Won't be our problem much longer,' I said, watching a few Ul Qoman tourists emerge into Besźel. 'Mahalia, I mean. Byela. Fulana Detail.'

CHAPTER SEVEN

TO FLY TO BESZEL from the east coast of the US involves changing planes at least once, and that's the best option. It is a famously complicated trip. There are direct flights to Besźel from Budapest, from Skopje, and, probably an American's best bet, from Athens. Technically Ul Qoma would have been harder for them to get to because of the blockade, but all they needed to do was nip into Canada and they could fly direct. There were many more international services to the New Wolf.

The Gearys were coming in to Besźel Halvic at ten in the morning. I had already made Corwi break the news of their daughter's death to them over the phone. I told her I would escort them to see the body myself, though she could join me if she chose. She did.

We waited at Besźel Airport, in case the plane came in early. We drank bad coffee from the Starbucks analogue in the terminal. Corwi asked me again about the workings of the Oversight Committee. I asked her if she had ever left Besźel.

'Sure,' she said. 'I've been to Romania. I've been to Bulgaria.'

'Turkey?'

'No. You?'

'There. And London. Moscow. Paris, once, a long time ago,

and Berlin. West Berlin as it was. It was before they joined.'

'Berlin?' she said. The airport was hardly crowded: mostly returning Besź, it seemed, plus a few tourists and Eastern European commercial travellers. It is hard to tourist in Besźel, or in Ul Qoma – how many holiday destinations set exams before they let you in? – but still, though I had not been I had seen film of the newish Ul Qoma Airport, sixteen or seventeen miles southeast, across Bulkya Sound from Lestov, and it got vastly more traffic than us, though their visitor conditions were not less strenuous than our own. When it had been rebuilt a few years previously, it had gone from somewhat smaller to much larger than our own terminal in a few months of frenetic construction. From above its terminals were concatenated half-moons of mirrored glass, designed by Foster or someone like that.

A group of foreign orthodox Jews were met by their, judging by clothes, much less devout local relatives. A fat security officer let his gun dangle to scratch his chin. There were one or two intimidatingly dressed execs from those gold-dust recent arrivals, our new high-tech, even American, friends, finding the drivers with signs for board members of Sear and Core, Shadner, VerTech, those executives who did not arrive in their own planes, or copter in to their own helipads. Corwi saw me reading the cards.

'Why the fuck would anyone invest here?' she said. 'Do you reckon they even remember agreeing to it? The government blatantly slips them Rohypnol at those junkets.'

'Typical Besź defeatist talk, Constable. That's what's doing our country down. Representatives Buric and Nyisemu and Syedr are doing precisely the job with which we entrust them.' Buric and Nyisemu made sense: it was extraordinary Syedr had got into organising the trade fairs. Some favour pulled in. The fact that, as these foreign visitors showed, there were even small successes was even more remarkable for that.

'Right,' she said. 'Seriously, watch these guys when they come out – I swear that's panic in their eyes. Have you seen those cars ferrying them around town, at tourist spots and cross-hatchings and whatever? "Seeing the sights." Right. Those poor sods are trying to find ways out.' I pointed at a display: the plane had landed.

'So you spoke to Mahalia's supervisor?' I said. 'I tried to call her a couple of times but can't get through and they won't give me her mobile.'

'Not for very long,' Corwi said. 'I got hold of her at the centre – there's like a research centre that's part of the dig in Ul Qoma. Professor Nancy, she's one of the bigwigs, she has a whole bunch of students. Anyway I called her and verified that Mahalia was one of hers, that no one had seen her for a while, et cetera et cetera. I told her we had reason to believe dot dot dot. Sent over a picture. She was very shocked.'

'Yeah?'

'Sure. She was . . . kept going on about what a great student Mahalia was, how she couldn't believe it, what had happened, so on. So you were in Berlin. Do you speak German then?'

'I used to,' I said. *'Ein bisschen.'*

'Why were you there?'

'I was young. It was a conference. "Policing Split Cities." They had sessions on Budapest and Jerusalem and Berlin, and Besźel and Ul Qoma.'

'Fuck!'

'I know, I know. That's what we said at the time. Totally missing the point.'

'*Split* cities? I'm surprised the acad let you go.'

'I know, I could almost feel my freebie evaporating in a gust of other people's patriotism. My super said it wasn't just a misunderstanding of our status it was *an insult to Besźel.* Not wrong, I suppose. But it was a subsidised trip abroad, was I going to say no? I had to persuade him. I did at least meet my first Ul Qomans, who'd obviously managed to overcome their own outrage, too. Met one in particular at the conference disco as I recall. We did our bit to ease international tensions over "99 Luftballons".' Corwi snorted, but passengers began to come through and we composed our faces, so they would be respectfully set when the Gearys emerged.

The immigration officer who escorted them saw us and nodded them gently over. They were recognisable from the photographs we had been sent by our American counterparts, but I would have known them anyway. They had the expression I have seen only on bereaved parents: their faces looked clayish, lumpy with exhaustion and grief. They shuffled into the concourse as if they were fifteen or twenty years older than they were.

'Mr. and Mrs. Geary?' I had been practicing my English.

'Oh,' she said, the woman. She reached out her hand. 'Oh yes, you are, you're Mr. Corwi are you, is that—'

'No, ma'am. I'm Inspector Tyador Borlú of the Besźel ECS.' I shook her hand, her husband's hand. 'This is constable Lizbyet Corwi. Mr. and Mrs. Geary, I, we, are very deeply sorry for your loss.'

The two of them blinked like animals and nodded and opened their mouths but said nothing. Grief made them look stupid. It was cruel.

'May I take you to your hotel?'

'No, thank you, Inspector,' Mr. Geary said. I glanced at Corwi, but she was following what was said, more or less – her comprehension was good. 'We'd like to . . . we'd like to do what it is we're here for.' Mrs. Geary clutched and unclutched at her bag. 'We'd like to see her.'

'Of course. Please.' I led them to the vehicle.

'Are we going to see Professor Nancy?' Mr. Geary asked as Corwi drove us. 'And May's friends?'

'No, Mr. Geary,' I said. 'We can't do that, I'm afraid. They are not in Beszel. They're in Ul Qoma.'

'You know that, Michael, you know how it works here,' his wife said.

'Yes yes,' he said to me, as if they had been my words. 'Yes, I'm sorry, let me . . . I just want to talk to her friends.'

'It can be arranged, Mr. Geary, Mrs. Geary,' I said. 'We'll see about phone calls. And . . .' I was thinking about passes through Copula Hall. 'We'll have to get you escorted into Ul Qoma. After we've dealt with things here.'

Mrs. Geary looked at her husband. He stared out at the buildup of streets and vehicles around us. Some of the overpasses we were approaching were in Ul Qoma, but I was certain he wouldn't forebear staring at them. He would not care even if he knew not to. En route there would be an illicit, breaching, view to a glitzy Ul Qoman Fast Economy Zone full of horrible but big public art.

The Gearys both wore visitors' marks in Besź colours, but as rare recipients of compassionate-entry stamps they had no tourist training, no appreciation of the local politics of boundaries. They would be insensitive with loss. The dangers of their breaching were high. We needed to protect them from unthinkingly committing acts that would get them deported, at least. Until the handover of the situation to Breach was made official, we were on babysitting duty: we would not leave the Gearys' sides while they were awake.

Corwi did not look at me. We would have to be careful. Had the Gearys been regular tourists, they would have had to undergo mandatory training and passed the not-unstringent entrance exam, both its theoretical and practical-role-play elements, to qualify for their visas. They would know, at least in outline, key signifiers of architecture, clothing, alphabet and manner, outlaw colours and gestures, obligatory details – and, depending on their Besź teacher, the supposed distinctions in national physiognomies – distinguishing Beszel and Ul Qoma, and their citizens. They would know a little tiny bit (not that we locals knew much more) about Breach. Crucially, they would know enough to avoid obvious breaches of their own.

After a two-week or however-long-it-was course, no one thought visitors would have metabolised the deep prediscursive instinct for our borders that Besź and Ul Qomans have, to have picked up real rudiments of unseeing. But we did insist that they acted as if they had. We, and the authorities of Ul Qoma, expected strict overt decorum, interacting with, and indeed obviously noticing, our crosshatched neighbouring city-state not at all.

While, or as, sanctions for breach are severe (the two cities depend on that), breach must be beyond reasonable doubt. We all suspect that, while we are long-expert in unseeing it, tourists to the Old Beszel ghetto are surreptitiously noticing Ul Qoma's glass-fronted Yal Iran Bridge, which in literal topology abuts it. Look up at the ribbon-streaming balloons of Beszel's Wind-Day parade, they doubtless can't fail (as we can) to notice the raised teardrop towers of Ul Qoma's palace district, next to them though a whole country away. So long as they do not point and coo (which is why except in rare exceptions no foreigners under eighteen are granted entry) everyone concerned can indulge the possibility that there is no breach. It is that restraint that the pre-visa training teaches, rather than a local's rigorous unseeing, and most students have the nous to understand that. We all, Breach included, give the benefit of the doubt to visitors when possible.

In the mirror of the car I saw Mr. Geary watch a passing truck. I unsaw it because it was in Ul Qoma.

His wife and he murmured to each other occasionally – my English or my hearing was not good enough to tell what they said. Mostly they sat in silence, each alone, looking out of windows on either side of the car.

Shukman was not at his laboratory. Perhaps he knew himself and how he would seem to those visiting the dead. I would not want to be met by him in these circumstances. Hamzinic led us to the storage room. Her parents moaned in perfect time as they entered and saw the shape below the sheet. Hamzinic waited with silent respect while they prepared, and when her mother nodded he showed Mahalia's face. Her parents moaned again. They stared at her, and after long seconds her mother touched her face.

'Oh, oh yes that's her,' Mr. Geary said. He cried. 'That's her, yes, that's my daughter,' as if we were asking formal identification of him, which we were not. They had wanted to see her. I nodded as if that were helpful to us and glanced at Hamzinic, who replaced the sheet and made himself busy as we led Mahalia's parents away.

*

94

'I DO WANT TO, to *go* to Ul Qoma,' Mr. Geary said. I was used to hearing that little stress on the verb from foreigners: he felt strange using it. 'I'm sorry, I know it's probably going to be . . . to be hard to organise but, I want to see, where she . . .'

'Of course,' I said.

'Of course,' Corwi said. She was keeping up with a reasonable amount of the English, and spoke occasionally. We were eating lunch with the Gearys at the Queen Czezille, a comfortable enough hotel with which the Besź Police had a long-standing arrangement. Its staff were experienced in providing the chaperoning, almost surreptitious imprisonment, that unqualified visitors required.

James Thacker, some middle-ranking twenty-eight- or -nine-year-old at the US embassy, had joined us. He spoke occasionally to Corwi in excellent Besź. The dining room looked out at the northern tip of Hustav Isle. Riverboats went by (in both cities). The Gearys picked at their peppercorned fish.

'We suspected that you might like to visit your daughter's place of work,' I said. 'We've been in discussion with Mr. Thacker and his counterparts in Ul Qoma for the paperwork to get you through Copula Hall. A day or two I think is all.' Not an embassy, in Ul Qoma, of course: a sulky US Interests section.

'And . . . you said that this is, this is for the Breach now?' Mrs. Geary said. 'You said it won't be the Ul Qomans investigating it but it'll be with this Breach, yes?' She stared at me with tremendous mistrust. 'So when do we talk to them?'

I glanced at Thacker. 'That will not happen,' I said. 'The Breach is not like us.'

Mrs. Geary stared at me. '"Us" the . . . the *policzai?*' she said. I had meant the 'us' to include her. 'Well, among other

95

things, yes. It . . . they aren't like the police in Besźel or in Ul Qoma.'

'I don't—'

'Inspector Borlú, I'll be happy to explain this,' Thacker said. He hesitated. He wanted me to go. Any explanation carried out in my presence would have to be moderately polite: alone with other Americans he could stress to them how ridiculous and difficult these cities were, how sorry he and his colleagues were for the added complications of a crime occurring in Besźel, and so on. He could insinuate. It was an embarrassment, an antagonism to have to deal with a dissident force like Breach.

'I don't know how much you know about Breach, Mr. and Mrs. Geary, but it is . . . it isn't like other powers. You have some sense of its . . . capabilities? The Breach is . . . It has unique powers. And it's, ah, extremely secretive. We, the embassy, have no contacts with . . . any representative of Breach. I do realise how strange that must sound, but . . . I can assure you Breach's record in the prosecution of criminals is, ah, ferocious. Impressive. We will receive word of its progress and of whatever action it takes against whoever it finds responsible.'

'Does that mean . . .?' Mr. Geary said. 'They have the death penalty here, right?'

'And in Ul Qoma?' his wife said.

'Sure,' Thacker said. 'But that's not really at issue. Mr. and Mrs. Geary, our friends in Besźel and the Ul Qoma authorities are about to invoke *Breach* to deal with your daughter's murder, so Besź laws and Ul Qoman laws are kind of irrelevant. The, ah, sanctions available to Breach are pretty limitless.'

'Invoke?' said Mrs. Geary.

'There are protocols,' I said. 'To be followed. Before Breach'll manifest to take care of this.'

Mr. Geary: 'What about the trial?'

'That will be *in camera*,' I said. 'Breach . . . tribunals,' I had tried out *decisions* and *actions* in my head, 'are secret.'

'We won't testify? We won't see?' Mr. Geary was aghast. This must all have been explained previously, but you know. Mrs. Geary was shaking her head in anger, but without her husband's surprise.

'I'm afraid not,' Thacker said. 'It is a unique situation here. I can pretty much guarantee you, though, that whoever did this will not only be caught but, be, ah, brought to pretty severe justice.' One could almost pity Mahalia Geary's killer. I did not.

'But that's—'

'I know, Mrs. Geary, I'm truly sorry. There are no other posts like this in the service. Ul Qoma and Besźel and Breach . . . These are unique circumstances.'

'Oh, God. You know, it's . . . it's all, this is all the stuff Mahalia was into,' Mr. Geary said. 'The city, the city, the other city. Besźel' – *Bezzel*, he said it – 'and Ul Qoma. And or seen it.' I didn't understand that.

'Or *seen* ee,' Mrs. Geary said. I looked up. 'It's not Orsinnit, it's Orciny, honey.'

Thacker pouted polite incomprehension and shook his head in question.

'What's that, Mrs. Geary?' I said. She fiddled with her bag. Corwi quietly took out a notebook.

'This is all this stuff Mahalia was into,' Mrs. Geary said. 'It's what she was studying. She was going to be a doctor of it.' Mr. Geary grimace-smiled, indulgent, proud, bewildered. 'She was doing real well. She told us a little bit about it. It sounds like that Orciny was like the Breach.'

'Ever since she first came here,' Mr. Geary said. 'This is the stuff she wanted to do.'

'That's right, she came here first. I mean ... here, this, Besźel, right? She came here first, but then she said she needed to go to Ul Qoma. I'm going to be honest with you, Inspector, I thought it was kind of the same place. I know that was wrong. She had to get special permission to go there, but because she's, was, a student, that's where she stayed to do all her work.'

'Orciny . . . it's a sort of folk tale,' I told Thacker. Mahalia's mother nodded; her father looked away. 'It is not so really like the Breach, Mrs. Geary. Breach is real. A power. But Orciny is . . .' I hesitated.

'The third city,' Corwi said in Besź to Thacker, who still furrowed his face. When he showed no comprehension, she said, 'A secret. Fairy tale. Between the other two.' He shook his head and looked, uninterestedly, *Oh*.

'She loved this place,' Mrs. Geary said. She looked longing. 'I mean, sorry, I mean Ul Qoma. Are we near where she lived?' Crudely physically, grosstopically, to use the term unique to Besźel and Ul Qoma, unnecessary anywhere else, yes we were. Neither Corwi nor I answered, as it was a complicated question. 'She'd been studying it all for years, since she first read some book about the cities. Her professors always seemed to think she was doing excellent in her work.'

'Did you like her professors?' I said.

'Oh, I never met them. But she showed me some of what they were doing; she showed me a website for the program, and the place she worked.'

'This is Professor Nancy?'

'That was her advisor, yes. Mahalia liked her.'

'They worked well together?' Corwi was watching me as I asked.

'Oh, I don't know.' Mrs. Geary even laughed. 'Mahalia seemed to argue with her all the time. Seemed they didn't agree on much, but when I said, 'Well how does *that* work?' she told me it was okay. She said they liked disagreeing. Mahalia said she learned more that way.'

'Did you keep up with your daughter's work?' I said. 'Read her essays? She told you about her Ul Qoman friends?' Corwi moved in her seat. Mrs. Geary shook her head.

'Oh no,' she said.

'Inspector,' said Thacker.

'The stuff she did just wasn't the sort of thing that I could . . . that I was real interested in, Mr. Borlú. I mean since she'd been over here, sure, stories in the paper about Ul Qoma would catch our eye a bit more than they had before, and sure I'd read them. But so long as Mahalia was happy, I . . . we were happy. Happy for her to get on with her thing, you know.'

'Inspector, when do you think we might be receiving the Ul Qoma transfer papers?' Thacker said.

'Soon, I think. And she was? Happy?'

'Oh, I think she . . .' Mrs. Geary said. 'There were always dramas, you know.'

'Yeah,' her father said.

'Now,' said Mrs. Geary.

'Oh?' I said.

'Well now it wasn't . . . only she'd been kind of stressed recently, you know. I told her she needed to come home for a vacation – I know, coming home hardly sounds like a vacation, but you know. But she said she was making real progress, like making a breakthrough in her work.'

'And some people were pissed about that,' Mr. Geary said.

'Honey.'

'They were. She told us.'

Corwi looked at me, confused. 'Mr. and Mrs. Geary . . .' While Thacker said that, I explained quickly to Corwi in Besz, 'Not "pissed" drunk. They're American – "angry". Who was pissed?' I asked them. 'Her professors?'

'No,' Mr. Geary said. 'Goddammit, who do you think did this?'

'Michael, please, please . . .'

'Goddammit, who the fuck are First Qoma?' Mr. Geary said. 'You haven't even asked us who we think did this. You haven't even asked us. You think we don't know?'

'What did she say?' I said. Thacker was standing now and patting the air, *Calm down everybody.*

'Some little bastard at a conference tells her her work was goddamn treason. Someone'd been gunning for her since the first time she came here.'

'Michael, stop, you're mixing it up. That first time, when that man said that, she was here, *here* here, Beszel-here, not in Ul Qoma, and that wasn't First Qoma, that was the other ones, here, nationalists or True Citizens, something, you remember . . .'

'Wait, what?' I said. 'First Qoma? And – someone said something to her when she was in Beszel? When?'

'Hold on boss, it's . . .' Corwi spoke quickly in Besz.

'I think we all need to take a minute,' Thacker said.

He placated the Gearys as if they had been wronged, and I apologised as if I had wronged them. They knew that they were expected to stay in their hotel. We had two officers stationed downstairs to ensure compliance. We told them that we would tell them as soon as we had news that their paperwork for travel had come through, and that we would be back the following day. In the meantime, if they needed anything or any information – I left them my numbers.

'He will be found,' Corwi said to them as we took leave. 'Breach will take who did this. I promise you that.' To me outside she said, 'Qoma First, not First Qoma, by the way. Like the True Citizens, only for Ul Qoma. As pleasant as our lot, by all accounts, but a lot more secretive and thank fuck not our headache.'

More radical in their Besźel-love even than Syedr's National Bloc, True Citizens were marchers in quasi-uniform and makers of frightening speeches. Legal but not by much. We had not succeeded in proving their responsibility for attacks on Besźel's Ul Qomatown, the Ul Qoman embassy, mosques and synagogues and leftist bookshops, on our small immigrant population. We – by which I mean we *policzai*, of course – had more than once found the perpetrators and that they were members of TC, but the organisation itself disavowed the attacks, just, just, and no judge had yet banned them.

'And Mahalia annoyed both lots.'

'So her dad says. He doesn't know . . .'

'We know she certainly managed to get the unificationists here mad, ages ago. And then she did the same to the nats over there? Any extremists she hasn't made angry?' We drove. 'You know,' I said, 'that meeting, of the Oversight Committee . . . it was pretty strange. Some of the things some people were saying . . .'

'Syedr?'

101

'Syedr, sure, among others, some of what they were saying didn't make much sense to me at the time. Maybe if I followed politics more carefully. Maybe I'll do that.' After a silence I said, 'Maybe we should ask around a bit.'

'The fuck, boss?' Corwi twisted in her seat. She did not look angry but confused. 'Why were you even grilling them like that? The muckamucks are invoking fucking *Breach* in a day or two to deal with this shit, and woe betide whoever did Mahalia then. You know? Even if we do find any leads now, we're going to be off the case any minute; this is just biding time.'

'Yeah,' I said. I swerved a little to avoid an Ul Qoman taxi, unseeing it as much as possible. 'Yeah. But still. I'm impressed with anyone who can piss off so many nutters. All of whom are at each other's throats as well. Besź Nats, Ul Qoman Nats, anti-Nats . . .'

'Let Breach deal. You were right. She deserves Breach, boss, like you said. What they can do.'

'She does deserve them. And she'll get them.' I pointed, drove on. '*Avanti*. For the next little while she's got us.'

CHAPTER EIGHT

EITHER HIS TIMING WAS PRETERNATURAL or Commissar Gadlem had had some techie rig up a cheat on his system – whenever I came into the office, any emails from him were invariably top of my inbox.

Fine, his latest said. *I gather Mr. & Mrs. G ensconced in hotel. Don't particularly want you tied up for days in paperwork (sure you agree) so polite chaperoning only please till formalities complete. Job done.*

Whatever information we had I would have to hand over when the time came. No point making work for myself, Gadlem was saying, nor costing the department my time, so take my foot off the accelerator. I made and read notes that would be illegible to everyone else, and to me in an hour's time, though I kept and filed them all carefully – my usual methodology. I reread Gadlem's message several times, rolling my eyes. I probably muttered something out loud to myself.

I spent some time tracking down numbers – online and through a real live operator on the end of the phone – and placed a call that made clucking noises as it ran through various international exchanges. 'Bol Ye'an offices.' I'd called twice before but previously had gone through a kind of automated system: this was the first time I'd had anyone pick up. His Illitan was good, but the accent was North American; so in English I said: 'Good afternoon, I'm trying to reach Professor Nancy. I've left messages on her voicemail, but—'

'Who's calling please?'

'This is Inspector Tyador Borlú of the Besźel Extreme Crime Squad.'

'Oh. *Oh.*' The voice was quite different now. 'This is about Ma-halia, isn't it? Inspector, I'm . . . Hold on I'm going to try to track down Izzy.' A long hollow-acousticked pause. 'This is Isabelle Nancy.' Anxious-sounding, American I'd have guessed if I hadn't known she was from Toronto. Not much like her voicemail voice.

'Professor Nancy, I'm Tyador Borlú of the Besźel *Policzai*, ECS. I think you have spoken to my colleague Officer Corwi? You got my messages maybe?'

'Inspector, yes, I'm . . . Please accept my apologies. I'd meant to call you back but it's been, everything's been, I'm very sorry . . .' She shifted between English and good Besź.

'I understand, Professor. I am sorry too about Miss Geary. I know this must be a very bad time for all of you and your colleagues.'

'I, we, we're all in shock here, Inspector. Real shock. I don't know what to tell you. Mahalia was a great young woman and—'

'Of course.'

'Where are you? Are you . . . local? Would you like to meet?'

'I'm afraid I'm calling internationally, Professor; I'm still in Besźel.'

'I see. So . . . how can I help you, Inspector? Is there any problem? I mean any problem other than, than *all* of this, I mean . . .' I heard her breath. 'I'm expecting Mahalia's parents any day now.'

'Yes, I just was with them actually. The embassy here is putting in paperwork for them, and they should come to you soon. No, I am calling you because I want to know more about Mahalia and what she was doing.'

'Forgive me, Inspector Borlú, but I was under the impression . . . this crime . . . will you not be invoking Breach, I thought . . .?' She had calmed and was speaking only Besź now, so what the hell I gave up on my English, which was no better than her Besź.

'Yes. The Oversight Committee . . . excuse me, Professor I don't know how much you know about how these matters go. But yes, responsibility for this will be passed over. You understand how that will work, then?'

'I think so.'

'Alright. I'm just doing some last work. I'm curious, is all. We hear interesting things about Mahalia. I want to know some things about her work. Can you help me? You were her advisor, yes? Do you have time to speak to me about that for a few minutes?'

'Of course, Inspector, you've waited long enough. I don't know quite what—'

'I want to know what she was working on. And about her history with you and with the program. And tell me about Bol Ye'an, too. She was studying Orciny, I understand.'

'What?' Isabelle Nancy was shocked. 'Orciny? Absolutely not. This is an archaeology department.'

'Forgive me, I'd been under the impression . . . What do you mean, this is archaeology?'

'I mean that if she were studying Orciny, and there might be excellent reasons to do so, she'd be doing her doctorate in Folklore or Anthropology or maybe Comp Lit. Granted, the edges of disciplines are getting vague. Also that Mahalia is one of a number of young archaeologists more interested in Foucault and Baudrillard than in Gordon Childe or in trowels.' She did not sound angry but sad and amused. 'But we wouldn't have accepted her unless her PhD was real archaeology.'

'So what was it?'

'Bol Ye'an's an old dig, Inspector.'

'Please tell me.'

'I'm sure you're aware of all the controversy around early artefacts in this region, Inspector. Bol Ye'an's uncovering pieces that are a good couple of millennia old. Whichever theory you subscribe to on Cleavage, split or convergence, what we're looking for predates it, predates Ul Qoma and Besźel. It's *root* stuff.'

'It must be extraordinary.'

'Of course. Also pretty incomprehensible. You understand we know next to nothing about the culture that produced all this?'

'I think so. That's why all the interest, yes?'

'Well . . . yes. That and the *kind* of things you have here. What Mahalia was doing was trying to decode what the title of her project called 'A Hermeneutics of Identity' from the layouts of gears and so on.'

'I'm not sure I understand.'

'Then she did a good job. The aim of a PhD's to ensure that no one, including your advisor, understands what you're doing after the first couple of years. I'm joking, you understand. What she was doing would have had ramifications for theories of the two cities. Where they came from, you know. She played her cards pretty close, so I was never sure month to month where she stood exactly on the issue, but she still had a couple of years to make up her mind. Or to just make something up.'

'So she was helping with the actual dig.'

'Absolutely. Most of our research students are. Some for primary research, some as part of their stipend deal, some a bit of both, some to suck up to us. Mahalia was paid a little bit, but mostly she needed to get her hands on the artefacts for her work.'

'I see. I'm sorry, Professor, I'd been under the impression that she'd been working on Orciny ...'

'She used to be interested in that. She first went to Besźel for a conference, some years ago.'

'Yes, I think I heard about that.'

'Right. Well, it caused a little stink because at that time she *was* very into Orciny, totally – she was a little Bowdenite, and the paper she gave didn't go down very well. Led to some remonstrations. I admired her guts, but she was on a hiding to nothing with all that stuff. When she applied to do her PhD – to be honest I was pretty surprised it was with me – I had to make sure she knew what would and wouldn't be ... acceptable. But ... I mean, I don't know what she was reading in her spare time, but what she was writing, when I got the updates on her PhD, they were, they were fine.'

'Fine?' I said. 'You don't sound ...'

She hesitated.

'Well ... Honestly I was a little, a little bit disappointed. She was smart. I know she was smart, because, you know, in seminars and so on she was terrific. And she worked super-

hard. She was a "grind," we'd say' – the word in English –
'always in the library. But her chapters . . .'

'Not good?'

'Fine. Really, they were okay. She'd pass her doctorate, no
problem, but it wasn't going to set the world on fire. It was
kind of lacklustre, you know? And given the number of hours
she was working, it was a bit *thin*. References and so on. I'd
spoken to her about it, though, and she promised that she was,
you know. Working on it.'

'Could I see it?'

'Sure.' She was taken aback. 'I mean, I suppose. I don't
know. I have to work out what the ethics of that are. I've got
the chapters she gave me, but they're very unfinished; she
wanted to work on them more. If she'd finished it it would be
public access, and no problem, but as it is . . . Can I get back
to you? She probably should have been publishing some of
them as papers in journals – that's kind of the done thing –
but she wasn't. We'd talked about that too; she said she was
going to do something about it.'

'What's a Bowdenite, Professor?'

'Oh.' She laughed. 'Sorry. It's the source of this Orciny stuff.
Poor David wouldn't thank me for using the term. It's someone
inspired by the early work of David Bowden. Do you know his
work?'

'. . . No.'

'He wrote a book, years ago. *Between the City and the City*.
Ring any bells? It was a huge thing for the later flower children. The first time for a generation anyone had taken Orciny
seriously. I guess it's not a surprise you haven't seen it; it's still
illegal. In Beszel and in Ul Qoma. You won't find it even in
the university libraries. In some ways it was a brilliant piece of

108

work – he did some fantastic archival investigations, and saw some analogies and connections that are . . . well, still pretty remarkable. But it was pretty crackpot ramblings.'

'How so?'

'Because he believed in it! He collated all these references, found new ones, put them together into a kind of ur-myth, then reinterpreted it as a secret and a cover-up. He . . . Okay I need to be a little bit careful here, Inspector, because honestly I never really, not *really*, thought he *did* believe it – I always thought it was kind of a game – but the book *said* he believed it. He came to Ul Qoma, from where he went to Beszél, managed I do not know how to go between the two of them – legally I assure you – several times, and he claimed to have found traces of Orciny itself. And he went further – said that Orciny wasn't just somewhere that had existed in the gaps between Qoma and Beszél since their foundings or coming together or splitting (I can't remember where he stood on the Cleavage issue): he said it was still here.'

'Orciny?'

'Exactly. A secret colony. A city between the cities, its inhabitants living in plain sight.'

'What? Doing what? How?'

'Unseen, like Ul Qomans to Besź and vice versa. Walking the streets unseen but overlooking the two. Beyond the Breach. And doing, who knows? Secret agendas. They're still debating that, I don't doubt, on the conspiracy theory websites. David said he was going to go into it and disappear.'

'Wow.'

'Exactly, wow. Wow is right. It's notorious. Google it, you'll see. Anyway, when we first saw Mahalia she was pretty unreconstructed. I liked her because she was spunky and because

Bowdenite she may have been but she had panache and smarts. But it was a joke, you understand? I even wondered if she knew it, if she was joking herself.'

'But she wasn't working on that anymore?'

'No one reputable would supervise a Bowdenite PhD. I had this stern word with her about it when she enrolled, but she even laughed. Said she'd left all that behind. As I say, I was surprised she'd come to me. My work's not as avant-garde as hers.'

'The Foucaults and the Žižieks not your thing?'

'I respect them of course, but—'

'Aren't there any of those, what should we say, theory types she could have gone with?'

'Yes, but she told me she needed to get her hands on the actual *objects*. I'm an artefact scholar. My more philosophically oriented colleagues would ... well, I wouldn't trust many of them to brush the dirt off an amphora.' I laughed. 'So I guess it made sense to her; she was really insistent on learning how to do that side of things. I was surprised but pleased. You understand these pieces are unique, Inspector?'

'I think so. I've heard all the rumours, of course.'

'You mean their magic powers? I wish, I wish. But even so these digs are incomparable. This material culture makes no sense at all. There is nowhere else in the world that you'll dig up what looks like cutting-edge late antiquity, really beautiful complicated bronzework mixed right up with frankly neolithic stuff. Stratigraphy looks like it goes out of the window with this. It was used as evidence against the Harris Matrix – wrongly, but you can see why. That's why these digs are popular with young archaeologists. And that's not even counting all the stories, which is all they are but which hasn't stopped

110

unlikely researchers pining for a chance to have a look. Still, I'd have thought Mahalia would have tried to go to Dave, not that she'd have had much luck with him.'

'Dave? Bowden? He's alive? He teaches?'

'Certainly he's alive. But even back when she was into this, Mahalia wouldn't have got him to supervise her. I'm willing to bet she must have spoken to him when she was first investigating. And I'm willing to bet she got pretty short shrift. He repudiated all this years ago. It's the bane of his life. Ask him. A burst of adolescence he's never been able to shake off. Never published anything else worth a damn – he's the Orciny man for the rest of his career. He'll tell you this himself if you ask him.'

'I may. You know him?'

'He's a colleague. It's not a big field, pre-Cleavage archaeology. He's at Prince of Wales too, at least part-time. He lives here, in Ul Qoma.'

She lived several months of the year in apartments in Ul Qoma, in its university district, where Prince of Wales and other Canadian institutions gleefully exploited the fact that the US state (for reasons now embarrassing even to most of its right-wingers) boycotted Ul Qoma. It was Canada, instead, that was enthusiastically forging links, academic and economic, with Ul Qoman institutions.

Besźel, of course, was a friend of both Canada and the US, but the enthusiasm with which the two countries combined plugged into our faltering markets was dwarfed by that with which Canada cosied up to what they called the New Wolf economy. We were a street mongrel, maybe, or a scrawny milkrat. Most vermin are interstitial. It is very hard to prove that the shy cold-weather lizards in cracks in Besź walls can live in Besźel only, as frequently claimed: certainly they die if exported into Ul Qoma (even more gently than by children's hands), but they tend to do so in Besź captivity as well. Pigeons, mice, wolves, bats live in both cities, are crosshatched animals. But by unspoken tradition, the majority of the local wolves – mean, bony things long-since adapted to urban scavenging – are generally if nebulously considered Besź: it is only those few of respectable size and none-too-vile pelt, the same notion held, that are Ul Qoman. Many citizens of Besźel avoid transgressing this – entirely unnecessary and invented – categorical boundary by never referring to wolves.

I had scared off a pair once, as they foraged through rubbish in the yard of my building. I had thrown something at them. They had been unusually kempt, and more than one of my neighbours had been shocked, as if I had breached.

Most of the Ul Qomanists, as Nancy described herself, were bilocated like her – she explained it with audible guilt, mentioning again and again that it must be a historical quirk that located the more fecund archaeological sites in areas of Ul Qoman totality, or heftily Ul Qoma-weighted crosshatching. Prince of Wales had reciprocal arrangements with several Ul Qoman academies. David Bowden lived more of each year in Ul Qoma, and less back in Canada. He was in Ul Qoma now. He had, she told me, few students, and not much of a teaching load, but I still could not get hold of him on the number she gave me.

A little ferreting online. It was not hard to confirm most of what Isabelle Nancy had told me. I found a page that listed Mahalia's PhD title (they had not yet taken her name offline, nor put up one of the online tributes I was sure would be coming). I found Nancy's list of publications, and David

Bowden's. His included the book Nancy had mentioned, from 1975, two articles from around the same time, one more article from a decade later, then mostly journalism, some of it collected into a volume.

I found fracturedcity.org, the main discussion site for the kooks of dopplurbanology, Ul-Qoma-and-Besźel obsession (the site's approach of conjoining the two as a single object of study would outrage polite opinion in both cities, but judging by comments on the forum it was commonly if mildly illegally accessed from both, too). From there a series of links (cheekily, confident in the indulgence or incompetence of our and the Ul Qoman censors, many were servers with .uq and .zb addresses) gave me a few paragraphs copied from *Between the City and the City*. It read as Nancy had suggested.

My phone startled me. I realised that it was dark, after seven.

'Borlú,' I said, sitting back.

'Inspector? Oh, shit, sir, we have a situation. This is Ceczoria.' Agim Ceczoria was one of the officers stationed at the hotel to look after Mahalia's parents. I rubbed my eyes and scanned my email to see if I'd missed any messages coming in. There was a noise behind him, a commotion. 'Sir, Mr. Geary . . . he went AWOL, sir. He fucking . . . he breached.'

'What?'

'He got out of the room, sir.' Behind him was a woman's voice, and she was shouting.

'What the hell happened?'

'I don't know how the fuck he got past us, sir, I just don't know. But he wasn't gone long.'

'How do you know? How did you get him?'

He swore again.

'We didn't. Breach did. I'm calling from the car, sir, we're

113

en route to the airport. Breach are . . . *escorting* us. Somewhere. They told us what to do. That's Mrs. Geary you can hear. He has to go. Now.'

CORWI HAD GONE, and she wasn't answering her phone. I took an unmarked squad car from the pool, but ran it with the sirens making their hysteric *gulp gulp* noises, so I could ignore traffic laws. (It was only the Besź rules which applied to me and which therefore I was with authority ignoring, but traffic law is one of the compromise areas where the Oversight Committee ensures close similarity between the rules of Besźel and Ul Qoma. Though the traffic cultures are not identical, for the sake of the pedestrians and cars who have, unseeing, to negotiate much foreign traffic, our vehicles and theirs run at comparable speeds in comparable ways. We all learn to tactfully avoid our neighbour's emergency vehicles, as well as our own.)

There were no flights out for a couple of hours, but they would sequester the Gearys, and in some hidden way Breach would watch them onto the plane, to make sure they were on it, and airborne. Our embassy in the US would already be informed, as well as the representatives in Ul Qoma, and a *no visa* flagged in their names on both our systems. Once they were out, they would not be back in. I ran through Besźel airport to the office of the *policzai*, showed my badge.

'Where are the Gearys?'

'In the cells, sir.'

Depending on what I saw I was ready with, *do you know what just happened to these people, whatever they've done they've just lost a daughter,* and so on, but it was not necessary. They had given them food and drink and treated them

114

gently. Ceczoria was with them in the little room. He was muttering to Mrs. Geary in his basic English.

She looked at me tearfully. Her husband was, I thought for a second, asleep on the bunk. I saw how very motionless he was and revised my opinion.

'Inspector,' Ceczoria said.

'What's happened to him?'

'He's . . . Breach did it, sir. He'll probably be okay, wake up in a bit. I don't know. I don't know what the hell they did to him.'

Mrs. Geary said, 'You've *poisoned* my *husband* . . .'

'Mrs. Geary, please.' Ceczoria rose and came closer to me, lowered his voice though he was talking now in Besź. 'We didn't know anything about it, sir. There was a little bit of a commotion outside and someone came into the lobby where we were.' Mrs. Geary was crying and talking to her unconscious husband. 'Geary kind of lurches in and passes out. The hotel security go at them, and they just look at this shape, someone behind Geary in the hallway, and the guards stop and wait. I hear this voice: 'You know what I represent. Mr. Geary breached. Remove him.'

'Ceczoria shook his head, helpless. 'Then, and I still can't see anything properly, whoever's speaking's gone.'

'How . . .?'

'Inspector, I don't fucking know. I . . . I take responsibility, sir. Geary must have got past us.'

I stared at him. 'Do you want a bloody biscuit? Of course it's your responsibility. What did he do?'

'Don't know. Breach were gone before I could say a word.'

'What about . . .' I nodded at Mrs. Geary.

'She wasn't deported: she didn't do anything.' He was

115

whispering. 'But when I told her we had to take her husband, she said she'd go with him. She doesn't want to stick around on her own.'

'Inspector Borlú.' Mrs. Geary was trying to sound controlled. 'If you're talking about me you should talk *to* me. Do you see what's been *done* to my husband?'

'Mrs. Geary, I'm terribly sorry.'

'You *should* be . . .'

'Mrs. Geary, I didn't do this. Neither did Ceczoria. Neither did any of my officers. Do you understand?'

'Oh *Breach Breach Breach* . . .'

'Mrs. Geary, your husband just did something very serious. Very serious.' She was quiet but for heavy breaths. 'Do you understand me? Has there been some mistake here? Were we less than clear in our explanations of the system of checks and balances between Besźel and Ul Qoma? Do you understand that this deportation is *nothing to do with us*, but that we have absolutely no power to do anything about it, and that he is, listen to me, he is *incredibly lucky* that's all he's got?' She said nothing. 'In the car I got the impression that your husband wasn't quite so clear on how it works here, so you tell me, Mrs. Geary, did something go wrong? Did he misunderstand our . . . advice? How did my men not see him leave? Where was he going?'

She looked still as if she might cry; then she glanced at her supine husband and her stance changed. She stood straighter and whispered something to him that I did not catch. Mrs. Geary looked at me.

'He was in the air force,' she said. 'You think you're looking at some fat old man?' She touched him. 'You never asked us who might have done this, Inspector. I don't know what to

116

make of you, I really don't. Like my husband said, *you think we don't know who did this?*' She clutched and folded and unfolded a piece of paper, without looking at it, took it out of a side pocket of her bag, put it in again. 'You think our daughter didn't talk to us? First Qoma, True Citizens, Nat Bloc ... Mahalia was *afraid*, Inspector.

'We haven't figured out exactly who did what, and we don't know why, but where was he going, you say? He was going to find out. I told him it wouldn't work – he didn't speak the language, he didn't read it – but he had addresses we got from the internet and a phrase book and, what, was I going to tell him *not* to go? Not to go? I'm so proud of him. Those people hated Mahalia for years, since she first came here.'

'Printed out from the internet?'

'And I mean *here*, Besźel. When she came to the conference. Then the same thing with others, in Ul Qoma. Are you going to tell me there's no connection? She knew she'd made enemies, she *told* us she'd made enemies. When she went looking into Orciny she made enemies. When she looked deeper she made more. They all hated her, because of what she was doing. What she knew.'

'Who hated her?'

'All of them.'

'What did she know?'

She shook her head and sagged. 'My husband was going to *investigate*.'

He had climbed out of a ground-floor bathroom window, to avoid my watching officers. A few steps across the road, what could have merely been a breaking of the rules we had set him, but he had blundered out of a crosshatching and into an alter area, a yard that existed only in Ul Qoma; and Breach, who must have watched him all the time, had come for him. I hoped they hadn't hurt him too badly. If they had I was pretty sure there wouldn't be any doctor back home who would be able to identify the agent of his injury. What could I say?

'I'm sorry for what happened, Mrs. Geary. Your husband shouldn't have tried to evade Breach. I . . . We are on the same side.' She looked at me carefully.

She whispered to me eventually, 'Let us go, then. Go on. We can walk back to the city. We have money. We . . . my husband's going *crazy*. He needs to be looking. He'll just come back. We'll come through Hungary and, or, we'll come up via Turkey or Armenia – there are ways we can get in, you know . . . We're going to find out who did this . . .'

'Mrs. Geary, Breach are watching us now. *Now.*' I raised my open hands slowly and filled them with air. 'You wouldn't get ten metres. What is it you think you can do? You don't speak Besź, Illitan. I . . . Let *me*, Mrs. Geary. Let me do my job for you.'

MR. GEARY WAS STILL UNCONSCIOUS when the plane boarded. Mrs. Geary looked at me with reproach and hope, and I tried to tell her again that there was nothing I could do, that Mr. Geary had done this himself.

There were not many other passengers. I wondered where Breach was. Our remit would end when the plane doors were sealed. Mrs. Geary cushioned her husband's head as he lolled in the stretcher in which we carried him. In the plane doorway, as they took the Gearys to their seats, I showed my badge to one of the attendants.

'Be good to them.'

'The deportees?'

118

'Yeah. Seriously.' He raised his brows but nodded.

I went to where the Gearys were seated. Mrs. Geary stared at me. I squatted.

'Mrs. Geary. Please pass my apologies to your husband. He shouldn't have done what he did, but I understand why.' I hesitated. 'You know ... if he'd known Besźel better, he could probably have avoided falling into Ul Qoma, and Breach couldn't have stopped him.' She just stared. 'Let me get that.' I stood, took her bag and put it overhead. 'Of course when we know what's happening, if we get any leads at all, any information, I'll tell you.' Still she didn't say anything. Her mouth was moving: she was trying to decide whether to plead with me or accuse me of something. I bowed a little, old-fashioned, turned and left the plane and the two of them.

Back in the airport building, I took out the paper I had taken from the side pocket of her bag and looked at it. The name of an organisation, True Citizens, copied from the internet. That his daughter must have told him hated her, and where Mr. Geary had been going with his own dissident investigations. An address.

CHAPTER NINE

CORWI COMPLAINED, more dutifully than with fervour. 'What's this all about, sir?' she said. 'Aren't they going to be invoking Breach any minute?'

'Yes. In fact they're taking their time. They should've done it by now; I don't know what the holdup is.'

'So what the fuck, sir? Why are we in such a rush to do this? Mahalia'll have Breach hunting for her killer soon.' I drove. 'Damn. You don't want to hand it over, do you?'

'Oh, I do.'

'So . . .'

'I just want to check some things first, in this unexpected little moment we have.'

She stopped staring at me when we arrived at the headquarters of the True Citizens. I had called in and got someone to check the address for me: it was as it was written on Mrs. Geary's paper. I had tried to contact Shenvoi, my acquaintance undercover, but couldn't get him, so relied on what I knew and could quickly read on the TCs. Corwi stood beside me, and I saw her touch the handle of her weapon.

A reinforced door, blocked-off windows, but the house itself was or had been residential, and the rest of the street remained so. (I wondered if there had ever been any attempt to close

120

the TC down on zoning charges.) The street almost looked crosshatched, its random-seeming variation between terraced and detached buildings, but it was not, it was total Besźel, the variation of styles an architectural quirk, though it was only a corner away from a very crosshatched area.

I had heard it alleged by liberals that this was more than irony, that the proximity of Ul Qoma gave the TC opportunities to intimidate the enemy. Certainly no matter how they unsaw them, the Ul Qomans in physical proximity must have registered at some level the paramilitary fatigues, the *Besźel First* patches. You could almost claim it was breach, though of course not quite.

They were milling as we approached, lounging, smoking, drinking, laughing loud. Their efforts to claim the street were so overt they might as well have been pissing musk. All but one were men. All eyed us. Words were spoken and most of them ambled into the building, leaving a few by the door. In leather, denim, one despite the cold in a muscle top his physiology deserved, staring at us. Bodybuilder, several men with cropped hair, one affecting an antique Besź-aristo cut like a fussy mullet. He leaned on a baseball bat – not a Besź sport but just plausible enough that he could not be done for Possessing Weapon with Intent. One man muttered to Haircut, spoke rapidly on a cell phone, clicked it shut. There were not many passersby. All there were of course were Besź, so they could and did stare at us and the TC crew, though most then looked away.

'You ready for this?' I said.

'Fuck off, boss,' Corwi muttered back. The bat holder swung it as if idly.

A few metres from the reception committee I said loudly

121

into my radio: 'At TC headquarters, four-eleven GyedarStrász, as planned. Check-in in an hour. Code alert. Ready backup.' I thumbed the radio off quickly before the operator had the chance to audibly respond along the lines of *What on earth are you on about, Borlú?*

The big man: 'Help you, Officer?' One of his comrades looked Corwi up and down and made a kiss-kiss noise that might be the chirrup of a bird.

'Yes, we're coming in to ask a few questions.'

'I don't think so.' Haircut smiled, but it was Muscles doing the talking.

'We really are, you know.'

'Not so much.' This was the man who had made the call, a blond suede-headed man, pushing in front of his big acquaintance. 'Got Entry and Search papers? No? Then you will not be coming in.'

I shifted. 'If you've got nothing to hide, why keep us out?' Corwi said. 'We've some questions ...' but Muscles and Haircut were laughing.

'Please,' Haircut said. He shook his head. 'Please. Who do you think you're talking to?'

The close-shorn man gestured him to shut up. 'We're done here,' he said.

'What do you know about Byela Mar?' I said. They looked without recognition, or uncertain. 'Mahalia Geary.' That time they knew the name. The telephoner made an *ah* noise; Haircut whispered to the big man.

'Geary,' Bodybuilder said. 'We read the papers.' He shrugged, *que sera*. 'Yes. A lesson in the dangers of certain behaviours?'

'How so?' I leaned against the doorjamb companionably,

forcing Mullet to back up a step or two. He muttered again to his friend. I could not hear what.

'No one's condoning attacks, but Miss *Geary*' – the man with the phone said the name with exaggerated American accent, and stood between us and all the others – 'had form and a reputation among patriots. We'd not heard from her for a while, true. Hoped she might have gained some perspective. Seems not.' He shrugged. 'If you denigrate Besźel, it'll come back to bite you.'

'What *denigration?*' Corwi said. 'What do you know about her?'

'Come on, Officer! Look at what she worked on! She was no friend of Besźel.'

'Alright,' Yellow said. 'Unif. Or worse, a spy.' I looked at Corwi and she at me.

'What?' I said. 'Which you going to go for?'

'She wasn't . . .' Corwi said. We both hesitated.

The men stayed in the doorway and would not even bicker with us anymore. Mullet seemed minded to, in response to my provocations, but Bodybuilder said, 'Leave it, Caczos,' and the man shut up, and only watched us from behind the bigger man's back, and the other who had spoken remonstrated with them quietly and they backed a few feet away but still watched me. I tried to reach Shenvoi, but he was away from his secure phone. It occurred to me that he might (I was not one of the few who knew his assignment) even be in the building before me.

'Inspector Borlú.' The voice came from behind us. A smart black car had pulled up behind ours, and a man was walking towards us, leaving the driver's door open. He was in his early fifties, I would say, portly, with a sharp, lined face. He wore a decent dark suit without a tie. What hair had not receded was grey and cut short. 'Inspector,' he said again. 'Time for you to leave.'

I raised an eyebrow. 'Of course, of course,' I said. 'Only forgive me . . . who in the name of the Virgin are you?'

'Harkad Gosz. Barrister for the True Citizens of Besźel.' Several of the thuggish men looked rather startled at that.

'Oh terrific,' whispered Corwi. I took Gosz in ostentatiously: he was clearly high-rent.

'Just popping by, are you?' I said. 'Or did you get a call?' I winked at the phone-man, who shrugged. Amiably enough. 'I take it you don't have a direct line to these donkeys, so who did it come through? They put the word to Syedr? Who dropped you a line?'

He raised an eyebrow. 'Let me guess why you're here, Inspector.'

'A moment, Gosz . . . How do you know who I am?'

'Let me guess – you're here asking questions about Mahalia Geary.'

'Absolutely. None of your boys seem too cut up about her death. And yet lamentably ignorant about her work: they're labouring under the delusion that she was a unificationist, which would make the unifs laugh very hard. Never heard of Orciny? And let me repeat – how do you know my name?'

'Inspector, are you really going to waste all our time? Orciny? However Geary wanted to spin it, whatever foolishness she wanted to pretend to, whatever stupid footnotes she wanted to stick in her essays, the thrust of everything she was working on was to undermine Besźel. This nation is not a plaything, Inspector. Understand me? Either Geary was stupid,

124

wasting her time with old wives' tales that manage to combine being meaningless with being insults, or she was not stupid, and all this work about the secret powerlessness of Besźel was designed to make a very different point. Ul Qoma seems to have been more congenial for her, after all, didn't it?'

'Are you joking with me? What's your point? That Mahalia *pretended* to be working on Orciny? She was an enemy of Besźel? What, an Ul Qoman agent . . .?'

Gosz came close to me. He motioned the TC-ers, who backed into their fortified house and half closed the door, waiting and watching.

'Inspector, you have no Entry and Search. Go. If you're going to insist on this, let me dutifully recite the following: continue this approach and I'll complain to your superiors about harassment of the, let's recall, entirely legal TC of B.' I waited a moment out. There was more he wanted to say. 'And ask yourself what you'd infer about someone who arrives here in Besźel; commences research on a topic long and justifiably ignored by serious scholars, that's predicated on the *uselessness and weakness* of Besźel; makes, unsurprisingly, enemies at every turn; leaves and then *goes straight to Ul Qoma*. And then anyway, which you appear to be unaware of, starts to quietly drop what was always an entirely unconvincing arena for research. She's not been working on Orciny for years – might as well have admitted the whole thing was a blind, for goodness' sake! She's working at one of the most contentious pro-Ul Qoman digs of the last century. Do I think there's reason to suspect her motives, Inspector? I do.'

Corwi was staring at him literally with her mouth open. 'Damn, boss, you were right,' she said without lowering her voice. 'They're *batshit*.' He looked at her coldly.

125

'How would you know all that, Mr. Gosz?' I said. 'About her work?'

'Her research? Please. Even without the newspapers fer-reting around, PhD topics and conference papers aren't state secrets, Borlú. There's a thing called the internet. You should try it.'

'And . . .'

'Just go,' he said. 'Tell Gadlem I sent my regards. Do you want a job, Inspector? No, not a threat, it's a question. Would you like a job? Would you like to keep the one you have? Are you for real, Inspector How-Do-I-Know-Your-Name?' He laughed. 'Do you think this' – a point at the building – 'is where things end?'

'Oh no,' I said. 'You got a call from someone.'

'Now go.'

'Which paper did you read?' I said with raised voice. I kept my eyes on Gosz but turned my head enough to show I was talking to the men in the doorway. 'Big man? Haircut? Which paper?'

'That's enough, now,' the crop-haired one said, as Muscles said to me, 'What?'

'You said you read it in the paper about her. Which one? Far as I know no one's mentioned her real name yet. She was still a Fulana Detail when I saw it. I'm obviously not reading the best press. So what should I be reading?' A mutter, a laugh.

'I pick things up.' Gosz did not tell the man to shut up. 'Who knows where I heard it?' I could not make too much of this. Information leaked fast, including from supposedly secure committees, and it was possible her name had got out and even been published somewhere, though I hadn't seen it – and if it had not, it would soon. 'And what should you be

126

reading? *Cry of the Spear,* of course!' He waved a copy of the TC newspaper.

'Well this is all very exciting,' I said. 'You're all so informed. Poor fuddled me, I suppose it'll be a relief to hand this over. I can't possibly keep hold of it. Like you say, I haven't got the right papers to ask the right questions. Of course Breach don't need any papers. They can *ask* anything they want, of anyone.'

That quietened them. I looked at them – at Muscles, Mullet, the telephoner and the lawyer – seconds more, before I walked, Corwi behind me.

'WHAT AN UNPLEASANT BUNCH OF FUCKERS'

'Ah well,' I said. 'We were fishing. A bit cheeky. Though I wasn't expecting to be spanked like quite such a naughty boy.'

'What was all that stuff . . .? How *did* he know who you are? And all that business about threatening you . . .'

'I don't know. Maybe it was real. Maybe he could make life hard if I pushed this. Not my problem very long.'

'I guess I have heard,' she said. 'About links, I mean. Everyone knows the TC are the street soldiers of the NatBloc, so he must know Syedr. Like you said that's probably the chain: they call Syedr, who calls him.' I said nothing. 'Probably is. Might be who they heard about Mahalia from, too. But would Syedr really be so dumb as to feed us to the TC?'

'You said yourself he is pretty dumb.'

'Okay, yeah, but why would he?'

'He's a bully.'

'True. They all are – that's how the politics work, you know? So maybe, yeah, that's what's going on, bluster to scare you off.'

'Scare me off what?'

'Scare you, I mean. Not "off" anything. They're congenital thugs, those guys.'

'Who knows? Maybe he's got something to keep to himself, maybe he hasn't. I admit I like the idea of the Breach hunting him and his. When the invocation finally comes.'

'Yeah. I just thought you seemed . . . We're still chasing stuff, I wondered if you were wishing you could . . . I wasn't expecting to do any more of this. I mean we're just waiting. For the committee . . .'

'Yeah,' I said. 'Well. You know.' I looked at her and away. 'It'll be good to give this one up; she needs Breach. But we haven't handed over just yet. The more we have to give them, the better I guess . . .' That was questionable.

Big breath in, out. I stopped and bought us coffee from a new place, before we went back to the HQ. American coffee, to Corwi's disgust.

'I thought you liked it *aj Tyrko*,' she said, sniffing it.

'I do, but even more than I like it *aj Tyrko*, I don't care.'

CHAPTER TEN

I WAS IN EARLY THE NEXT MORNING but had no time to orient myself to anything. '*El jefe* wants you, Tyad,' said Tsura, on desk duty, as I entered.

'Shit,' I said. 'He in already?' I hid behind my hand and whispered, 'Turn away, turn away, Tsura. Be on a piss break at my ingress. You didn't see me.'

'Come on, Tyad.' She waved me away and covered her eyes. But there was a note on my desk. *See me IMMEDIATELY.* I rolled my eyes. Canny. If he had emailed it to me or left it as a voicemail I could have claimed to not see it for a few hours. I couldn't avoid him now.

'Sir?' I knocked and poked my head around his door. I considered ways to explain my visit to the True Citizens. I hoped Corwi was not too loyal or honourable to blame me if she was taking shit herself for it. 'You wanted me?'

Gadlem looked at me over the rim of his cup and beckoned, motioned me to sit. 'Heard about the Gearys,' he said. 'What happened?'

'Yes sir. It was . . . it was a cock-up.' I had not tried to contact them. I did not know if Mrs. Geary knew where her paper had gone. 'I think they were, you know, they were just distraught and they did a stupid thing . . .'

'A stupid thing with a lot of preplanning. Quite the most organised spontaneous foolishness I've ever heard of. Are they lodging a complaint? Am I going to hear stern words from the US embassy?'

'I don't know. It would be a bit cheeky if they did. They wouldn't have much to stand on.' They had breached. It was sad and simple. He nodded, sighed, and offered me his two closed fists.

'Good news or bad news?' he said.

'Uh . . . bad.'

'No, you get the good news first.' He shook his left hand and opened it dramatically, spoke as if he had released a sentence. 'The good news is that I have a tremendously intriguing case for you.' I waited. 'The bad news.' He opened his right hand and slammed it on his desk with genuine anger. 'The bad news, Inspector Borlú, is that it's the same case you're already working on.'

'. . . Sir? I don't understand . . .'

'Well no, Inspector, who among us understands? To which of us poor mortals is *understanding* given? You're still on the case.' He unfolded a letter and waggled it at me. I saw stamps and embossed symbols above the text. 'Word from the Oversight Committee. Their official response. You remember, the little formality? They're not handing the Mahalia Geary case over. They're refusing to invoke Breach.'

I sat back hard. 'What? *What?* What the hell . . .?'

His voice was flat. 'Nyisemu for the committee informs us that they've reviewed the evidence presented and have concluded that there's insufficient evidence to suppose any breach occurred.'

'This is bullshit.' I stood. 'You saw my dossier, sir, you know

130

what I gave them, you know there's no way this wasn't breach. What did they say? What were their reasons? Did they do a breakdown of the voting? Who signed the letter?'

'They're not obliged to give any reasons.' He shook his head and looked disgusted at the paper he held in fingertips like tongs.

'God *damn* it. Someone's trying to . . . Sir, this is ridiculous. We need to invoke Breach. They're the only ones who can . . . How am I supposed to investigate this shit? I'm a Beszél cop, is all. Something fucked is going on here.'

'Alright, Borlú. As I say they're not obliged to give any reasons, but doubtless anticipating something of our polite surprise, they have in fact included a note, and an enclosure. According to this imperious little missive, the issue wasn't your presentation. So take comfort in the fact that no matter how cack-handed you were, *you* more or less convinced them this was a case of breach. What happened, they explain, is that as part of their 'routine investigations,' 'his scare quotes were like birds' claws, 'more information came to light. To whit.'

He tapped one of the pieces of mail or junk on his desk, threw it to me. A videocassette. He pointed me to the TV/VCR in the corner of his office. The image came up, a poor sepia-tinted and static-flecked thing. There was no sound. Cars puttered diagonally across the screen, in not-heavy but steady traffic, above a time-and-date stamp, between pillars and the walls of buildings.

'What am I looking at?' I worked out the date – the small hours, a couple of weeks ago. The night before Mahalia Geary's body was found. 'What am I looking at?'

The few vehicles sped up, beetled with tremendous jerky

business. Gadlem waved his hand in bad-tempered play, conducting the fast-forwarding image with the remote control as if it were a baton. He sped through minutes of tape.

'Where is this? This picture is shit.'

'It's a lot less shit than if it was one of ours, which is rather the point. Here we are,' he said. 'Deep of the night. Where are we, Borlú? Detect, detective. Watch the right.'

A red car passed, a grey car, an old truck, then – 'Hello! Voilà!' shouted Gadlem – a dirty white van. It crawled from the lower right to the upper left of the picture toward some tunnel, paused perhaps at an unseen traffic signal, and passed out of the screen and out of sight.

I looked at him for an answer. 'Mark the stains,' he said. He was fast-forwarding, making little cars dance again. 'They've trimmed us a bit. An hour and change later. *Hello!*' He pressed *play* and one, two, three other vehicles, then the white van – it must be the same one – reappeared, moving in the opposite direction, back the way it came. This time the angle of the little camera captured its front plates.

It went by too quick for me to see. I pressed the buttons on the built-in VCR, hurtling the van backwards into my line of sight, then bringing it a few metres forward, pausing it. It was no DVD, this, the paused image was a fug of ghost lines and crackles, the stuttering van not really still but trembling like some troubled electron between two locations. I could not read the number plate clearly, but in most of its places what I saw seemed to be one of a couple of possibilities – a *vye* or a *bye*, *zsec* or *kho*, a 7 or a 1, and so on. I took out my notebook and flicked through it.

'There he goes,' murmured Gadlem. 'He's onto something. He has something, ladies and gentlemen.' Back through pages and days. I stopped. 'A lightbulb, I see it, it's straining to come on, to glow illumination across the situation . . .'

'Fuck,' I said.

'Indeed fuck.'

'It is. That's Khurusch's van.'

'It is, as you say, the van of Mikyael Khurusch.' The vehicle in which Mahalia's body had been taken, and from which it had been dumped. I looked at the time on the image. As I looked at it onscreen it almost certainly contained dead Mahalia. 'Jesus. Who found this? What is it?' I said. Gadlem sighed and rubbed his eyes. 'Wait, wait.' I held up my hand. I looked at the letter from the Oversight Committee, which Gadlem was using to fan his face. 'That's the corner of Copula Hall,' I said. 'God damn it. That's Copula Hall. And this is Khurusch's van going out of Besźel into Ul Qoma and coming back in again. Legally.'

'Bing,' said Gadlem, like a tired game-show buzzer. 'Bing bing bloody bing.'

AS PART, WE WERE TOLD – and to which, I told Gadlem, we would return – of the background investigations pursuant to any invocation of Breach, CCTV footage of the night in question had been investigated. That was unconvincing. This had looked so clear a case of breach no one had any reason to pore so hard through hours of tape. And besides, the antique cameras in the Besź side of Copula Hall would not give clear enough pictures to identify the vehicle – these were from outside, from a bank's private security system, that some investigator had commandeered.

With the help of the photographs provided by Inspector Borlú and his team, we heard, it had been ascertained that one of the vehicles passing through an official checkpoint in Copula Hall, into Ul Qoma from Besźel and back again, had been that in which the deceased body had been transported. Accordingly, while a heinous crime had been committed and must be investigated as a matter of urgency, the passage of the body from the murder site, though it appears it was in Ul Qoma, to the dumping ground in Besźel had not, in fact, involved breach. Passage between the two cities had been legal. There were, accordingly, no grounds to invoke Breach. No breach had been committed.

This is the sort of juridical situation to which outsiders react with understandable bewilderment. Smuggling, they regularly insist, for example. Smuggling is breach, yes? Quintessentially, yes? But no.

Breach has powers the rest of us can hardly imagine, but its calling is utterly precise. It is not the passage itself from one city to the other, not even with contraband: it is the manner of the passage. Throw felid or cocaine or guns from your Besź rear window across a crosshatched yard into an Ul Qoman garden for your contact to pick up – that is breach, and Breach will get you, and it would still be Breach if you threw bread or feathers. Steal a nuclear weapon and carry it secretly with you through Copula Hall when you cross *but cross that border itself*? At that official checkpoint where the cities meet? Many crimes are committed in such an act, but breach is not one of them.

Smuggling itself is not breach, though most breach is committed in order to smuggle. The smartest dealers, though, make sure to cross correctly, are deeply respectful of the cities' boundaries and pores, so if they are caught they face only the laws of one or other or both places, not the power of Breach.

134

Perhaps Breach considers the details of those crimes once a breach is committed, all the transgressions in Ul Qoma or Beszel or both, but if so it is only once and because those crimes are functions of breach, the only violation Breach punishes, the existential disrespect of Ul Qoma's and Beszel's boundaries.

The theft of the van and the dumping of the body in Beszel were illegal. The murder in Ul Qoma was horribly so. But what we had assumed was the particular transgressive connection between the events had never taken place. All passage had appeared scrupulously legal, effected through official channels, paperwork in place. Even if the permits were faked, the travel through the borders in Copula Hall made it a question of illegal entry, not of breach. That is a crime you might have in any country. There had been no breach.

'THIS IS FUCKING BULLSHIT.'

I walked back and forth between Gadlem's desk and the frozen car on-screen, the conveyance of the victim. 'This is bullshit. We've been screwed.'

'It is bullshit, he tells me,' Gadlem said to the world. 'He tells me we've been screwed.'

'We've been screwed, sir. We *need* Breach. How the hell are we supposed to do this? Someone somewhere is trying to freeze this where it stands.'

'We've been screwed he tells me, and I note he tells me so as if I am disagreeing with him. Which when last I looked I was not doing.'

'Seriously what . . .'

'In fact it could be said I agree with him on a startling scale. Of *course* we've been screwed, Borlú. Stop spinning like a drunk dog. What do you want me to say? Yes, yes, yes this is bullshit; yes someone has done this to us. What would you have me do?'

'Something! There must be something. We could appeal . . .'

'Look, Tyador.' He steepled his fingers. 'We are both in accord about what's happened here. We're both pissed off that you are still on this case. For different reasons perhaps but—' He waved that away. 'But here's the problem you're not addressing. While yes we can both agree the sudden recovery of this footage smells not a little, and that we appear to be bits of tinfoil-on-string to some malevolent government kitten, yes yes yes *but*, Borlú, however they've come by the evidence, *this is the correct decision.*'

'Have we checked with the border guards?'

'Yes, and there's bugger all, but you think they keep records of everyone they wave through? All they needed was to see some vaguely plausible pass. You can't argue with that.' He waved his hand at the television.

He was right. I shook my head.

'As that footage shows,' he said, 'the van did *not* breach, and, therefore, what appeal would we be making? We *can't* invoke Breach. Not for this. Nor, frankly, should we.'

'So what now?'

'What now is you are continuing this investigation. You started it, finish it.'

'But it's . . .'

'. . . in Ul Qoma, yes, I know. You're going over.'

'What?'

'This has become an international investigation. Ul Qoma cops weren't touching it while it looked like a Breach matter, but now this is their murder investigation, on the what-looks-like convincing evidence that it occurred on their soil. You are going to get to experience the joys of international collaboration. They've requested our help. On-site. You're going to Ul Qoma as the guest of the UQ *militsya*, where you'll be consulting with officers from their Murder Team. No one knows the status of the investigation better than you.'

'This is ridiculous. I can just send them a report . . .'

'Borlú, don't sulk. This has crossed our borders. What's a report? They need more than a bit of paper. This case has already turned out to be more convoluted than a dancing worm, and you're the man on it. It needs cooperation. Just *go over*, talk them through it. See the bloody sights. When they find someone we're going to want to bring charges against them here, too, for the theft, the body-dumping, and so on. Don't you know this is an exciting new era of cross-border policing?' It was a slogan from a booklet we had received when last we upgraded our computer equipment.

'The chance of us finding the killer just dropped hard. We needed Breach.'

'He tells me. I agree. So go and improve the odds.'

'How long am I going to be gone for?'

'Check in every couple of days with me. We'll see how it goes. If it's stretching more than a couple of weeks we'll review – it's a big enough pain that I'm losing you for those days.'

'So don't.' He looked at me sardonically: *What's the choice?* 'I'd like Corwi to come with me.'

He made a rude noise. 'I'm sure you would. Don't be stupid.'

I ran my hands through my hair. 'Commissar, I need her help. If anything she knows more about the case than I do. She's been integral to it from the beginning. If I'm going to take this over the border . . .'

137

'Borlú, you're not taking anything anywhere; you're a *guest*. Of our neighbours. You want to saunter over with your own Watson? Anyone else you'd like me to supply? Masseuse? Actuary? Get this in your head: over there *you're* the assistant. Jesus, it's bad enough that you press-ganged her in the first place. Under what authority, please? Instead of focusing on what you've lost, I suggest you remember the good times you had together.'

'This is—'

'Yes, yes. Don't tell me again. You want to know what's bullshit, Inspector?' He pointed the remote control at me, as if he could stop me or rewind me. 'What's bullshit is a senior officer of the Beszel ECS stopping off, with the subordinate officer he's quietly commandeered as his personal property, for an unauthorised, unnecessary, and unhelpful confrontation with a group of thugs with friends in high places.'

'. . . Right. You heard about that, then. From the lawyer?'

'What lawyer would you be speaking of? It was representative Syedr who was good enough to call this morning.'

'Syedr called you himself? Damn. Sorry, sir. I'm surprised. What, was he telling me to leave them alone? I thought part of the deal was that he was never quite open about being connected to TCs. Hence sending for that lawyer, who seemed a tad out of the league of the tough guys.'

'Borlú, I know only that Syedr had just heard about the previous day's tête-à-tête and was aghast to hear that he'd been mentioned, phoned in no small spleen to threaten various sanctions against you for slander should his name come up again in any such context, et cetera. I don't know and don't want to what led to that particular little investigative cul-de-sac, but you might ask yourself about the parameters of coincidence, Borlú. It was this same morning, only hours after your fabulously fruitful public argument with the patriots, that this footage popped up, and that Breach was called off. And no I have no idea what that might mean either, but it's an interesting fact, is it not?'

'DON'T ASK ME, BORLÚ,' Taskin said when I phoned her. 'I don't know. I just found out. I get rumours is all I get. Nyisemu's not happy about what happened, Buric is livid, Katrinya's confused, Syedr's delighted. That's the whisper. Who leaked what, who's messing with who, I don't have anything. I'm sorry.'

I asked her to keep her ears out. I had a couple of days to prepare. Gadlem had passed on my details to the relevant departments in Besźel and to a counterpart in Ul Qoma who would be my contact. 'And answer your damn messages,' he said. My pass and orientation would be organised for me. I went home and looked at clothes, put my old suitcase on my bed, picked up and put down books.

One of the books was new. I had received it in the mail that morning, having paid extra for expedited shipping. I'd ordered it online from a link on fracturedcity.org.

My copy of *Between the City and the City* was old and bruised, intact but with the cover folded back and its pages stained and annotated by at least two hands. I had paid an outrageous price for it despite these deficits because of its illegality in Besźel. It was not much of a risk, having my name on the dealer's list. It had been easy for me to ascertain that the book's status was, in Besźel at least, more a mildly embarrassing throwback than due to any ongoing sense of sedition. The majority of illegal books in the city were only vaguely so:

sanctions were rarely applied, even the censors rarely cared.

It was published by a long-gone anarcho-hippy press, though judging by the tone of the opening pages it was far drier than its florid, druggy cover would suggest. The print wobbled rather up and down the pages. There was no index, which made me sigh.

I lay on the bed and called the two women I saw, told them I was going to Ul Qoma. Biszaya, the journalist, said, 'Cool, make sure you go to the Brunai gallery. There's a Kounellis exhibition. Buy me a postcard.' Sariska the historian sounded more surprised, and disappointed that I might be gone for I did not know how long.

'Have you read *Between the City and the City*?' I said.

'When I was an undergrad, sure. My cam-cover was *The Wealth of Nations*.' During the 1960s and '70s, some banned literature could be bought bound in the stripped covers of legal paperbacks. 'What about it?'

'What did you think?'

'At the time, that it was amazing, man. Plus that I was unspeakably brave to be reading it. Subsequently that it was ridiculous. Are you finally going through adolescence, Tyador?'

'Could be. No one understands me. I didn't *ask* to be born.' She had no memories of the book, in particular.

'I cannot fucking believe this,' Corwi said when I called her and told her. She kept repeating it.

'I know. That's what I told Gadlem.'

'They're taking me off the case?'

'I don't think there's a "they". But unfortunately, yes, no, you can't come.'

'So that's it? I'm just dropped off?'

'I'm sorry.'

140

'Son of a *bitch*. The question,' she said after a minute we'd spent without saying anything, only listening to each other's silence and breath, like teenagers in love, 'is who would have released that footage. No, the question is how did they *find* that footage? Why? How many fucking hours of tape are there, how many cameras? Since when do they have the time to go through that shit? Why this one time?'

'I don't have to leave immediately. I'm just thinking . . . I've got my orientation the day after tomorrow . . .'

'So?'

'Well.'

'So?'

'Sorry, I've been thinking this through. About this footage that's just slapped us upside the head. Do you want to do a last little investigating? Couple of phone calls and a visit or two. There's one thing in particular I have to sort out before my visa and whatnot comes through – I've been thinking about that van swanning over to foreign lands. This could get you in trouble.' I said this last jokingly, as if it were something appealing. 'Of course you're off the case, now, so it's a bit unauthorised.' That wasn't true. She was in no danger – I could okay anything she did. I might get in trouble but she would not.

'Fuck, yes, then,' she said. 'If authority's stiffing you, unauthorised is all you've got.'

CHAPTER ELEVEN

'YES?' Mikyael Khurusch looked at me more closely from behind the door to his shabby office. 'Inspector. It's you. What . . . Hello?'

'Mr. Khurusch. Small point.'

'Let us in, please, sir,' Corwi said. He opened the door wider to see her, too, sighed and opened to us.

'How can I help you?' He clasped, unclasped his hands.

'Doing okay without your van?' Corwi said.

'It's a pain in the arse, but a friend's helping me out.'

'Good of him.'

'Isn't it?' Khurusch said.

'When did you get an AQD visa for your van, Mr. Khurusch?' I said.

'I, what, what?' he said. 'I don't, I have no—'

'Interesting that you stall like that,' I said. His response verified the guess. 'You're not so stupid as to out-and-out deny it, because, hey, passes are matters of record. But then what are we asking for? And why aren't you just answering? What's the trouble with that question?'

'Can we see your pass, please, Mr. Khurusch?'

He looked at Corwi several seconds.

'It's not here. It's at my house. Or—'

'Shall we not?' I said. 'You're lying. That was a little last chance for you, courtesy of us, and oh, you pissed it up a wall. You don't have your pass. A visa, Any Qualified Driver, for multiple entry-reentry into and out of Ul Qoma. Right? And you don't have it because it's been stolen. It was stolen when your van was stolen. It was, in fact, *in* your van when your van was stolen, along with your antique street map.'

'Look,' he said, 'I've told you, I wasn't there, I don't *have* a street map, I have GPS on my phone. I don't know anything—'

'Not true, but true that your alibi checks out. Understand, no one here thinks you committed this murder, or even dumped the body. That's not why we're ticked off.'

'Our concern,' Corwi said, 'is that you never told us about the pass. The question is who took it, and what you got for it.' Colour left his face.

'Oh God,' he said. His mouth worked several times and he sat down hard. 'Oh God, wait. I had nothing to do with anything, I didn't get *anything* . . .'

I had watched the CCTV footage repeatedly. There had been no hesitation in the van's passage, on that guarded and official route through Copula Hall. Far from breaching, slipping along a cross-hatched street, or changing plates to match some counterfeit permission, the driver had had to show the border guards papers that raised no eyebrows. There was one kind of pass in particular that might have expedited so uncomplicated a journey.

'Doing someone a favour?' I said. 'An offer you couldn't refuse? Blackmail? Leave the papers in the glove compartment. Better for them if you don't know anything.'

'Why else would you not tell us you'd lost your papers?' Corwi said.

'One and only chance,' I said. 'So. What's the score?'

'Oh God, look.' Khurusch looked longingly around. 'Please, look. I know I should've taken the papers in from the van. I do normally, I swear to you, I swear. I must have forgotten this one time, and that's the time the van gets stolen.'

'That's why you never told us about the theft, wasn't it?' I said. 'You never told us the van was stolen because you knew you'd have to tell us eventually about the papers, and so you just hoped the whole situation would sort itself out.'

'Oh God.'

Visiting Ul Qoman cars are generally easy to identify as visitors with rights of passage, with their licence plates, window stickers and modern designs: as are Besź cars in Ul Qoma, from their passes and their, to our neighbours, antiquated lines. Vehicular passes, particularly AQD multiple-entry, are neither cheap nor effortless to get hold of, and come hedged with conditions and rules. One of which is that a visa for a particular vehicle is never left unguarded in that vehicle. There's no point making smuggling easier than it is. It is, though, a not-uncommon oversight, or crime, to leave such papers in glove compartments or under seats. Khurusch knew he was facing at the very least a large fine and the revocation of any travel rights to Ul Qoma forever.

'Who did you give your van to, Mikyael?'

'I swear to Christ, Inspector, no one. I don't know who took it. I seriously do not know.'

'Are you saying that it was *total coincidence?* That someone who needed to pick up a body from Ul Qoma just happened to steal a van with pass papers still in it, waiting? How handy.'

'On my life, Inspector, I don't know. Maybe whoever nicked the van found the papers and sold them to someone else . . .'

'They found someone who needed trans-city transport the same night they stole it? These are the luckiest thieves ever.'

Khurusch slumped. 'Please,' he said. 'Go through my bank accounts. Check my wallet. No one's paying me dick. Since the van got taken I've not been able to do fucking anything, no business at all. I don't know what to do . . .'

'You're going to make me cry,' said Corwi. He looked at her with a ragged expression.

'On my life,' he said.

'We've looked up your record, Mikyael,' I said. 'I don't mean your *police* record – that's what we checked last time. I mean your record with the Besźel border patrol. You got random audited a few months after you first got a pass. A few years ago. We saw First Warning marks on several things, but the biggest by far was that you'd left the papers in the car. It was a car at the time, right? You'd left it in the glove compartment. How'd you get away with that one? I'm surprised they didn't revoke it there and then.'

'First offence,' he said. 'I begged them. One of the guys who found it said he'd have a word with his mate and get it commuted to an official warning.'

'Did you bribe him?'

'Sure. I mean, something. I can't remember how much.'

'Why not? I mean, that's how you got it in the first place, right? Why even bother?'

A long silence. AQD vehicle passes are generally advertised as for businesses with a few more employees than Khurusch's sketchy concern, but it is not uncommon for small traders to help their applications with a few dollars – Besźmarques being unlikely to move the Besź middlemen or issuing clerks at the Ul Qoman embassy.

145

'In case,' he said hopelessly, 'I ever needed help picking stuff up. My nephew's done the test, couple of mates, could've driven it, helped me out. You never know.'

'Inspector?' Corwi was looking at me. She'd said it more than once, I realised. 'Inspector?' She glanced at Khurusch, *What are we doing?*

'Sorry,' I said to her. 'Just thinking.' I motioned her to follow me to the corner of the room, warning Khurusch with a pointed finger to stay put.

'I'm going to take him in,' I said quietly, 'but something's . . . Look at him. I'm trying to work something out. Look, I want you to chase something up. As quick as you can, because tomorrow I'm going to have to go to this damn orientation, so I think tonight's going to be a long night. Are you okay with that? What I want is a list of all the vans reported stolen in Besźel that night, and I want to know what happened in each case.'

'*All* of them . . . ?'

'Don't panic. It'll be a lot for all vehicles, but factor out everything but vans round about this size, and it's only for one night. Bring me everything you can on each of them. Including all paperwork associated, okay? Quick as possible.'

'What are you going to do?'

'See if I can make this sleazy sod tell the truth.'

CORWI, through cajoling, persuasion and computer expertise, got hold of the information within a few hours. To be able to do that, so quickly, to speed up official channels, is voodoo.

For the first couple of hours as she went through things, I sat with Khurusch in a cell, and asked him in various ways

146

and in several different formulations *Who took your van?* and *Who took your pass?* He whined and demanded his lawyer, which I told him he would have soon. Twice he tried getting angry, but mostly he just repeated that he did not know, and that he had not reported the thefts, of van and papers, because he had been afraid of the trouble he would bring on himself. 'Especially because they already warned me on that, you know?'

It was after the end of the working day when Corwi and I sat together in my office to work through it. It would be, as I warned her again, a long night.

'What's Khurusch being held for?'

'At this stage Inappropriate Pass Storage and Failure to Report Crime. Depending on what we find tonight I might add Conspiracy to Murder, but I have a feeling—'

'You don't think he's in on whatever, do you?'

'He's hardly a criminal genius, is he?'

'I'm not suggesting he planned anything, boss. Maybe even that he knew about anything. Specific. But you don't think he knew who took his van? Or that they were going to do something?'

I wagged my head. 'You didn't see him.' I pulled the tape of his interrogations out of my pocket. 'Take a listen if we have a bit of time.'

She drove my computer, pulling the information she had into various spreadsheets. She translated my muttered, vague ideas into charts. 'This is called *data mining*.' She said the last words in English.

'Which of us is the canary?' I said. She did not answer. She only typed and drank thick coffee, 'made fucking properly,' and muttered complaints about my software.

147

'So this is what we have.' It was past two. I kept looking out of my office window at the Besźel night. Corwi smoothed out the papers she had printed. Beyond the window were the faint hoots and quietened mutter of late traffic. I moved in my chair, needing a piss from caffeinated soda.

'Total number of vans reported stolen that night, thirteen.' She scanned through with her fingertip. 'Of which three then turn up burnt out or vandalised in some form or other.'

'Joyriders.'

'Joyriders, yes. So ten.'

'How long before they were reported?'

'All but three, including the charmer in the cells, reported by the end of the following day.'

'Okay. Now where's the one where you have . . . How many of these vans have Ul Qoma pass papers?'

She sifted. 'Three.'

'That sounds high – three out of thirteen?'

'There are going to be way more for vans than for vehicles as a whole, because of all the import-export stuff.'

'Still though. What are the statistics for the cities as a whole?'

'What, of vans with passes? I can't find it,' she said after a while of typing and staring at the screen. 'I'm sure there must be a way to find out, but I can't figure out a way to do it.'

'Okay, if we have time we'll chase that. But I'm betting it's less than three out of thirteen.'

'You could . . . It does sound high.'

'Alright, try this. Of those three with passes that got stolen, how many owners have previous warnings for condition-transgressions?'

She looked through papers and then at me. 'All three of them. Shit. All three for inappropriate storage. *Shit*.'

'Right. That does sound unlikely, right? Statistically. What happened to the other two?'

'They were . . . Hold on. Belonged to Gorje Feder and Salya Ann Mahmud. Vans turned up the next morning. Dumped.'

'Anything taken?'

'Smashed up a bit, a few tapes, bit of change from Feder's, an iPod from Mahmud's.'

'Let me look at the times – there's no way of proving which of these were stolen first, is there? Do we know if these other two still have their passes?'

'Never came up, but we could find out tomorrow.'

'Do if you can. But I'm going to bet they do. Where were the vans taken from?'

'Juslavsja, Brov Prosz, and Khurusch's from Mashlin.'

'Where were they found?'

'Feder's in . . . Brov Prosz. Jesus. Mahmud's in Mashlin. Shit. Just off ProspekStrász.'

'That's about four streets from Khurusch's office.'

'Shit.' She sat back. 'Talk this out, boss.'

'Of the three vans that get stolen that night that have visas, all have records for failing to take their paperwork out of their glove compartments.'

'The thief *knew*?'

'Someone was visa-hunting. Someone with access to border-control records. They needed a vehicle they could get through Copula. They knew exactly who had form for not bothering to take their papers with them. Look at the positions.' I scribbled a crude map of Beszel. 'Feder's is taken first, but good on Mr. Feder, he and his staff have learned their lesson, and he takes his paperwork with him now. When they realise that our criminals use it instead to drive *here*, to near where Mahmud

149

parks hers. They jack it, fast, but Ms. Mahmud keeps her pass in the office now too, so after having made it look like a robbery, they dump it near the *next* in the list and move on.'

'And the next one's Khurusch's.'

'And he's remained true to his previous tendency, and leaves his in the van. So they've got what they need, and it's off to Copula Hall, and Ul Qoma.' Quiet.

'What the fuck is this?'

'It's . . . looking dodgy, is what it is. It's a very inside job. Inside what, I don't know. Someone with access to arrest records.'

'What the fuck do we do? What do we do?' she said again after I was quiet too long.

'I don't know.'

'We need to tell someone . . .'

'Who? Tell them what? We don't have anything.'

'Are you . . .' She was about to say *joking*, but she was intelligent enough to see the truth of it.

'Correlations might be enough for us, but it's not evidence, you know – not enough to do anything with.' We stared at each other. 'Anyway . . . whatever this is . . . whoever . . .' I looked at the papers.

'They've got access to stuff that . . .' Corwi said.

'We need to be careful,' I said. She met my eyes. There was another set of long moments when neither of us spoke. We looked slowly around the room. I do not know what we were looking for but I suspect that she felt, in that moment, as suddenly hunted and watched and listened-to as she looked like she did.

'So what do we do?' she said. It was unsettling to hear alarm like that in Corwi's voice.

150

'I guess what we've been doing. We investigate.' I shrugged slowly. 'We have a crime to solve.'

'We don't know who it's safe to talk to, boss. Anymore.'

'No.' There was nothing else I could say, suddenly. 'So maybe don't talk to anyone. Except me.'

'They're taking me off this case. What can I . . .?'

'Just answer your phone. If there's stuff I can get you to do I'll call.'

'Where does this go?'

It was a question that did not, at that point, mean anything. It was merely to fill the near noiselessness in the office, to cover up what noises there were, that sounded baleful and suspicious – each tick and creak of plastic an electronic ear's momentary feedback, each small knock of the building the shift in position of a sudden intruder.

'What I would really like,' she said, 'is to invoke Breach. Fuck them all, it would be just great to sic Breach on them. It would be great if this weren't our problem.' Yes. The notion of Breach exacting revenge on whomever, for whatever this was. 'She found something out. Mahalia.'

The thought of Breach had always seemed right. I remembered though, suddenly, the look on Mrs. Geary's face. Between the cities, Breach watched. None of us knew what it knew.

'Yeah. Maybe.'

'No?'

'Sure, it's just . . . we can't. So . . . we have to try to focus on this ourselves.'

'We? The two of us, boss? Neither of us knows what the fuck's going on.'

Corwi was whispering by the end of the last sentence.

151

Breach were beyond our control or ken. Whatever situation or thing this was, whatever had happened to Mahalia Geary, we two were its only investigators, so far as we could trust, and she would soon be alone, and I would be alone, too, and in a foreign city.

PART TWO

UL QOMA

CHAPTER TWELVE

THE INNARD ROADS OF COPULA HALL seen from a police car. We did not travel fast and our siren was off, but in some vague pomp our light flickered and the concrete around us was staccato blue-lit. I saw my driver glance at me. Constable Dyegesztan his name was, and I had not met him before. I had not been able to get Corwi even as my escort.

We had gone on the low flyovers through Besźel Old Town into the convolutes of Copula Hall's outskirts, and down at last into its traffic quadrant. Past and under the stretches of facade where caryatids looked at least somewhat like figures from Besź history, towards where they were Ul Qoman, into the hall itself, where a wide road overlit by windows and grey lights was sided at the Besź end by a long line of pedestrians seeking day entry. In the distance beyond the red taillights we were faced by the tinted headlights of Ul Qoman cars, more gold than ours.

'Been to Ul Qoma before, sir?'

'Not for a long time.'

When the border gates came into view Dyegesztan spoke to me again. 'Did they have it like this before?' He was young.

'More or less.'

Apoliczai car, we were in the official lane, behind dark imported Mercedeses that probably carried politicians or businesspeople on fact-finding missions. A way off was the engine-grumbling line of quotidian travellers in cheaper cars, spivs and visitors.

'Inspector Tyador Borlú.' The guard looked at my papers.

'That's right.'

He went carefully over everything written. Had I been a tourist or trader wanting a day-pass, passage might well have been quicker and questioning more cursory. As an official visitor, there was no such laxity. One of those everyday bureaucratic ironies.

'Both of you?'

'It's right there, Sergeant. Just me. This is my driver. I'm being picked up, and the constable here'll be coming straight back. In fact if you look, I think you can see my party over in Ul Qoma.'

There, uniquely at that convergence, we could look across a simple physical border and see into our neighbour. Beyond, beyond the stateless space and the backwards-to-us-facing Ul Qoman checkpoint, a small group *of militsya* officers stood around an official car, its lights stuttering as pompously as our own, but in different colours and with a more modern mechanism (true on-off, not the twisting blinder that our own lamps contained). Ul Qoman police lights are red and darker blue than the cobalt in Besźel. Their cars are charcoal and streamlined Renaults. I remember when they drove ugly little local-made Yadajis, more boxy than our own vehicles.

The guard turned and glanced at them. 'We're due about now,' I told him.

The *militsya* were too far for any details to be clear. They were waiting for something though. The guard took his time of course – *You may be* policzai *but you get no special treat-*

156

ment, we watch the borders – but without excuses to do otherwise eventually saluted somewhat sardonically and pointed us through as the gate rose. After the Besź road itself the hundred metres or so of no-place felt different under our tyres, and then through the second set of gates and we were on the other side, with uniformed *militsya* coming towards us.

There was the gunning of gears. The car we had seen waiting sped in a sudden tight curve around and in front of the approaching officers, calling out one truncated and abrupt *whoop* from the siren. A man emerged, putting on his police cap. He was a bit younger than me, thickset and muscular and moving with fast authority. He wore official *militsya* grey with an insignia of rank. I tried to remember what it meant. The border guards had stopped in surprise as he held out his hand.

'That'll do,' he shouted. He waved them away. 'I got this. Inspector Borlú?' He was speaking Illitan. Dyegesztan and I climbed out of the car. He ignored the constable. 'Inspector Tyador Borlú, Besźel Extreme Crime, right?' Shook my hand hard. Pointed to his car, in which his own driver waited. 'Please. I'm Senior Detective Qussim Dhatt. You got my message, Inspector? Welcome to Ul Qoma.'

COPULA HALL HAD OVER CENTURIES SPREAD, a patchwork of architecture defined by the Oversight Committee in its various historic incarnations. It sat across a considerable chunk of land in both cities. Its inside was complicated – corridors might start mostly total, Besźel or Ul Qoma, become progressively crosshatched along their length, with rooms in one or other city along them, and numbers also of those strange rooms and areas that were in neither or both cities, that were in *Copula Hall only,* and of which the Oversight Committee and its bodies were the only government. Legended diagrams of the buildings inside were pretty but daunting meshes of colours.

At ground level, though, where the wide road jutted into the first set of gates and wire, where the Besź Border Patrol waved arrivals to a stop in their separated lines – pedestrians, handcarts, and animal-drawn trailers, squat Besź cars, vans, sub-lines for various kinds of passes, all moving at different speeds, the gates rising and lowering out of any phase – the situation was simpler. An unofficial but ancient market where Copula Hall vents into Besźel, within sight of the gates. Illegal but tolerated street hawkers walked the lines of waiting cars with roasted nuts and paper toys.

Beyond the Besźel gates, below the main mass of Copula Hall, a no-man's-land. The tarmac was unpainted: this was neither a Besź nor an Ul Qoman thoroughfare, so what system of road markings would be used? Beyond towards the other end of the hall the second set of gates, which we on the Besźel side could not but notice were better kept than our own, with weapon-wielding Ul Qoman guards staring, most of them away from us at their own efficiently shepherded lines of visitors to Besźel. Ul Qoman border guards are not a separate wing of government, as they are in Besźel: they are *militsya*, police, like the *policzai*.

It is bigger than a coliseum, but Copula Hall's traffic chamber is not complicated – an emptiness walled by antiquity. From the Besźel threshold you can see over the crowds and crawling vehicles to daylight filtering in from Ul Qoma, beyond. You can see the bobbing heads of Ul Qoman visitors or returning fellow countrymen approaching, the ridges of Ul Qoman razorwire beyond the hall's midpoint, beyond that empty stretch between

158

checkpoints. You can just make out the architecture of Ul Qoma itself through the enormous gateway hundreds of metres off. People strain to see, across that junction.

On our way there I had had the driver take us, to his raised eyebrows, a long way round to the Besźel entrance on a route that took us on KarnStrász. In Besźel it is an unremarkable shopping street in the Old Town, but it is crosshatched, some-what in Ul Qoma's weight, the majority of buildings in our neighbour, and in Ul Qoma its topolganger is the historic, famous Ul Maidin Avenue, into which Copula Hall vents. We drove as if coincidentally by the Copula Hall exit into Ul Qoma.

I had unseen it as we took KarnStrász, at least ostensibly, but of course grosstopically present near us were the lines of Ul Qomans entering, the trickle of visitor-badge-wearing Besź emerging into the same physical space they may have walked an hour previously, but now looking around in astonishment at the architecture of Ul Qoma it would have been breach to see before.

Near the Ul Qoma exit is the Temple of Inevitable Light. I had seen photos many times, and though I had unseen it dutifully when we passed I was aware of its sumptuous crenel-lations, and had almost said to Dyegesztan that I was looking forward to seeing it soon. Now light, foreign light, swallowed me as I emerged, at speed, from Copula Hall. I looked every-where. From the rear of Dhatt's car, I stared at the temple. I was, suddenly, rather astonishingly and at last, in the same city as it.

'First time in Ul Qoma?'

'No, but first time in a long time.'

*

IT WAS YEARS since I had first taken the tests: my passmark was long expired and in a defunct passport. This time I had undergone an accelerated orientation, two days. It had only been me and the various tutors, Ul Qomans from their Besź embassy. Illitan immersion, the reading of various documents of Ul Qoman history and civic geography, key issues of local law. Mostly, as with our own equivalents, the course was concerned to help a Besź citizen through the potentially traumatic fact of actually *being in* Ul Qoma, unseeing all their familiar environs, where we lived the rest of our life, and seeing the buildings beside us that we had spent decades making sure not to notice.

'Acclimatisation pedagogy's come a long way with computers,' said one of the teachers, a young woman who praised my Illitan constantly. 'We've got so much more sophisticated ways of dealing with stuff now; we work with neuroscientists, all sorts of stuff.' I got spoiled because I was *policzai*. Everyday travellers would undergo more conventional training, and would take considerably longer to qualify.

They sat me in what they called an Ul Qoma simulator, a booth with screens for inside walls, on which they projected images and videos of Besźel with the Besź buildings highlighted and their Ul Qoman neighbours minimised with lighting and focus. Over long seconds, again and again, they would reverse the visual stress, so that for the same vista Besźel would recede and Ul Qoma shine.

How could one not think of the stories we all grew up on, that surely the Ul Qomans grew up on too? Ul Qoman man and Besź maid, meeting in the middle of Copula Hall, returning to their homes to realise that they live, grosstopically, next door to each other, spending their lives faithful and alone, rising at the same time, walking crosshatched streets close like a couple, each in their own city, never breaching, never quite touching, never speaking a word across the border. There were folktales of renegades who breach and avoid Breach to live between the cities, not exiles but in-siles, evading justice and retribution by consummate ignorability. Pahlaniuk's novel *Diary of an Insile* had been illegal in Besźel (and, I was sure, in Ul Qoma), but like most people I had skimmed a pirated edition.

I did the tests, pointing with a cursor at an Ul Qoman temple, an Ul Qoman citizen, an Ul Qoman lorry delivering vegetables, as quick as I could. It was faintly insulting stuff, designed to catch me inadvertently seeing Besźel. There had been nothing like this the first time I had done such studies. Not very long ago the equivalent tests would have involved being asked about the different national character of Ul Qomans, and judging who from various pictures with stereotyped physiognomies was Ul Qoman, Besź, or 'Other' (Jewish, Muslim, Russian, Greek, whatever, depending on the ethnic anxieties of the time).

'Seen the temple?' Dhatt said. 'And that there used to be a college. Those are apartment blocks.' He jabbed his finger at buildings as we passed, told his driver, to whom he had not introduced me, to go various routes.

'Weird?' he said to me. 'Guess it must be strange.'

Yes. I looked at what Dhatt showed me. Unseeing, of course, but I could not fail to be aware of all the familiar places I passed grosstopically, the streets at home I regularly walked, now a whole city away, particular cafés I frequented that we passed, but in another country. I had them in the background now, hardly any more present than Ul Qoma was when I was

161

at home. I held my breath. I was unseeing Besźel. I had forgotten what this was like; I had tried and failed to imagine it. I was seeing Ul Qoma.

Day, so the light was that of the overcast cold sky, not the twists of neon I had seen in so many programs about the neighbouring country, which the producers evidently thought it easier for us to visualise in its garish night. But that ashy daylight illuminated more and more vivid colours than in my old Besźel. The Old Town of Ul Qoma was at least half transmuted these days into a financial district, curlicued wooden rooflines next to mirrored steel. The local street hawkers wore gowns and patched-up shirts and trousers, sold rice and skewers of meat to smart men and a few women (past whom my nondescript compatriots, I tried to unsee, walked on their way to Besźel's more quiet destinations) in the doorways of glass blocks.

After mild censure from UNESCO, a finger-wag tied to some European investment, Ul Qoma had recently passed zoning laws to stop the worst of the architectural vandalism its boomtime occasioned. Some of the ugliest recent works had even been demolished, but still the traditional baroque curlicues of Ul Qoma's heritage sights were made almost pitiful by their giant young neighbours. Like all Besźel dwellers, I had become used to shopping in the foreign shadows of foreign success.

Illitan everywhere, in Dhatt's running commentary, from the vendors, taxi drivers and insult-hurling local traffic. I realised how much invective I had been unhearing on crosshatched roads at home. Each city in the world has its own road-grammar, and though we were not in any total Ul Qoma areas yet, so these streets shared the dimensions and shapes of those I knew, they felt in the sharp turns we took more intricate. It was as strange as I had expected it would be, seeing and unseeing, being in Ul Qoma. We went by narrow byways less frequented in Besźel (deserted there though bustling in Ul Qoma), or which were pedestrian-only in Besźel. Our horn was constant.

'Hotel?' Dhatt said. 'Probably want to get cleaned up and have something to eat, right? Where then? I know you must have some ideas. You speak good Illitan, Borlú. Better than my Besź.' He laughed.

'I've got a few thoughts. Places I'd like to go.' I held my notebook. 'You got the dossier I sent?'

'Sure did, Borlú. That's the lot of it, right? That's where you're at? I'll fill you in about what we've been up to but' – he held up his hands in mock surrender – 'truth is there's not that much to tell. We thought Breach was going to be invoked. Why didn't you give them it? You like making work for yourself?' Laugh. 'Anyway, I only got assigned all this in the last couple of days, so don't expect too much. But we're on it now.'

'Any idea where she was killed yet?'

'Not so much. There's only CCTV of that van coming through Copula Hall; we don't know where it went then. No leads. Anyway, things . . .'

A visiting Besź van, one might assume, would be memorable in Ul Qoma, as an Ul Qoman one would be in Besźel. The truth is that unless someone saw the sign in the windscreen, people's assumption would be that such a foreign vehicle was not in their home city, and accordingly it would remain unseen. Potential witnesses would generally not know there was anything to witness.

'That's the main thing I want to track down.'

163

'Absolutely. Tyador, or is it Tyad? Got a preference?'

'And I'd like to talk to her advisors, her friends. Can you take me to Bol Ye'an?'

'Dhatt, Quss, whichever's fine by me. Listen, just to get this out of the way, avoid confusions, I know your *commissar* told you this' – he relished the foreign word – 'but while you're here this is an Ul Qoman investigation, and you don't have police powers. Don't get me wrong – we're totally grateful for the cooperation, and we're going to work out what we do together, but I've got to be the officer here. You're a consultant, I guess.'

'Of course.'

'Sorry, I know turf bullshit is bullshit. I was told – did you speak to my boss yet? Colonel Muasi? – anyway, he wanted to make sure we were cool before we talked. Of course you're an honoured guest of the Ul Qoman *militsya*.'

'I'm not restricted to . . . I can travel?'

'You've got your permit and stamp and all that.' A single-entry trip, a month renewable. 'Sure if you have to, if you want take a tourist day or two, but you're strictly a tourist when you're on your own. Cool? It might be better if you didn't. I mean shit, no one's going to stop you, but we all know it's harder to cross over without a guide; you could breach without meaning to, and then what?'

'So. What would you do next?'

'Well look.' Dhatt turned in his seat to look at me. 'We'll be at the hotel soon. Anyway listen: like I'm trying to tell you, things are getting . . . I guess you haven't heard about the other one . . . No, we don't even know if there's anything there and we only just got sniff ourselves. Look, there may be a complication.'

164

'What? What are you talking about?'

'We're here, sir,' the driver said. I looked out but stayed in the car. We were by the Hilton in Asyan, just outside the Ul Qoma Old Town. It was at the edge of a total street of low, modern concrete Ul Qoman residences, at the corner of a plaza of Besź brick terraces and Ul Qoman faux pagodas. Between them was an ugly fountain. I had never visited it: the buildings and pavements at its rim were crosshatched, but the central square itself was total Ul Qoma.

'We don't know for sure yet. Obviously we've been up to the dig, talked to Iz Nancy, all Geary's supervisors, all her classmates and that. No one knew anything; they just thought she'd fucked off for a couple of days. Then they heard what had happened. Anyway, the point is that after we spoke to a bunch of the students, we got a phone call from one of them. It was only yesterday. About Geary's best friend – we saw her the day we went in to tell them, another student. Yolanda Rodriguez. She was totally in shock. We didn't get much out of her. She was collapsing all over the place. She said she had to go, I said did she want any help, blah blah, she said she had someone to look after her. Local boy, one of the others said. Once you've tried Ul Qoman . . .' He reached over and opened my door. I did not get out.

'So she called?'

'No, that's what I'm saying, the kid who called wouldn't give us his name, but he was calling *about* Rodriguez. It seems like – and he was saying he's not sure, could be nothing, et cetera et cetera. Anyway. No one's seen her for a little while. Rodriguez. No one can get her on her phone.'

'She's disappeared?'

'Holy Light, Tyad, that's melodramatic. She might just be

sick, she might have turned her phone off. I'm not saying we don't go looking, but don't let's panic yet, right? We don't know that she's disappeared . . .'

'Yeah we do. Whatever's happened, whether anything's happened to her at all, no one can find her. That's pretty definitional. She's disappeared.'

Dhatt glanced at me in the mirror and then at his driver.

'Alright, Inspector,' he said. 'Yolanda Rodriguez has disappeared.'

CHAPTER THIRTEEN

'WHAT'S IT LIKE, BOSS?' There was a lag on the hotel's line to Beszel, and Corwi and I were stutteringly trying not to overlap each other.

'Too early to say. Weird to be here.'

'You saw her rooms?'

'Nothing helpful. Just student digs, with a bunch of others in a building leased by the university.'

'Nothing of hers?'

'Couple of cheap prints, some books complete with scribbled margin notes, of which none are interesting. A few clothes. A computer which either has really industrial-strength encryption or nothing germane on it. And on that I have to say I trust Ul Qoman geeks more than ours. Lots of *Hi Mom love you* emails, a few essays. She probably used proxies and a cleaner-upper online too, because there was bugger-all of interest in her cache.'

'You have no idea what you're saying, do you, boss?'

'None at all. I had the techies write it all out phonetically for me.' Perhaps one day we would be finished with I-don't-understand-the-internet jokes. 'On which topic she hadn't updated her MySpace since moving to Ul Qoma.'

'So you didn't figure her all out?'

'Sadly no, the force was not with me.' It really had been a startlingly bland and uninformative room. Yolanda's, by contrast, a corridor over, into which we had also peered, had been crammed with hipster toys, novels and DVDs, moderately flamboyant shoes. Her computer was gone.

I had gone carefully through Mahalia's room, referring often to the photographs of how it had been when the *militsya* entered, before the books and few bits and pieces had been tagged and processed. The room was cordoned, and officers kept the students away, but when I glanced out of the door over the little pile of wreaths I could see Mahalia's classmates in knots at either end of the corridor, young women and men with little visitors' marks discreetly on their clothes. They whispered to each other. I saw more than one weeping.

We found no notebooks and no diaries. Dhatt had acquiesced to my request for copies of Mahalia's textbooks, the copious annotations of which appeared to be her preferred study method. They were on my table: whoever had photocopied them had been rushed, and the print and handwriting yawed. As I spoke to Corwi I read a few cramped lines of Mahalia's telegraphic arguments with herself in A *People's History of Ul Qoma*.

'What's your contact like?' Corwi said. 'Your Ul Qoman me?'

'Actually I think I'm his you.' The phrase was not best chosen but she laughed.

'What's their office like?'

'Like ours with better stationery. They took my gun.'

In fact the police station had been rather different from our own. It did have better fittings, but it was large and open-plan, full of whiteboards and cubicles over which neighbouring officers debated and bickered. Though I am sure most of the local *militsya* must have been informed that I was coming, I left a wake of unabashed curiosity as I followed Dhatt past his own office – he was ranked enough to get a little room – to his boss's. Colonel Muasi had greeted me boredly with something about what a good sign of the changing relationships between our countries, herald of future cooperation, any help at all I needed, and had made me surrender my weapon. That had not been agreed beforehand, and I had tried to argue it but had given in quickly rather than sour things so early.

When we had left it had been to another roomful of not-very-friendly stares. 'Dhatt,' someone had greeted him in passing, in a pointed way. 'Ruffling feathers, am I?' I had asked, and Dhatt had said, 'Touchy touchy. You're Besź, what did you expect?'

'Fuckers!' said Corwi. 'They did not.'

'No valid Ul Qoman licence, here in advisory role, et cetera.' I went through the bedside cupboard. There was not even a Gideon Bible. I did not know whether that was because Ul Qoma is secular, or because of lobbying by its disestablished but respected Lux Templars.

'Fuckers. So nothing to report?'

'I'll let you know.' I glanced over the list of code phrases we had agreed to, but none of them – *I miss Besź dumplings = am in trouble*, *Working on a theory = know who did it* – were remotely germane. 'I feel fucking stupid,' she had said as we came up with them. 'I agree,' I had said. 'I do too. Still.' Still, we could not assume that our communications would not be listened to, by whatever power it was that had outmanoeuvred us in Besźel. Is it more foolish and childish to assume there is a conspiracy, or that there is not?

'Same weather over here as back home,' I said. She laughed. That cliché witticism we had arranged meant *nothing to report*.

'What next?' she said.

'We're going to Bol Ye'an.'

'What, now?'

'No. Sadly. I wanted to go earlier today, but they didn't get it together and it's too late now.' After I had showered and eaten, and wandered around the drab little room, wondering if I would recognise a listening device if I saw one, I had called the number Dhatt gave me three times before getting through to him.

'Tyador,' he had said. 'Sorry, did you try to call? Been flat out, got caught tying up some stuff here. What can I do for you?'

'It's getting on. I wanted to check about the dig site . . .'

'Oh, shit, yeah. Listen, Tyador, it's not going to happen tonight.'

'Didn't you tell people to expect us?'

'I told them to *probably* expect us. Look, they'll be glad to go home, and we'll go first thing in the morning.'

'What about What's-her-name Rodriguez?'

'I'm still not convinced she's actually . . . no, I'm not allowed to say that, am I? I'm not convinced that the fact that she's missing is suspicious, how's that? It's hardly been very long. But if she's still gone tomorrow, and not answering her email or her messages or anything, then it's looking worse, I grant you. We'll get Missing Persons on it.'

'So . . .'

'So look. I'm not going to get a chance to come over tonight. Can you . . .? You've got stuff you can do, right? I'm sorry about this. I'm couriering over a bunch of stuff, copies of our notes,

170

and that info you wanted, about Bol Ye'an and the university campuses and all that. Do you have a computer? Can you go online?'

'. . . Yeah.' A departmental laptop, a hotel Ethernet connection at ten dinar a night.

'Alright then. And I'm sure they've got video-on-demand. So you won't be lonely.' He laughed.

I READ *Between the City and the City* for a while, but stalled. The combination of textual and historic minutiae and tendentious *therefores* was wearing. I watched Ul Qoman television. There were more feature films than on Besź TV, it seemed, and more and louder game shows, all a channel-hop or two from newsreaders listing the successes of President Ul Mak and the New Reform packages: visits to China and Turkey, trade missions to Europe, praise from some in the IMF, whatever Washington's sulk. Ul Qomans were obsessed with economics. Who could blame them?

'Why not, Corwi?' I took a map and made sure all of my papers, my *policzai* ID, my passport and my visa were in my inside pocket. I pinned my visitor's badge to my lapels and went into the cold.

Now there was the neon. All around me in knots and coils, effacing the weak lights of my far-off home. The animated yammering in Illitan. It was a busier city than Besźel at night: now I could look at the figures at business in the dark that had been unseeable shades until now. I could see the homeless dossing down in side streets, the Ul Qoman rough sleepers that we in Besźel had had to become used to as protubs to pick our unseeing ways over and around.

I crossed Wahid Bridge, trains passing to my left. I watched

171

the river, that was here the Shach-Ein. Water – does it cross-hatch with itself? If I were in Beszel, as these unseen passersby were, I would be looking at the River Colinin. It was quite a way from the Hilton to Bol Ye'an, an hour along Ban Yi Way. Aware that I was crisscrossing Beszel streets I knew well, streets mostly of very different character than their Ul Qoman topol-gangers. I unsaw them but knew that the alleys off Ul Qoma's Modrass Street were in Beszel only, and that the furtive men entering and emerging from them were customers of the cheapest Besz prostitutes, who if I failed to unsee them I might have made out as miniskirted phantoms in that Beszel dark-ness. Where were Ul Qoma's brothels, near what Beszel neighbourhoods? I policed a music festival once, early in my career, in a crosshatched park, where the attendees got high in such numbers that there was much public fornication. My partner at the time and I had not been able to forebear amuse-ment at the Ul Qoman passersby we tried not to see in their own iteration of the park, stepping daintily over fucking couples they assiduously unsaw.

I considered taking the subway, which I never had (there is nothing like it in Beszel), but it was a good thing to walk. I tested my Illitan on conversations I overheard; I saw the groups of Ul Qomans unsee me because of my clothes and the way I held myself, double-take and see my visitor's mark, see me. There were groups of young Ul Qomans outside amusement arcades that rang with sound. I looked at, could see, gasrooms, small vertically oriented blimps contained within integuments of girders: once urban crow's nests to guard against attack, for many decades now architectural nostalgias, kitsch, these days used to dangle advertisements.

There was a siren I quickly unheard, of a Besz *policzai* car, that passed. I focused instead on the locals moving quickly and without expression to get out of its way: that was the worst kind of protub. I had marked Bol Ye'an on my street map. Before coming to Ul Qoma I had considered travelling to its topolganger, the physically corresponding area of Beszel, to accidentally glimpse that unseen dig, but I would not risk it. I did not even travel to the edges where the ruins and park trip over tinily into Beszel itself. Unimpressive, people said, like most of our antique sites: the large majority of the great remnants were on Ul Qoman soil.

Past an old Ul Qoman edifice, though of European style, I – having planned this route – stared down a slope the length of Tyan Ulma Street, heard distantly (across a border, before I thought to un-hear) the bell of a tram crossing the street in Beszel a half mile in front of me in the country of my birth, and I saw filling the plateau at the street's end under the half-moon the parkland, and ruins of Bol Ye'an.

Hoardings surrounded them, but I was above and could look down over those walls. An up-down treed and flowered landscape, some parts wilder, some coiffed. At the northern end of the park, where the ruins themselves were, what looked at first like a wasteland, was scrub punctuated with old stones of fallen temples, canvas-covered walkways linking marquees and prefab office buildings in some of which lights were still on. Ground showed the marks of digging: most of the excavation was hidden and protected by tough tents. Lights dotted and shone down at the winter-dying grass. Some were broken, and shed nothing but excess shadow. I saw figures walking. Security guards, keeping safe these forgotten then remembered memories.

In places the park and the site itself were edged right up

to its rubble and boscage by the rear of buildings, most in Ul Qoma (some not) that seemed to jostle up against it, against history. The Bol Ye'an dig had about a year before the exigencies of city growth would smother it: money would breach the chipboard and corrugated iron boundary, and with official expressions of regret and necessity, another (Besźel-punctuated) block of offices would rise in Ul Qoma.

I traced on my map the proximity and route between Bol Ye'an and the offices of Ul Qoma University used by the Prince of Wales Archaeology Department. 'Hey.' It was a *militsya* officer, his hand on the butt of his weapon. He had a partner a pace behind.

'What are you doing?' They peered at me. 'Hey.' The officer at the rear pointed at my visitor's sign.

'What are you doing?'

'I'm interested in archaeology.'

'The fuck you are. Who are you?' Finger click for papers. The few unseeing Besź pedestrians crossed without probably being conscious that they did so to the other side of the street. There is little more unsettling than nearby foreign trouble. It was late, but there were some Ul Qomans close enough to hear the exchange, and they did not pretend not to listen. Some stopped to watch.

'I'm . . .' I gave them my papers.

'Tye Adder Borlo.'

'More or less.'

'Police?' They stared all confused at me.

'I'm here assisting the *militsya* with an international inves-tigation. I suggest you contact Senior Detective Dhatt of the Murder Team.'

'Fuck.' They conferred out of my hearing. One radioed

something through. It was too dark to take a shot of Bol Ye'an on my cheap cell phone camera. The smell of some heavy-scented street food reached me. This was increasingly the prime candidate for the smell of Ul Qoma.

'Alright, Inspector Borlú.' One of them returned my documents.

'Sorry about that,' his colleague said.

'It's quite alright.' They looked annoyed, and waited. 'I'm on my way back to the hotel anyway, officers.'

'We'll escort you, Inspector.' They would not be deterred.

When Dhatt came to pick me up the next morning, he said nothing beyond pleasantries when he came into the dining hall to find me trying 'Traditional Ul Qoman Tea,' which was flavoured with sweet cream and some unpleasant spice. He asked how the room was. Only when I had finally got into his car and he lurched away from the kerb faster and more violently than even his officer the previous day had done did he say to me finally, 'I wish you hadn't done that last night.'

THE STAFF AND STUDENTS of the Prince of Wales University Ul Qoman Archaeology program were mostly at Bol Ye'an. I arrived at the site for the second time in less than twelve hours.

'I didn't make us appointments,' Dhatt said. 'I spoke to Professor Rochambeaux, the head of the project. He knows we're coming again, but the rest of them I thought we'd take by chance.'

Unlike for my distance viewing of the night, up close the walls blocked off the site from watchers. *Militsya* were stationed at points outside, security guards within. Dhatt's badge got us immediately into the little complex of makeshift offices. I had a list of the staff and students. We went first to Bernard

175

Rochambeaux's office. He was a wiry man about fifteen years my senior, who spoke Illitan with a strong Quebecois accent.

'We're all devastated,' he told us. 'I didn't know the girl, you understand? Only to see in the common room. By reputation.' His office was in a portacabin, folders and books on the temporary shelves, photographs of himself in various dig sites. Outside we heard young people walking past and talking. 'Any help we can give you, of course. I don't know many of the students myself, not well. I have three PhD students at the moment. One is in Canada, the other two being, I think, over there.' He indicated the direction of the main dig. 'Them I know.'

'What about Rodriguez?' He looked at me and signalled confusion. 'Yolanda? One of your students? Have you seen her?'

'She's not one of my three, Inspector. I'm afraid there's not much I can tell you. Have we . . . Is she missing?'

'She is. What do you know about her?'

'Oh my God. She's missing? I don't know anything about her. Mahalia Geary I knew by reputation of course, but we had literally never exchanged words other than at a welcome-new-students party a few months ago.'

'A lot longer than that,' Dhatt said. Rochambeaux stared at him.

'There you go – it's impossible to keep track of time. Is it really? I can tell you about her all the things you already know. Her supervisor's the one who can really help you. Have you met Isabelle?'

He had his secretary print a list of staff and students. I did not tell him we had one already. When Dhatt did not offer it to me I took it. Judging by the names, and in accordance with law, two of the archaeologists detailed were Ul Qoman.

'He's got an alibi for Geary,' Dhatt said when we left. 'He's one of the very few who does. Most of them, you know, it was late in the night, no one can vouch, so alibi-wise at least they're all fucked. He was on a conference call to a colleague in an uncongenial time zone roundabout the time she was killed. We checked it.'

We were looking for Isabelle Nancy's office when someone called my name. A trim man in his early sixties, grey beard, glasses, hurrying between temporary rooms towards us. 'Is it Inspector Borlú?' He glanced at Dhatt, but seeing the Ul Qoman insignia looked back at me. 'I heard you might be coming. I'm glad to coincide with you. I'm David Bowden.'

'Professor Bowden.' I shook his hand. 'I'm enjoying your book.'

He was visibly taken aback. He shook his head. 'I take it you mean my first one. No one ever means the second one.' He dropped my hand. 'That'll get you arrested, Inspector.' Dhatt was looking at me in surprise.

'Where's your office, Professor? I'm Senior Detective Dhatt. I'd like to talk to you.'

'I don't have one, SD Dhatt. I'm only in here a day a week. And it's not *professor*. Plain doctor. Or David is fine.'

'How long will you be here this morning, Doctor?' I said. 'Could we grab a word with you?'

'I . . . of course, if you'd like, Inspector, but as I say, I've no office. Normally I meet students at my flat.' He gave me a card and when Dhatt raised an eyebrow he gave Dhatt one too. 'My number's on that. I'll wait around if you'd like; we can probably find a place to talk.'

'Did you not come in to see us, then?' I said.

'No, this is chance. I wouldn't normally be in today at all, but my supervisee didn't turn up yesterday and I thought I might find her here.'

'Your supervisee?' Dhatt said.

'Yes, they only trust me with the one.' He smiled. 'Hence no office.'

'Who is it you're looking for?'

'Her name's Yolanda, SD. Yolanda Rodriguez.'

He was horrified when we told him that she was unreachable. He stammered for something to say.

'She's gone? After what happened to Mahalia, now Yolanda? Oh my God, Officers, do you—'

'We're looking into it,' Dhatt said. 'Don't jump to conclusions.'

Bowden looked stricken. We had similar reactions from his colleagues. One by one we went through the four academics we could find on-site, including Thau'ti, the senior of the two Ul Qomans, a young taciturn man. Only Isabelle Nancy, a tall well-dressed woman with two pairs of glasses of different prescriptions on chains around her neck, was aware that Yolanda had disappeared.

'It's good to meet you, Inspector, Senior Detective.' She shook our hands. I had read her statement. She claimed she had been at home when Mahalia was murdered but could not prove it. 'Anything I can do to help,' she kept saying.

'Tell us about Mahalia. I get the sense she was well-known here, if not by your boss.'

'Not so much anymore,' Nancy said. 'At one point maybe. Did Rochambeaux say he didn't know her? That's a bit . . . disingenuous. She'd ruffled some feathers.'

'At the conference,' I said. 'Back in Besźel.'

178

'That's right. Down south. He was there. Most of us were. I was, David, Marcus, Asina. Anyway she'd been raising eyebrows at more than one session, asking questions about *dissensi*, about Breach, that sort of thing. Nothing explicitly illegitimate, but a bit *vulgar*, you could say, the sort of thing you'd expect from Hollywood or something, not the nuts-and-bolts stuff of Ul Qoman or pre-Cleavage or even Besź research. You could see the bigwigs who'd come along to open proceedings and dedicate ceremonies and whatnot were getting a bit leery. Then finally she out and starts raving about Orciny. So David's mortified, of course; the university's embarrassed; she nearly gets chucked out – there were some Besź representatives there who made a big hoo-ha about it.'

'But she didn't?' Dhatt said.

'I think people decided she was young. But someone must have given her a talking-to, because she simmered down. I remember thinking the Ul Qoman opposite numbers, some of whom had also turned up, must be pretty sympathetic to the Besź reps who were so put out. When I found out she was coming back for a PhD with us I was surprised she'd been allowed in, with dubious opinions like that, but she'd grown out of it. I've already made a statement about all this. But tell me, do you have any idea what's happened to Yolanda?'

Dhatt and I looked at each other. 'We're not even sure anything's happened to her at all,' Dhatt said. 'We're checking into it.'

'It's probably nothing,' she said again and again. 'But I normally see her around, and it's a good few days now, I think. That's what makes me . . . I think I mentioned that Mahalia disappeared a bit before she was . . . found.'

'She and Mahalia knew each other?' I said.

179

'They were best friends.'

'Anyone who might know anything?'

'She's seeing a local boy. Yolanda, I mean. That's the rumour. But who it was I couldn't tell you.'

'Is that allowed?' I asked.

'These are adults, Inspector, SD Dhatt. Young adults, yes, but we can't stop them. We, ah, make them aware of the dangers and difficulties of life, let alone love, in Ul Qoma, but what they do while they're here . . .' She shrugged.

Dhatt tapped a foot when I spoke to her. 'I'd like to speak to them,' he said.

Some were reading articles in the tiny make-do library. Several, when finally Nancy escorted us to the site of the main dig itself, stood, sat and worked in that deep, straight-edged hole. They looked up from below striae discernable in shades of earth. That line of dark – the residue of an ancient fire? What was that white?

At the edges of the big marquee was wild-looking scrubland, thistled and weedy between a litter of broken-off architecture. The dig was almost the size of a soccer pitch, subdivided by its matrix of string. Its base was variously depthed, flat-bottomed. Its floor of compacted earth was broken by inorganic shapes, strange breaching fish: shattered jars, crude and uncrude statuettes, verdigris-clogged machines. The students looked up from the section they were in, each at various careful depths, through various cord borders, clutching pointed trowels and soft brushes. A couple of the boys and one girl were Goths, much rarer in Ul Qoma than in Besźel or in their own homes. They must have got a lot of attention. They smiled at Dhatt and me sweetly from beneath eyeliner and the muck of centuries.

'Here you see,' Nancy said. We stood a way from the excavations. I looked down at the many markers in the layered dirt. 'You understand how it is here?' It might be anything that we could see beneath the soil.

She spoke quietly enough that her students, though they must have realised that we were talking, could probably not make out about what. 'We've never found written records from Precursor Age except a few poem fragments to make sense of any of it. Have you heard of the Gallimaufrians? For a long time when the pre-Cleavage stuff was first unearthed, after archaeologist-error was grudgingly ruled out,' she laughed, 'people made them up as an explanation for what was being fished up. A hypothetical civilisation before Ul Qoma and Besźel that systematically dug up all artefacts in the region, from millennia ago to their own grandmother's bric-a-brac, mixed them all up and buried them again or chucked them away.'

Nancy saw me looking at her. 'They didn't exist,' she reassured me. 'That's agreed now. By most of us, anyway. This' – she gestured at the hole – 'is *not* a mix. It is the remnants of a material culture. Just one we're still not very clear on. We had to learn to stop trying to find and follow a sequence and just look.'

Items that should have spanned epochs, contemporaneous. No other culture in the region made any but the scantest, seductively vague references to the pre-Cleavage locals, these peculiar men and women, witch-citizens by fairy tale with spells that tainted their discards, who used astrolabes that would not have shamed Arzachel or the Middle Ages, dried-mud pots, stone axes that my flat-browed many-greats grandfather might have made, gears, intricately cast insect toys,

181

and whose ruins underlay and dotted Ul Qoma and, occasionally, Besźel.

'This is Senior Detective Dhatt of the *militsya* and Inspector Borlú of the *policzai*,' Nancy was telling the students in the hole. 'Inspector Borlú's here as part of the investigation into the . . . into what happened to Mahalia.'

Several of them gasped. Dhatt crossed off names, and I copied him, as one by one the students came to talk to us in the common room. They had all been interviewed before but came docile as lambs, and answered questions they must have been sick of.

'I was relieved when I realised you were here for Mahalia,' the Goth woman said. 'That sounds awful. But I thought you'd found Yolanda and something'd happened.' Her name was Rebecca Smith-Davis, she was a first year, working on pot reconstruction. She got teary when she spoke about her dead friend and her missing friend. 'I thought you'd found her and it was . . . you know, she'd been . . .'

'We're not even sure Rodriguez is missing,' Dhatt said.

'You say. But you know. With Mahalia, and everything.' Shook her head. 'Them both being into strange stuff.'

'Orciny?' I said.

'Yeah. And other stuff. But yeah, Orciny. Yolanda's more into that stuff than Mahalia was, though. People said Mahalia used to be way into it when she first started, but not so much now, I guess.'

Because they were younger and partied later, several of the students, unlike their teachers, had alibis for the night of Mahalia's death. At some unspoken point Dhatt deemed Yolanda an official missing person, and his questions grew more precise, the notes he took longer. It did not do us much good. No one was sure of the last time they had seen her, only that they hadn't seen her for days.

'Do you have any idea what might have happened to Mahalia?' Dhatt asked all the students. We got no after no.

'I'm not into conspiracies,' one boy said. 'What happened was ... unbelievably horrible. But, you know, the idea that there's some big secret ...' He shook his head. He sighed. 'Mahalia was ... she could piss people off, and what happened happened because she went to the wrong part of Ul Qoma, with the wrong person.' Dhatt made notes.

'No,' said a girl. 'No one knew her. You maybe thought you did, but then you realise she was doing all kinds of secret stuff you didn't know anything about. I think I was a bit scared of her. I liked her, I did, but she was kind of intense. And smart. Maybe she was seeing someone. Some local crazy. That's the kind of thing she'd have ... She was into weird stuff. I'd always see her in the library – we've got like reading cards for the university library here? – and she'd be making all those little notes in her books.' She made cramped writing motions and shook her head, inviting us to agree on how strange that was.

'Weird stuff?' Dhatt said.

'Oh, you know, you hear stuff.'

'She pissed someone off, yo.' This young woman spoke loud and quickly. 'One of the crazies. You heard about her first time to the cities? Over in Besźel? She nearly got into a fight. With like academics and like *politicians*. At an *archaeology* conference. That's hard to do. It's amazing she ever got let back in anywhere.'

'Orciny.'

'Orciny?' Dhatt said.

'Yeah.'

This last speaker was a thin and straightlaced boy wearing a grubby T-shirt featuring what must have been the character from a children's television show. His name was Robert. He looked mournfully at us. He blinked desperately. His Illitan was not good.

'Do you mind if I speak to him in English?' I said to Dhatt.

'No,' he said. A man put his head round the corner of the door and stared at us. 'You go on,' Dhatt said to me. 'I'll be back in a minute.' He left, closing the door behind him.

'Who was that?' I said to the boy.

'Doctor UlHuan,' he said. The other of the Ul Qoman academics on-site. 'Will you find who did this?' I might have answered with the usual kind, meaningless certainties, but he looked too stricken for them. He stared at me and bit his lip. 'Please,' he said.

'What did you mean about Orciny?' I said eventually.

'I mean' – he shook his head – 'I don't know. Just keep thinking about it, you know? Makes you nervy. I know it's stupid but Mahalia used to be right up in that, and Yolanda was getting more and more into it – we used to rip shit out of her for it, you know? – and then both of them disappear . . .' He looked down and closed his eyes with his hand, as if he did not have the strength to blink. 'It was me who called about Yolanda. When I couldn't find her. I don't know,' he said. 'It just makes you wonder.' He ran out of what to say.

'WE'VE GOT SOME STUFF,' Dhatt said. He was pointing me along the walkways between the offices, back out of Bol Ye'an. He looked at the masses of notes he had made, sorted through the business cards and phone numbers on scraps. 'I don't know yet what it is that we've got, but we've got stuff. Maybe. Fuck.'

'Anything from UlHuan?' I said.

'What? No.' He glanced at me. 'Backed up most of what Nancy said.'

'You know what it's interesting that we didn't get?' I said.

'Eh? Not following,' Dhatt said. 'Seriously, Borlú,' he said as we neared the gate. 'What d'you mean?'

'That was a group of kids from Canada, right . . .'

'Most of them. One German, one a Yank.'

'All Anglo-Euro-American, then. Let's not kid ourselves – it might seem a bit rude to us, but we both know what outsiders to Beszel and Ul Qoma are most fascinated with. You notice what not a single one of them brought up, in any context, as even possibly to do with anything?'

'What do you . . .'. Dhatt stopped. 'Breach.'

'None of them mentioned Breach. Like they were nervous. You know as well as I do that normally it's the first and only thing foreigners want to know about. Granted this lot have gone a bit more native than most of their compatriots, but still.' We waved thanks to the guards who opened the gate, and we stepped out. Dhatt was nodding carefully. 'If someone we knew just disappeared without a single damned trace and out of nowhere like this, it's one of the first things we'd consider, right? However much we might not want to?' I said. 'Let alone people who must find it a whole lot harder than us not to breach every minute.'

'Officers!' It was one of the security detail, an athletic-looking young man with a mid-period David Beckham Mohican. He was younger than most of his colleagues. 'Officers, please?' He jogged towards us.

'I just wanted to know,' he said. 'You're investigating who killed Mahalia Geary, right? I wanted to know . . . I wanted to know if you knew anything. If you got anywhere. Could they have got away?'

'Why?' said Dhatt eventually. 'Who are you?'

'I, no one, no one. I just . . . It's sad, it's terrible, and we all, me and the rest of us, the guards, we feel bad and we want to know if, whoever, if who did this . . .'

'I'm Borlú,' I said. 'What's your name?'

'I'm Aikam. Aikam Tsueh.'

'You were a friend of hers?'

'I, sure a little bit. Not really, but you know I knew her. To say hello. I just want to know if you found anything.'

'If we did, Aikam, we can't tell you,' said Dhatt.

'Not now,' I said. Dhatt glanced at me. 'Have to work things out first. You understand. But maybe we can ask you a few questions?' He looked alarmed for a moment.

'I don't know anything. But sure, I guess. I was worried if they could get out of the city, past the *militsya*. If there was a way you could do that. Is there?'

I made him write his phone number in my notebook before he went back to his station. Dhatt and I watched his back.

'Did you question the guards?' I said, watching Tsueh go.

'Of course. Nothing very interesting. They're security guards, but this site's under ministry aegis, so the checks are a bit more stringent than usual. Most of them had alibis for the night of Mahalia's death.'

'Did he?'

'I'll check, but I don't remember his name being red-flagged, so he probably did.'

Aikam Tsueh turned at the gate and saw us watching. Raised his hand hesitantly in a good-bye.

CHAPTER FOURTEEN

SIT HIM IN A COFFEE SHOP – a teahouse, really, we were in Ul Qoma – and Dhatt's aggressive energy dissipated somewhat. He still drummed his fingers on the edge of the table in a complicated rhythm I could not have mimicked, but he met my eyes, did not shift in his seat. He listened and made serious suggestions for how we might proceed. He twisted his head to read the notes I made. He took messages from his centre. While we sat there he did a gracious job, in truth, of obscuring the fact that he did not like me.

'I think we need to get some *protocol* in place about questioning,' was all he said, when first we sat, 'too many cooks,' to which I murmured some half apology.

The tea shop staff would not take Dhatt's money: he did not offer it very hard. '*Militsya* discount,' the serving woman said. The café was full. Dhatt eyed a raised table by the front window until the man who sat there noticed the scrutiny, rose, and we sat. We overlooked a Metro station. Among the many posters on a nearby wall was one I saw then unsaw: I was not sure it was not the poster I had had printed, to identify Mahalia. I did not know if I was right, if the wall was alter to me now, total in Besźel, or crosshatched and a close patchwork of information from different cities.

Ul Qomans emerged from below the street and gasped at the temperature, shrank into their fleeces. In Besźel, I knew – though I tried to unsee the Besź citizens doubtless descending from Yan-jelus Station of the overland transit, which was by chance a few scores of metres from the submerged Ul Qoman stop – people would be wearing furs. Among the Ul Qoman faces were people I took to be Asian or Arab, even a few Africans. Many more than in Besźel.

'Open doors?'

'Hardly,' Dhatt said. 'Ul Qoma needs people, but everyone you see's been carefully vetted, passed the tests, knows the score. Some of them are having kids. Ul Qoman pickaninnies!' His laugh was delighted. 'We've got more than you lot, but not because we're lax.' He was right. Who wanted to move to Besźel?

'What about the ones that don't make it through?'

'Oh, we have our camps, same as you, here and there, round the outskirts. The UN's not happy. Neither's Amnesty. Giving you shit about conditions too? Want smokes?' A cigarette kiosk was a few metres from the entrance to our café. I had not realised I was staring at it.

'Not really. Yes, I guess. Curiosity. I haven't smoked Ul Qoman I don't think ever.'

'Hold on.'

'No, don't get up. I don't anymore; I gave up.'

'Oh come on, consider it ethnography, you're not at home . . . Sorry, I'll stop. I hate people who do that.'

'That?'

'Pimping stuff on people who've given up. And I'm not even a smoker.' He laughed and sipped. 'Then at least it would be some fucked-up resentment at your success in quitting. I must

188

just generally resent you. Malicious little bastard I am.' He laughed.

'Look, I'm sorry about, you know, jumping in like that . . .'

'I just think we need protocols. I don't want you to think—'

'I appreciate that.'

'Alright, no worries. How about I handle the next one?' he said. I watched Ul Qoma. It was too cloudy to be so cold.

'You said that guy Tsueh has an alibi?'

'Yeah. They called it in for me. Most of those security guys are married and their wives'll vouch, which okay isn't worth a turd, but we couldn't find any link from any of them to Geary except nods in a corridor. That one, Tsueh, actually was out that night with a bunch of the students. He's young enough to fraternise.'

'Convenient. And unusual.'

'Sure. But he's got no connections between anyone and anything. The kid's nineteen. Tell me about the van.' I went over it again. 'Light, am I going to have to come back with you?' he said. 'Sounds like we're looking for someone Besź.'

'Someone in Besźel drove the van through the border. But we know Geary was killed in Ul Qoma. So unless the killer murdered her, raced over to Besźel, grabbed a van, raced back, grabbed her, raced back again to dump the body, and why, we might add did they dump the body where they dumped it?, we're looking at a cross-border phone call followed by a favour. So two perps.'

'Or breach.'

I moved.

'Yeah,' I said. 'Or breach. But from what we know someone's gone to a fair bit of trouble to *not* breach. And to let us know that.'

189

'The notorious footage. Funny how that turned up . . .'

I looked at him, but he did not seem to be mocking. 'Isn't it?'

'Oh come on, Tyador, what, are you surprised? Whoever's done this, smart enough to know not to fuck with the borders, gives a friend over your side a call, and now's shitting rocks that Breach is going to appear for him. And that would be unfair. So they've got some little helper in Copula Hall or Traffic or something and they've given them a whisper what time they crossed. It isn't as if Besź bureaucrats are irreproachable.'

'Hardly.'

'There you go, then. See, you look happier.'

It would be a smaller conspiracy that way, than some of the other looming possibilities. Someone had known which vans to look for. Pored over a bunch of videos. What else? In that freezing but pretty day, cold muting Ul Qoma's colours to everyday shades, it was hard and felt absurd to see Orciny in any corners.

'Let's retrace,' he said. 'We're not going to get anywhere hunting for this fucking van driver. Hopefully your lot are on that. We've got *nothing* except a description of the van, and who in Ul Qoma's going to admit having even maybe seen a Besź van, with or without permit to be there? So let's go back to square one. What was your break?' I looked at him. I looked at him carefully and thought over the order of events. 'When did she stop being Unknown Corpse One? What started it?'

In my room at the hotel were the notes I had taken from the Gearys. Her email address and phone number were in my notebook. They did not have their daughter's body nor could they return to collect it. Mahalia Geary lay in the freezer waiting. For me, you could say.

'A phone call.'

'Yeah? A snitch?'

'. . . Sort of. It was his lead got me to Drodin.' I saw him remember the dossier, that this was not how it was described there.

'What are you . . . Who?'

'Well this is the thing.' I paused a long time. Eventually I looked at the table and drew shapes in my spilled tea. 'I'm not sure what to . . . It was a phone call from here.'

'Ul Qoma?' I nodded. 'What the fuck? From who?'

'I don't know.'

'Why were they calling?'

'They saw our posters. Yeah. Our posters *in Besźel*.'

Dhatt leaned in. 'The *fuck* they did. Who?'

'You realise that this puts me in—'

'Of course I do.' He was intent, spoke quickly. 'Of course I do, but come on, you're police, you think I'm going to fuck you over? Between us. Who was it?'

It was not a small thing. If I was accessory to breach, he was now accessory to accessory. He did not seem nervous about it. 'I think they were unifs. You know, unificationists?'

'They said so?'

'No, but it was what they said and how they said it. Anyway, I know it was totally not-on, but it was that got me on the right track . . . What?' Dhatt was sitting back. His fingers drummed faster now, and he was not looking at me.

'Fuck, we've *got* something. I cannot fucking believe you didn't mention this before.'

'Hold on, Dhatt.'

191

'Okay, I can really – I can see that this puts you in a bit of a position.'

'I don't know anything about who this was.'

'We're still in time; we can maybe hand it over and explain that you were just a bit late . . .'

'Hand what over? We don't have anything.'

'We have a unif bastard who knows something is what we have. Let's go.' He stood and jiggled his car keys.

'Go where?'

'Go fucking detecting!'

'OF BLOODY COURSE,' Dhatt said. He was tearing up Ul Qoma streets, the car's siren gasping. He turned, shouting abuse at scuttling Ul Qoman civilians, swerved wordlessly to avoid Besź pedestrians and cars, accelerating with the expressionless anxiety foreign emergencies occasion. If we hit one of them it would be a bureaucratic disaster. A breach now would not be helpful.

'Yari, it's Dhatt.' He shouted into his cell phone. 'Any clue if the cc of the unifs are in at the moment? Excellent, thanks.' He slapped it shut.

'Looks like at least some of them are. I knew you'd spoken to Besź unifs, of course. Read your report. But what kind of fool am I' – slap slap of his forehead with the heel of his hand – 'didn't occur to me to go talk to our own little homegrowns. Even though of *course* those fuckers, those fuckers more than any other fuckers – and we have our share of fuckers, Tyad – are all talking to each other. I know where they hang out.'

'Is that where we're going?'

'I hate those little sods. I hope . . . Goes without saying, I mean, that I've met some great Besź in my time.' He glanced at me. 'Nothing against the place and I hope I get to visit, and it's great that we're all getting on so well these days, you know, better than it used to be – what was the fucking point of all that shit? But I'm Ul Qoman and I'm fucked if I want to be anything else. You imagine unification?' He laughed. 'Fucking catastrophe! Unity is strength my Ul Qoman arse. I know they say crossbreeding makes animals stronger, but what if we inherited, shit, Ul Qoman sense of timing and Besź optimism?'

He made me laugh. We passed between ancient age-mottled roadside stone pillars. I recognised them from photographs, remembered too late that the one on the eastern side of the road was the only one I should see – it was in Ul Qoma, the other in Besźel. So most people said, anyway: they were one of the cities' controversial disputed loci. The Besź buildings I couldn't help fail to completely unsee were, I glimpsed, sedate and tidy, but in Ul Qoma wherever we were was an area of decay. We passed canals, and for several seconds I did not know which city they were in, or if it was both. By a weed-flecked yard, where nettles poked out from below a long-immobile Citroën like a hovercraft's skirt of air, Dhatt braked hard and got out before I had even undone my seatbelt.

'Time was,' Dhatt said, 'we'd have locked every one of these fuckers away.' He strode towards a tumbledown door. There are no legal unificationists in Ul Qoma. There are no legal socialist parties, fascist parties, religious parties in Ul Qoma. Since the Silver Renewal almost a century before under the tutelage of General Ilsa, Ul Qoma had had only the People's National Party. Many older establishments and offices still displayed portraits of Ya Ilsa, often above 'Ilsa's Brothers' Atatürk and Tito. The cliché was that in older offices there was always

193

a faded patch between those two, where erstwhile brother Mao had once beamed.

But this is the twenty-first century, and President Ul Mak (whose portrait you can also see where managers are most obsequious), like President Umbir before him, had announced certainly not a repudiation but a development of the National Road, an end to restrictive thinking, a *glasnostroika*, as Ul Qoman intellectuals hideously neologised. With the CD-and-DVD shops, the software startups and galleries, the bullish Ul Qoman financial markets, the revalued dinar, came, they said, New Politics, a very vaunted openness to hitherto dangerous dissidence. Not to say that radical groups, let alone parties, were legalised, but their ideas were sometimes acknowledged. So long as they displayed restraint in meetings and proselytisation, they were indulged. So one heard.

'Open!' Dhatt slammed on the door. 'This is the unif hangout,' he said to me. 'They're constantly on the phone to your lot in Beszel – that's kind of their *deal*, right?'

'What's their status?'

'You're about to hear them say they're just a group of friends meeting for a chat. No membership cards or anything, they're not stupid. Shouldn't take a fucking bloodhound for us to track down some contraband, but that's not really what I'm here for.'

'What are we here for?' I looked around at decrepit Ul Qoman facades, Illitan graffiti demanding that so-and-so fuck off and informing that such-and-such person sucked cock. Breach must be watching.

He looked at me levelly. 'Whoever made that phone call to you did it from here. Or frequents this place. Pretty much guarantee it. Want to find out what our seditionist pals know. *Open*.' That to the door. 'Don't be fooled by their whole *who us?* thing;

they're perfectly happy to smack shit out of anyone quote working against unification unfuckingquote. *Open.*'

The door obeyed this time, a crack onto a small young woman, the sides of her head shaved, showing tattooed fish and a few letters in a very old alphabet.

'Who . . .? What do you want?'

Perhaps they had sent her to the door hoping her size would shame anyone out of what Dhatt did next, which was to shove the door hard enough to send her stumbling backwards into the grotty hallways.

'Everyone here now,' he shouted, striding through the corridor, past the dishevelled punkess.

After confused moments when the thought of attempting to get out must have crossed their minds and been overruled, the five people in the house gathered in their kitchen, sat on the unstable chairs where Dhatt put them, and did not look at us. Dhatt stood at the head of the table and leaned over them.

'Right,' he said. 'Here it is. Someone made a phone call that my esteemed colleague here is keen to recall, and we're keen to find out who it was who was so helpful on the phone. I won't waste your time by pretending I think any of you are going to admit it, so instead we're going to go round the table and each of you is going to say, "Inspector, I have something to tell you."' They stared at him. He grinned and waved them begin. They did not, and he cuffed the man nearest him, to the cries of his companions, the man's own shout of pain and a noise of surprise from me. When the man looked slowly up his forehead was stained with incoming bruise.

'"Inspector, I have something to tell you,"' Dhatt said. 'We're just going to have to keep going till we get our man. Or woman.' He glanced at me; he had forgotten to check.

'That's the thing with cops.' He got ready for a backwards swipe across the same man's face. I shook my head and raised my hands a bit, and the unificationists gathered around the table made various moans. The man Dhatt threatened tried to rise but Dhatt grabbed his shoulder with his other hand and shoved him back into the chair.

'Yohan, just say it!' the punk girl shouted.

'Inspector, I've got something to tell you.'

Around the table it went. 'Inspector, I have something to tell you.' 'Inspector, I have something to tell you.'

One of the men spoke slowly enough, at first, that it might have been a provocation, but Dhatt raised an eyebrow at him and slapped his friend yet again. Not as hard, but this time blood came.

'Holy fucking Light!'

I dithered by the door. Dhatt made them all say it again, and their names.

'Well?' he said to me.

It had been neither of the two women, of course. Of the men, one's voice was reedy and his Illitan accent, I presumed, from a part of the city I didn't recognise. It could have been either of the other two. One in particular – the younger, named, he told us, Dahar Jaris, not the man Dhatt menaced, but a boy in a battered denim jacket with NoMeansNo written on the back in English print that made me suspect it was the name of a band, not a slogan – had a voice that was familiar. Had I heard him say exactly the words my interlocutor had used, or had I heard him speak in the same long-dead form of language, it might have been easier to be sure. Dhatt saw me looking at him and pointed questioningly. I shook my head.

'Say it again,' Dhatt said to him.

'No,' I said, but Jaris was gabbling pointlessly through the phrase. 'Anyone speak old Illitan or Besź? Root-form stuff?' I said. They looked at each other. 'I know, I know,' I said. 'There's no Illitan, no Besź, and so on. Do any of you speak it?'

'All of us,' said the older man. He did not wipe the blood from his lip. 'We live in the city and it's the language of the city.'

'Careful,' said Dhatt. 'I could charge you on that. It's this one, right?' He pointed at Jaris again.

'Leave it,' I said.

'Who knew Mahalia Geary?' Dhatt said. 'Byela Mar?'

'Marya,' I said. 'Something.' Dhatt fished in his pocket for her photograph. 'But it's none of them,' I said. I was in the door frame, and moving out of the room. 'Leave it. It's no one. Let's go. Let's go.'

He approached me close, looking quizzical. 'Hmm?' he whispered. I shook my head minutely. 'Fill me in, Tyador.'

Eventually he pursed his lips and turned back to the unificationists. 'Stay careful,' he said. He left and they stared after him, five faces frightened and bewildered, one of them bloody and dripping. My own was set, I suspect, from the effort of not showing anything.

'You've got me confused, Borlú.' He drove much more slowly than we had come on the return. 'I can't work out what just happened. You backed away from that, and it was our best lead. The only thing that makes sense is that you're worried about complicity. Because sure, if you got a call and went with it, if you took them up on that information, then yeah that's breach. But no one's going to give a shit about you, Borlú. It's a little tiny breach, and you know as well as I do that they'll let that go if we sort out something bigger.'

'I don't know how it is in Ul Qoma,' I said. 'In Besźel breach is breach.'

'Bullshit. What does that even mean? Is that what this is? That's it?' He slowed behind a Besź tram; we rocked over the foreign rails in the crosshatched road. 'Fuck, Tyador, we can sort it out; we can come up with something, no problem, if that's what's worrying you.'

'That's not it.'

'I fucking hope that's it. I really do. What else is your beef? Listen, you wouldn't have to incriminate yourself or anything—'

'That's not it. None of those were the ones that made the phone call. I don't know for sure the phone call was even from abroad. From here. I don't know anything for sure. Could have been a crank call.'

'Right.' When he dropped me at the hotel he did not get out. 'I've got paperwork,' he said. 'I'm sure you do too. Take a couple of hours. We should talk to Professor Nancy again, and I want to have another word with Bowden. Does that meet with your approval? If we drove there and asked a few questions, would those methods be acceptable?'

After a couple of tries I got Corwi. At first we tried to stick to our stupid code, but it did not last.

'I'm sorry boss, I'm not bad at this shit, but there's no way I'm going to be able to snag Dhatt's personnel files from the *militsya*. You'll cause a sodding international incident. What do you want, anyway?'

'I just want to know what his story is.'

'Do you trust him?'

'Who knows? They're old-school here.'

'Yeah?'

'Robust interrogations.'

'I'll tell Naustin, he'll love it, get an exchange. You sound rattled, boss.'

'Just do me a favour and see if you can get anything, okay?' When I had rung off I picked up *Between the City and the City* and put it down again.

CHAPTER FIFTEEN

'STILL NO LUCK WITH THE VAN?' I said.

'Not pitching up on any cameras we can find,' Dhatt said. 'No witnesses. Once it's through Copula Hall from your side it's mist.' We both knew that with its make and its Besź number plates, anyone in Ul Qoma who glimpsed it would likely have thought it elsewhere and quickly unseen it, without noticing its pass.

When Dhatt showed me on the map how close Bowden's flat was to a station, I suggested we go by public transport. I had travelled on the Paris and Moscow Metros and the London Tube. The Ul Qoma transit used to be more brutalist than any – efficient and to a certain taste impressive, but pretty unrelenting in its concrete. Something over a decade ago it was renewed, at least all those stations in its inner zones. Each was given to a different artist or designer, who were told, with exaggeration but not as much as you might think, that money was no object.

The results were incoherent, sometimes splendid, variegated to a giddying extent. The nearest stop to my hotel was a camp mimicry of Nouveau. The trains were clean and fast and full and on some lines, on this line, driverless. Ul Yir Station, a few turns from the pleasant, uninteresting neighbourhood where Bowden lived, was a patchwork of Constructivist lines and Kandinsky colours. It was, in fact, by a Besź artist.

'Bowden knows we're coming?'

Dhatt lifted a hand for me to wait. We had ascended to street level and he had his cell to his ear, was listening to a message.

'Yeah,' he said after a minute, shutting the phone. 'He's waiting for us.'

David Bowden lived in a second-floor apartment, in a skinny building, giving him the whole storey to himself. He had crammed it with art objects, remnants, antiquities from the two cities and, to my ignorant eye, their precursor. Above him, he told us, was a nurse and her son: below him a doctor, originally from Bangladesh, who had lived in Ul Qoma even longer than he had.

'Two expats in one building,' I said.

'It's not exactly a coincidence,' he said. 'Used to be, before she passed away, that upstairs was an ex-Panther.' We stared. 'A Black Panther, made it out after Fred Hampton was killed. China, Cuba and Ul Qoma were the destinations of choice. When I moved here, when your government liaison officer told you an apartment had come up, you took it, and blow me if all the buildings we were housed in weren't full of foreigners. Well, we could moan together about whatever it was we missed from home. Have you heard of Marmite? No? Then you've obviously never met a British spy in exile.' He poured me and Dhatt, unbidden, glasses of red wine. We spoke in Illitan. 'This was years ago, you understand. Ul Qoma didn't have a pot to piss in. It had to think about efficiencies. There was always one Ul Qoman living in each of these buildings. Much easier for a single person to keep an eye on several foreign visitors if they were all in one place.'

Dhatt met his eye. *Fuck off, these truths don't intimidate me*, his expression said. Bowden smiled a little bashfully.

'Wasn't it a bit insulting?' I said. 'Honoured visitors, sympaticos being watched like that?'

'Might have been for some of them,' Bowden said. 'The Philbys of Ul Qoma, the real fellow travellers, were probably rather put out. But then they'd also be the ones most likely to put up with anything. I never particularly objected to being watched. They were right not to trust me.' He sipped his drink. 'How are you getting on with *Between*, Inspector?'

His walls were painted beiges and browns in need of renovation, and busy with bookshelves and books and the folk art in Ul Qoman and Besź styles, antique maps of both cities. On surfaces were figurines and the remnants of pottery, tiny clockwork-looking things. The living room was not large, and so full of bits and pieces it was cramped.

'You were here when Mahalia was killed,' Dhatt said.

'I have no alibi, if that's what you mean. My neighbour might have heard me puttering about, ask her, but I don't know.'

'How long have you lived here?' I said. Dhatt pursed his lips without looking at me.

'God, years.'

'And why here?'

'I don't understand.'

'So far as I can tell you have at least as much Besź stuff as local.' I pointed at one of the many old or reproduction Besź icons. 'Is there a particular reason you ended up here rather than Beszel? Or anywhere else?'

Bowden turned his hands so that his palms faced the ceiling.

'I'm an archaeologist. I don't know how much you know about this stuff. Most of the artefacts that are worth looking at, including the ones that look to us now like they were made by Besź craftsmen, are in Ul Qoman soil. That's just how it's always been. The situation was never helped by Besźel's idiotic willingness to sell what little heritage it could dig up to whoever wanted it. Ul Qoma's always been smarter about that.'

'Even a dig like Bol Ye'an?'

'You mean under foreign direction? Sure. The Canadians don't technically own any of it; they just have some handling and cataloguing rights. Plus the kudos they get from writing up, and a warm glow. And dibs on museum tours, of course. The Canadians are happy as Larry about the US blockade, believe me. Want to see a very vivid green? Tell an American archaeologist you work in Ul Qoma. Have you seen Ul Qoma's laws on antiquities export?' He closed his hands, fingers interlocking like a trap. 'Everyone who wants to work on Ul Qoma, or Besźel, let alone if they're into Precursor Age, ends up here if they can get here.'

'Mahalia was an American archaeologist . . .' Dhatt said.

'Student,' Bowden said. 'When she finished her PhD she'd have had a harder time staying.'

I was standing, glancing into his study. 'Could I . . .?' I indicated in.

'I . . . sure.' He was embarrassed at the tiny space. It was if anything even more cramped with the tat of antiquity than his living room. His desk was its own archaeology of papers, computer cables, a street-finder map of Ul Qoma, battered and several years old. Amid the mess of papers were some in a strange and very ancient script, neither Illitan nor Besź, pre-Cleaved. I could not read any of it.

'What's this?'

'Oh . . .' He rolled his eyes. 'It arrived yesterday morning. I still get crank mail. Since *Between*. Stuff that people put together and say is in the script of Orciny. I'm supposed to *decode* it for them. Maybe the poor sods really believe it's something.'

'Can you decode that one?'

'Are you kidding? No. It doesn't mean anything.' He closed the door. 'No news of Yolanda?' he said. 'This is seriously worrying.'

'I'm afraid not,' said Dhatt. 'Missing Persons are on it. They're very good. We're working closely with them.'

'We absolutely have to find her, Officers. I'm . . . This is crucial.'

'Do you have any idea who might have any grievance against Yolanda?'

'Yolanda? My God no, she's sweet, I can't think of anyone. Mahalia was a bit different. I mean . . . Mahalia was . . . what happened to her was utterly appalling. Appalling. She was smart, very smart, and opinionated, and brave, and it isn't quite so . . . What I'm saying is I can imagine Mahalia getting people angry. She did that. It's the kind of person she was, and I mean that as a compliment. But there was always that fear that Mahalia might one day piss off the wrong person.'

'Who might she have pissed off?'

'I'm not talking specifics, Senior Detective, I have no idea. We didn't have very much contact, Mahalia and I. I hardly knew her.'

'Small campus,' I said. 'Surely you all knew everyone.'

'True. But honestly I avoided her. We hadn't spoken for a long time. We didn't get off to a very auspicious start. Yolanda, though, I know. And she's nothing like that. She's not as clever, maybe, but I cannot think of a single person who doesn't like her, nor why anyone would want to do anything to her. Everyone's horrified. Including the locals who work there.'

'Would they have been devastated about Mahalia, too?' I said.

'I doubt any of them knew her, to be frank.'

'One of the guards seemed to. Made a point of asking us about her. About Mahalia. I thought he might be her boyfriend or something.'

'One of the guards? Absolutely not. Sorry, that sounded a bit peremptory. What I mean is that I'd be amazed. Knowing what I do of Mahalia, I mean.'

'Which isn't much, you said.'

'No. But, you know, you pick up on who's doing what, which students do what. Some of them – Yolanda's one – hang out with the Ul Qoman staff, but not Mahalia. You will tell me if you find anything out about Yolanda? You have to find her. Or even if you just have theories about where she is, please, this is terrible.'

'You're Yolanda's supervisor?' I said. 'What's her PhD on?'

'Oh.' He waved. '"Representing Gender and the Other in Precursor Age Artefacts." I still prefer "pre-Cleavage" but it makes an unfortunate pun in English, so Precursor Age is the newly preferred term.'

'You said she's not smart?'

'I did not say that. She's perfectly intelligent enough. It's fine. She's just . . . There aren't that many people like Mahalia in any postgraduate program.'

'So why weren't you her supervisor?'

He stared at me as if I was mocking him.

'Because of her *bullshit*, Inspector,' he said at last. He stood and turned his back, seemed to want to walk around the room, but it was too small. 'Yes, these were the tricky circumstances under which we met.' He turned back to us. 'Senior Detective Dhatt, Inspector Borlú. Do you know how many PhD students I have? One. Because no one else wanted her. Poor thing. I have no office at Bol Ye'an. I have no tenure nor am I on tenure track. Do you know what my official title is, at Prince of Wales? I'm a *Corresponding Lecturer*. Don't ask me what that means. Actually, I can tell you what it means – it means *We are the world's leading institution for Ul Qoma, Besźel and Precursor Age studies, and we need all the names we can get, and we may even entice a few rich kooks onto our program with your moniker, but we are not so stupid as to give you a real job.*'

'Because of the book?'

'Because of *Between the City and the City*. Because I was a stoned young man with a neglectful supervisor and a taste for the arcane. No matter that you turn around a little later and say 'Mea culpa, I messed up, no Orciny, my apologies.' No matter that eighty-five percent of the research *still holds up and is still used*. Hear me? No matter what else you do, ever. You can never walk away from it no matter how hard you try.

'So when, as happens regularly, someone comes to me and tells me that the work that fucked things up is so great, and that she'd *love* to work with me – and this is what Mahalia did at the conference over in Besźel where I first met her – and that it's *such a travesty* that the truth is still banned in both cities, and that she's *on my side* . . . Did you know by the way that when she first arrived here she not only smuggled a copy of *Between* into Besźel but told me she was going to shelve it in the history section of the University Library, for Christ's sake? For people to find? She told me that proudly. I told her to get rid of it immediately or I would set the *policzai* on her. Anyway, when she tells me all that, yes, I got shirty.

'I meet these people pretty much every conference I go to. I tell them *I was wrong* and they think either that I've been bought off by the Man, or that I'm afraid for my life. Or that I've been replaced by a robot or something.'

'Did Yolanda ever talk about Mahalia? Wasn't it hard, you feeling like that about her best friend . . .'

'Feeling like what? There was nothing, Inspector. I told her I wouldn't supervise her; she accused me of cowardice or ca-pitulation or something, I can't remember; that was the last of it. I gathered that she'd more or less shut up about Orciny in the years since she'd been on the program. I thought good, she's grown out of it. That was it. And I heard she was clever.'

'I got the impression Professor Nancy was a bit disappointed with her.'

'Maybe. I don't know. She wouldn't be the first person to be a let-down in writing, but she still had a reputation.'

'Yolanda wasn't into Orciny stuff? That's not why she was studying with you?'

He sighed and sat down again. It was unimpressive, his lack-lustre up-down.

'I thought not. I wouldn't have supervised her. And no, not at first . . . but she'd mentioned it recently. Brought up *dis-sensi*, what might live there, all that. She knew my feelings, so she was trying to act as if it was all hypotheticals. It sounds

207

ridiculous, but it honestly hadn't even occurred to me that it was because of Mahalia's influence. Was she talking to her about it? Do you know?'

'Tell us about the *dissensi*,' Dhatt said. 'Do you know where they are?'

He shrugged. 'You know where some are, SD. There's no secret about lots of them. A few paces of back yard here, a deserted building there. The central five metres or so of Nuistu Park? *Dissensus*. Ul Qoma claims it; Besźel claims it. They're effectively crosshatched or out of bounds in both cities while the bickering goes on. There's just not that much exciting about them.'

'I'd like a list from you.'

'If you want, but you'll get it quicker via your own department, and mine is probably twenty years out of date. They do get resolved, time to time, and new ones emerge. And then you might hear of the secret ones.'

'I'd like a list. Hang on, secret? If no one knows they're disputed, how can they be?'

'Quite. They're *secretly* disputed, SD Dhatt. You have to get your head into the right mindset for this foolishness.'

'Doctor Bowden . . .' I said. 'Do you have any reason to think anyone might have anything against *you*?'

'Why?' He was very abruptly alarmed. 'What have you heard?'

'Nothing, only . . .' I said, and paused. 'There's some speculation that someone is targeting people who've been investigating Orciny.' Dhatt made no move to interrupt me. 'Perhaps you should be careful.'

'What? I *don't* study Orciny, I haven't for years . . .'

'As you say yourself, once you've started this stuff, Doctor

. . . I'm afraid you're the doyen whether you like it or not. Have you received anything that could be construed as a threat?'

'No . . .'

'You were burgled.' That was Dhatt. 'A few weeks ago.' We both looked at him. Dhatt was unembarrassed by my surprise. Bowden's mouth worked.

'But that was just a burglary,' he said. 'Nothing was even taken . . .'

'Yes, because they must've got startled – that was what we said at the time,' Dhatt said. 'Could be it was never their intent to take anything.'

Bowden, and more surreptitiously I, looked around the room, as if some malevolent gris-gris or electronic ear or painted threat might jump suddenly to light.

'SD, Inspector, this is utterly absurd; there is no Orciny . . .'

'But,' Dhatt said, 'there are such things as nutters.'

'Some of whom,' I said, 'for whatever reason are interested in some of the ideas being explored by yourself and Miss Rodriguez, Miss Geary . . .'

'I don't think either of them were *exploring ideas* . . .'

'Whatever,' Dhatt said. 'The point is they got someone's attention. No, we're not sure why, or even if there is a why.'

Bowden was staring absolutely aghast.

209

CHAPTER SIXTEEN

DHATT TOOK THE LIST Bowden gave him and sent an underling to supplement it, sent officers to the itemised lots, derelict buildings, patches of kerb and little promenade spaces on the river's shore, to scuff stones and probe at the edges of disputed, functionally crosshatched patches. I spoke to Corwi again that night – she made a joke about hoping this was a secure line – but we were unable to say anything useful to each other.

Professor Nancy had sent a printout of Mahalia's chapters to the hotel. There were two more or less finished, two somewhat sketchy. I stopped reading them after not very long, looked instead at the photocopies of her annotated textbooks. There was a vivid disparity between the sedate, somewhat dull tone of the former, and the exclamation points and scribbled interjections of the latter, Mahalia arguing with her earlier selves and with the main text. The marginalia were incomparably the more interesting, to the extent that you could make any sense of them. I put them down eventually for Bowden's book.

Between the City and the City was tendentious. You could see it. There are secrets in Besźel and in Ul Qoma, secrets everyone knows about: it was unnecessary to posit secret secrets. Still, the old stories, the mosaics and bas-reliefs, the

210

artefacts the book referred to were in some cases astonishing – beautiful and startling. Young Bowden's readings of some still-unsolved mysteries of Precursor or Pre-Cleavage age works were ingenious and even convincing. He had an elegantly argued claim that the incomprehensible mechanisms euphemistically slanged as 'clocks' were not mechanisms at all, but intricately chambered boxes designed solely to hold the gears they contained. His leaps to the *therefore* were lunatic, as he now admitted.

Of course there would be paranoia, for a visitor to this city, where the locals would stare and stare furtively, where I would be watched by Breach, of which snatched glances would not feel like anything I had experienced.

My cell phone rang, later, while I was sleeping. It was my Besź phone, showing an international call. It would piss credit, but it was on the government.

'Borlú,' I said.

'Inspector . . .' Illitan accent.

'Who is this?'

'Borlú I don't know why you . . . I can't talk long. I . . . thank you.'

'Jaris.' I sat up, put my feet on the floor. The young unif. 'It's . . .'

'We're not fucking comrades, you know.' He was not speaking in Old Illitan this time, but quickly in his own everyday language.

'Why would we be?'

'Right. I can't stay on the line.'

'Okay.'

'You could tell it was me, couldn't you? Who called you in Besźel.'

211

'I wasn't sure.'

'Right. This call never fucking happened.' I said nothing. 'Thanks for the other day,' he said. 'For not saying. I met Marya when she came over here.' I had not given her that name for a while, but for the moment when Dhatt had questioned the unifs. 'She told me she knew our brothers and sisters over the border; she'd worked with them. But she wasn't one of us, you know.'

'I know. You set me on that track in Besźel ...'

'Shut up. Please. I thought she was at first, but the stuff she was asking about, it was ... She was into stuff you don't even know about.' I would not preempt him. '*Orciny*.' He must have interpreted my silence as awe. 'She didn't give a shit about unification. She was putting everyone in danger so she could use our libraries and our contacts lists ... I really liked her, but she was trouble. She only cared about Orciny.

'Borlú, she fucking *found* it, Borlú.'

'Are you there? Do you understand? She found it ...'

'How do you know?'

'She told me. None of the others knew. When we realised how ... dangerous she was she was banned from meetings. They thought she was, like, a spy or something. She wasn't that.'

'You stayed in touch with her.' He said nothing. 'Why, if she was so ...?'

'I ... she was ...'

'Why'd you call me? In Besźel?'

'... She deserved better than a potter's field.'

I was surprised he knew the term. 'Were you together, Jaris?' I said.

'I hardly knew anything about her. Never asked. Never met her friends. We're careful. But she told me about Orciny.

Showed me all her notes about it. She was . . . Listen, Borlú, you won't believe me but she'd *made contact*. There are places—'

'*Dissensi?*'

'No, shut up. Not disputed: places that everyone in Ul Qoma thinks are in Besźel, and everyone in Besźel thinks are in Ul Qoma. They're not in either one. They're Orciny. She found them. She told me she was helping.'

'Doing what?' I only spoke at last because the silence went on so long.

'I don't know much. She was saving them. They wanted something. She said. Something like that. But when I said to her once "How d'you know Orciny's on our side?" she just laughed and said "I don't, they're not." She wouldn't tell me a lot. I didn't want to know. She didn't talk about it much at all. I thought she might be crossing, through some of these places, but . . .'

'When did you last see her?'

'I don't know. A few days before she . . . before. Listen, Borlú, this is what you need to know. She knew she was in trouble. She got really angry and upset when I said something about Orciny. The last time. She said I didn't understand anything. She said something like she didn't know if what she was doing was restitution or criminal.'

'What does that mean?'

'I don't know. She said Breach was *nothing*. I was shocked. Can you imagine? She said everyone who knew the truth about Orciny was in danger. She said there weren't many but anyone that did wouldn't even know how much shit they were in, wouldn't believe it. I said "Even me?" she said "Maybe, I maybe already told you too much."'

213

'What do you think it means?'

'What do you know about Orciny, Borlú? Why the fuck would anyone think Orciny was safe to fuck with? How d'you think you stay hidden for centuries? By playing nice? Light! I think somehow she got mixed up working for Orciny, is what I think happened, and I think they're like parasites, and they told her she was helping them but she found something out, and when she realised they *killed* her.' He gathered himself. 'She carried a knife at the end, for protection. From *Orciny*.' A miserable laugh. 'They killed her, Borlú. And they're going to kill everyone who might trouble them. Everyone who's ever brought attention to them.'

'What about you?'

'I'm fucked, is what. She's gone, so I'm gone too. Ul Qoma can go fuck itself and so can Besźel and so can Or-fucking-ciny. This is my good-bye. Can you hear the sound of wheels? In a minute this phone is going out the fucking window when we're done and sayonara. This call's a good-bye present, for her sake.'

By the last words he was whispering. When I realised he had rung off I tried to call him back but his number was blocked.

I RUBBED MY EYES for long seconds, too long. I scribbled notes on the hotel-headed paper, nothing I would ever look at again, just trying to organise thoughts. I listed people. I saw the clock and did a time-zone calculation. I dialled a long-distance number on the hotel phone.

'Mrs. Geary?'

'Who is this?'

'Mrs. Geary, this is Tyador Borlú. Of the Besźel police.' She said nothing. 'We . . . May I ask how Mr. Geary is?' I walked barefoot to the window.

'He's alright,' she said finally. 'Angry.' She was very careful. She could not decide about me. I pulled the heavy curtains back a little, looked out. No matter that it was the small hours, there were a few figures visible in the street, as there always are. Now and then a car passed. So late, it was harder to tell who was local and who foreign and so unseeable in the day: the colours of clothes were obscured by streetlamp light and the huddled quick night-walking blurred body language.

'I wanted to say again how sorry I was about what happened and to make sure you were alright.'

'Have you got anything to tell me?'

'You mean have we caught who did this to your daughter? I'm sorry, Mrs. Geary, we have not. But I wanted to ask you . . .' I waited, but she did not hang up, nor say anything. 'Did Mahalia ever tell you she was seeing anyone here?'

She only made some sound. When I had waited several seconds I continued. 'Do you know Yolanda Rodriguez? And why was it the *Besź* nationalists Mr. Geary was looking for? When he breached. Mahalia lived in Ul Qoma.'

She made the sound and I realised that she was crying. I opened my mouth but could only listen to her. Too late as I woke up more I realised that I should perhaps have called from another phone, if my and Corwi's suspicions were right. Mrs. Geary did not break the connection, so after a little while I said her name.

'Why are you asking me about Yolanda?' she said finally. She had pulled her voice together. 'Of course I met her, she's Mahalia's friend. Is she . . .?'

'We're just trying to get hold of her. But . . .'

215

'Oh my God, is she *missing*? Mahalia confided in her. Is that why . . .? Is she . . .?'

'Please don't, Mrs. Geary. I promise you there's no evidence of anything untoward; she may have just taken a few days away. Please.' She started again but controlled herself.

'They hardly spoke to us on that flight,' she said. 'My husband woke up near the end and realised what had happened.'

I said, 'Mrs. Geary, was Mahalia involved with anyone here? That you know of? In Ul Qoma, I mean?'

'No.' She sighed it. 'You're thinking 'How would her mother know?' but I would. She didn't tell me details, but she . . .' She gathered herself. 'There was someone who hung around with her, but she didn't like him that way. Said it was too *complicated*.'

'What was his name?'

'Don't you think I'd have told you? I don't know. She met him through politics, I think.'

'You mentioned Qoma First.'

'Oh, my girl made them all mad.' She laughed a bit. 'She got people sore on all sides of it. And even the unifiers, is that what they are? Michael was going to check them all. It was easier to find names and addresses for Besźel. That's where we were. He was going to check them all out, one at a time. He wanted to find them all, because . . . one of them *did* this.'

I promised her all the things she wanted me to, rubbing my forehead and staring at Ul Qoma's silhouettes.

Not later enough, I was woken by Dhatt's phone call.

'Are you still in fucking bed? Get up.'

'How long before you . . .' It was morning, not that early.

'I'm downstairs. Hurry up, come on. Someone sent a bomb.'

CHAPTER SEVENTEEN

IN BOL YE'AN men of the Ul Qoma bomb squad lounged out-side the tiny ersatz postroom, talking to several awed security guards, chewing, squat in their protective clothes. The squad wore their visors up, angling from their foreheads.

'You Dhatt? It's cool, SD,' one said, glancing at Dhatt's insignia. 'You can go in.' He eyed me and opened the door onto the cupboard-sized room.

'Who caught it?' Dhatt said.

'One of the security boys. Sharp. Aikam Tsueh. What? What?' Neither of us said anything, so he shrugged. 'Said he didn't like how it felt; he went out to the *militsya* outside, asked them to take a look at it.'

Pigeonholes covered the walls, and large brown parcels, opened and unopened, lay in corners and plastic bins, on tabletops. Displayed on a stool in the centre, surrounded by ripped envelope and fallen letters trodden with footprints, was a package splayed, electronic innards jutting like wire stamens from a flower.

'This is the mechanism,' the man said. I read the Illitan on his Kevlar: his name was Tairo. He spoke to Dhatt, not me, pointing with a little laser pen, red-dotting what he referred to. 'Two layers of envelope.' Scribbling with the light all over the paper. 'Open the first one, nothing. Inside's another one. Open *that . . .*' Clicked his fingers. Indicating the wires. 'Nicely done. Classic.'

'Old-fashioned?'

'Nah, just nothing fancy. But nicely done. Not just *son et lumiere* either – this wasn't made to scare someone, it was made to fuck someone up. And I tell you what also. See this? Very directed. It's linked up with the tag.' The remnants of it visible in the paper, a red strip on the inner envelope, printed in Besź *Pull here to open.* 'Whoever does is going to get a faceful of bang and fall down. But short of pretty bad luck, anyone standing next to them's only going to need a new hairdo. The blast is directed.'

'It's defused?' I asked Tairo. 'Can I touch it?' He did not look at me but at Dhatt, who nodded him to answer.

'Fingerprints,' Tairo said, but shrugged. I took a ballpoint from one of the shelves and took out its cartridge, not to mark anything. I prodded gently at the paper, smoothing down the inner envelope. Even scored open by the defusers, it was easy to read the name written on it: David Bowden.

'Check this,' Tairo said. He rummaged gently. Below the parcel on the inside of the outer envelope, someone had scribbled, in Illitan, *The heart of a wolf.* I recognised the line but could not place it. Tairo sang it and grinned.

'It's an old motherland song,' Dhatt said.

'It wasn't a scare and it wasn't for generalised mayhem either,' Dhatt said to me quietly. We sat in the office we had commandeered. Opposite us, trying politely to avoid eavesdropping, Aikam Tsueh. 'That was a kill-shot. What the fuck?'

'With Illitan written on it, sent from Besźel,' I said.

218

Dusting didn't turn anything up. Both envelopes had been scrawled on, the address on the outer and Bowden's name on the inner in a chaotic script. The package was sent from Besźel from a post office that was grosstopically not far from the dig itself, though of course the package would have been imported a long way round through Copula Hall.

'We'll get the techs on it,' Dhatt said. 'See if we can trace it backwards, but we've got nothing to point to anyone. Maybe your lot'll turn something up.' The chances were low to nil we could reconstruct its journey backwards through both the Ul Qoman and Besź postal services.

'Listen.' I made sure Aikam could not hear. 'We know Mahalia had pissed off some hardcore nats back home. I get it, such organisations cannot possibly exist in Ul Qoma, of course, but if by some inadvertent glitch any of them *are* out here too, the chances are reasonable that she might have pissed them off too, no? She was mixed up in stuff that could have been designed to annoy them. You know, undermining the power of Ul Qoma, secret groups, porous boundaries, all that. You know.'

He watched me without expression. 'Right,' he said eventually.

'Two out of two students with special interests in Orciny are out of the picture. And now we've got a bomb to Mr. *Between Cities*.'

We looked at each other.

After a moment, louder now, I said, 'Well done, Aikam. That was really something that you did.'

'Have you held a bomb before, Aikam?' Dhatt said.

'Sir? No.'

'Not in national service?'

219

'I haven't done mine yet, Officer.'

'So how do you know what a bomb feels like?'

Shrug. 'I didn't, I don't, I just . . . It was wrong. Too heavy.'

'I bet this place gets a lot of books in the mail,' I said. 'Maybe computer stuff too. They're pretty heavy. How did you know this was different?'

'. . . Different heavy. It was harder. Under the envelopes. You could tell it wasn't paper, it was like metal or something.'

'Matter of fact is it even your job to be checking mail?' I said.

'No, but I was in there, just because. I was thinking that I could bring it out. I wanted to, and then I felt that one and it was . . . there was something about it.'

'You have good instincts.'

'Thank you.'

'Did you think about opening it?'

'No! It wasn't to me.'

'Who was it to?'

'It wasn't to anyone.' That outer envelope had named no recipient, only the dig. 'That's another reason, that's why I looked at it, maybe, because I thought that was weird.'

We conferred. 'Okay, Aikam,' Dhatt said. 'You gave your address to the other officer, in case we need to get hold of you again? When you go out would you send in your boss and Professor Nancy, please?'

He hesitated in the doorway. 'Do you have any information about Geary yet? Do you know what happened yet? Who killed her?' We told him no.

Kai Buidze, the chief guard, a muscular fifty-year-old, ex-army I'd guess, came in with Isabelle Nancy. She, not Rochambeaux, had offered her help in any way she could. She was rubbing her eyes. 'Where's Bowden?' I said to Dhatt. 'Does he know?'

'She called him when the bomb squad opened the outer envelope and there was his name.' He nodded at Nancy. 'She heard one of them reading it out. Someone's gone to get him. Professor Nancy.' She looked up. 'Does Bowden get a lot of mail here?'

'Not so much. He doesn't even have an office. But a bit. Quite a lot from foreigners, a few from prospective students, people who don't know where he lives or who assume he's based here.'

'Do you send it on?'

'No, he comes in to check it every few days. Throws most of it away.'

'Someone's really . . .' I said quietly to Dhatt. Hesitated. 'Trying to outrun us, know what we're doing.' With everything that was happening, Bowden might be wary now of any packages to his home. With the outer envelope and its foreign postmark discarded, he might even have thought something with only his name written on it an internal communication, something from one of his colleagues, and torn the strip. 'Like someone knew he'd been warned to be careful.' After a moment I said, 'They're bringing him in?' Dhatt nodded.

'Mr. Buidze,' Dhatt said. 'You had any trouble like this before?' 'Not like this. Sure, we get, you know, we had some letters from fuckups. Excuse me.' A glance at an unruffled Nancy. 'But you know, we get warnings from Leave-the-Past-Alone types, people who say we're betraying Ul Qoma, all that shit, UFO watchers and junkies. But an actual . . . but *this*? A bomb?' He shook his head.

'That's not true,' Nancy said. We stared at her. 'This

221

happened before. Not here. But to him. Bowden's been targeted before.'

'Who by?' I said.

'They never proved anything, but he got a lot of people angry when his book came out. The right. People who thought he was disrespectful.'

'Nats,' Dhatt said.

'I don't even remember which city it was from. Both lots had it in for him. Probably the only thing they agreed on. But this was *years* ago.'

'Someone's remembered him,' I said. Dhatt and I stared at each other and he pulled me aside.

'From *Besźel*,' he said. 'With a little *Illitan* fuck-you on it.' He threw up his hands: *Any ideas?*

'What's the name of those people?' I said after a silence. 'Qoma First.'

He stared. 'What? Qoma First?' he said. 'It came from *Besźel*.'

'Maybe a contact there.'

'A spy? A nat Qoman in Besźel?'

'Sure. Don't look like that – it's not so hard to believe. They'd send it from over there to cover their tracks.'

Dhatt wagged his head noncommittally. 'Okay . . .' he said. 'Still a hell of a thing to organize, and you're not—'

'They never liked Bowden. Maybe they figure if he's got wind that they're after him he might have alarm bells, but *not* with a package from Besźel,' I said.

'I get the idea,' he said.

'Where's Qoma First hang out?' I said. 'That's what they're called, right? Maybe we should visit—'

'That's what I keep trying to tell you,' he said. 'There's

nowhere to go. There is no "Qoma First," not like that. I don't know how it is in Besźel, but here . . .'

'In Besźel I know exactly where our own versions of these characters hang out. Me and my constable went round there recently.'

'Well congratulations but it doesn't work that way here. There's not like a fucking *gang* with little membership cards and a house they all live in; they're not unifs and they're not The Monkees.'

'You're not saying you've got no ultranationalists . . .'

'Right, I'm *not* saying that, we've got plenty, but I'm saying I don't know who they are or where they live, very sensibly they keep it that way, and I'm saying Qoma First's just a term some press guy came up with.'

'How come the unificationists congregate but this lot don't? Or can't?

'Because the unifs are clowns. Dangerous clowns some-times, alright, but still. The sort of people you're talking about now are serious. Old soldiers, that sort of thing. I mean you got to . . . respect that . . .'

No wonder they could not be allowed to gather visibly. Their hard nationalism might rebuke the People's National Party on its own terms, which the rulers would not permit. The unifs, by contrast, were free or free-ish to unite the locals in loathing.

'What can you tell us about him?' Dhatt said, raising his voice to the others who watched us.

'Aikam?' Buidze said. 'Nothing. Good worker. Dumb as a brick. Okay look, I'd have said that until today, but given what he just did, scratch that. Not nearly as tough as he looks. All pecs and no teeth, that one. Likes the kids, makes him feel good to hobnob with clever foreigners. Why? Tell me you're not eyeballing him, SD. That parcel came from *Besźel*. How the hell would he—'

'Absolutely it did,' Dhatt said. 'No one here's accusing anyone, least of all the hero of the hour. Standard questions.'

'Tsueh got on with the students, you said?' Unlike Tairo, Buidze did not look for permission to answer me. He met my eye and nodded. 'Anyone in particular? Good friends with Mahalia Geary?'

'Geary? Hell no. Geary probably never even knew his name. Rest her.' He made the Sign of Long Sleep with his hand. 'Aikam's friends with some of them, but not Geary. He hangs out with Jacobs, Smith, Rodriguez, Browning . . .'

'Just that he asked us—'

'He was very keen to know about any leads in the Geary case,' Dhatt said.

'Yeah?' Buidze shrugged. 'Well that got everyone really upset. Of course he wants to know about it.'

'I'm wondering . . .' I said. 'This is a complicated site, and I notice that even though it's mostly total, there's a couple of places where it crosshatches a bit. And that's got to be a nightmare to watch. Mr. Buidze, when we spoke to the students, not a single one of them mentioned Breach. At all. Didn't bring it up. A group of foreign kids? You know how much foreigners are obsessed with that stuff. One of their friends is disappeared and they're not even mentioning the most notorious bogeyman of Ul Qoma and Besźel, which is even *real*, and they don't mention it? Which couldn't help but make us wonder what are they afraid of?'

Buidze stared at me. He glanced at Nancy. He looked around the room. After long seconds he laughed.

'You're joking. Okay then. Alright then, Officers. Yeah

224

they're scared alright, but not that someone's breaching from fuck knows where to mess with them. Is that what you're thinking?' He shook his head. 'They're scared because they don't want to get caught.' He held up his hands in surrender. 'You've got me, Officers. There is breaching going on that we're not able to stop. These little sods breach all the damn time.'

He met our stares. Not defensive. He was matter-of-fact. Did I look as shocked as Dhatt? Professor Nancy's expression was if anything embarrassed.

'You're right, of course,' Buidze said. 'You can't avoid all breach, not in a place like this, and not with kids like these. These aren't locals, and I don't care how much training you give them, they've never seen anything like this before. Don't tell me it's not the same back in your place, Borlú. You think they're going to play loyal? You think while they wander around town they're *really* unseeing Besźel? Come on. Best any of us can hope for's they've got the sense not to make a big thing of it, but of *course* they're seeing across the border. No we can't prove it, which is why Breach wouldn't come unless they really fuck up. Oh it's happened. But much rarer than you think. Not for a long time.'

Professor Nancy still looked down at the table. 'You think *any* of the foreigners don't breach?' Buidze said, and leaned in towards us, spreading his fingers. 'All we can get from them's a bit of politeness, right? And when you get a bunch of young people together, they're going to push it. Maybe it's not just looks. Did you always do what you're told? But these are smart kids.'

He sketched maps on the table with his fingertips. 'Bol Ye'an crosshatches *here*, *here*, and the park it's in *here* and *here*. And yeah, over at the edges in this direction, it even creeps into Besźel total. So when this lot get drunk or whatever, don't they egg each other on to go stand in a crosshatch bit of the park? And then, who knows if they don't, maybe standing still there, without a single word, without even moving, cross over into Besźel, then back again? You don't have to take a step to do that, not if you're in a crosshatch. All here.' Tapped his forehead. 'No one can prove shit. Then maybe next time when they're doing that they reach down, grab a souvenir, straighten back up into Ul Qoma with a rock from Besźel or something. If that's where they were when they picked it up, that's where it's from, right? Who knows? Who could prove it?

'So long as they don't flaunt it, what can you do? Even Breach can't watch for breach all the time. Come on. If they did, not a single one of this foreign lot would still be here. Isn't that right, Professor?' He looked at her not unkindly. She said nothing but looked at me in embarrassment. 'None of them mentioned Breach, SD Dhatt, because they're all guilty as hell.' Buidze smiled. 'Hey, don't get me wrong: they're only human, I like them. But don't make this more than it is.'

As we ushered them out, Dhatt got a call that had him scribbling notes and muttering. I closed the door.

'That was one of the uniforms we sent to get Bowden. He's gone. They got to his apartment and no one's answering. He's not there.'

'They told him they were coming?'

'Yeah, and he knew about the bomb. But he's gone.'

CHAPTER EIGHTEEN

'I WANT TO GO BACK AND TALK to that kid again,' Dhatt said.

'The unificationist?'

'Yeah, Jaris. I know, I know, "It wasn't him." Right. You said. Well, whatever, he knows something and I want to talk to him.'

'You won't find him.'

'What?'

'Good luck. He's gone.'

He fell behind me a few steps and made a phone call.

'You're right. Jaris is nowhere. How did you know? What the fuck are you playing at?'

'Let's go to your office.'

'Fuck the office. The office can wait. Repeat, how the fuck did you know about Jaris?'

'Look . . .'

'I'm getting a bit spooked by your occult abilities, Borlú. I didn't sit on my arse – when I heard I'd be babysitting you, I looked you up, so I know a little bit, I know you're no one to fuck with. I'm sure you did the same, so you know the same.' I should have done. 'So I was geared up to be working with a detective. Even some hot shit. I wasn't expecting this lugubrious tutting bugger. How the fuck did you know about Jaris, and why are you *protecting* that little shit?'

'Okay. He phoned me last night from a car or I think from the train and told me he was going.'

He stared at me. 'Why the fuck did he call *you*? And why the fuck did you not tell me? Are we working together or not, Borlú?'

'Why did he call me? Maybe he wasn't bananas about your interrogation style, Dhatt. And are we working together? I thought the reason I was here was to obediently give you everything I've got, then watch TV in my hotel room while you find the bad guy. When did Bowden get burgled? When were you going to tell me that? I didn't see you rushing to spill whatever shit you found out from Ul-Huan at the dig, and he should have the choicest info – he is the bloody government mole, isn't he? Come on, it's no big deal, all public works have them. What I object to is you cutting me out then coming the "How could you?"'

We stared at each other. After a long moment he turned and walked to the kerb.

'Put out a warrant for Jaris,' I said to his back. 'Put a stop on his passports, inform the airports, stations. But he only called me because he was en route, to tell me what he thinks happened. His phone's probably smashed up by the tracks in the middle of Cucinis Pass, halfway to the Balkans by now.'

'So what is it he *thinks happened*?'

'Orciny.'

He turned in disgust and waved the word away.

'Were you even going to fucking tell me this?' he said.

'I told you, didn't I?'

'He's just done a runner. Doesn't that tell you anything? The goddamn *guilty* run.'

'What, you talking about Mahalia? Come on, what's his

228

motive?' I said that but remembered some of what Jaris had told me. She had not been one of their party. They had driven her out. I hesitated a little. 'Or you mean Bowden? Why the hell and *how* the hell would Jaris organise something like that?'

'I don't know, both. Who knows what makes these fuckers do what they do?' Dhatt said. 'There'll be some fucked-up justification or other, some conspiracy thing.'

'Doesn't make sense,' I said carefully, after a minute. 'It was . . . Okay, it was him who called me from here in the first place.'

'I *knew* it. You fucking *covered* for him . . .'

'I didn't know. I couldn't tell. When he called last night he told me. Wait, wait, listen, Dhatt: why would he call me in the first place if it was him who killed her?'

He stared at me. After a minute he turned and hailed a cab. He opened its door. I watched. The cab had halted skew-whiff on the road: Ul Qoman cars sounded their horns as they went past, Besź drivers cut quietly around the protub, the law-abiding not even whispering cusses.

Dhatt stood there half-in, half-out, and the cabbie made some remonstrance. Dhatt snapped something and showed him his ID.

'I don't know why,' he said to me. 'Something to find out. But it's a bit fucking much, isn't it? That he's gone?'

'If he was in on it there's no sense him drawing my attention to *anything*. And how's he supposed to have got her to Besźel?'

'Called his friends over there; they did it . . .'

I shrugged a doubting *maybe*. 'It was the Besź unifs who gave us our first lead on all this, guy called Drodin. I've heard of misdirection, but we didn't have anything to misdirect. They don't have the smarts or contacts to know which van to steal – not the ones I've met. Plus there's more *policzai* agents than members on their books anyway. If this was unifs it was some secret hardcore we've not seen.

'I spoke to Jaris . . . He's scared,' I said. 'Not guilty: scared and sad. He was into her, I think.'

'Alright,' Dhatt said after a while. He looked at me, motioned me into the cab. He stayed standing outside for several seconds, giving orders into his phone too quiet and quick for me to follow. 'Alright. Let's change the record.' He spoke slowly as the cab drove.

'Who gives a fuck what's gone down between Besźel and Ul Qoma, right? Who gives a fuck what my boss is telling me or what yours is telling you? You're police. I'm police. Let's fix this. Are we working together, Borlú? I could do with some help on a case that's getting more fucked by the minute, how about you? UlHuan doesn't know fuck, by the way.'

Where he took me, a place very close to his office, was not as dark as a cop bar in Besźel would have been. It was more salubrious. I still would not have booked a wedding reception there. It was, if only just, during working hours, but the room was more than half-full. It cannot have all been local *militsya*, but I recognised many of the faces from Dhatt's office. They recognised me, too. Dhatt entered to greetings, and I followed him past whispers and those so-charmingly frank Ul Qoman stares.

'One definite murder and now two disappearances,' I said. I watched him very carefully. 'All people who are known to have looked at this stuff.'

'There is no fucking Orciny.'

'Dhatt, I'm not saying that. You said yourself there are such things as cults and lunatics.'

230

'Seriously fuck off. The most culty lunatic we've met just fled the scene of the crime, and you gave him a free pass.'

'I should have said first thing this morning, I apologise.'

'You should've called last night.'

'Even if we could find him I thought we didn't have enough to hold him. But I apologise.' Held my hands open.

I stared at him some time. He was overcoming something. 'I want to solve this,' he said. The pleasant burr of Illitan from the customers. I heard the clucks as one or two saw my visitor's mark. Dhatt bought me a beer. Ul Qoman, flavoured with all kinds of whatnot. It would not be winter for weeks, and though it was no colder in Ul Qoma than in Besźel, it felt colder to me. 'What do you say? If you won't even fucking trust me . . .'

'Dhatt, I've already told you stuff that—' I lowered my voice. 'No one else knows about that *first* phone call. I don't know what's going on. I don't understand any of this. I'm not solving anything. I'm, by some fluke that I do not know the whys of any more than you, being used. For some reason I've been a repository for a bunch of information that I don't know what to do with. I hope there's a *yet* after that, but I don't know, just like I don't know anything.'

'What does *Jaris* think happened? I'm going to track that fucker down.' He would not.

'I should've called, but I could . . . He's not our guy. You know, Dhatt. You know. How long you been an officer? Sometimes you *know*, right?' I tapped my chest. I was right, he liked that, nodded.

I told him what Jaris had said. 'Fucking crap,' he said, when I was done.

'Maybe.'

'What the fuck is this Orciny stuff? *That's* what he was running from? You're reading that book. The dodgy one Bowden wrote. What's it like?'

'There's a lot in it. A lot of stuff. I don't know. Of course it's ludicrous, like you say. Secret overlords behind the scene, more powerful even than Breach, puppetmasters, hidden cities.'

'Crap.'

'Yeah, but the point is that it's crap a bunch of people believe. And' – I opened my hands at him – '*something* big's going on, and we have no idea what it is.'

'Maybe I'll take a look at it after you,' Dhatt said. 'Who the fuck knows anything.' He said the last word carefully.

'Qussim.' A couple of his colleagues, men of about his age or mine, raising their glasses to him, just about to me. There was something in their eyes, they were moving in like curious animals. 'Qussim, we've not had a chance to meet our guest. You've been hiding him away.'

'Yura,' Dhatt said. 'Kai. How's tricks? Borlú, these are detectives blah and blah.' He waved his hands between them and me. One of them raised his eyebrow at Dhatt.

'I just wanted to find out how Inspector Borlú was finding Ul Qoma,' the one called Kai said. Dhatt snorted and finished his beer.

'Fuck's sake,' he said. He sounded as amused as angry. 'You want to get drunk and get into an argument with him, maybe even if you're far gone enough, Yura, a fight. You'll bring up all manner of unfortunate international incidents. The fucking war might get dusted off. You might even say something about your dad. His dad was in the UQ Navy,' he said to me. 'Got tinnitus or some shit in a fucking idiot's skirmish with a Besź tugboat over some disputed lobster pots or whatever.' I glanced, but neither of our interlocutors looked particularly outraged. There was even a trace of humour on Kai's face. 'I'll save you the trouble,' Dhatt said. 'He's as much of a Besź wanker as you think, and you can spread that around the office. Come on, Borlú.'

We went via his station's garage and he picked up his car. 'Hey ...' He indicated me the steering wheel. 'It never even occurred to me, maybe you want to give the Ul Qoman roads a go.'

'No, thanks. I think it would be a bit confusing.' Driving in Besźel or Ul Qoma is hard enough when you are in your home city, negotiating local and foreign traffic. 'You know,' I said. 'When I was first driving ... it must be the same here, as well as seeing all the cars on the road you've got to learn to unsee all the other cars, the ones abroad, but unsee them fast enough to get out of their way.' Dhatt nodded. 'Anyway, when I was a kid first driving we had to get used to zooming past all these old bangers and stuff in Ul Qoma, donkey carts in some parts and what have you. That you unsaw, but you know ... Now years later most of the unseens have been overtaking me.'

Dhatt laughed. Almost embarrassed. 'Things go up and down,' he said. 'Ten years from now it'll be you lot doing the overtaking again.'

'Doubt it.'

'Come on,' he said. 'It'll shift; it always does. It's already started.'

'Our expos? A couple of little pity investments. I think you'll be top wolf for a while.'

'We're blockaded!'

233

'Not that you seem to be doing too bad on it. Washington loves us, and all we've got to show for it is Coke.'

'Don't knock that,' Dhatt said. 'Have you tasted Canuck Cola? All this is old Cold War bullshit. Who gives a fuck who the Americans want to play with, anyway? Good luck with them. *Oh Canada* . . .' He sang the line. Dhatt said to me, 'What's the food like at that place?'

'Okay. Bad. No worse than any other hotel food.'

He yanked the wheel, took us off the route I'd come to know. 'Sweet?' he said into his phone. 'Can you chuck some more stuff on for supper? Thanks, beautiful. I want you to meet my new partner.'

Her name was Yallya. She was pretty, quite a lot younger than Dhatt, but she greeted me very poised, playing a role and enjoying it, waiting at the door of their apartment to triple-kiss me hello, the Ul Qoman way.

On the way to the house, Dhatt had looked at me and said 'You okay?' It was quickly obvious that he lived within a mile, in grosstopic terms, of my own house. From their living room I saw that Dhatt and Yallya's rooms and my own overlooked the same stretch of green ground, that in Besźel was Majdlyna Green and in Ul Qoma was Kwaidso Park, a finely balanced crosshatch. I had walked in Majdlyna myself often. There are parts where even individual trees are crosshatched, where Ul Qoman children and Besź children clamber past each other, each obeying their parents' whispered strictures to unsee the other. Children are sacks of infection. That was the sort of thing that spread diseases. Epidemiology was always complicated here and back home.

'How you liking Ul Qoma, Inspector?'

'Tyador. Very much.'

'Bullshit, he thinks we're all thugs and idiots and being invaded by secret armies from hidden cities.' Dhatt's laughter was not without edge. 'Anyway we're not getting much chance to exactly go sightseeing.'

'How's the case?'

'There is no case,' he told her. 'There's a series of random and implausible crises that make no sense other than if you believe the most dramatic possible shit. And there's a dead girl at the end of it all.'

'Is that true?' she said to me. They were bringing out food in bits and pieces. It was not home cooking, and seemed to include a lot of convenience and prepackaged food, but it was better quality than I'd been eating, and was more Ul Qoman, though that is not an unmitigated good. The sky darkened over the crosshatched park, with night and with wet clouds.

'You miss potatoes,' Yallya said.

'Is it written on my face?'

'It's all you eat, isn't it?' She thought she was being playful. 'This too spicy for you?'

'There's someone watching us from the park.'

'How can you tell from here?' She glanced over my shoulder. 'Hope for their sake they're in Ul Qoma.' She was an editor at a financial magazine and had, judging by the books I saw and the posters in the bathroom, a taste for Japanese comics.

'Are you married, Tyador?' I tried to answer Yallya's questions though they came too fast really for that. 'Is this the first time you've been here?'

'No, but the first time for a long time.'

'So you don't know it.'

235

'No. I might once have claimed to know London, but not for years.'

'You're well travelled! And now with all this are you mixing with insiles and breachers?' I did not find this line adorable. 'Qussim says you're spending your time where they're digging up old hex stuff.'

'It's like most places, much more bureaucratic than it sounds, no matter how weird the stories are.'

'It's ridiculous.' She looked contrite, quite suddenly. 'I shouldn't make jokes about it. It's just because I don't know almost anything about the girl who died.'

'You never ask,' Dhatt said.

'Well, it's ... Do you have a picture of her?' Yallya said. I must have looked surprised because Dhatt shrugged at me. I reached into my inner pocket jacket, but remembered when I touched it that the only picture I had – a small copy of a copy taken in Besźel, tucked into my wallet – was of Mahalia dead. I would not show that.

'I'm sorry, I don't.' In the little quiet it occurred to me that Mahalia was only a few years younger than Yallya.

I stayed longer than I had expected. She was a good host, particularly when I got her off this stuff – she let me steer the conversation away. I watched her and Dhatt perform gentle bickering. The proximity of the park and of other people's affection was moving, to the point of distracting. Watching Yallya and Dhatt made me think of Sariska and Biszaya. I recalled the odd eagerness of Aikam Tsueh.

When I left, Dhatt took me down to the street and headed for the car, but I said to him, 'I'll make my own way.'

He stared. 'Are you okay?' he said. 'You've been funny all night.'

236

'I'm fine, sorry. I'm sorry, I don't mean to be rude; it was very kind of you. Really it was a good night, and Yallya ... you're a lucky man. I just, I'm trying to think things through. Look, I'm okay to go. I've money. Ul Qoman money.' I showed him my wallet. 'I've got all my papers. Visitor's badge. I know it makes you uncomfortable having me out and about, but seriously, I'd like to walk; I need to be out for a bit. It's a beautiful night.'

'What the fuck are you talking about? It's raining.'

'I like rain. Anyway, this is drizzle. You wouldn't last a day in Beszel. We get *real* rain in Beszel.' An old joke but he smiled and surrendered.

'Whatever. We have to work this out, you know; we're not getting very far.'

'No.'

'And us the best minds our cities have, right? And Yolanda Rodriguez remains unfound, and now we've lost Bowden, too. We're not going to win medals for this.' He looked around. 'Seriously, what is going on?'

'You know everything I know,' I said.

'What bugs me,' he said, 'isn't that there's no way to make sense of this shit. It's that there is a way to make sense of it. And it's not a way I want to go. I don't believe in . . .' He waved at malevolent hidden cities. He stared the length of his street. It was total, so none of the lights from windows above was foreign. It was not so late, and we were not alone. People were silhouetted by the lights of a road perpendicular to Dhatt's street, a road mostly in Beszel. For a moment I thought one of the black figures had, for seconds long enough to constitute breach, watched us, but then they moved on.

When I started walking, watching the wet-edged shapes of

the city, I was not going anywhere in particular. I was moving south. Walking alone past people who were not, I indulged the idea of walking to where Sariska or Biszaya lived, or even Corwi – something of that melancholy connection. They knew I was in Ul Qoma: I could find them and could walk alongside them in the street and we would be inches apart but unable to acknowledge each other. Like the old story.

Not that I would ever do such a thing. Having to unsee acquaintances or friends is a rare and notoriously uncomfortable circumstance. What I did do was walk past my own house.

I half expected to see one of my neighbours, none of whom, I think, knew I was abroad, and who might therefore be expected to greet me before noticing my Ul Qoman visitor's badge and hurriedly attempting to unbreach. Their lights were on, but they were all indoors.

In Ul Qoma I was in Ioy Street. It is pretty equally crosshatched with RosidStrász where I lived. The building two doors along from my own house was a late-night Ul Qoman liquor store, half the pedestrians around me in Ul Qoma, so I was able to stop grosstopically, physically close to my own front door, and unsee it of course, but equally of course not quite, with an emotion the name of which I have no idea. I came slowly closer, keeping my eyes on the entrances in Ul Qoma.

Someone was watching me. It looked like an old woman. I could hardly see her in the dark, certainly not her face in any detail, but something was curious in the way she stood. I took in her clothes and could not tell which city she was in. That is a common instant of uncertainty, but this one went on for much longer than usual. And my alarm did not sub-side, it grew, as her locus refused to clarify.

I saw others in similar shadows, similarly hard to make sense of, emerging, sort of, not approaching me, not even moving but holding themselves so they grew more in focus. The woman continued to stare at me, and she took a step or two in my direction, so either she was in Ul Qoma or breaching.

That made me step back. I kept backing away. There was an ugly pause, until as if in belated echo she and those others did the same, and were gone suddenly into shared dark. I got out of there, not quite running but fast. I found better-lit avenues.

I did not walk straight to the hotel. After my heart had slowed and I had spent some minutes in a not-empty spot, I walked to the same vantage point I had taken before, overlooking Bol Ye'an. I was much more careful in my scrutiny than I had been, and tried to affect Ul Qoman bearing, and for the hour I watched that unlit excavation, no *militsya* came. So far they tended to be either violently present or altogether absent. Doubtless there was a method of ensuring subtle intervention from the Ul Qoman police, but I did not know it.

At the Hilton I requested a 5 a.m. wakeup call, and asked the woman behind the desk if she would print me up a message, as the tiny room called a 'business centre' was closed. First she did so on marked Hilton paper. 'Would you mind doing it on plain?' I said. I winked. 'Just in case it's intercepted.' She smiled, not sure what intimacy it was she was privy to. 'Can you read that back to me?'

'"Urgent. Come ASAP. Don't call."'

'Perfect.'

239

I was back overlooking the site the next morning, having taken a circuitous walked route through the city. Though as law demanded I wore my visitor's mark, I had placed it at the very edge of my lapel, where cloth folded, only visible to those who knew to look. I wore it on a jacket that was a genuine Ul Qoman design and was, like my hat, not new but new to me. I had set out some hours before any shops were open, but a surprised Ul Qoman man at the farthest reach of my walk was several dinar richer and lighter his outer clothes.

Nothing guaranteed that I was not watched, but I did not think I was by the *militsya*. It was not long after dawn, but Ul Qomans were everywhere. I would not risk walking closer to Bol Ye'an. As the morning wore on the city filled with hundreds of children: those in the strict Ul Qoman school uniforms, and dozens of street children. I attempted to be moderately unobtrusive, watched from behind the overlong headlines of the *Ul Qoma Nasyona*, eating fried street food for breakfast. People began to arrive at the dig. Arriving often in little groups, they were too far away for me to tell who was who as they entered, showing their passes. I waited a while.

The little girl I approached in her outsized trainers and cutoff jeans looked at me sceptically. I held up a five-dinar note and a sealed envelope.

'You see that place? You see the gate?' She nodded, guarded. They were opportunist couriers, these kids, among everything else.

'Where you from?' she said.

'Paris,' I said. 'But that's a secret. Don't tell anyone. I have a job for you. Do you think you could persuade those guards to call someone for you?' She nodded. 'I'm going to tell you a name, and I want you to go there, and find the person with that name, and only that person, and I want you to hand over this message.'

She was either honest or realised, smart girl, that from where I stood I could see almost her entire route to the door of Bol Ye'an. She delivered it. She threaded in and out of the crowds, tiny and quick – the sooner this lucrative task was done the sooner she could get another. It was easy to see why she and the other homeless children like her had the nickname 'job-mice.'

A few minutes after she reached the gates, someone emerged, moving fast, bundled up, head down, walking stiffly and quickly away from the dig. Though he was far away, alone like that and expected, I could tell that it was Aikam Tsueh.

I HAD DONE THIS BEFORE. I could keep him in sight, but in a city I didn't know it was hard to do so while ensuring that I could not be seen. He made it easier than it should have been, never once looking behind him, taking in all but a couple of places the largest, most crowded and crosshatched roads, which I presumed were the most direct routes.

The most complicated point came when he took a bus. I was close to him, and was able to huddle behind my paper and keep him in sight. I winced when my phone rang, but it was not the first in the bus to do so, and Aikam did not glance at me. It was Dhatt. I diverted the call and switched the ringer off.

Tsueh disembarked, and led me to a desolate total zone of Ul Qoman housing projects, out past Bisham Ko, way out from the centre. No pretty corkscrew towers or iconic gasrooms here. The concrete warrens were not deserted but full of noise and

241

people between the stretches of garbage. It was like the poorest estates of Besźel, though even poorer, with a soundtrack in a different language, and children and hustlers in other clothes. Only when Tsueh entered one of the dripping towerblocks and ascended did I have to exercise real care, padding as soundlessly as I could up the concrete stairs, past graffiti and animal shit. I could hear him racing ahead of me, stopping at last, and knocking softly. I slowed.

'It's me,' I heard him say. 'It's me, I'm here.'

An answering voice, alarm, though that impression may have been because I expected alarm. I continued to quietly and carefully climb. I wished I had my gun.

'You *told* me to,' Tsueh said. 'You *said*. Let me in. What is it?'

The door creaked a little, and the second voice came whispering, but just a little louder. I was one stained pillar away now. I held my breath.

'But you *said* . . .' The door opened more and I heard Aikam step forward, and I turned and went fast across the little landing behind him. He did not have time to register me, or to turn. I shoved him hard, and he barrelled into the ajar door, slamming it open, pushing aside someone beyond him, falling and sprawling on the floor of the hallway beyond. I heard a scream, but I had followed him through the door and slammed it closed behind me. I stood against it, blocking exit, looking along a gloomy corridor between rooms, down at where Tsueh wheezed and struggled to stand, at the screaming young woman backing away, staring at me in terror.

I put my finger to my lips and, surely by coincidence of her breath running out, she ebbed to silence.

'No, Aikam,' I said. 'She didn't say. The message wasn't from her.'

'Aikam,' she blubbered.

'Stop,' I said. I put my finger to my lips again. 'I'm not going to hurt you, I'm *not* here to hurt you, but we both know there are others who want to. I want to help you, Yolanda.'

She cried again and I could not tell if it was fear or relief.

CHAPTER NINETEEN

AIKAM GOT TO HIS FEET and tried to attack me. He was muscular and held his hands as if he had studied boxing but if he had he was not a good student. I tripped him and pushed his face down onto the stained carpet, pinioned an arm behind his back. Yolanda shouted his name. He half rose, even with me straddling him, so I pushed his face down again, ensuring that his nose bled. I stayed between both of them and the door.

'That's enough,' I said. 'Are you ready to calm down? I'm not here to hurt her.' Strength to strength, eventually he would overpower me unless I broke his arm. Neither eventuality was desirable. 'Yolanda, for God's sake.' I caught her eye, riding his shuffles. 'I have a gun – don't you think I'd have shot you if I wanted to hurt you?' I switched to English for the lie.

''Kam,' she said at last, and almost instantly he grew calm. She stared at me, backed into the wall at the corridor's end, her hands flat against it.

'You hurt my arm,' Aikam said beneath me.

'Sorry to hear it. If I let him up, is he going to behave?' That in English again to her. 'I'm here to help you. I know you're scared. You hear me, Aikam?' Switching between two foreign languages was not hard, so adrenalised. 'If I let you up, you going to go look after Yolanda?'

He did nothing to clear away the blood that dripped from his nose. He cradled his arm and, unable to put it comfortably around Yolanda, sort of loomed lovingly over and around her. He put himself between me and her. She looked out at me from behind him with wariness, not terror.

'What do you want?' she said.

'I know you're scared. I'm not Ul Qoma *militsya* – I don't trust them any more than you do. I'm not going to call them. Let me help you.'

IN WHAT YOLANDA RODRIGUEZ called the living room she cowered in an old chair they had probably pulled in from an abandoned flat in the same tower. There were several such pieces, broken in various ways but clean. The windows overlooked the courtyard, from which I could hear Ul Qoman boys playing a rough makeshift version of rugby. They were invisible through the whitewash on the glass.

Books and other things sat in boxes around the room. A cheap laptop, a cheap inkjet printer. No power, though, so far as I could tell. There were no posters on the walls. The door to the room was open. I stood leaning by it, looking at the two pictures on the floor: one of Aikam; the other, in a better frame, of Yolanda and Mahalia smiling behind cocktails.

Yolanda stood, sat again. She would not meet my eye. She did not try to hide her fear, which had not abated though I was no longer its immediate object. She was afraid to show or indulge her growing hope. I had seen her expression before. It is not uncommon for people to crave deliverance.

'Aikam's been doing a good job,' I said. I was back to English. Though he did not speak it, Aikam did not ask for translation. He stood by Yolanda's chair and watched me. 'You

245

had him trying to find out how to get out of Ul Qoma, below the radar. Any luck?'

'How did you know I was here?'

'Your boy's been doing just what you told him to. He's been trying to find out what's going on. What did he ever care about Mahalia Geary? They never spoke. Now you, though, he cares about. So there's something odd when, like you told him to, he's been asking all about her. Gets you thinking. Why would he do that? You, you did care about her, and you do care about yourself.'

She stood again and turned her face to the wall. I waited for her to say something, and when she did not I continued. 'I'm flattered you'd get him to ask me. The one police you think just might possibly not be part of what's happening. The outsider.'

'You don't know!' She turned to me. 'I *don't* trust you—'

'Okay, okay, I never said you did.' A strange reassurance. Aikam watched us jabbering. 'So do you never leave?' I said. 'What do you eat? Tins? I guess Aikam comes, but not often . . .'

'Can't come often. How did you even *find* me?'

'He can explain. He got a message to come back. For what it's worth he was trying to look after you.'

'He does that.'

'I can see.' Dogs began to fight outside, noise told us. Their owners joined in. My phone buzzed, audible even with the ringer off. She started and backed away as if I might shoot her with it. The display told me it was Dhatt.

'Look,' I said. 'I'm turning it off. I'm turning it off.' If he was paying attention, he would know his call was rerouted to voice-mail before the rings had all sounded out. 'What happened?

Who got to you? Why did you run when you did?'

'I didn't give them the chance. You saw what happened to Mahalia. She was my *friend*. I tried to tell myself it wasn't going down like that, but she's *dead*.' She said it with what sounded almost like awe. Her face collapsed and she shook her head. 'They *killed* her.'

'Your parents haven't heard from you . . .'

'I can't. I can't, I have to . . .' She bit her nails and glanced up. 'When I get out . . .'

'Straight to the embassy next country along? Through the mountains? Why not here? Or in Besźel?'

'You know why.'

'Say I don't.'

'Because *they're* here, and they're there too. They *run* things. Looking for me. It's just 'cause I got away when I did that they haven't found me. They're ready to kill me like they killed my *friend*. Because I know they're there. Because I know they're real.' Her tone alone was enough reason for Aikam to hug her then.

'Who?' Let's hear it.

'The third place. Between the city and the city. Orciny.'

A WEEK OR SO would have been long enough ago for me to tell her she was being foolish or paranoid. The hesitation – when she told me about the conspiracy, there were those seconds when I was tacitly invited to tell her she was wrong, during which I was silent – vindicated her beliefs, gave her to think I agreed.

She stared and thought me a co-conspirator, and not knowing what was occurring I behaved like one. I could not tell her her life was not in danger. Nor that Bowden's was not

247

– perhaps he was dead already – nor mine, nor that I could keep her safe. I could tell her almost nothing.

Yolanda had stayed hidden in this place, that her loyal Aikam had found and tried to prepare, in this part of town that she had never intended to so much as visit and of which she did not know the name the day before she arrived here, after an arduous, circuitous and secret midnight dash. He and she had done what they could to make the place bearable, but it was an abandoned hovel in a slum, that she could not quit for terror of being spotted by the unseen forces she knew wanted her dead.

I would say that she could never have seen the like of this place before, but that may not be true. Maybe she had once or twice watched a documentary named something like *The Dark Side of the Ul Qoma Dream* or *The Sickness of the New Wolf or* what have you. Films about our neighbour were not generally popular in Besźel, were rarely distributed, so I could not vouch, but it would not be surprising if some blockbuster had been made with the backdrop of gangs in the Ul Qoma slums – the redemption of some not-too-hardcore drug-runner, the impressive murder of several others. Perhaps Yolanda had seen footage of the failed estates of Ul Qoma, but she would not have meant to visit.

'Do you know your neighbours?'

She did not smile. 'By voice.'

'Yolanda I know you're afraid.'

'They got Mahalia, they got Doctor Bowden, now they're going to get me.'

'I know you're afraid, but you have to help me. I am going to get you out of here, but I need to know what happened. If I don't know, I can't help you.'

248

'Help me?' She looked around the room. 'You want me to tell you what's up? Sure, you ready to bunk down here? You'll have to, you know. If you know what's going on, they'll come for you too.'

'Alright.'

She sighed and looked down. Aikam said to her, 'Is it okay?' in Illitan, and she shrugged, *Maybe*.

'HOW DID SHE FIND ORCINY?'

'I don't know.'

'Where is it?'

'I don't know and I do not want to. There are access points,' she said. She didn't tell me any more and that was alright by me.'

'Why didn't she tell anyone but you?' She seemed to know nothing of Jaris.

'She wasn't crazy. You've seen what happened to Doctor Bowden? You don't admit you want to know about Orciny. That was always what she was here for, but she wouldn't tell anyone. That's how they want it. Orcinians. It's perfect for them that no one thinks they're real. That's just what they want. That's how they rule.'

'Her PhD . . .'

'She didn't care about it. She was just doing enough to keep Prof Nance off her back. She was here for Orciny. Do you realise they contacted *her*.' She stared at me intently. 'Seriously. She was a bit . . . the first time she was at a conference, in Beszel, she sort of said a load of stuff. There was a load of politicians and stuff there as well as academics and it caused a bit of—'

'She made enemies. I heard about it.'

249

'Oh, we all knew the *nats* had their eyes on her, nats on both sides, but that wasn't the issue. It was *Orciny* who saw her then. They're everywhere.'

Certainly she had made herself visible. Shura Katrinya had seen her: I remembered her face at the Oversight Committee when I mentioned the incident. As had Mikhel Buric, I recalled, and a couple of others. Perhaps Syedr had seen her too. Perhaps there had been interested unknown others. 'After she first started writing about them, after she was reading all that stuff in *Between*, and writing it up, and researching, making all her mad little notes' – she made tiny scribbling motions – 'she got a letter.'

'Did she show you?'

She nodded. 'I didn't understand it when I saw it. It was in the root form. Precursor stuff, old script, before Besź and Illitan.'

'What did it say?'

'She told me. It was something like: *We are watching you. You understand. Would you like to know more?* There were others too.'

'She showed you?'

'Not straightaway.'

'What were they saying to her? Why?'

'Because she worked them out. They could tell she wanted to be part of it. So they *recruited* her. Had her do stuff for them, like, like initiation. Give them information, deliver things.' This was impossible stuff. With a look she challenged me to mock and I was silent. 'They gave her addresses where she should leave letters and things. In *dissensi*. Messages back and forth. She was writing back. They were telling her things. About Orciny. She told me a little bit about it, and the history

250

and that, and it was like . . . Places no one can see because they think they're in the other city. Besź think it's here; Ul Qomans think it's in Beszél. The people in Orciny, they're not like us. They can do things that aren't . . .'

'Did she meet them?'

Yolanda stood beside the window pane, staring out and down at an angle that kept her from being framed by its white-wash-diffused light. She turned to look at me and said nothing. She had calmed into despondency. Aikam came closer to her. His eyes went between us like a spectator at a tennis match. Finally Yolanda shrugged. 'I don't know.'

'Tell me.'

'She wanted to. I don't know. I know at first they said no.' *Not yet*, they had said. 'They told her stuff, history, stuff about what we were doing. This stuff, the Precursor Age stuff . . . it's *theirs*. When Ul Qoma digs it up, or even Beszél, there's this whole thing about whose is it, where was it found, you know, all that? It's not Ul Qoma's or Beszél's. It's Orciny's; it always was. They told her about stuff we'd found that *no one who hadn't put it there could know*. This is their history. They were here before Ul Qoma and Beszél split, or joined, around them. They never went away.'

'But it was just lying there until a bunch of Canadian archae-ologists—'

'That's where they *kept* it. That stuff wasn't lost. The earth under Ul Qoma and Beszél's their storeroom. It's all Orciny's. It was all theirs, and we were just . . . I think she was telling them where we were digging, what we were finding.'

'She was stealing for them.'

'We were stealing *from* them . . . She never breached, you know.'

'What? I thought all of you—'

'You mean . . . like games? Not Mahalia. She couldn't. Too much to lose. Too likely someone was watching, she said. She *never* breached, not even in one of those ways that you can't tell, standing there, you know? She wouldn't give Breach a chance to take her.' She shivered again. I squatted down and looked around. 'Aikam,' she said in Illitan. 'Can you get us something to drink?' He did not want to leave the room, but he could see she was not afraid of me anymore.

'What she did do,' she said, 'was go to these places where they'd leave her letters. The *dissensi* are entrances to Orciny. She was so close to being part of it. She thought. At first.' I waited, and at last she continued. 'I kept asking her what was up. Something was really wrong, in the last couple of weeks. She stopped going to the dig, meetings, everything.'

'I heard.'

"What is it?' I kept saying, and at first she was like, 'Nothing,' but in the end she told me she was scared. 'Something's wrong,' she said. She'd been frustrated I think because Orciny wouldn't let her in, and she'd been going mad with work. She was studying harder than I'd ever seen. I asked her what it was. She just kept saying she was scared. She said she'd been going over and over her notes, and that she was figuring stuff out. Bad stuff. She said we could be thieves without even knowing.'

Aikam came back. He carried for me and for Yolanda warm cans of Qora-Oranja.

'I think she'd done something to make Orciny *angry*. She knew she was in trouble, and Bowden too. She said so just before she—'

'Why would they kill him?' I said. 'He doesn't even believe in Orciny any more.'

252

'Oh, God, of course he knows they're real. Of course he does. He's denied it for years because he needs work, but have you read his book? They're going after everyone who knows about them. Mahalia told me he was in trouble. Just before she disappeared. He knew too much, and I do too. And now you do too.'

'What are you intending to do?'

'Stay here. Hide. Get out.'

'How's that going?' I said. She looked at me in misery. 'Your boy did his best. He was asking me how a criminal might get out of the city.' She even smiled. 'Let me help you.'

'You can't. They're everywhere.'

'You don't know that.'

'How can you keep me safe? They're going to get you now too.'

Every few seconds there came the sounds of someone ascending outside the apartment, shouts and the noise of a handheld MP3 player, rap or Ul Qoman techno played loud enough to be insolent. Such everyday noises could be camouflage. Corwi was a city away. Listening now it seemed that every few noises paused by the door to the apartment.

'We don't know what the truth is,' I said. I had intended to say more, but realising that I was not sure whom I was trying to convince of what, I hesitated, and she interrupted me.

'Mahalia did. What are you doing?' I had taken out my phone. I held it up as if surrendering, both hands. 'Don't panic,' I said. 'I was just thinking . . . we need to work out what we're going to do. There are people who might be able to help us—'

'Stop,' she said. Aikam looked as if he might come for me

again. I got ready to sidestep but waved the phone so she could see it was not on.

'There's an option you never pursued,' I said. 'You could go outside, cross the road a little bit down the way there, and walk into YahudStrász. It's in Besźel.' She looked at me as though I was crazy. 'Stand there, wave your hands. You could breach.' Her eyes got wider.

Another loud man ran upstairs outside, and we three waited. 'Did you ever think it was worth a try? Who can touch *Breach*? If Orciny's out to get you . . .' Yolanda was staring at the boxes of her books, her boxed-up self. 'Maybe you'd be safer, even.'

'Mahalia said they were enemies,' she said. She sounded far away. 'She once said the whole history of Besźel and Ul Qoma was the history of the war between Orciny and Breach. Besźel and Ul Qoma were set up like chess moves, in that war. They might do anything to me.'

'Come on,' I interrupted. 'You know most foreigners who breach are just ejected—' But she interrupted back.

'*Even if* I knew what they'd do, which neither of us do, think about it. A secret for like more than a thousand years, in between Ul Qoma and Besźel, watching us all the time, whether we know it or not. With its own agenda. You think I'd be safer if Breach had me? In the *Breach*? I'm not Mahalia. I'm not sure Orciny and the Breach are enemies at all.' She looked at me then and I did not disdain her. 'Maybe they work together. Or maybe when you *invoke* you've been handing power to Orciny for centuries, while you all sit there telling each other it's a fairy tale. I think Orciny is the name Breach calls itself.'

CHAPTER TWENTY

FIRST SHE HAD NOT WANTED ME TO ENTER; then Yolanda did not want me to leave. 'They'll see you! They'll find you. They'll take you and then they'll come for *me*.'

'I can't stay here.'

'They'll get you.'

'I can't stay here.'

She watched me walk the width of the room, to the window and back to the door.

'Don't – you can't make a phone call from here—'

'You have to stop panicking.' But I stopped myself, because I was not sure that she was wrong to do so. 'Aikam, are there other ways out of this building?'

'Not the way we came in?' He looked intently and emptily a moment. 'Some of the apartments downstairs are empty, and maybe you could go through them . . .'

'Okay.' It had begun to rain, fingertipping against the obscured windows. Judging by the halfhearted darkening of the white windows, it was only just overcast. Washed out of colour, perhaps. Still it felt safer to escape than if it had been clear or coldly sunny, as it had that morning. I paced the room.

'You're alone in Ul Qoma,' Yolanda whispered. 'What can you do?' I looked at her at last.

'Do you trust me?' I said.

'No.'

'Too bad. You've no choice. I'm going to get you out. I'm not in my element here, but . . .'

'What do you want to do?'

'I'm going to get you out of here, back to home ground, back to where I can make things happen. I'm going to get you to Besźel.'

She protested. She had never been to Besźel. Both cities were controlled by Orciny, both were overlooked by Breach. I interrupted her.

'What else are you going to do? Besźel's my city. I can't negotiate the system here. I have no contacts. I don't know my way around. But I can get you out from Besźel, and you can help me.'

'You can't—'

'Yolanda, shut up. Aikam, don't move another step.' No time for this immobility. She was right, I could promise her nothing but an attempt. 'I can get you out, but not from here. One more day. Wait here. Aikam, your job's finished. You don't work at Bol Ye'an any more. Your job's to stay here and look after Yolanda.' He would provide little protection, but his continued interventions at Bol Ye'an would eventually attract other people's attention than my own. 'I will be back. You understand? And I'll get you out.'

She had food for some days, a diet of tins. This little living room/bedroom, another, smaller, filled with only damp, the kitchen with its electricity and gas supplies disconnected. The bathroom was not good but it would not kill them another day or two: from some standpipe Aikam had brought buckets that stood ready to flush. The many air fresheners he had bought made a stink different than it would otherwise have been.

'Stay,' I said. 'I'll be back.' Aikam recognised the phrase, though it was in English. He smiled and so I said the words again for him in an Austrian accent. Yolanda did not get it. 'I will get you out,' I said to her.

On the ground floor a few shoves at doors yielded me an empty apartment, a long time since fire-damaged but still smelling of carbon. I stood in its glassless kitchen and watched the hardiest girls and boys outside refuse to get out of the rain. I watched for a long time, looking into all the shadows I could see. I saw only those children. My sleeves pulled over my fingertips in case of a fringe of glass, I vaulted out into the yard, where if any of the kids saw me emerge they did not remark.

I know how to watch to ensure I am not followed. I walked quickly through the byway meanders of the project, between its bins and cars, graffiti and children's playgrounds, until I made it out of cul-de-sac land into the streetscape of Ul Qoma, and Besźel. With relief at being one of several pedestrians rather than the only purposeful figure in sight, I breathed out a little, I took on the same rain-avoidance gait as everyone else, and at last turned on my phone. It scolded me with how many messages I had missed. All from Dhatt. I was starving and uncertain of how to get back to the Old Town. I wandered, looking for a Metro but finding a phone box. I called him.

'Dhatt.'

'It's Borlú.'

'Where the *fuck* are you? Where've you been?' He was angry but conspiratorial, his voice quieter as he turned and muttered into his phone, not louder. A good sign. 'I've been trying to call you for fucking hours. Is everything . . . Are you alright? What the fuck's going on?'

'I'm alright, but . . .'

'Something happened?' Anger but not only anger in his voice.

'Yeah, something happened. I can't talk about it.'

'The fuck you can't.'

'Listen. *Listen.* I need to talk to you but I don't have time for this. You want to know what's been going on, meet me, I don't know' – flipping through my street map – 'in Kaing Shé, in the square by the station, in two hours, and Dhatt, do *not* bring anyone else. This is serious shit. There's more going on here than you know. I don't know who to talk to. Now are you going to help me?'

I made him wait an hour. I watched him from the corner as he must surely have known I would. Kaing Shé Station is the city's major terminus, so the square outside it bustled with Ul Qomans in cafés, street performers, people buying DVDs and electronics from stalls. The topolganger square in Besźel was not quite empty, so unseen Besź citizens were grosstopically there too. I stayed in the shadows of one of the cigarette kiosks shaped in homage to an Ul Qoman temporary hut, once common on the wetlands where scavengers sifted through the crosshatched mud. I saw Dhatt look for me, but I stayed out of sight while it grew dark and watched to see if he made any calls (he did not) or hand signals (he did not). He only set his face more and more as he drank teas and glowered in the shadows. At last I stepped into his line of sight and moved my hand in a little regular motion that caught his eye and beckoned him over.

'What the fuck is going on?' he said. 'I've had your boss on the phone. And Corwi. Who the fuck is she anyway? What's happening?'

'I don't blame you being angry, but you're keeping your voice low, so you're being careful and you want to know what's going on. You're right. Something's up. I found Yolanda.'

When I would not tell him where she was he was enraged enough to start threatening an international incident. 'This is not your fucking city,' he said, 'you come here and use our resources, you fucking hold up our investigations,' and so on, but still he kept his voice low and walked with me, so I let his anger ebb out a bit and began to tell him how Yolanda was afraid.

'We both know we can't reassure her,' I said. 'Come on. Neither of us knows the truth about what the hell's going on. About the unifs, the nats, the bomb, about *Orciny*. Shit, Dhatt, for all we know . . .' He stared at me, so I said, 'Whatever this is' – I glanced around to indicate everything that was happening – 'it goes somewhere bad.'

We were both silent a while. 'So why the fuck are you talking to me?'

'Because I need someone. But yeah, you're right, it might be a mistake. You're the only person who might understand . . . the scale of what might be going on. I want to get her out. Listen to me: this is *not* about Ul Qoma. I don't trust my own lot any more than you. I want to get that girl out, away from Ul Qoma *and* Besźel. And I can't do it from here; this isn't my patch. She's watched here.'

'Maybe I could.'

'You volunteering?' He said nothing. 'Right. I am. I have contacts back home. You don't cop for this long without being able to score tickets and false papers. I can hide her; I can talk to her in Besźel before I get her out, get some more sense of all this. This isn't about giving up: the opposite. If we get her out of harm's way we've got a much better chance of not getting blindsided. We can maybe work out what's going on.'

'You said Mahalia had already made enemies back in Besźel. I thought you wanted them for this.'

'The nats? That doesn't make much sense anymore. A, all this is way beyond Syedr and his boys, and B, *Yolanda* hasn't pissed off *anyone* back home; she's never been there. I can do my job there.' I could go beyond my job, I meant – could pull strings and favours. 'I'm not trying to cut you out, Dhatt. I'll tell you what I know if I get any more from her, maybe even come back and we can go hunting criminals, but I want to get that girl out of here. She's scared to death, Dhatt, and can we really say she's wrong to be?'

Dhatt kept shaking his head. He was neither agreeing nor disagreeing with me. After a minute he spoke again, tersely. 'I sent my crew back to the unifs. No sign of Jaris. We don't even know the little fucker's real name. If any of his mates know where he is or that he was seeing her they're not saying.'

'Do you believe them?'

He shrugged. 'We've been checking them out. Can't find anything. Doesn't look like they know shit. One or two of them it's obvious "Marya" rings a bell, but most of them never even met her.'

'This is all beyond them.'

'Oh, they're up to all kinds of shit, don't you worry; we've got moles say they're going to do this and that, they're going to break the boundaries, planning all sorts of revolutions . . .'

'That's not what we're talking about. And you hear that stuff all the time.'

He was silent while I listed for him again what had happened on our watch. We slowed down in the dark and sped up in the pools of lamplight. When I told him that according to Yolanda, Mahalia had said that Bowden was in danger too, he halted. We stood in that freezing silence for seconds.

'Today while you were fucking around with Little Miss Paranoid we searched Bowden's flat. There's no sign of forced entry, no sign of struggle. Nothing. Food left on the side, books pagedown on the chair. We did find a letter on his desk.'

'From who?'

'Yallya told me you'd be onto something. The letter doesn't say. It's not in Illitan. It was just a single word. I thought it was in weird-looking Besź but it isn't. It's in Precursor.'

'What? What does it say?'

'I took it to Nancy. She said it's an old version of the script she hasn't seen before and she wouldn't want to swear to it yadda yadda, but she's pretty sure it's a warning.'

'A warning of what?'

'Just a warning. Like a skull-and-crossbones. A word that is a warning.' It was dark enough that we could not see each other's faces well. Not deliberately, I had steered us close to an intersection with a total Besź street. Those squat brick buildings in their brown light, the men and women walking beneath them in long coats under the swinging sepia signs that I unsaw bisected the Ul Qoman sodium-lit strip of glass fronts and imports like something old and recurrent.

'So who might use that kind of . . .?'

'Don't fucking tell me about secret cities. Don't.' Dhatt looked haunted and hunted. He looked sick. He turned and bundled himself into the corner of a doorway, punched his

261

own palm furiously several times. 'What the fuck?' he said, looking into the dark.

What lived like Orciny would live, if one indulged Yolanda's and Mahalia's ideas? Something so small, so powerful, lodged in the crevices of another organism. Willing to kill. A parasite. A tick-city, quite ruthless.

'Even if . . . even if, say, something is wrong with my lot and your lot, whatever,' Dhatt said at last.

'Controlled. Bought.'

'Whatever. Even if.'

We whispered under the foreign shriek of a flap above us in Besźel swinging in the wind. 'Yolanda's convinced that Breach is Orciny,' I said. 'I'm not saying I agree with her – I don't know what I'm saying – but I promised her I'd get her out.'

'Breach would get her out.'

'You prepared to swear she's wrong? You prepared to abso-bloody-lutely swear she's got nothing to worry about from them?' I was whispering. This was dangerous talk. 'They've no way in yet – nothing's fucking breached – and she wants to keep it that way.'

'So what do you want to do?'

'I want to get her away. I'm not saying anyone here's got her in their sights, I'm not saying she's right about anything she's saying, but *someone* killed Mahalia, and someone got to Bowden. Something's going on in Ul Qoma. I'm asking for your help, Dhatt. Come with me. We can't do this officially; she won't cooperate with anything official. I promised her I'd look after her, and this is not my city. You going to help me? No, we can't risk doing this by the book. So are you going to help me? I need to get her to Besźel.'

We did not go back to the hotel room that night, nor to Dhatt's house. Not overcome by anxiety but indulging it, behaving *as if* this all might be true. We walked instead.

'Fuck's sake, can't believe I'm doing this,' he kept saying. He looked behind us more than I did.

'We can find a way to blame me,' I told him. It was not what I might have expected, despite that I'd risked telling him what I had, to have him be part of this, to put himself so on this line.

'Stick us to crowds,' I told him. 'And to crosshatching.' More people, and where the two cities are close up they make for interference patterns, harder to read or predict. They are more than a city and a city; that is elementary urban arithmetic.

'I've got an exit anytime on my visa,' I said. 'Can you get her a pass out?'

'I can get one for me, sure. I can get one for a fucking *cop*, Borlú.'

'Let me rephrase that. Can you get an exit visa for Officer Yolanda Rodriguez?' He stared at me. We were still whispering. 'She won't even have an Ul Qoman passport . . .'

'So *can you get her* through? I don't know what your border guards are like.'

'Oh what the fuck?' he said again. As the numbers of walkers fell our pedestrianism ceased being camouflage and risked becoming its opposite. 'I know a place,' Dhatt said. A drinking club, the manager of which greeted him with almost convincing pleasure, in the basement opposite a bank in the outskirts of Ul Qoma Old Town. It was full of smoke and men who eyed Dhatt, knowing what he was, despite that he was in civilian clothes. It looked for a second as if they thought him there to bust the drag act, but he waved at them to get on with it. Dhatt gestured for the manager's phone. Lips thinned, the man passed it to him over the counter and he passed it to me.

'Holy Light, let's do this, then,' he said. 'I can get her through.' There was music, and the growl of conversation was very loud. I stretched the phone to the extent of its cord and huddled down, squatting, by the bar, at stomach-level of the men around me. It felt quieter. I had to go through an operator to get an international line, which I did not like to do.

'Corwi, it's Borlú.'

'Christ. Give me a minute. Christ.'

'Corwi, I'm sorry to call so late. Can you hear me?'

'Christ. What time . . . Where are you? I can't fucking hear a word, you're all—'

'I'm in a bar. Listen, I'm sorry about the time. I need you to organise something for me.'

'Christ, boss, are you fucking kidding?'

'No. Come on. Corwi, I need you.' I could almost see her rubbing her face, maybe walking phone in hand and sleepy to the kitchen and drinking cold water. When she spoke again she was more focused.

'What's going on?'

'I'm coming back.'

'Serious? When?'

'That's what I'm calling about. Dhatt, the guy I'm working with here, he's coming over to Besźel. I need you to meet us. Can you get everything in motion and keep it on the QT? Corwi – black-ops stuff. Serious. Walls have ears.'

Long pause. 'Why me, boss? And why at two-thirty in the morning?'

'Because you're good, and because you're the soul of discretion. I need no noise. I need you in a car, with your gun and preferably one for me, and that's it. And I need you to book a hotel for them. Not one of the department's usuals.' Another long silence. 'And listen . . . he's bringing another officer.'

'What? Who?'

'She's *undercover*. What do you think? She wanted a free trip.' I glanced apology at him, though he could not hear me over the criminal din. 'Keep this low, Corwi. Just a little moment in the investigation, okay? And I'm going to want your help getting something, getting a package, out of Besźel. You understand?'

'. . . Think so, boss. Boss, someone's been calling for you. Asking what's going on with your investigation.'

'Who? What do you mean, what's going on?'

'Who I don't know, won't leave his name. He wants to know, Who are you arresting? When are you back? Have you found the missing girl? What are the plans? I don't know how he got my desk number, but he blatantly knows something.'

I was clicking at Dhatt to pay attention. 'Someone's asking questions,' I said to him. 'Won't say his name?' I asked Corwi.

'No, and I don't recognise his voice. Crap line.'

'What does he sound like?'

'Foreign. American. And scared.' On a bad, an international, line.

'God *damn*,' I said to Dhatt, hand over the receiver. 'Bowden's out there. He's trying to find me. He must be avoiding our numbers here in case he's traced . . . Canadian, Corwi. Listen, when did he call?'

'Every day, yesterday and today, won't leave his details.'

'Right. Listen. When he calls again, tell him this. Give him this message from me. Tell him he's got one chance. Hold on,

I'm thinking. Tell him we're . . . Tell him I'll make sure he's okay, I can get him out. We *have* to. I know he's afraid with everything going on, but he's got no chance on his own. Keep this to yourself, Corwi.'

'Jesus, you're determined to fuck my career.' She sounded tired. I waited silently until I was sure she would do it.

'Thank you. Just trust me he'll understand and please don't ask me anything. Tell him we know more now. Shit, I can't go into this.' A loud burst from the sequined Ute Lemper look-alike made me wince. 'Just tell him we know more and tell him he has to call us.' I looked around as if inspiration might jump to me, and it did. 'What's Yallya's mobile number?' I asked Dhatt.

'Huh?'

'He doesn't want to call us on mine or yours, so just . . .' He recited it to me and I to Corwi. 'Tell our mystery man to call *that* number, and we can help him. And you call me back on that, too, okay? From tomorrow on.'

'What the fuck?' said Dhatt. 'What the fuck are you doing?'

'You're going to have to borrow her phone; we need one so Bowden can find us – he's too scared to, we don't know who's listening to ours. If he contacts us, you might have to . . .' I hesitated.

'What?'

'Jesus, Dhatt, not *now*, okay? Corwi?'

She was gone, the line disconnected, by her or by the old exchanges.

CHAPTER TWENTY-ONE

I EVEN CAME WITH DHATT into his office the next day. 'The more you're a no-show, the more people wonder what the fuck's going on and the more they're going to notice you,' he said. As it was there were plenty of stares from his office colleagues. I nodded at the two who had tried halfheartedly to start an altercation with me.

'I'm getting paranoid,' I said.

'Oh no, they're really watching you. Here.' He handed me Yallya's cell phone. 'I think that's the last time you're getting invited to supper.'

'What did she say?'

'What do you think? It's her fucking phone; she was seriously pissed off. I told her we needed it, she told me to fuck off, I begged, she said no, I took it and blamed you.'

'Can we get hold of a uniform? For Yolanda ...' We huddled over his computer. 'Might get her through easier.' I watched him use his more up-to-date version of Windows. The first time Yallya's phone rang we froze and looked at each other. A number appeared that neither of us knew. I connected without a word, still meeting his eyes.

'Yall? Yall?' A woman's voice in Illitan. 'It's Mai, are you ... Yall?'

'Hello, this isn't Yallya actually . . .'

'Oh, hey, Qussim . . .?' but her voice faltered. 'Who is this?'
He took it from me.

'Hello? Mai, hey. Yeah, he's a friend of mine. No, well spotted. I had to borrow Yall's phone for a day or two, have you tried the house? Alright then, take care.' The screen went dark and he handed it back. 'That's another fucking reason you can field this shit. You're going to get a pissload of calls from her friends asking you if you still want to go for that facial or if you've seen the Tom Hanks movie.'

After the second and third such call, we no longer started when the cell rang. There were not many, however, despite what Dhatt said, and none on those topics. I imagined Yallya on her office phone, making countless angry calls denouncing her husband and his friend for the inconvenience.

'Do we want to put her in a uniform?' Dhatt spoke low.

'You're going to be in yours, right? Isn't it always best to hide in plain sight?'

'You want one too?'

'Is it a bad idea?'

He shook his head slowly. 'It'll make life easier for some of it . . . I think I can get through my side on police papers and my say-so.' *Militsya*, let alone senior detectives, trumped Ul Qoman border guards, without much trouble. 'Alright.'

'I'll do the talking at the Besźel entrance.'

'Is Yolanda okay?'

'Aikam's with her. I can't go back . . . Not again. Every time we do . . .' We still had no idea how, or by whom, we might be watched.

Dhatt moved too much, and after the third or fourth time he had snapped at one of his colleagues for some imagined

268

infraction I made him come with me for an early lunch. He glowered and would not speak, staring at everyone who passed us.

'Will you stop?' I said.

'I am going to be so fucking glad when you're gone,' he said. Yallya's phone rang and I held it to my ear without speaking.

'Borlú?' I tapped the table for Dhatt's attention, pointed at the phone.

'Bowden, where are you?'

'I'm keeping myself safe, Borlú.' He spoke in Besź to me.

'You don't sound like you feel safe.'

'Of course not. I'm not safe, am I? The question is, how much trouble am I in?' His voice was very strained.

'I can get you out.' Could I? Dhatt shrugged an exaggerated *what the fuck?* 'There are ways out. Tell me where you are.'

He sort of laughed. 'Right,' he said. 'I'll just tell you where I am.'

'What else do you propose? You can't spend your life in hiding. Get out of Ul Qoma and I can maybe do something. Besźel's my turf.'

'You don't even know what's going on . . .'

'You've got one chance.'

'Help me like you did Yolanda?'

'She's not stupid,' I said. 'She's letting me help.'

'What? You've *found* her? What . . .'

'Like I told you, I told her. I can't help either of you here. I *might* be able to help you in Besźel. Whatever's going on, whoever's after you . . .' He tried to say something, but I did not let him. 'I know people there. Here I can't do a thing. Where are you?'

269

'. . . Nowhere. Doesn't matter. I'll . . . Where are *you*? I don't want to —'

'You've done well to stay out of sight this long. But you can't do it forever.'

'No. No. I'll find you. Are you . . . crossing now?'

I couldn't help glancing around and lowering my voice again. 'Soon.'

'When?'

'Soon. I'll tell you when I know. How do I contact you?'

'You don't, Borlú. I'll contact you. Keep this phone.'

'What if you miss me?'

'I'll just have to call every couple of hours. I'm afraid I'm going to have to *bother* you, a lot.' He disconnected. I stared at Yallya's phone, looked up at last at Dhatt.

'Do you have any fucking idea how much I hate not knowing where I can look?' Dhatt whispered. 'Who I can trust?' He shuffled papers. 'What I should be saying to whom?'

'I do.'

'What's going on?' he said. 'Does he want out too?'

'He wants out too. He's afraid. He doesn't trust us.'

'I don't blame him one bit.'

'Neither do I.'

'I don't have any papers for him.' I met his eye and waited. 'Holy *Light*, Borlú, you going to fucking . . .' He whispered furiously. 'Alright, alright, I'll see what I can do.'

'Tell *me* what to do,' I said to him, without breaking my gaze, 'who to call, what corners to cut, and you can fucking blame me. Blame me, Dhatt. *Please*. But bring a uniform in case he comes.' I watched him, poor man, agonise.

It was after 7 p.m. that night that Corwi called me. 'We're go,' she said. 'I've got the paperwork.'

270

'Corwi, I owe you, I owe you.'

'Do you think I don't know that, boss? It's you, your guy Dhatt, and his ahem "colleague," right? I'll be waiting.'

'Bring your ID and be ready to back me up with Immigration. Who else? Who else knows?'

'No one. I'm your designated driver, again, then. What time?'

The question, what is the best way to disappear? There must be a graph, a carefully plotted curve. Is something more invisible if there are no others around, or if it is one of many? 'Not too late. Not like two in the morning.'

'I'm glad to fucking hear it.'

'We'd be the only ones there. But not in the middle of the day either; there's too much risk someone might know us or something.' After dark. 'Eight,' I said. 'Tomorrow evening.' It was winter and the nights came early. There would be crowds still, but in the dim colours of evening, sleepy. Easy not to see.

IT WAS NOT ALL LEGERDEMAIN; there were tasks we should and did perform. Reports of progress to finesse, and families to contact. I watched and with occasional over-the-shoulder suggestions helped Dhatt construct a letter saying polite and regretful nothing to Mr. and Mrs. Geary, whose main liaison now was with the Ul Qoma *militsya*. It was not a good feeling of power, to be present a ghost in that holding message, knowing them, seeing them from inside the words which would be like one-way glass, so they could not look back in and see me, one of the writers.

I told Dhatt a place – I did not know the address, had to describe it in vague topography, which he recognised – a piece of parkland walking distance from where Yolanda hid, to meet

271

me at the end of the following day. 'Anyone asks, tell them I'm working from the hotel. Tell them about all the ridiculous paperwork hoops they make us jump through in Besźel, that keep me busy.'

'It's all we ever fucking talk about, Tyad.' Dhatt could not stay in one place, he was so anxious, so frenetic with lack of trust, in anything, so troubled. He did not know where to look. 'Blame you or not, I'm going to be on school liaison for the rest of my fucking career.'

We had agreed there was a good possibility we would not hear from Bowden again, but I got a call on poor Yallya's phone half an hour after midnight. I was sure it was Bowden though he said nothing. He called again just before seven the next morning.

'You sound bad, Doctor.'

'What's happening?'

'What do you want to do?'

'Are you going? Is Yolanda with you? Is she coming?'

'You have one shot, Doctor.' I scribbled times on my notepad. 'If you're not going to let me come for you. You want out, be outside the main traffic gate of Copula Hall at seven p.m.'

I disconnected. I tried to make notes, plans on paper, could not. Bowden did not call me back. I kept the phone on the table or in my hand throughout my early breakfast. I did not check out of the hotel – no telegraphing of movements. I sorted through my clothes for anything I could not afford to leave, and there was nothing. I carried my illegal volume of *Between the City and the City*, and that was all.

I took almost the whole day to get to Yolanda and Aikam's hide. My last day in Ul Qoma. I took taxis in stages to the ends of the city. 'How long you staying?' the last driver asked me.

'A couple of weeks.'

'You like it here,' he said, in enthusiastic beginner's Illitan. 'Best city in the world.' He was Kurdish.

'Show me your favourite parts of town, then. You don't get trouble?' I said. 'Not everyone's welcoming to foreigners, I heard . . .'

He made a pooh-poohing noise. 'Are fools all over everywhere, but is the best city.'

'How long have you been here?'

'Four years and some. I was one year in camp . . .'

'A refugee camp?'

'Yeah, in the camp, and three years study for Ul Qoma citizenship. Speaking Illitan and learning, you know, not to, you know, to unsee the other place, so not to breach.'

'Did you ever think of going to Besźel?'

Another snort. 'What's in Besźel? Ul Qoma is the best place.'

He took me first past the Orchidarium and the Xhincis Kann Stadium, a tourist route he had obviously taken before, and when I encouraged him to indulge more personal preferences he started to show me the community gardens where alongside Ul Qoman natives those Kurds, Pakistanis, Somalis and Sierra Leoneans who got through the stringent conditions for entry played chess, the various communities regarding each other with courteous uncertainty. At a crossroads of canals he, careful not to say anything unequivocally illegal, pointed out to me where the barges of the two cities – pleasure craft in Ul Qoma, a few working transport boats unseen in Besźel – wove between each other.

'You see?' he said.

A man on the opposite side of a nearby lock, half-hidden in people and little urban trees, was looking straight at us. I met his eye – for a moment I was not sure but then decided he must be in Ul Qoma, so it was not breach – until he looked away. I tried to watch where he went, but he was gone.

When I expressed choices between the various sights the driver proposed, I made sure the resulting route crisscrossed the city. I watched the mirrors as he, delighted with this fare, drove. If we were followed it was by very sophisticated and careful spies. I paid him a ridiculous amount, in a much harder currency than I was paid in, after three hours of escorting, and I had him drop me where back-street hackers abutted cheap secondhand shops, around the corner from the estate where Yolanda and Aikam hid.

For moments I thought they had skipped out on me, and I closed my eyes, but I kept repeating in a whisper up close to the door, 'It's me, it's Borlú, it's me,' and at last it opened, and Aikam ushered me in.

'Get ready,' I said to Yolanda. She looked dirty to me, thinner and more startled like an animal than even when I had last seen her. 'Get your papers. Be ready to agree with whatever me or my colleagues say to anyone at the border. And get lover-boy used to the idea that he's not coming, because we're not having a scene at Copula Hall. We're getting you out.'

SHE MADE HIM STAY IN THE ROOM. He looked as if he would not do as she asked, but she made him. I did not trust him to be unobtrusive.

He demanded to know again and again why he could not come. She showed him where she had his number, and she swore that she would call him from Besźel, and from Canada, and that she would call for him there. It took her several such promises until he stood at last miserable as a neglected thing, staring as we closed the door on him and walked fast through the shadowing light to the corner of the park, where Dhatt was waiting in an unmarked police car.

'Yolanda.' He nodded to her from the driver's seat. 'Pain in my arse.' He nodded to me. We set off. 'What the fuck? Who exactly *have* you pissed off, Miss Rodriguez? You've got me fucking my life and collaborating with this foreign wacko. There's clothes in the back,' he said. 'Course I'm out of work, now.' He very well might not be exaggerating.

Yolanda stared at him until he glanced into the mirror and snapped at her, 'For fuck's sake, what, you think I'm *peeping?*' and she scootched down in the rear seat and began to wriggle out of her clothes, replacing them with the *militsya* uniform he had brought for her, that almost fit.

'Miss Rodriguez, do as I say and stick close. There's fancy dress for our possible-other-guest too. And that's for you, Borlú. Might save us a bit of shit.' A jacket with a fold-down *militsya* blazon on it. I made it visible. 'I wish they had rank on them. I'd've fucking demoted you.'

He did not meander, nor make the mistake of the guilty nervous and drive more slowly, more carefully than the cars around us. We took the main streets, and he flicked on and off the headlights at other drivers' infractions as Ul Qoman drivers do, little messages of road-rage code like aggressive Morse, *flick flick, you cut me up, flick flick flick, make up your mind.*

'He called again,' I said to Dhatt quietly. 'He might be there. In which case . . .'

'Come on, pain in my arse, say it again. In which case he's going over, right?'

275

'He's got to get out. Did you get spare papers?'

He swore and punched the steering wheel. 'Fuck I really wish I'd thought of a way to talk myself out of this fucking shit. I hope he doesn't come. I hope fucking Orciny *does* get him.' Yolanda stared at him. 'I'll sound out whoever's on duty. Get ready to crack out your wallet. If push comes to shove I'll give him my fucking papers.'

We saw Copula Hall over the roofs and through cables of telephone exchanges and gasrooms many minutes before we arrived at it. The way we came, we first passed, as unseeing as we could, the building's rear-to-Ul Qoma, its entryway in Besźel, the queues of Besź and returning Ul Qoman passengers siphoning in in patient dudgeon. A Besź police light was flashing. We were obliged not to and did not see any of it, but we could not but be aware as we did so that we would be on that side soon. We rounded the huge building to its Ul Maidin Avenue entrance, opposite the Temple of Inevitable Light, where the slow line into Besźel proceeded. There Dhatt parked – a bad job not corrected, skewed from the kerb with the swagger of *militsya*, keys hanging ready – and we emerged to cross through the night crowds towards the great forecourt and the borders of Copula Hall.

The outer guards of *militsya* did not ask a thing or even speak to us as we cut across the lines of people, walked over the roads weaving through stationary traffic, only ushered us through the restricted gates and on into the grounds proper of Copula Hall, where the huge edifice waited to eat us.

I looked everywhere as we came. Our eyes never stopped moving. I walked behind Yolanda, moving uneasily in her disguise. I raised my stare above the sellers of food and tat, the guards, the tourists, the homeless men and women, the other

276

militsya. Of the many entrances we had chosen the most open, wide and unconvoluted under a vault of old brickwork, with a view clear through the yawning interstitial space, over the mass of crowds filling the great chamber on both sides of the checkpoint – though more, noticeably, on the Besźel side, wanting to come in to Ul Qoma.

From this position, this vantage angle, for the first time in a long time we did not have to unsee the neighbouring city: we could stare along the road that linked Ul Qoma to it, over the border, the metres of no-man's-land and the border beyond, directly into Besźel itself. Straight ahead. Blue lights awaited us. A Besź bruise just visible beyond the lowered gate between the states, the flashing we had unseen minutes before. As we passed the outer fringes of Copula Hall's architecture, I saw at the far end of the hall standing on the raised platform where the Besź guards watched the crowds a figure in *policzai* uniform. A woman – she was very distant yet, on the Besźel side of the gates.

'Corwi.' I did not know I'd said her name aloud until Dhatt said to me, 'That her?' I was about to tell him it was too far off to know, but he said to me, 'Hold on a second.'

He was looking back the way we had come. We stood somewhat apart from most of those heading into Besźel, between lines of aspirant travellers and on a thin fringe of pavement vehicles travelling slowly. There was, Dhatt was right, something about one of the men behind us that was disconcerting. There was nothing about his appearance which stood out: he was bundled against the cold in a drab Ul Qoman cloak. But he walked or shuffled towards us somewhat across the directionality of the line of his fellow pedestrians, and I saw behind him disgruntled faces. He was pushing out of his turn, walking towards us. Yolanda saw where we were looking, and gave a little whimper.

'Come on,' Dhatt said, and put his hand to her back and walked her more quickly towards the entrance of the tunnel, but seeing how the figure behind us tried as far as the constraints of those around him would permit to raise his speed as well, to exceed our own, to come towards us, I turned around suddenly and began to move toward him.

'Get her over there,' I said to Dhatt behind me, without looking. 'Go, get her to the border. Yolanda, go to the *policzai* woman over there.' I accelerated. 'Go.'

'Wait,' Yolanda said to me but I heard Dhatt remonstrate with her. I was focused now on the approaching man. He could not fail to see that I was coming towards him, and he hesitated and reached into his jacket, and I fumbled at my side but remembered I had no gun in that city. The man backed up a step or two. The man threw up his hands and unwrapped his scarf. He was shouting my name. It was Bowden.

He pulled out something, a pistol dangling in his fingers as if he were allergic to it. I dived for him and heard a hard exhalation behind me. Behind me another spat-out breath and screams. Dhatt shouted and shouted my name.

Bowden was staring over my shoulder. I looked behind me. Dhatt was crouched between cars a few metres away. He was wrapping himself up in himself and bellowing. Motorists were hunched in their vehicles. Their screams were spreading to the lines of pedestrian travellers in Beszel and in Ul Qoma. Dhatt huddled over Yolanda. She lay as if tossed. I could not see her clearly, but there was blood across her face. Dhatt was gripping his shoulder.

'I'm hit!' he shouted. 'Yolanda's ... Light, Tyad, she's shot, she's down ...'

A commotion started in the hall a long way off. Over the sedately moving traffic I saw at the farthest end of the enormous room a surge in the crowd in Besźel, a movement like animal panic. People scattering away from a figure, who leaned on, no, raised, something in both hands. Aiming, a rifle.

CHAPTER TWENTY-TWO

ANOTHER OF THOSE ABRUPT LITTLE SOUNDS, hardly audible over the rising screams the length of the tunnel. A shot, silenced or muffled by acoustics, but by the time I heard it I was on Bowden and had pushed him down, and the explosive percussion of the bullet into the wall behind him was louder than the shot itself. Architecture sprayed. I heard Bowden's panicked breath, put my hand on his wrist and squeezed until he dropped his weapon, kept him down out of the sightline of the sniper targeting him.

'Down! Everybody down!' I was shouting that. So sluggishly it was hard to believe, the crowds were falling to their knees, their cowering and their screams more and more exaggerated as they realised the danger. Another sound and another, a car braking violently and with an alarm, another implosive gasp as bricks took a bullet.

I kept Bowden on the tarmac. 'Tyad!' It was Dhatt.

'Talk to me,' I shouted to him. The guards were all over the place, raising weapons, looking everywhere, yelling idiot point-less orders at each other.

'I'm hit, I'm okay,' he replied. 'Yolanda's head-shot.'

I looked up, no more firing. I looked up further, to where Dhatt rolled and gripped his wound, to where Yolanda lay

280

dead. Rose slightly more and saw *militsya* approaching Dhatt and the corpse he guarded, and way off *policzai* running towards where the shots had come from. In Besźel the police were buffeted and blocked by the hysterical crowd. Corwi was looking in all directions – could she see me? I was shouting. The shooter was running.

His way was blocked, but he swung his rifle like a club when he had to, and people were clearing from around him. Orders would be going out to block the entrance, but how fast would they go? He was moving into a part of the crowd who had not seen him shoot, and were surrounding him, and good as he was he would drop or hide his weapon.

'God *damn* it.' I could hardly see him. No one was stopping him. He had some way to go before he was out. I looked, carefully, item by item, at his hair and clothes: cropped; grey tracksuit top with a hood behind; black trousers. All nondescript. Did he drop his weapon? He was into the crowd.

I stood holding Bowden's gun. A ridiculous P38, but loaded and well kept. I stepped towards the checkpoint, but there was no way I could get through it, all that chaos, not ever and not now with both lines of guards in uproar flailing guns around; even if my Ul Qoman uniform got me through the Ul Qoman lines, the Besź would stop me, and the shooter was too far for me to catch. I hesitated. 'Dhatt, radio help, watch Bowden,' I shouted, then turned and ran the other way, out into Ul Qoma, towards Dhatt's car.

The crowds got out of my way; they saw me coming with my *militsya* emblazoning, saw the pistol I held, and scattered. The *militsya* saw one of their own, in pursuit of something, and did not stop me. I turned the emergency lights on and started the engine.

I sent the car breakneck, dodging local and foreign cars, screaming outside the length of Copula Hall. The siren confused me, I was not used to Ul Qoman sirens, a *ya ya ya* more whining than our own cars'. The shooter was, must be, fighting his way through the terrified and confused thronging tunnel of travellers. My lights and alarm cleared the roads before me, ostentatiously in Ul Qoma, on the topolganger streets in Besźel with the typical unstated panic of a foreign drama. I yanked the wheel and the car snapped right, bumped over Besź tram tracks.

Where was Breach? But no breach had occurred.

No breach had occurred though a woman had been killed, brazenly, across a border. Assault, a murder and an attempted murder, but those bullets had travelled across the checkpoint itself, in Copula Hall, across the meeting place. A heinous, complex, vicious killing, but in the assiduous care the assassin had taken – to position himself just so at the point where he could stare openly along the last metres of Besźel over the physical border and *into* Ul Qoma, could aim precisely down this one conduit between the cities – that murder had been committed with if anything a *surplus* of care for the cities' boundaries, the membrane between Ul Qoma and Besźel. There was no breach, Breach had no power here, and only Besź police were in the same city as the killer now.

I turned right again. I was back where we had been an hour before, in Weipay Street in Ul Qoma, which shared the cross-hatched latitude-longitude with the Besź entrance to Copula Hall. I drove the car as close as the crowds let me, braked hard. I got out and jumped on its roof – it would not be long before Ul Qoman police would come to ask me, their supposed colleague, what I was doing, but now I jumped on the roof. After a second's hesitation I did not stare into the tunnel at the oncoming Besź escaping the attack. I looked instead all around, into Ul Qoma, and then in the direction of the hall, not changing my expression, giving away nothing that suggested that I might be looking anywhere other than at Ul Qoma. I was unimpeachable. The car's stuttering police lights turned my legs red and blue.

I let myself notice what was happening in Besźel. Many more travellers were still trying to enter Copula Hall than leave it, but as the panic within spread there was a dangerous contraflow. There was commotion, lines backing up, those behind who did not know what it was they had seen or heard blocking those who knew very well and were trying to flee. Ul Qomans unsaw the Besź melee, looked away and crossed the road to avoid the foreign trouble.

'Get out, get out—'

'Let us in, what's . . .?'

Among the clots and grots of panicked escapees I saw a hurrying man. He caught my attention by the care with which he tried not to run too fast, not to be too large, to raise his head. I believed it was, then that it was not, then that it was, the shooter. Pushing his way past a last shouting family and a chaotic line of Besź *policzai* trying to impose order without knowing what it was they should do. Pushing his way out and turning, walking with his hurried careful step away.

I must have made a sound. Certainly those scores of yards away the killer glanced backwards. I saw him see me and reflexively unsee, because of my uniform, because I was in Ul Qoma, but even as he dropped his eyes he recognised something and walked even faster away. I had seen him before, I could not think where. I looked around desperately, but none of the *policzai* in Besźel knew to follow him, and I was in Ul Qoma. I jumped off the roof of the car and walked quickly after the murderer.

Ul Qomans I shoved out of the way: Besź tried to unsee me but had to scurry to get out of my path. I saw their startled looks. I moved faster than the killer. I kept my eyes not on him but looking at some spot or other in Ul Qoma that put him in my field of vision. I tracked him without focusing, just legally. I crossed the plaza and two Ul Qoman *militsya* I passed called some tentative query at me which I ignored.

The man must have heard the sound of my step. I had come within a few tens of metres when he turned. His eyes widened in astonishment at the sight of me, which, careful even then, he did not hold. He registered me. He looked back into Besźel and sped up, trotting diagonally away toward ErmannStrász, a high street, behind a Kolyub-bound tram. In Ul Qoma, the road we were on was Saq Umir Way. I accelerated too.

He glanced back again and went faster, jogging through the Besź crowds, looking quickly to either side into the cafés lit by coloured candles, into the bookshops of Besźel – in Ul Qoma these were quieter alleys. He should have entered a shop. Perhaps he did not because there were crosshatched crowds he would have to negotiate on both pavements, perhaps his body rebelled at dead ends, cul-de-sacs, while pursued. He began to run.

The murderer ran left, into a smaller alley, where still I followed him. He was fast. He was faster than me now. He ran like a soldier. The distance between us grew. The stallholders and walkers in Besź stared at the killer; those in Ul Qoma stared at me. My quarry vaulted a bin that blocked his way, with greater ease than I knew I would manage. I knew where he was going. The Old Towns of Besźel and Ul Qoma are closely crosshatched: reach their edges, separations begin, alter and total areas. This was not, could not be, a chase. It was only two accelerations. We ran, he in his city, me close behind him, full of rage, in mine.

I shouted wordlessly. An old woman stared at me. I was not looking at him, I was still not looking at him, but fervently, legally, at Ul Qoma, its lights, graffiti, pedestrians, always at Ul Qoma. He was by iron rails curled in traditional Besź style. He was too far. He was by a total street, a street in Besźel only. He paused to look up in my direction as I gasped for breath.

For that sliver of time, too short for him to be accused of any crime, but certainly deliberate, he looked right at me. I knew him, I did not know from where. He looked at me at the threshold to that abroad-only geography and made a tiny triumphant smile. He stepped toward space where no one in Ul Qoma could go.

I raised the pistol and shot him.

I SHOT HIM IN THE CHEST. I saw his astonishment as he fell. Screaming from everywhere, at the shot, first, then his body and the blood, and almost instantly from all the people who had seen, at the terrible kind of transgression.

'Breach.'

'Breach.'

I thought it was the shocked declaration by those who had witnessed the crime. But unclear figures emerged where there had been no purposeful motion instants before, only the milling of no ones, the aimless and confused, and those suddenly appeared newcomers with faces so motionless I hardly

285

recognised them as faces were saying the word. It was statement of both crime and identity.

'*Breach.*' A grim-featured something gripped me so that there was no way I could break out, had I wanted to. I glimpsed dark shapes draped over the body of the killer I had killed. A voice close up to my ear. '*Breach.*' A force shoving me effortlessly out of my place, fast fast past candles of Beszàel and the neon of Ul Qoma, in directions that made sense in neither city.

'Breach,' and something touched me and I went under into black, out of waking and all awareness, to the sound of that word.

PART THREE

BREACH

CHAPTER TWENTY-THREE

IT WAS NOT A SOUNDLESS DARK. It was not without intrusions. There were presences within it that asked me questions I could not answer, questions I was aware of as urgencies at which I failed. Those voices again and again said to me, *Breach.* What had touched me sent me not into mindless silence but into a dream arena where I was quarry.

I REMEMBERED THAT LATER. In the moment I woke it was without a sense of time having passed. I closed my eyes in the crosshatched streets of the Old Towns; I opened them again and gasped for breath and looked into a room.

It was grey, without adornment. It was a small room. I was in a bed, no, on it. I lay on top of the sheets in clothes I did not recognise. I sat up.

Grey floor in scuffed rubber, a window admitting light at me, tall grey walls, stained in places and cracked. A desk and two chairs. Like a shabby office. A dark glass half-globe in the ceiling. There was no sound at all.

I was blinking, standing, nowhere near as groggy as I felt I should have been. The door was locked. The window was too high for me to see through. I jumped up, which did send a little spin through my head, but I saw only sky. The clothes I wore were clean and terribly nondescript. They fit me well enough. I remembered what had been with me in the dark, then, and my heart and my breath began to speed.

The soundlessness was enervating. I gripped the lower rim of the window and pulled myself up, my arms trembling. With nothing on which to brace my feet I could not stay in the position long. Roofs spread out below me. The slates, satellite dishes, flat concrete, ajut girders and antennae, the onion domes, corkscrew towers, gasrooms, the backs of what might be gargoyles. I could not tell where I was, nor what might be listening beyond the glass, guarding me from outside.

'Sit.'

I dropped hard at the voice. I struggled to my feet and turned.

Someone stood in the doorway. Light behind him, he was a cutout of darkness, a lack. When he stepped forward he was a man fifteen or twenty years my senior. Tough and squat, in clothes as vague as my own. There were others behind him: a woman my age, another man a little older. Their faces were without anything approaching expressions. They looked like people-shaped clay in the moments before God breathed out.

'Sit.' The older man pointed to a chair. 'Come out of the corner.'

It was true. I was flattened into the corner. I realised it. I slowed my lungs and stood straighter. I took my hands away from the walls. I stood like a proper person.

After a long time I said, 'How embarrassing.' Then, 'Excuse me.' I sat where the man indicated. When I could control my voice I said, 'I'm Tyador Borlú. And you?'

He sat and looked at me, his head to one side, abstract and curious like a bird.

'Breach,' he said.

'BREACH,' I SAID. I took a shaky breath. 'Yes, Breach.'

Finally he said, 'What were you expecting? What are you expecting?' Was that too much? Another time I might have been able to tell. I was looking around nervily as if to catch sight of something almost invisible in the corners. He pointed his right hand at me fork-fingered, index and middle digits one at each of my eyes, then at his own: *Look at me.* I obeyed.

The man glanced at me from under his brows. 'The situation,' he said. I realised we were both speaking Besź. He did not sound quite Besź, nor Ul Qoman, but was certainly not European or North American. His accent was flat.

'You breached, Tyador Borlú. Violently. You killed a man by it.' He watched me again. 'You shot from Ul Qoma right into Beszel. So you are in the Breach.' He folded his hands together. I watched how his thin bones moved under his skin: just like mine. 'His name was Yorjavic. The man you killed. Do you remember him?'

'I . . .'

'You knew him from before.'

'How do you know?'

'You told us. It's up to us how you go under, how long you stay there, what you see and say while you're there, when you come out again. If you come out. Where did you know him from?'

I shook my head but – 'The True Citizens,' I said suddenly. 'He was there when I questioned them.' Who had called Gosz the lawyer. One of the tough, cocky nationalist men.

'He was a soldier,' the man said. 'Six years in the BAF. A sniper.'

No surprise. It was an amazing shot. 'Yolanda!' I looked up. 'Jesus, Dhatt. What happened?'

'Senior Detective Dhatt will never fully move his right arm again, but he's recovering. Yolanda Rodriguez is dead.' He watched me. 'What hit Dhatt was intended for her. It was the second shot that went through her head.'

'God *damn*.' For seconds I could only look down. 'Do her family know?'

'They know.'

'Was anyone else hit?'

'No. Tyador Borlú, you breached.'

'He *killed* her. You don't know what else he's—' The man sat back. I was already nodding an apology, a hopelessness, when he said, 'Yorjavic didn't breach, Borlú. He shot over the border, in Copula Hall. He never breached. Lawyers might have an argument: was the crime committed in Besźel where he pulled the trigger, or Ul Qoma where the bullets hit? Or both?' He held out his hands in an elegant *who cares?* 'He never breached. You did. So you are here, now, in the Breach.'

WHEN THEY LEFT, food came. Bread, meat, fruit, cheese, water. When I had eaten I pushed and pulled at the door, but there was no way I could move it. I fingertipped its paint, but it was only splitting paint or its messages were in a more arcane code than I could decrypt.

Yorjavic was not the first man I had shot, nor even the first I had killed, but I had not killed many. I had never before shot someone not raising a gun at me. I waited for shakes. My heart was slamming but it was with where I was, not guilt.

292

I was alone a long time. I walked the room every way, watched the globe-hidden camera. I pulled myself up to stare out of the window at the roofs again. When the door opened again, it was twilight looking down. The same trio entered.

'Yorjavic,' the older man said, in Besź again. 'He did breach in one way. When you shot him you made him. Victims of breach always breach. He interacted hard with Ul Qoma. So we know about him. He had instructions from somewhere. Not from the True Citizens. Here's how it is,' he said. 'You breached, so you're ours.'

'What happens now?'

'Whatever we want. Breach, and you belong to us.'

They could disappear me without difficulty. There were only rumours about what that would mean. No one ever heard even stories about those who had been taken by Breach and – what? – served their time. Such people must be impressively secretive, or never released.

'Because you may not see the justice of what we do doesn't mean it's unjust, Borlú. Think of this, if you want, as your trial.

'Tell us what you did and why, and we might see ways to perform actions. We have to fix a breach. There are investigations to be carried out: we can talk to those who haven't breached, if it's relevant and we prove it. Understand? There are less and more severe sanctions. We have your record. You're police.'

What was he saying? Does that make us colleagues? I did not speak.

'Why did you do this? Tell us. Tell us about Yolanda Rodriguez, and tell us about Mahalia Geary.'

I said nothing for a long time but had no plan. 'You know? What do you know?'

'Borlú.'

'What's out there?' I pointed at the door. They had left it a little open.

'You know where you are,' he said. 'What's out there you'll see. Under what conditions depends on what you say and do now. Tell us what got you here. This fool's conspiracy that's recurred, for the first time in a long time. Borlú, tell us about Orciny.'

THE SEPIA ILLUMINATION from the corridor was all they let light me, in a wedge, a slice of inadequate glow that kept my interrogator in shade. It took hours to tell them the case. I did not dissemble because they must already know everything.

'Why did you breach?' the man said.

'I hadn't meant to. I wanted to see where the shooter went.'

'That was breach then. He was in Besźel.'

'Yes, but you know. You know that happens all the time. When he smiled, the look he had, I just . . . I was thinking about Mahalia and Yolanda . . .' I paced closer to the door.

'How did he know you'd be there?'

'I don't know,' I said. 'He's a nat, and a crazy one, but he's obviously got contacts.'

'Where is *Orciny* supposed to be in this?'

We looked at each other. 'I've told you everything I know,' I said. I held my face in my hands, looked over my fingertips. It looked as if the man and woman in the doorway weren't paying attention. I ran hard at them, I thought without any warning. One – I do not know which – hooked me in midair and sent me across the room into the wall and down. Someone hit me, the woman it must be, because my head was tugged

294

up and the man stood leaning still in the doorway. The older man sat at the table waiting.

The woman straddled my back and held me in some neck-lock. 'Borlú, you are in Breach. This room is where your trial is taking place,' the older man said. 'This can be where it's finished. You're beyond law now; this is where decision lives, and we are it. Once more. Tell us how this case, these people, these murders, connects to this story of Orciny.'

After many seconds he said to the woman, 'What are you doing?'

'He's not choking,' she said.

I was, so far as her hold would allow, laughing.

'This isn't about me,' I said at last, when I was able. 'My God. You're investigating Orciny.'

'There is no such place as Orciny,' the man said.

'So everyone tells me. And yet things keep happening, people keep disappearing or dying, and there's that word again and again, Orciny.' The woman got off me. I sat on the floor and shook my head at it all.

'You know why she never came to you?' I said. 'Yolanda? She thought *you* were Orciny. If you said *How could there be a place between the city and the city?* she'd say *Do you believe in the Breach? Where's that?* But she was wrong, wasn't she? You're not Orciny.'

'There is no Orciny.'

'So why are you asking all this? What have I been running from for days? I just *saw* Orciny or something a lot like it shoot my partner. You know I've breached: what do you care about the rest of it? Why aren't you just punishing me?'

'As we say—'

'What, this is mercy? Justice? Please.'

'If there's something *else* between Besźel and Ul Qoma, where does that leave you? You're hunting. Because it's suddenly back. You don't know where Orciny is, or what's going on. You're . . .' *Hell with it.* 'You're afraid.'

THE YOUNGER MAN AND WOMAN left and returned with an old film projector, trailing a lead into the corridor. They fiddled with it and it hummed, and made the wall a screen. It projected scenes from an interrogation. I scooted back to see better, still sitting on the floor.

The subject was Bowden. A snap of static and he was speaking in Illitan, and I saw that his interrogators were *militsya*.

'. . . don't know what happened. Yes, *yes* I was hiding because someone was coming after me. Someone was trying to kill me. And when I heard Borlú and Dhatt were getting out, I didn't know if I could trust them but I thought maybe they could get me out too.'

'. . . have a gun?' The voice of the interrogator was muffled.

'Because someone was trying to kill me, is why. Yes, I had a gun. You can get one on half the street corners in East Ul Qoma, as well you know. I've lived here for years, you know.'

Something.

'No.'

'Why not?' That was audible.

'Because there is *no such thing as Orciny*,' Bowden said.

Something. 'Well, I don't give a damn what you think, or what Mahalia thought, or what Yolanda said, or what Dhatt's been insinuating, and no I have no idea who called me. But there's *no such place*.'

A big loud crack of distressed image-sound, and there was

296

Aikam. He was just weeping and weeping. Questions came, and he ignored them to weep.

The picture changed again and Dhatt was in Aikam's place. He was not in uniform and his arm was in a sling.

'I fucking do not know,' he shouted. 'Why the fuck are you asking me? Go get Borlú, because he seems to have a damn sight more of an idea what the fuck is going on than I do. Orciny? No I fucking don't, because I'm not a child, but here's the thing, *even though* it's goddamn obvious Orciny's a pile of shit, something is still going on, people are still getting hold of information they should not be able to, and other people are still being shot in the head by forces unknown. Fucking kids. *That* is why I agreed to help Borlú, illegal be fucked, so if you're going to take my badge go the fuck ahead. And be my guest – disbelieve in Orciny all you want, I fucking do. But keep your head down in case that nonexistent fucking city shoots you in the face. Where is Tyador? What've you done?'

The picture went still on the wall. The interrogators looked at me in the light of Dhatt's oversized monochrome snarl.

'So,' the older man said. He nodded at the wall. 'You heard Bowden. What's happening. What do you know about Orciny?'

THE BREACH WAS NOTHING. It is nothing. This is a commonplace; this is simple stuff. The Breach has no embassies, no army, no sights to see. The Breach has no currency. If you commit it it will envelop you. Breach is void full of angry police.

This trail that led and led again to Orciny suggested systemic transgression, secret para-rules, a parasite city where there should be nothing but nothing, nothing but Breach. If Breach was not Orciny, what would it be but a mockery of

297

itself, to have let that go for centuries? That was why my questioner, when he asked me *Does Orciny exist?*, put it like this, 'So, are we at war?'

I brought our collaboration to their attention. I, daring, bargained. 'I'll help you . . .' I kept saying, with a drawn-out pause, an ellipsis implying *if*. I wanted the killers of Mahalia Geary and Yolanda Rodriguez and they could tell that, but I was not too noble to bargain. That there was room to barter, a way, a small chance that I might get out of Breach again, was intoxicating.

'YOU ALMOST CAME for me once before,' I said. They had been watching, when I came grosstopically close to my house. 'So are we partners?' I said.

'You're a breacher. But it'll go better if you help us.'

'You really think Orciny killed them?' the other man said.

Would they finish with me when there was even a possibility that Orciny was here, emerging, and still unfound? Its population walking the streets, unseen by the populations of Besźel and Ul Qoma, each thinking they were in the other. Hiding like books in a library.

'What is it?' the woman said, seeing my face.

'I've told you what I know, and it's not much. It's Mahalia who really knew what was happening, and she's dead. But she left something behind. She told a friend. She told Yolanda that she'd realised the truth when she was going through her notes. We never found anything like that. But I know how she worked. I know where they are.'

CHAPTER TWENTY-FOUR

WE LEFT THE BUILDING – the station, call it – in the morning, me in the company of the older man, Breach, and I realised I did not know what city we were in.

I had stayed up much of the night watching films of interrogations, from Ul Qoma and from Beszél. A Besz border guard and an Ul Qoman, passersby from both cities who knew nothing. 'People started screaming . . .' Motorists over whom bullets had gone.

'Corwi,' I said, when her face appeared on the wall.

'So where is he?' A quirk of recording made her voice far away. She was angry and controlling herself. 'What the fuck has boss-man got himself into? Yes, he wanted me to help him get someone through.' That was all they established, repeatedly, her Besz questioners. They threatened her job. She was as contemptuous of that as Dhatt, though more careful how she phrased it. She knew nothing.

Breach showed me brief shots of someone questioning Biszaya and Sariska. Biszaya cried. 'I'm not impressed with this,' I said. 'This is just cruel.'

The most interesting films were those of Yorjavic's comrades among the extreme nationalists of Beszél. I recognised some who had been with Yorjavic. They stared sulky at their questioners, the *policzai*. A few refused to speak except in the company of their lawyers. There was hard questioning, an officer leaning across the table and punching a man in the face.

'Fuck's sake,' the bleeding man shouted. 'We're on the same fucking side, you fuck. You're Besź, you're not fucking Ul Qoman and you're not fucking Breach . . .'

With arrogance, neutrality, resentment or, often, compliance and collaboration, the nationalists denied any knowledge of Yorjavic's action. 'I've never fucking heard of this foreign woman; he never mentioned her. She's a student?' one said. 'We do what's right for Besźel, you know? And you don't have to know why. But . . .' The man we watched agonised with his hands, made shapes to try to explain himself without recrimination.

'We're fucking soldiers. Like you. For Besźel. So if you hear that something has to be done, if you get instructions, like someone has to be warned, reds or unifs or traitors or UQ or the fucking Breach-lickers are gathering or whatever, something has to be done, okay. But you know why. You don't ask, but you can see it's got to be done, most of the time. But I don't know why this Rodriguez girl . . . I don't believe he did and if he *did* I don't . . .' He looked angry. 'I don't know why.'

'Of course they have contacts in the deep state,' my Breach interlocutor said. 'But with something as hard to parse as this, you can see the possibility, that Yorjavic maybe wasn't a True Citizen. Or not only, but a representative of a more hidden organisation.'

'A more hidden place maybe,' I said. 'I thought you watched everything.'

'No one breached.' He put papers in front of me. 'Those

300

are the findings of the Besźel *policzai* who searched Yorjavic's apartment. Nothing linking him to anything like Orciny. Tomorrow we're leaving early.'

'How did you get all this?' I said as he and his companions stood. He looked at me with a motionless but withering face as he left.

HE RETURNED AFTER A SHORT NIGHT, alone this time. I was ready for him.

I waved the papers. 'Presuming my colleagues did a good job, there's nothing. A few payments come in time to time, but not that much – could be anything. He passed the exam a few years back, could cross – not so unusual, although with his politics . . .' I shrugged. 'Subscriptions, bookshelves, associates, army record, criminal record, hangouts, and all that mark him out as a run-of-the-mill violent nat.'

'Breach has watched him. Like all dissidents. There's been no sign of unusual connections.'

'Orciny, you mean.'

'No sign.'

He ushered me finally out of the room. The corridor had the same scabbing paint, a worn colourless carpet, a succession of doors. I heard the steps of others, and as we turned into a stairwell a woman passed us, with a moment's acknowledgement to my companion. Then a man passed, and then we were in a hallway with several other people. What they wore would be legal in either Besźel or in Ul Qoma.

I heard conversation in both languages and a third thing, a mongrel or antique that combined them. I heard typing. I never considered rushing or attacking my companion and trying to escape. I admit that. I was very observed.

On the walls of an office we passed were corkboards thick with memos, shelves of folders. A woman tore paper from a printer. A telephone rang.

'Come on,' the man said. 'You said you know where the truth is.'

There were double doors, doors to an outside. We stepped through, and that, when the light ate me up, was when I realised I did not know which city we were in.

AFTER PANIC AT THE CROSSHATCH, I realised we must be in Ul Qoma: that was where our destination was. I followed my escort down the street.

I was breathing deep. It was morning, noisy, overcast but without rain, boisterous. Cold: the air made me gasp. I was pleasantly disoriented by all the people, by the motion of coated Ul Qomans, the growl of cars moving slowly on this mostly pedestrian street, the shouts of hawkers, the sellers of clothes and books and food. I unsaw all else. There was the thrum of cables above us as one of the Ul Qoman inflates butted against the wind.

'I don't need to tell you not to run,' the man said. 'I don't need to tell you not to shout. You know I can stop you. And you know I'm not alone in watching you. You're in Breach. Call me Ashil.'

'You know my name.'

'While you're with me you're Tye.'

Tye, like Ashil, was not traditional Besź, nor Ul Qoman, could just plausibly be either. Ashil walked me across a courtyard, below facades of figures and bells, video screens with stock information. I did not know where we were.

'You're hungry,' Ashil said.

'I can wait.' He steered me to a side street, another cross-hatched side street where Ul Qoman stalls by a supermarket offered software and knickknacks. He took my arm and guided me, and I hesitated because there was no food in sight except, and I pulled against him a moment, there were dumpling stations and bread stalls, but they were in Besźel.

I tried to unsee them but there could be no uncertainty: that source of the smell I had been unsmelling was our destination. 'Walk,' he said, and he walked me through the membrane between cities; I lifted my foot in Ul Qoma, put it down again in Besźel, where breakfast was.

Behind us was an Ul Qoman woman with raspberry punk hair selling the unlocking of mobile phones. She glanced in surprise then consternation; then I saw her quickly unsee us as Ashil ordered food in Besźel.

Ashil paid with Besźmarques. He put the paper plate in my hand, walked me back across the road into the supermarket. It was in Ul Qoma. He bought a carton of orange juice with dinar, gave it to me.

I held the food and the drink. He walked me down the middle of the crosshatched road.

My sight seemed to untether as with a lurching Hitchcock shot, some trickery of dolly and depth of field, so the street lengthened and its focus changed. Everything I had been unseeing now jostled into sudden close-up.

Sound and smell came in: the calls of Besźel; the ringing of its clocktowers; the clattering and old metal percussion of the trams; the chimney smell; the old smells; they came in a tide with the spice and Illitan yells of Ul Qoma, the clatter of a *militsya* copter, the gunning of German cars. The colours of Ul Qoma light and plastic window displays no longer

303

effaced the ochres and stone of its neighbour, my home.

'Where are you?' Ashil said. He spoke so only I could hear. 'I . . .'

'Are you in Beszel or Ul Qoma?'

'. . . Neither. I'm in Breach.'

'You're with me here.' We moved through a crosshatched morning crowd. 'In Breach. No one knows if they're seeing you or unseeing you. Don't creep. You're not in neither: you're in both.'

He tapped my chest. 'Breathe.'

HE TOOK US BY METRO in Ul Qoma, where I sat still as if the remnants of Beszel clung to me like cobwebs and would frighten fellow passengers, out and onto a tram in Beszel, and it felt good, as if I were back home, misleadingly. We went by foot through either city. The feeling of Beszel familiarity was replaced by some larger strangeness. We stopped by the glass-and-steel frontage of UQ University Library.

'What would you do if I ran?' I said. He said nothing.

Ashil took out a nondescript leather holder and showed the guard the sigil of Breach. The man stared at it for seconds, then jumped to his feet.

'My God,' he said. He was an immigrant, from Turkey judging from his Illitan, but he had been here long enough to understand what he saw. 'I, you, what can I . . .?' Ashil pointed him back to his chair and walked on.

The library was newer than its Besz counterpart. 'It will have no classmark,' Ashil said.

'That's the point,' I said. We referred to the map and its legend. The histories of Beszel and Ul Qoma, carefully separately listed but shelved close to each other, were on the fourth floor. The students in their carrels looked at Ashil as he passed. There was in him an authority unlike that of parents or tutors.

Many of the titles we stood before were not translated, were in their original English or French. *The Secrets of the Precursor Age; The Literal and the Littoral: Besźel, Ul Qoma and Maritime Semiotics.* We scanned for minutes – there were many shelves. What I was looking for, and there at last on the second-to-top shelf three rows back from the main walkway found, pushing past a confused young undergraduate as if I were the one with authority here, was a book marked by lack. It was unadorned at the bottom of its spine with a printed category mark.

'Here.' The same edition I had had. That psychedelic doors-of-perception-style illustration, a long-haired man walking a street made patchwork from two different (and spurious) architectural styles, from the shadows of which watched eyes. I opened it in front of Ashil. *Between the City and the City.* Markedly worn.

'If all this is true,' I said quietly, 'then we're being watched. You and me, now.' I pointed to one of the pairs of eyes on the cover.

I riffled the pages. Ink flickers, most pages annotated in tiny scrawl: red, black, and blue. Mahalia had written in an extra-fine nib, and her notes were like tangled hair, years of annotations of the occult thesis. I glanced behind me, and Ashil did the same. No one was there.

NO, we read in her hand. NOT AT ALL, and REALLY? CF HARRIS ET AL, and LUNACY!! *MAD!!!* and so on. Ashil took it from me.

'She understood Orciny better than anyone,' I said. 'That's where she kept the truth.'

305

CHAPTER TWENTY-FIVE

'THEY'VE BOTH BEEN TRYING TO FIND OUT what's happened to you,' Ashil said. 'Corwi and Dhatt.'

'What did you tell them?'

A look: *We don't speak to them at all.* That evening he brought me colour copies, bound, of every page, and inside and outside covers, of Mahalia's Ul Qoma copy of *Between*. This was her notebook. With effort and attention, I could follow a particular line of reasoning from each tangled page, could track each of her readings in turn.

That evening Ashil walked with me in that both-cities. The sweep and curves of Ul Qoman byzanterie ajut over and around the low *mittel*-continental and middle-history brick-work of Beszel, its bas-relief figures of scarfed women and bombardiers, Beszel's steamed food and dark breads fugging with the hot smells of Ul Qoma, colours of light and cloth around grey and basalt tones, sounds now both abrupt, schwa-staccatoed-sinuous *and* throaty swallowing. Being in both cities had gone from being in Beszel and Ul Qoma to being in a third place, that nowhere-both, that Breach.

Everyone, in both cities, seemed tense. We had returned through the two crosshatched cities not to the offices where I had woken – they were in Rusai Bey in Ul Qoma or

TushasProspekta in Beszél, I had back-figured-out – but to another, a middling-smart apartment with a concierge's office, not too far from that larger HQ. On the top floor the rooms extended across what must be two or three buildings, and in the warrens of that, Breach came and went. There were anonymous bedrooms, kitchens, offices, outdated-looking computers, phones, locked cabinets. Terse men and women.

As the two cities had grown together, places, spaces had opened between them, or failed to be claimed, or been those controversial *dissensi*. Breach lived there.

'What if you get burgled? Doesn't that happen?'

'Time to time.'

'Then . . .'

'Then they're in Breach, and they're ours.'

The women and men stayed busy, carrying out conversations that fluctuated through Besź, Illitan, and the third form. The featureless bedroom into which Ashil put me had bars on its windows, another camera somewhere, for sure. There was an en-suite toilet. He did not leave. Another two or three Breach joined us.

'Look at this,' I said. 'You're evidence this could all be real.' The interstitiality which made Orciny so absurd to most citizens of Beszél and Ul Qoma was not only possible but inevitable. Why would Breach disbelieve life could thrive in that little gap? The anxiety was now rather something like *We have never seen them*, a very different concern.

'It can't be,' Ashil said.

'Ask your superiors. Ask the powers. I don't know.' What other, higher or lower, powers were there in Breach? 'You know we're watched. Or they were – Mahalia, Yolanda, Bowden – by something somewhere.'

'There's nothing linking the shooter to anything.' That was one of the others, speaking Illitan.

'Alright.' I shrugged. I spoke in Besź. 'So he was just a random, very lucky right-winger. If you say so. Or maybe you think it's insiles, doing this?' I said. None of them denied the existence of the fabled scavenging interstitial refugees. 'They used Mahalia, and when they were done they killed her. They killed Yolanda, in a way exactly so you couldn't chase them. As if of all the things in Besźel, Ul Qoma, or anywhere, what they're most scared of is Breach.'

'But' – a woman pointed at me – 'look what you did.'

'Breached?' I had given them a way in to whatever this war was. 'Yes. What did Mahalia know? She worked something out about what they had planned. They killed her.' The overlaid glimmer of nighttime Ul Qoma and Besźel lit me through the window. I made my ominous point to a growing audience of Breach, their faces like owls'.

They locked me in overnight. I read Mahalia's annotations. I could discern phases of annotation, though not in any page-wise chronology – all the notes were layered, a palimpsest of evolving interpretation. I did archaeology.

Early on, in the lowest layers of marks, her handwriting was more careful, the notes longer and neater, with more references to other writers and to her own essays. Her idiolect and unorthodox abbreviations made it hard to be sure. I started page on page trying to read, transcribe, those early thoughts. Mostly what I discerned was her anger.

I felt a something-stretched-out over the night streets. I wanted to talk to those I had known in Besźel or Ul Qoma, but I could only watch.

Whatever unseen bosses, if any, waited in the Breach's

bowels, it was Ashil who came for me again the next morning, found me going over and over those notes. He led me the length of a corridor to an office. I imagined running – no one seemed to be watching me. They would stop me, though. And if they did not, where would I go, hunted in-betweener refugee?

There were twelve or so Breach in the cramped room, sitting, standing, precarious on the edge of desks, low muttering in two or three languages. A discussion midway. Why was I shown this?

'. . . Gosharian says it hasn't, he just called . . .'

'What about SusurStrász? Wasn't there some talk . . .?'

'Yes, but everyone's accounted for.'

This was a crisis meeting. Mutterings into phones, quick checks against lists. Ashil said to me, 'Things are moving.' More people came and joined the talk.

'What now?' The question, spoken by a young woman wearing the headscarf of a married Beszel woman from a traditional family, was addressed to me, prisoner, condemned, consultant. I recognised her from the previous night. Silence went through the room, leaving itself behind, with all the people watching me. 'Tell me again about when Mahalia was taken,' she said.

'Are you trying to close in on Orciny?' I said. I had nothing to suggest to her, though something felt close to my reach.

They continued their quick back-and-forth, using shorthands and slang I did not know, but I could tell they were debating each other, and I tried to understand over what – some strategy, some question of direction. Periodically everyone in the room murmured something final-sounding and paused, and raised or did not raise a hand, and glanced around to count how many did which.

'We have to understand what got us here,' Ashil said. 'What would you do to find out what Mahalia knew?' His comrades were growing agitated, interrupting each other. I recalled Jaris and Yolanda talking about Mahalia's anger at the end. I sat up hard.

'What is it?' Ashil said.

'We need to go to the dig.' I said. He regarded me.

'Ready with Tye,' Ashil said. 'Coming with me.' Three-quarters of the room raised their hands briefly.

'Said my piece about him,' said the headscarfed woman, who did not raise hers.

'Heard,' Ashil said. 'But.' He pointed her eyes around the room. She had lost a vote.

I left with Ashil. It was there on the streets, that something fraught.

'You feel this?' I said. He even nodded. 'I need . . . can I call Dhatt?' I said.

'No. He's still on leave. And if you see him . . .'

'Then?'

'You're in Breach. Easier for him if you leave him alone. You'll see people you know. Don't put them in positions. They need to know where you are.'

'Bowden . . .'

'He's under surveillance by *militsya*. For his protection. No one in Besźel or Ul Qoma can find any link between Yorjavic and him. Whoever tried to kill him—'

'Are we still saying it's not Orciny? There's no Orciny?'

'—might try again. The leaders of True Citizens are with the *policzai*. But if Yorj and any other of their members were some secret cell, they don't seem to know. They're angry about it. You saw the film.'

'Where are we? Which way is the dig?'

HE TOOK US BY THAT AWESOME SUCCESSION of breaching transport, worming through the two cities, leaving a tunnel of Breach in the shape of our journey. I wondered where he carried what weapon. The guard at the gate of Bol Ye'an recognised me and smiled a smile that quickly faltered. He had perhaps heard I had disappeared.

'We're not approaching the academics, we're not questioning the students,' Ashil said. 'You understand we're here to investigate the background to and terms of your breach.' I was police on my own crime.

'It would be easier if we could talk to Nancy.'

'None of the academics, none of the students. Begin. You know who I am?' This to the guard.

We went to Buidze, who stood with his back to the wall of his office, stared at us, at Ashil in great and straightforward fear, at me in fear that was more bewildered: *Can I speak of what we spoke of before?* I saw him think, *Who is he?* Ashil manoeuvred me with him to the back of the room, found a shaft of shadow.

'I haven't breached,' Buidze kept whispering.

'Do you invite investigation?' Ashil said.

'Your job's to stop smuggling,' I said. Buidze nodded. What was I? Neither he nor I knew. 'How's that going?'

'Holy Light . . . Please. The only way any of these kids could do it would be to slip a memento straight in their pockets from the ground, so it never gets catalogued, and they can't because everyone's searched when they leave the site. No one could sell this stuff anyway. Like I said, the kids go for walks around the site, and they might be breaching when they stand still.

311

What can you do? Can't prove it. Doesn't mean they're thieves.'

'She told Yolanda you could be a thief without knowing it,' I said to Ashil. 'At the end. What have you lost?' I asked Buidze.

'Nothing!'

He took us to the artefact warehouse, stumbling eager to help us. On the way two students I somewhat recognised saw us, stopped still – something about Ashil's gait, that I was mimicking – backed away. There were the cabinets where the finds were, in which the latest dusted-off things born from the ground were stored. Lockers full of the impossible variety of Precursor Age debris, a miraculous and obstinately opaque rubble of bottles, orreries, axe heads, parchment scraps.

'Goes in, whoever's in charge that night makes sure everyone puts whatever's been found away, locks up, leaves the key. Doesn't get out the grounds without we search them. They don't even give us shit about that; they know that's how it is.'

I motioned Buidze to open the cabinet. I looked into the collection, each piece nestled in its little house, its segment of polystyrene, in the drawer. The topmost drawers had not yet been filled. Those below were full. Some of the fragile pieces were wrapped in lint-free cloth, swaddled from view. I opened the drawers one below the other, examining the ranked findings. Ashil came to stand beside me and looked down into the last as if it were a teacup, as if the artefacts were leaves with which one could divine.

'Who has the keys each night?' Ashil said.

'I, I, it depends.' Buidze's fear of us was wearing, but I did not believe he would lie. 'Whoever. It's not important. They all do it sometimes. Whoever's working late. There's a schedule, but they're always ignoring it . . .'

'After they've given the keys back to security, they leave?'

'Yeah.'

'Straightaway?'

'Yeah. Usually. They might go to their office a bit, walk in the grounds, but they don't usually stick around.'

'The grounds?'

'It's a park. It's . . . nice.' He shrugged helpless. 'There's no way out, though; its alter a few metres in, they have to come back through here. They don't leave without being searched.'

'When did Mahalia last lock up?'

'Loads of times. I don't know . . .'

'Last time.'

'. . . The night she disappeared,' he said at last.

'Give me a list of who did it when.'

'I can't! They keep one, but like I say half the time they just do each other favours . . .'

I opened the lowest drawers. Between the tiny crude figures, the intricate Precursor lingams and ancient pipettes, there were delicates wrapped. I touched the shapes gently.

'Those are old,' Buidze said, watching me. 'They were dug up ages ago.'

'I see,' I said, reading the labels. They had been disinterred in the early days of the dig. I turned at the sound of Professor Nancy entering. She stopped hard, stared at Ashil, at me. She opened her mouth. She had lived in Ul Qoma many years, was trained to see its minutiae. She recognised what she saw. 'Professor,' I said. She nodded. She stared at Buidze and he at her. She nodded and backed out.

'When Mahalia was in charge of the keys, she went for walks after locking up, didn't she?' I said. Buidze shrugged, bewildered. 'She offered to lock up when it wasn't her turn, too.

313

More than once.' All the small artefacts were in their cloth-lined beds. I did not rummage, but I felt around at the rear of the drawer without what I imagined was the preferred care.

He shifted, but Buidze would not challenge me. At the rear of the third shelf up, of things brought to light still more than a year ago, one of the cloth-wrapped items gave under my finger in a way that made me pause. 'You have to wear gloves,' Buidze said.

I unwrapped it and within was newspaper, and in the twist of paper was a piece of wood still flecked with paint and marked by where screws had held it. Not ancient nor carved: the offcut of a door, an absolute piece of nothing.

Buidze stared. I held it up. 'What dynasty's this?' I said.

'Don't,' said Ashil to me. He followed me out. Buidze came behind us.

'I'm Mahalia,' I said. 'I've just locked up. I've just volunteered to do it, though it's someone else's turn. Now a little walk.'

I marched us out into the open air, past the carefully layered hole where students glanced at us in surprise, on into the wasteland, where there was that rubble of history, and beyond it out of the gate that would open to a university ID, that opened for us because of where and what we were, that we propped open, into the park. Not much of a park this close to the excavation, but scrub and a few trees crossed by paths. There were Ul Qomans visible, but none too close. There was no unbroken Ul Qoman space between the dig and the bulk of the Ul Qoman park. Besźel intruded.

We saw other figures at the edges of the clearing: Besź sitting on the rocks or by the crosshatched pond. The park was only slightly in Besźel, a few metres at the edge of vegetation, a rill of crossover in paths and bushes, and a little stretch of totality cutting the two Ul Qoman sections off from each other. Maps made clear to walkers where they might go. It was here in the crosshatch that the students might stand, scandalously, touching distance from a foreign power, a pornography of separation.

'Breach watches fringes like this,' Ashil said to me. 'There are cameras. We'd see anyone emerge into Besźel who didn't come in by it.'

Buidze was hanging back. Ashil spoke so he could not hear. Buidze was trying not to watch us. I paced.

'Orciny . . .' I said. No way in or out of here in Ul Qoma but back through Bol Ye'an dig. '*Dissensi?* Bullshit. That's not how she delivered. This is what she was doing. Have you seen *The Great Escape?*' I walked to the edge of the crosshatched zone, where Ul Qoma ended for metres. Of course I was in Breach now, could wander on into Besźel if I wanted, but I stopped as if I were only in Ul Qoma. I walked to the edge of the space it shared with Besźel, where Besźel became briefly total and separated it from the rest of Ul Qoma. I made sure Ashil was watching me. I mimed placing the piece of wood in my pocket, stuffing it in fact down past my belt, down the inside of my trousers. 'Hole in her pockets.'

I walked a few steps in the crosshatch, dropping the thankfully unsplintering wood down my leg. I stood still when it hit the ground. I stood as if contemplating the skyline and moved my feet gently, letting it onto the earth, where I trod it in and scuffed plant muck and dirt onto it. When I walked away, without looking back, the wood was a nothing shape, invisible if you did not know it was there.

'When she goes, someone in Beszél – or someone who looks like they are, so there's nothing for you to notice – comes by,' I said. 'Stands and looks at the sky. Kicks their heels. Kicks something up. Sits on a rock for a moment, touches the ground, puts something in their pocket.

'Mahalia wouldn't take the recent stuff because it was just put away, much too noticeable. But while she's locking up, because it only takes a second, she opens the *old* drawers.'

'What does she take?'

'Maybe it's random. Maybe she's following instructions. Bol Ye'an searches them every night, so why would they think anyone's stealing? She never had anything on her. It was sitting here in the crosshatch.'

'Where someone came to take it. Through Beszél.'

I turned and looked slowly in all directions.

'Do you feel watched?' Ashil said.

'Do you?'

A very long quiet. 'I don't know.'

'Orciny.' I turned again. 'I'm tired of this.' I stood. 'Really.' I turned. 'This is wearing.'

'What are you thinking?' Ashil said.

A noise of a dog in the woods made us look up. The dog was in Beszél. I was ready to unhear, but of course I did not have to.

It was a lab, a friendly dark animal that sniffed out of the undergrowth and trotted to us. Ashil held out his hand for it. Its owner emerged, smiled, started, looked away in confusion and called his dog to heel. It went to him, looking back at us. He was trying to unsee, but the man could not forebear looking at us, wondering probably why we would risk playing with an animal in such an unstable urban location. When Ashil met his eye the man looked away. He must have been able to tell where and so what we were.

ACCORDING TO THE CATALOGUE the wood offcut was a replacement for a brass tube containing gears encrusted into position by centuries. Three other pieces were missing, from those early digs, all from within wrappings, all replaced by twists of paper, stones, the leg of a doll. They were supposed to be the remains of a preserved lobster's claw containing some proto-clockwork; an eroded mechanism like some tiny sextant; a handful of nails and screws.

We searched the ground in that fringe zone. We found pot-holes, cold scuffs, and the near-wintry remains of flowers, but no shallow-buried priceless treasures of the Precursor Age. They had been picked up, long ago. No one could sell them.

'That makes it breach then,' I said. 'Wherever these Orciny-ites came from or went, they can't have picked the stuff up in Ul Qoma, so it was in Besźel. Well, maybe to them they never left Orciny. But to most people they were put down in Ul Qoma and picked up in Besźel, so it's breach.'

ASHIL CALLED THROUGH TO SOMEONE on our way back, and when we arrived at the quarters Breach were bickering and voting in their fast loose way on issues alien to me. They entered the room in the middle of the strange debate, made cell phone calls, interrupted at speed. The atmosphere was fraught, in that distinct expressionless Breach way.

There were reports from the two cities, with muttered add-itions from those holding telephone receivers, delivering messages from other Breach. 'Everyone on guard,' Ashil kept saying. 'This is starting.'

317

They were afraid of head shots and breach mugging-murders. The number of small breaches was increasing. Breach were where they could be, but there were many they missed. Someone said graffiti were appearing on walls in Ul Qoma in styles that suggested Besźel artists.

'It hasn't been this bad, since, well . . .' Ashil said. He whispered explanations to me as the discussion continued. 'That's Raina. She's unremitting on this.' 'Samun thinks even mentioning Orciny's to give ground.' 'Byon doesn't.'

'We need to be ready,' the speaker said. 'We stumbled on something.'

'She did, Mahalia. Not us,' Ashil said.

'Alright, she did. Who knows when whatever's going to happen will? We're in the dark and we know war's come, but can't see where to aim.'

'I can't deal with this,' I said to Ashil quietly.

He escorted me back to the room. When I realised he was locking me in I shouted in remonstration. 'You need to remember why you're here,' he said through the door.

I sat on the bed and tried to read Mahalia's notes a new way. I did not try to follow the thread of a particular pen, the tenor of a particular period of her studies, to reconstruct a lineage of thought. Instead I read all the annotations on each page, years of opinions set together. I had been trying to be an archaeologist of her marginalia, separating the striae. Now I read each page out of time, no chronology, arguing with itself.

On the inside of the back cover among layers of irate theory I read in big letters written over earlier smaller ones BUT CF SHERMAN. A line from that to an argument on the facing page: ROSEN'S COUNTER. These names were familiar from my earlier investigations. I turned a couple of pages backwards.

In the same pen and late hurried hand I read, abutting an older claim: NO – ROSEN, VIJNIC.

Assertion overlaid with critique, more and more exclamation-marked clauses in the book. NO, a pointer connecting the word not to the original printed text but to an annotation, to her own older, enthusiastic annotations. An argument with herself. WHY A TEST? WHO?

'Hey,' I shouted. I did not know where the camera was. 'Hey, Ashil. Get Ashil.' I did not stop making noise until he arrived. 'I need to get online.'

He took me to a computer room, to what looked like a 486 or something similarly antique, with an operating system I did not recognise, some jury-rigged imitation of Windows, but the processor and connection were very fast. We were two of several in the office. Ashil stood behind me as I typed. He watched my researches, as well, certainly, as ensuring I did not email anyone.

'Go wherever you need,' Ashil told me, and he was right. Pay sites guarded by password protection needed only an empty *return* to roll over.

'What kind of connection is this?' I did not expect or get any answer. I searched *Sherman, Rosen, Vijnic*. On the forums I had recently visited, the three writers were subjected to ferocious contumely. 'Look.'

I got the names of their key works, checked listings on Amazon for a quick-and-dirty appreciation of their theses. It took minutes. I sat back.

'Look. *Look*. Sherman, Rosen, Vijnic are all absolute hate figures on these fractured-city boards,' I said. 'Why? Because they wrote books claiming Bowden was full of shit. That the whole argument's bollocks.'

'So does he.'

'That's not the point, Ashil. Look.' Pages and pages in *Between the City and the City*. I pointed to Mahalia's early remarks to herself, then her later ones. 'The point is that *she's* citing them. At the end. Her last notes.' Turning more pages, showing him.

'She changed her mind,' he said finally. We looked at each other a long time.

'All that stuff about parasites and being wrong and finding out she was a thief,' I said. 'God damn. She wasn't killed because she was, some, one of the bloody elect few who knew the awesome secret that the third city existed. She wasn't killed because she realised Orciny was lying to her, was using her. That's not the lies she was talking about. Mahalia was killed because she *stopped* believing in Orciny at all.'

CHAPTER TWENTY-SIX

THOUGH I BEGGED and grew angry, Ashil and his colleagues would not let me call Corwi or Dhatt.

'Why the hell not?' I said. 'They could do this. Alright then, do whatever the hell it is you do, find out. Yorjavic's still our best connection, him or some of his partners. We know he's involved. Try to get the *exact* dates Mahalia locked up, and if possible we need to know where Yorjavic was every one of those evenings. We want to work out if he picked up. The *policzai* watch the TC; they might know. Maybe the leaders'll even tell, if they're that disgruntled. And check out where Syedr was too – someone with access to stuff from Copula Hall's involved.'

'We're not going to be able to get every day Mahalia did the keys. You heard Buidze: half of them weren't planned.'

'Let me call Corwi and Dhatt; they'd know how to sift them.'

'You.' Ashil spoke hard. 'Are in Breach here. Don't forget. You don't get to demand things. Everything we're doing is an investigation into *your* breach. Do you understand?'

They would not give me a computer in the cell. I watched the sun rising, the air beyond my window growing light. I had not realised how late it was. I fell asleep at last, and woke with Ashil back in the room with me. He drank something – it was the first time I had seen him eat or drink anything. I rubbed my eyes. It was morning enough to be day. Ashil did not seem an iota tired. He tossed papers onto my lap, indicated a coffee and a pill by my bed.

'Wasn't as hard as that,' he said. 'They sign off when they put the keys back, so we got all the dates. You've got the original schedules there, that changed, and the signings sheets themselves. But there are loads. We can't put a bead on Yorjavic let alone Syedr or any other nat for this many nights. This stretches over more than two years.'

'Hold on.' I held the two lists against each other. 'Forget when she was scheduled in advance – she was obeying orders, don't forget, from her mysterious contact. When she *wasn't* down to take the keys but did it anyway, that's what we should be looking at. No one loves the job – you have to stay late – so those are the days she suddenly turns around and says to whoever's turn it is "I'll do it." These are the days she got a message. She got told to deliver. So let's see who was doing what *then*. Those are the dates. And there aren't nearly so many.'

Ashil nodded – counted the evenings in question. 'Four, five. Three pieces are missing.'

'So a couple of those days nothing happened. Maybe they were legitimate changes, no instructions at all. They're still the ones to chase.' Ashil nodded again. 'That's when we're going to see the nats moving.'

'How did they organise this? Why?'

'I don't know.'

'Wait here.'

'This would be easier if you'd just let me come with you. Why are you shy now?'

'Wait.'

More waiting, and though I did not shout at the unseen camera, I glared at all the walls in turn, so it would see me.

'No.' Ashil's voice came from a loudspeaker I could not see. 'Yorjavic was under *policzai* observation at least two of those nights. He didn't go near the park.'

'What about Syedr?' I addressed the emptiness. 'No. Accounted for on four of the nights. Could be another of the nat bigwigs, but we've seen what Besźel has on them all, and there's nothing red-flagging.'

'Shit. What do you mean Syedr's "accounted for"?'

'We know where he was, and he was nowhere near. He was in meetings those evenings and the days after them.'

'Meetings with whom?'

'He's on the Chamber of Commerce. They had trade events those days.' Silence. When I did not speak a long time he said, 'What? What?'

'We've been thinking wrong.' I pincered my fingers in the air, trying to catch something. 'Just because it was Yorjavic who shot, and because we know Mahalia pissed off the nats. But doesn't it seem like a hell of a coincidence that those trade things would happen on the very nights that Mahalia volunteers to lock up?' Another long quiet. I remembered the delay before I could see the Oversight Committee, for one of those events. 'There are receptions afterwards, for the guests, aren't there?'

'Guests.'

'The companies. The ones Besźel's schmoozing – that's what those things are for, when they bicker for contracts. Ashil, find out who was there on those dates.'

'At the Chamber of Commerce . . .'

'Check the guest lists for the parties afterwards. Check press releases a few days afterwards and you'll see who got what contract. Come on.'

'Jesus fucking Christ,' I said minutes later in silence, when I still stalked back and forth in my room without him. 'Why the fuck don't you just let me out? I'm *policzai*, God damn it, this is what I do. You're good at being bogeymen but you're shit at this.'

'You're a breacher,' Ashil said, pushing open the door. 'It's you we're investigating.'

'Right. Did you wait outside till I said something you could make an entrance to?'

'This is the list.' I took the paper.

Companies – Canadian, French, Italian and British, a couple of smaller American ones – next to the various dates. Five names were ringed in red.

'The rest were there on one or other fair, but the ones in red, those ones are the ones that were there on every one of the nights Mahalia did the keys,' Ashil said.

'ReddiTek's software. Burnley – what do they do?'

'Consultancy.'

'CorIntech are electronics components. What's this written next to them?' Ashil looked.

'The man heading their delegation was Gorse, from their parent company, Sear and Core. Came to meet up with the local head of CorIntech, guy runs the division in Beszel. They both went to the parties with Nyisemu and Buric and the rest of the chamber.'

'Shit,' I said. 'We . . . Which time was he here?'

'All of them.'

'All? The CEO of the parent company? Sear and Core? Shit.'

'Tell me,' he said, eventually.

'The nats couldn't pull this off. Wait.' I thought. 'We know there's an insider in Copula Hall but . . . what the hell could Syedr do for these guys? Corwi's right – he's a clown. And what would be his angle?' I shook my head. 'Ashil, how does this work? You can just siphon this information, right, from either city. Can you . . . What's your status internationally? Breach, I mean.

'We need to go for the company.'

I'M AN AVATAR OF BREACH, Ashil said. Where breach has occurred I can do whatever. But he made me run through it a long time. His manner ossified, that opacity, the glimmerlessness of any sense of what he thought – it was hard to tell if he even heard me. He did not argue nor agree. He stood, while I told him what I claimed.

No, they can't sell it, I said, that's not what this is about. We had all heard rumours about Precursor artefacts. Their questionable physics. Their properties. They want to see what's true. They've got Mahalia to supply them. And to do it they've got her thinking she's in touch with Orciny. But she realised.

Corwi had said something once about the visitors' tours of Beszel those companies' representatives endured. Their chauffeurs might take them anywhere total or crosshatched, any pretty park to stretch their legs.

Sear and Core had been doing R&D.

Ashil stared at me. 'This doesn't make sense,' he said. 'Who'd put money into superstitious nonsense . . .?'

'How sure are you? That there's nothing to the stories? And even if you're right, the CIA paid millions of dollars to men trying to kill goats by staring at them,' I said. 'Sear and Core

325

pay, what, a few thousand dollars to set this up? They don't have to believe a word of it: it's worth that kind of money just on the *off chance* that any of the stories turn out to have anything at all to them. It's worth that for curiosity.'

Ashil took out his cell and began to make calls. It was the early part of the night. 'We need a conclave,' he said. 'Big stake. Yes, make it.' 'Conclave. At the set.' He said more or less the same many times.

'You can do anything,' I said.

'Yes. Yes . . . We need a show. Breach in strength.'

'So you believe me? Ashil, you do?'

'How would they do it? How would outsiders like that get word to her?'

'I don't know, but that's what we have to find out. Paid off a couple of locals – we know where that money came to Yorj from.' They had been small amounts.

'They could not possibly, not possibly create Orciny for her.'

'They wouldn't have the CEO *of their parent* here for these piddling little glad-handers, let alone every time Mahalia locks up. Come on. Besźel's a basket case, and they've already thrown us a bone by being here. There's got to be a connection . . .'

'Oh, we'll investigate. But these aren't citizens nor citizens, Tye. They don't have the . . .' A silence.

'The fear,' I said. That Breach freeze, that obedience reflex shared in Ul Qoma and Besźel.

'They don't have a certain response to us, so if we do anything we need to show weight – we need many of us, a presence. And if there's truth to this, it's the shutdown of a major business in Besźel. It'll be a crisis for the city. A catastrophe. And no one will like that.

'It isn't unknown for a city or a city to argue with Breach, Tye. It's happened. There've been *wars* with Breach.' He waited while that image hung. 'That doesn't help anyone. So we need to have presence.' Breach needed to intimidate. I understood.

'Come on,' I said. 'Hurry.'

But the ingathering of Breach avatars from wherever they had posted themselves, the attempt with that diffuse authority, a corralling of chaos, was not efficient. Breach answered their phones, agreed, disagreed, said they would come or said they would not, said they would hear Ashil out. This was to judge from his side of the conversations.

'How many do you need?' I said. 'What are you waiting for?'

'We need a *presence*, I said.'

'You feel what's going on out there?' I said. 'You've felt it in the air.'

There had been more than two hours of this. I was wired by something in the food and drink I had been given, pacing and complaining of my incarceration. More calls began to come in to Ashil. More than the messages he had left – word had gone viral. In the corridor was commotion, quick steps, voices, shouting and responding to shouts.

'What is it?'

Ashil was listening on his phone, not to the sound outside. 'No,' he said. His voice betrayed nothing. He said it again several times until he closed the phone and looked at me. For the first time that set face looked like an evasion. He did not know how to say what he had to say.

'What's happened?' The shouting outside was greater, and now there was noise from the street too.

'A crash.'

'A car crash?'

327

'Buses. Two buses.'

'They breached?'

He nodded. 'They're in Beszel. They jackknifed on Finn Square.' A big crosshatched piazza. 'Skidded into a wall in Ul Qoma.' I did not say anything. Any accident leading to breach obviously necessitated Breach, a few avatars gusting into view, sealing off the scene, sorting out parameters, ushering out the blameless, holding any breachers, handing authority back as quickly as possible to the police in the two cities. There was nothing in the fact of a traffic breach to lead to the noise I heard outside, so there must be more.

'They were buses taking refugees to camps. They're out, and they haven't been trained; they're breaching everywhere, wandering between the cities without any idea what they're doing.'

I could imagine the panic of bystanders and passersby, let alone those innocent motorists of Beszel and Ul Qoma, having swerved desperately out of the path of the careening vehicles, of necessity in and out of the topolganger city, trying hard to regain control and pull their vehicles back to where they dwelt. Faced then with scores of afraid, injured intruders, without intent to transgress but without choice, without language to ask for help, stumbling out of the ruined buses, weeping children in their arms and bleeding across borders. Approaching people they saw, not attuned to the nuances of nationality – clothes, colours, hair, posture – oscillating back and forth between countries.

'We've called a closure,' Ashil said. 'Complete lockdown. Clearing both the streets. Breach is out in force, everywhere, until this is finished.'

'What?'

Martial Breach. It had not happened in my lifetime. No

entrance to either city, no passage between them, ultrahard enforcement of all Breach rules. The police of each city on mopping-up standby under Breach injunctions, adjuncts for the duration to the shutdown of borders. That was the sound I could hear, those mechanised voices over the growing roar of sirens: loudspeakers announcing the closure in both languages. *Get off the streets.*

'For a bus crash . . .?'

'It was *deliberate*,' Ashil said. 'It was ambushed. By unificationists. It's happened. They're all over. There's reports of breaches everywhere.' He was regaining himself.

'Unifs in which city . . .?' I said, and my question petered out as I guessed the answer.

'Both. They're working in concert. We don't even know if it was Besź unifs who stopped the buses.' Of course they worked together; that we knew. But that those little bands of eager utopians could do this? Could untether this breakdown, could make this happen? 'They're everywhere in both cities. This is their insurrection. They're trying to merge us.'

ASHIL WAS HESITATING. That kept me talking, only that, that he was there in the room minutes more than he needed to be. He was checking the contents of his pockets, preparing himself into soldierly alertness. All Breach were called out. He was expected. The sirens continued, the voices continued.

'Ashil, for Christ's sake listen to me. Listen to me. You think this is coincidence? Come *on*. Ashil, don't open that door. You think we get to this, you think we figure *this* out, get this far and all of a sudden there's a fucking uprising? Someone's doing this, Ashil. To get you and all the Breach out and away from them.

329

'How did you find out about which companies were here when? The nights Mahalia delivered.'

He was motionless. 'We're Breach,' he said eventually. 'We can do whatever we need . . .'

'*Damn* it, Ashil. I'm not some breacher for you to scare; I need to know. How do you investigate?'

At last: 'Taps. Informants.' Glance up at the window, at a welling-up of the crisis sound. He waited by the door for more from me.

'Agents or systems in offices in Beszel and Ul Qoma tell you what you need to know, right? So someone somewhere was going through databases trying to find out who was where, when, in the Besź Chamber of Commerce.

'It's been red-flagged, Ashil. You sent someone looking, and them pulling up files has been *seen*. What better evidence do you need that we're onto something? You've seen the unifs. They're nothing. Beszel and Ul Qoma, doesn't make a difference, they're a tiny bunch of dewy-eyed punks. There's more agents than agitators; someone's given an order. Someone's engineered this because they've realised we're onto them.

'Wait,' I said. 'The lockdown . . . It's not just Copula Hall, right? All borders to everywhere are closed, and no flights in or out, right?'

'BesźAir and Illitania are grounded. The airports aren't taking incoming traffic.'

'What about private flights?'

'. . . The instruction's the same, but they're not under our authority like the national carriers, so it's a bit more—'

'That's what this is. You can't lock them down, not in time. Someone's getting out. We have to get to the Sear and Core building.'

'That's where—'

'That's where what's happening's happening. This ...' I pointed at the window. We heard the shattering of glass, the shouts, the frenetics of vehicles in panicked rush, the fight sounds. 'This is a decoy.'

CHAPTER TWENTY-SEVEN

IN THE STREETS we went through the last throes, the nerve twitches of a little revolution that had died before it was born, and had not known it. Those dying flails remained dangerous, though, and we were in a soldierly way. No curfew could contain this panic.

People were running, in both cities, along the street in front of us while the barks of public announcements in Besź and Illitan warned them this was a Breach lockdown. Windows broke. Some figures I saw run did so with more giddiness than terror. Not unifs, too small and too aimless: teenagers throwing stones, in their most transgressive act ever, little hurled breaches breaking glass in the city they did not live or stand in. An Ul Qoman fire crew sped in its bleating engine the length of the road, towards where the night sky glowed. A Besź wagon followed seconds behind it: they were still trying to maintain their distinctions, one fighting the fire in one part of the conjoined facade, the other in the other.

Those kids had better get out of the street fast, because Breach were everywhere. Unseen by most still out that night, maintaining their covert methods. Running I saw other Breach moving in what could pass as the urban panic of citizens of Beszel and Ul Qoma but was a somewhat different motion, a more purposeful, predatory motion like Ashil's and mine. I could see them because of recent practice, as they could see me.

We saw a unif gang. It was shocking to me even then after days of interstitial life to see them running together, from both chapters, in clothes which despite their transnational punk-and-rocker jackets and patches clearly marked them, to those attuned to urban semiosis, as from, whatever their desire, *either* Besźel *or* Ul Qoma. Now they were grouped as one, dragging a grassroots breach with them as they went from wall to wall spraying slogans in a rather artful combine of Besź and Illitan, words that, perfectly legible if somewhat filigreed and seriffed, read *TOGETHER! UNITY!* in both languages.

Ashil reached. He carried a weapon he had prepared before we left. I had not seen it closely.

'We don't have time . . .' I started to say, but from the shadows around that insurgence a small group of figures did not so much emerge as come into focus. Breach. 'How do you move like that?' I said. The avatars were outnumbered, but they moved without fear into that group, where with sudden not dramatic but very brutal locks and throws they incapacitated three of the gang. Some of the others rallied, and the Breach raised weapons. I did not hear anything but two unifs dropped.

'Jesus,' I said, but we were moving.

With a key and a quick expert twist Ashil opened a random parked car, selected by unclear criteria. 'Get in.' He glanced back. 'Cessation's best done out of sight; they'll move them. This is an emergency. Both cities are Breach now.'

'Jesus . . .'

'Only where it can't be avoided. Only to secure the cities and the Breach.'

'What about the refugees?'

'There are other possibilities.' He started the engine.

There were few cars on the streets. The trouble always seemed to be around corners from us. Small groups of Breach were moving. Several times someone, Breach, appeared in the chaos and seemed about to stop us; but each time Ashil stared or slapped his sigil or drummed in some secret fingercode, and his status as avatar was noted and we were away.

I had begged for more Breach to come with us. 'They won't,' he had said. 'They won't believe. I should be with them.'

'What do you mean?'

'Everyone's dealing with this. I don't have time to win the argument.'

He said this, and it had been abruptly clear how few Breach there were. How thin a line. The crude democracy of their methodology, their decentralised self-ordering, meant that Ashil could do this mission the importance of which I had convinced him, but the crisis meant we were alone.

Ashil took us across lanes of highway, through straining borders, avoiding little anarchies. *Militsya* and *policzai* were on corners. Sometimes Breach would emerge from the night with that uncanny motion they perfected and order the local police to do something – to take some unif or body away, to guard something – then disappear again. Twice I saw them escorting terrified north African men and women from somewhere to somewhere, refugees made the levers of this breakdown.

'It isn't possible, this, we've . . .' Ashil interrupted himself, touched his earpiece as reports came in.

There would be camps full of unificationists after this. We were in a moment of outright foregone conclusion, but the unifs still fought to mobilise populations deeply averse to their mission. Perhaps the memory of this joint action would buoy up whichever of them remained after that night. It must be an intoxication to step through the borders and greet their foreign comrades across what they made suddenly one street, to make their own country even if just for seconds at night in front of a scrawled slogan and a broken window. They must know by now that the populaces were not coming with them, but they did not disappear back to their respective cities. How could they go back now? Honour, despair, or bravery kept them coming.

'It isn't possible,' Ashil said. 'There is no way the head of Sear and Core, some *outsider*, could have constructed this . . . We've . . .' He listened, set his face. 'We've lost avatars.' What a war, this now bloody war between those dedicated to bringing the cities together and the force charged with keeping them apart.

UNITY had been half written across the face of the Ungir Hall which was also the Sul Kibai Palace, so now in dripping paint the building said something nonsense. What passed as Beszel's business districts were nowhere near the Ul Qoman equivalent. The headquarters of Sear and Core were on the banks of the Colinin, one of the few successes in the attempts to revivify Beszel's dying dockside. We passed the dark water.

We both looked up at percussion in the otherwise empty locked-down sky. A helicopter the only thing in the air, backlit by its own powerful lights as it left us below.

'It's them,' I said. 'We're too late.' But the copter was coming in from the west, towards the riverbank. It was not an exit; it was a pickup. 'Come on.'

Even in such a distracting night Ashil's driving prowess cowed me. He veered across the dark bridge, took a one-way total street in Beszel the wrong way, startling pedestrians trying to get out of the night, through a crosshatch plaza then a total Ul Qoma street. I was leaning to watch the helicopter descend into the roofscape by the river, half a mile ahead of us.

'It's down,' I said. 'Move.'

There was the reconfigured warehouse, the inflatable gasrooms of Ul Qoman buildings to either side of it. No one was in the square, but there were lights on throughout the Sear and Core building, despite the hour, and there were guards in the entrance. They came towards us aggressively when we entered. Marbled and fluorescently lit, the S&C logo in stainless steel and placed as if it were art on the walls, magazines and corporate reports made to look like magazines on tables by sofas.

'Get the fuck out,' a man said. Besz ex-military. He put his hand to his holster and led his men towards us. He came up short a moment later: he saw how Ashil moved.

'Stand down,' Ashil said, glowering to intimidate. 'The whole of Beszel's in Breach tonight.' He did not have to show his sigil. The men fell back. 'Unlock the lift now, give me the keys to reach the helipad, and stand down. No one else comes in.'

If the security had been foreign, had come from Sear and Core's home country, or been drafted in from its European or North American operations, they might not have obeyed. But this was Beszel and the security was Besz, and they did as Ashil said. In the elevator, he drew out his weapon. A big pistol of unfamiliar design. Its barrel encased, muzzled in some dramatic silencer. He worked the key the security had given us, to the corporate levels, all the way up.

*

THE DOOR OPENED onto gusts of hard cold air amid surrounds of vaulting roofs and antennae. The tethers of the Ul Qoman gas-rooms, a few streets off the mirrored fronts of Ul Qoman businesses, the spires of temples in both cities, and there in the darkness and the wind ahead of us, behind a thicket of safety rails, the helipad. The dark vehicle waiting, its rotor turning very slowly, almost without noise. Gathered before it a group of men.

We could not hear much except the bass of the engine, the siren-infested putting down of unification riots all around us. The men by the helicopter did not hear us as we approached. We stayed close to cover. Ashil led me towards the aircraft, the gang who did not yet see us. There were four of them. Two were large and shaven-headed. They looked like ultranats: True Citizens on secret commission. They stood around a suited man I did not know and someone I could not see from the way he stood, in deep and animated conversation.

I heard nothing, but one of the men saw us. There was a commotion and they turned. From his cockpit the pilot of the helicopter swivelled the police-strength light he held. Just before it framed us the gathered men moved and I could see the last man, staring straight at me.

It was Mikhel Buric. The Social Democrat, the opposition, the other man on the Chamber of Commerce.

Blinded by the floodlight I felt Ashil grab me and pull me behind a thick iron ventilator pipe. There was a moment of dragged-out quiet. I waited for a shot but no one shot.

'Buric,' I said to Ashil. '*Buric*. I knew there was no way Syedr could do this.'

Buric was the contact man, the organiser. Who knew Mahalia's predilections, who had seen her on her first visit to

Besźel, when she angered everyone at the conference with her undergraduate dissidence. Buric the operator. He knew her work and what she wanted, that abhistory, the comforts of paranoia, a cosseting by the man behind the curtain. In the Chamber of Commerce as he was, he was in a position to provide it. To find an outlet for what she stole at his behest, for the invented benefit of Orciny.

'It was all geared stuff that got stolen,' I said. 'Sear and Core are investigating the artefacts. This is a science experiment.'

It was his informers – he like all Besź politicians had them – who had told Buric that investigations had occurred into Sear and Core, that we were chasing down the truth. Perhaps he thought we had understood more than we had, would be shocked at how little of this we could have predicted. It would not take so much for a man in his position to order the government provocateurs in the poor foolish unificationists to begin their work, to forestall Breach so he and his collaborators could get away.

'They're armed?' Ashil glanced out and nodded.

'Mikhel Buric?' I shouted. '*Buric?* What are True Citizens doing with a liberal sellout like you? You getting good soldiers like Yorj killed? Bumping off students you think are getting too close to your bullshit?'

'Piss off, Borlú,' he said. He did not sound angry. 'We're all patriots. They know my record.' A noise joined the noise of the night. The helicopter's engine, speeding up.

Ashil looked at me and stepped out into full view.

'Mikhel Buric,' he said, in his frightening voice. He kept his gun unwavering and walked behind it, as if it led him, towards the helicopter. 'You're answerable to Breach. Come with me.' I followed him. He glanced at the man beside Buric.

'Ian Croft, regional head of CorIntech,' Buric said to Ashil. He folded his arms. 'A guest here. Address your remarks to me. And fuck yourself.' The True Citizens had their own pistols up. Buric moved towards the helicopter.

'Stay where you are,' Ashil said. 'You will step *back*,' he shouted at the True Citizens. 'I am *Breach*.'

'So what?' Buric said. 'I've spent *years* running this place. I've kept the unifs in line, I've been getting *business for Beszel*, I've been taking their damned gewgaws out from *under Ul Qoman noses*, and what do you do? You gutless Breach? You protect Ul Qoma.'

Ashil actually gaped a moment at that.

'He's playing to them,' I whispered. 'To the True Citizens.'

'Unifs have one thing right,' Buric said. 'There's only one city, and if it weren't for the superstition and cowardice of the populace, kept in place by you goddamned *Breach*, we'd all know there was only one city. And *that city is called Beszel*. And you're telling patriots to obey *you*? I warned them, I *warned* my comrades you might turn up, despite it being made clear you have no business here.'

'That's why you leaked the footage of the van,' I said. 'To keep Breach out of it, send the mess to the *militsya* instead.'

'Breach's priorities are *not* Beszel's,' Buric said. 'Fuck the Breach.' He said it carefully. 'Here we recognise only one authority, you pissing little neither-nor, and that is *Beszel*.'

He indicated Croft to precede him into the helicopter. The True Citizens stared. They were not quite ready to fire on Ashil, to provoke Breach war – you could see a kind of blasphemy-drunkenness in their look at the intransigence they were already showing, disobeying Breach even this far – but they would not lower their guns either. If he shot they would

339

shoot back, and there were two of them. High on their obedience to Buric they did not need to know anything about where their paymaster was going or why, only that he had charged them to cover his back while he did. They were fired with jingo bravery.

'I'm not Breach,' I said.

Buric turned to look at me. The True Citizens stared at me. I felt Ashil's hesitation. He kept his weapon up.

'I'm not Breach.' I breathed deep. 'I am Inspector Tyador Borlú. Besźel Extreme Crimes Squad. I'm not here for Breach, Buric. I represent the Besźel *policzai*, to enforce Besź law. Because you broke it.

'Smuggling's not my department; take what you want. I'm not a political man – I don't care if you mess with Ul Qoma. I'm here because you're a murderer.

'Mahalia wasn't Ul Qoman, nor an enemy of Besźel, and if she seemed to be, it was only because she believed the crap *you* told her, so you could sell what she supplied you, for this *foreigner's* R and D. Doing it for Besźel, my arse: you're just a fence for foreign bucks.'

The True Citizens looked uneasy.

'But she realised she'd been lied to. That she wasn't righting antique wrongs or learning any hidden truth. That you'd made her a thief. You sent Yorjavic over to get rid of her. That makes it an Ul Qoman crime, so even with the links we will find between you and him, nothing I can do. But that's not the end of it. When you heard Yolanda was hiding, you thought Mahalia'd told her something. Couldn't risk her talking.

'You were smart to get Yorj to take her out from his side of the checkpoint, keep Breach off your backs. But that makes his shot, and the order you gave for it, Besź. And that makes you mine.

'Minister Mikhel Buric, by the authority vested in me by the government and courts of the Commonwealth of Besźel, you are under arrest for Conspiracy to Murder Yolanda Rodriguez. You are coming with me.'

SECOND AFTER SECOND of astonished silence. I stepped slowly forward, past Ashil, towards Mikhel Buric.

It would not last. The True Citizens mostly had not much more respect for we who they believed were the weak local police than for many other of the herdlike masses of Besźel. But those were ugly charges, in Besźel's name, that did not sound like the politics for which they were signed up, or the reasons they might have been given for those killings, if they even knew about them. The two men looked at each other uncertainly.

Ashil moved. I breathed out. 'Fuck damn,' Buric said. From his pocket he took his own small pistol and raised it and pointed it at me. I said, 'Oh,' or something as I stumbled back. I heard a shot but it did not sound as I expected. Not explosive; it was a hard-breathed gust of breath, a rush. I remember thinking that and being surprised that I would notice such a thing as I died.

Buric leapt into instant backward scarecrow motion, his limbs crazy and a rush of colour on his chest. I had not been shot; he had been shot. He threw his little weapon away as if deliberately. It was the silenced blast of Ashil's pistol I had heard. Buric fell, his chest all blood.

Now, there, *that* was the sound of shots. Two, quickly, a third. Ashil fell. The True Citizens had fired on him.

'Stop, stop,' I screamed. 'Hold your fucking fire!' I scrabbled crabwise back to him. Ashil was sprawled across the concrete, bleeding. He was growling in pain.

'You two are under fucking arrest,' I shouted. The True Citizens stared at each other, at me, at the unmoving dead Buric. This escort job had become suddenly violent and utterly confusing. You could see them glimpse the scale of the web that snagged them. One muttered to the other and they backed away, jogged towards the lift shaft.

'Stay where you are,' I shouted, but they ignored me as I knelt by wheezing Ashil. Croft still stood motionless by the helicopter. 'Don't you goddamn move,' I said, but the True Citizens pulled open the door to the roof and disappeared back down into Besźel.

'I'm alright, I'm alright,' Ashil gasped. I patted him to find his injuries. Below his clothes he was wearing some kind of armour. It had stopped what would have been the killing bullet, but he had been also hit below his shoulder and was bleeding and in pain. 'You,' he managed to shout to Sear and Core's man. 'Stay. You may be protected in Besźel but you're not *in* Besźel if I say you're not. You're in Breach.'

Croft leaned into the cockpit and said something to the pilot, who nodded and sped up the rotor.

'Are you finished?' Croft said.

'Get out. That vehicle's grounded.' Even through pain-gritted teeth and having dropped his pistol, Ashil made his demand.

'I'm neither Besź nor Ul Qoman,' Croft said. He spoke in English, though he clearly understood us. 'I'm neither interested in nor scared of you. I'm leaving. "Breach."' He shook his head. 'Freak show. You think anyone beyond these odd

342

little cities cares about you? *They* may bankroll you and do what you say, ask no questions, they may need to be scared of you, but no one else does.' He sat next to the pilot and strapped himself in. 'Not that I think you could, but I strongly suggest you and your colleagues don't try to stop this vehicle. "Grounded." What do you think would happen if you provoked my government? It's funny enough the idea of either Besźel or Ul Qoma going to war against a real country. Let alone you, Breach.'

He closed the door. We did not try to get up for a while, Ashil and I. He lay there, me kneeling behind him, as the helicopter grew louder and the distended-looking thing eventually bobbed up as if dangled from string, pouring air down on us, ripping our clothes every way and buffeting Buric's corpse. It tore away between the low towers of the two cities, in the airspace of Besźel and Ul Qoma, once again the only thing in the sky.

I watched it go. An invasion of Breach. Paratroopers landing in either city, storming the secret offices in their contested buildings. To attack Breach an invader would have to breach Besźel and Ul Qoma.

'Wounded avatar,' Ashil said into his radio. He gave our location. 'Assist.'

'Coming,' the machine said.

He sat back against the wall. In the east the sky was beginning faintly to lighten. There were still noises of violence from below, but fewer and ebbing. There were more sirens, Besź and Ul Qoman, as the *policzai* and *militsya* reclaimed their own streets, as Breach withdrew where it could. There would be a day more of lockdown to clear last nests of unifs, to return to normalcy, to corral the lost refugees back to the camps, but we were past the worst of it. I watched the dawn-lit clouds begin. I checked Buric's body, but he carried nothing on him.

ASHIL SAID SOMETHING. His voice was weak, and I had to have him repeat himself.

'I still can't believe it,' he said. 'That he could have done this.'

'Who?'

'Buric. Any of them.'

I leaned against a chimney and watched him. I watched the sun coming.

'No,' I said finally. 'She was too smart. Young but . . .'

'. . . Yes. She worked it out in the end, but you wouldn't think Buric could have taken her in to begin with.'

'And then the way it was done,' I said slowly. 'If he had someone killed we wouldn't find the body.' Buric was not competent enough at one end, too competent at the other, to make sense of this story. I sat still in the slowly growing light as we waited for help. 'She was a specialist,' I said. 'She knew all about the history. Buric was clever, but not like that.'

'What are you thinking, Tye?' There were sounds from one of the doors that jutted onto the roof. A slamming and it flew open, disgorging someone I vaguely recognised as Breach. She came towards us, speaking into her radio.

'How did they know where Yolanda would be?'

'Heard your plans,' he said. 'Listening to your friend Corwi's phone . . .' He offered the idea.

'Why did they shoot at Bowden?' I said. Ashil looked at me. 'At Copula Hall. We thought it was Orciny, going for him, because he inadvertently knew the truth. But it wasn't Orciny.

344

It was . . .' I looked at dead Buric. 'His orders. So why would he go for Bowden?'

Ashil nodded. He spoke slowly. 'They thought Mahalia told Yolanda what she knew, but . . .'

'Ashil?' the approaching woman shouted, and Ashil nodded. He even stood, but sat down again, heavily.

'Ashil,' I said.

'Okay, okay,' he said. 'I just . . .' He closed his eyes. The woman came faster. He opened them suddenly and looked at me. 'Bowden told you all along Orciny wasn't true.'

'He did.'

'Move,' the woman said. 'I'll get you out of here.'

'What are you going to do?' I said.

'Come on Ashil,' she said. 'You're weak . . .'

'Yes I am.' He interrupted her himself. 'But . . .' He coughed. He stared at me and I at him.

'We have to get him out,' I said. 'We have to get Breach to . . .' But they were still engaged in the end of that night, and there was no time to convince anyone.

'A second,' he said to the woman. He took his sigil out of his pocket and gave it to me, along with a ring of keys. 'I authorize it,' he said. She raised an eyebrow but did not argue. 'I think my gun went over there. The rest of Breach is still . . .'

'Give me your phone. What's its number? Now go. Get him out of here. Ashil, I'll do it.'

345

CHAPTER TWENTY-EIGHT

THE BREACH WITH ASHIL did not ask me for help. She shooed me away.

I found his weapon. It was heavy, its silencer almost organic-looking, like something phlegmy coating the muzzle. I had to look for far too long before I could find the safety catch. I did not risk trying to release the clip to check it. I pocketed it and took the stairs.

As I descended I scrolled through the numbers in the phone's contacts list: they were meaningless-seeming strings of letters. I hand-dialled the number I needed. On a hunch I did not prefix a country code, and I was right – the connection made. When I reached the foyer it was ringing. The security looked at me uncertainly, but I held out the Breach sigil and they backed away.

'What . . . who is this?'

'Dhatt, it's me.'

'Holy Light, *Borlú*? What . . . where are you? Where've you been? What's going on?'

'Dhatt, shut up and listen. I know it's not morning yet, but I need you to wake up and I need you to help me. Listen.'

'Light, Borlú, you think I'm sleeping? We thought you were

with *Breach* . . . Where are you? Do you know what's going on?'

'I am with Breach. Listen. You're not back at work, right?'

'Fuck no, I'm still fucked—'

'I need you to help me. Where's Bowden? You lot took him in for questioning, right?'

'Bowden? Yeah, but we didn't hold him. Why?'

'Where is he?'

'Holy Light, Borlú.' I could hear him sitting up, pulling himself together. 'At his flat. Don't panic; he's watched.'

'Send them in. Hold him. Till I get there. Just do it, please. Send them now. Thanks. Call me when you have him.'

'Wait, wait. What number is this? It isn't showing on my phone.'

I told him. In the square, I watched the lightening sky and the birds wheel over both cities. I walked back and forth, one of few but not the only person out at that hour. I watched the others who passed close, furtively. I watched them trying to retreat to their home city – Besźel, Ul Qoma, Besźel, whichever – out of the massive Breach that was at last ebbing around them.

'Borlú. He's gone.'

'What do you mean?'

'There was a detail on his apartment, right? For protection, after he got shot? Well, when stuff started going mad tonight it was all hands to the pump and they got pulled off onto some other job. I don't know the ins and outs – no one was there for a little while. I sent them back – things are calming down a bit, the *militsya* and your lot are trying to sort out boundaries again – but it's still fucking lunacy on the streets. Anyway I sent them back and they've just tried his door. He's not there.'

'Son of a bitch.'

'Tyad, what the fuck is going on?'

'I'm getting there. Can you make a . . . I don't know it in Illitan. *Put out an APB on him.*' I said it in English, copying the films.

'Yeah, we call it 'send the halo.' I'll do it. But fuck, Tyad, you seen what chaos it is tonight. You think anyone's going to see him?'

'We have to try. He's trying to get out.'

'Well no problem, he's fucked then, all the borders are closed, so wherever he turns up he'll just get stopped. Even if he got through to Besźel earlier, your lot aren't so incompetent they're going to let people out.'

'Okay but still, put a halo on him?'

'*Send,* not put. Alright. We're not going to find him, though.'

There were more rescue vehicles on the roads, in both cities, racing to the sites of continued crisis, here and there civilian vehicles, ostentatiously obeying their own city's traffic laws, negotiating around each other with unusual legal care, like the few pedestrians. They must have good and defensible reasons to be out. The assiduousness of their unseeing and seeing was marked. The crosshatching is resilient.

It was predawn cold. With his skeleton key but without Ashil's aplomb I was breaking into an Ul Qoman car when Dhatt called back. His voice was very different. He was – there was no other way to hear it – in some kind of awe.

'I was wrong. We've found him.'

'What? Where?'

'Copula Hall. The only *militsya* who weren't sent onto the streets were the border guards. They recognised his photos. Been there for hours, they told me, must've headed there as

348

soon as it all kicked off. He was inside the hall earlier, with everyone else who got trapped when it locked down. But listen.'

'What's he doing?'

'Just waiting.'

'Have they got him?'

'Tyad, listen. They can't. There's a problem.'

'What's going on?'

'They . . . They don't think he's in Ul Qoma.'

'He crossed? We need to talk to Besźel border patrol then—'

'No, *listen*. They *can't tell* where he is.'

'. . . What? What? What the hell's he doing?'

'He's just . . . He's been standing there, just outside the entrance, in full view, and then when he saw them moving towards him he started walking . . . but the way he's moving . . . the clothes he's wearing . . . they *can't tell* whether he's in Ul Qoma or Besźel.'

'Just check if he passed through before it closed.'

'Tyad, it's fucking chaos here. No one's been keeping track of the paperwork or the computer or whatever, so we don't know if he did or not.'

'You have to get them to—'

'Tyad, listen to me. It was all I could do to get that out of them. They're fucking terrified that even seeing him and saying *that's* breach, and they're not fucking wrong because you know what? It might be. Tonight of all nights. Breach are all over the place; there was just a fucking *closure*, Tyad. The last thing anyone's going to do is risk breaching. That's the last information you're going to get unless Bowden moves so they can tell he's definitely in Ul Qoma.'

'Where is he now?'

349

'How can I know? They won't risk watching him. All they'd say was that he started walking. Just walking, but so no one can tell where he is.'

'No one's stopping him?'

'They don't even know if they can *see* him. But he's not breaching either. They just . . . can't tell.' Pause. 'Tyad?'

'Jesus Christ, of course. He's been *waiting* for someone to notice him.'

I sped the car towards Copula Hall. It was several miles away. I swore.

'What? Tyad, what?'

'This is what he wants. You said it yourself, Dhatt; he'll be turned back from the border by the guard of whichever city he's in. Which is?'

There were seconds of silence. 'Fuck me,' Dhatt said. In that uncertain state, no one would stop Bowden. No one could.

'Where are you? How close are you to Copula Hall?'

'I can be there in ten minutes, but—'

But he would not stop Bowden either. Agonised as Dhatt was, he would not risk Breach by seeing a man who might not be in his city. I wanted to tell him not to be concerned, I wanted to beg him, but could I tell him he was wrong? I did not know he would not be watched. Could I say he was safe?

'Would the *militsya* arrest him on your say-so if he was definitely in Ul Qoma?'

'Sure, but they won't follow him if they can't risk seeing him.'

'Then you go. Dhatt, please. Listen. Nothing's stopping you just going for a walk, right? Just going out there to Copula Hall and going wherever you want, and if it happens that someone

350

who happens to be always in your vicinity tips a hand and turns out to be in Ul Qoma, then you could arrest him, right?' No one had to admit a thing, even to themselves. So long as there was no interaction while Bowden was unclear, there would be plausible deniability. 'Please, Dhatt.'

'Alright. But listen, if I'm going for a fucking walk and someone in my maybe-grosstopic proximity does *not* turn out for *certain* into Ul Qoma, then I can't arrest him.'

'Hold on. You're right.' I could not ask him to risk breaching. And Bowden might have crossed and be Besźel, in which case Dhatt was powerless. 'Okay. Go for your walk. Let me know when you're at Copula Hall. I have to make another call.'

I disconnected and dialled another number, also without an international code, though it was in another country. Despite the hour the phone was answered almost immediately, and the voice that answered was alert.

'Corwi,' I said.

'Boss? Jesus, *boss*, where *are* you? What's happening? Are you okay? What's going on?'

'Corwi. I'll tell you everything, but right now I can't; right now I need you to move, and move fast, and not ask any questions and to just do exactly as I say. I need you to go to Copula Hall.'

I CHECKED MY WATCH and glanced at the sky, which seemed resistant to morning. In their respective cities Dhatt and Corwi were on their way to the border. It was Dhatt who called me first.

'I'm here, Borlú.'

'Can you see him? Have you found him? Where is he?' Silence. 'Alright, Dhatt, listen.' He would not see what he was not sure was in Ul Qoma, but he would not have called me had there been no point to the contact. 'Where are you?'

'I'm at the corner of Illya and Suhash.'

'Jesus, I wish I knew how to do conference calls on this thing. I've got call waiting figured, so stay on the damn phone.' I connected to Corwi. 'Corwi? Listen.' I had to pull up by the kerb and compare the map of Ul Qoma in the car's glove compartment with my knowledge of Beszel. Most of the Old Towns were crosshatched. 'Corwi, I need you to go to ByulaStrász and . . . and WarszaStrász. You've seen the photos of Bowden, right?'

'Yeah. . .'

'I know, I know.' I drove. 'If you're not sure he's in Beszel you won't touch him. Like I said, I'm just asking you to go walking so that if anyone *were* to turn out to be in Beszel, you could arrest him. And tell me where you are. Okay? Careful.'

'Of what, boss?'

It was a point. Bowden would not likely attack either Dhatt or Corwi: do so and he would declare himself a criminal, in Beszel or Ul Qoma. Attack both and he would be in Breach, which, unbelievably, he was not yet. He walked with equipoise, possibly in either city. Schrödinger's pedestrian.

'Where are you, Dhatt?'

'Halfway up Teipei Street.' Teipei shared its space grosstopically with MirandiStrász in Beszel. I told Corwi where to go. 'I won't be long.' I was over the river now, and the number of vehicles on the street was increasing.

'Dhatt, where is he? Where are you, I mean?' He told me. Bowden had to stick to crosshatched streets. If he trod on a total area, he'd be committing to that city, and its police could take him. In the centres the most ancient streets were too

352

narrow and twisted for the car to save me any time and I deserted it, running through the cobbles and overhanging eaves of Besźel Old Town by the intricate mosaics and vaults of Ul Qoma Old Town. 'Move!' I shouted at the few people in my way. I held out the Breach sigil, the phone in my other hand.

'I'm at the end of MirandiStrász, boss.' Corwi's voice had changed. She would not admit she could see Bowden – she did not, nor quite did she unsee him, she was between the two – but she was no longer simply following my directions. She was close to him. Perhaps he could see her.

One more time I examined Ashil's gun, but it made little sense to me. I could not work it. I returned it to my pocket, went to where Corwi waited in Besźel, Dhatt in Ul Qoma, and to where Bowden walked no one was quite sure where.

I SAW DHATT FIRST. He was in his full uniform, his arm in a sling, his phone to his ear. I tapped him on the shoulder as I passed him. He started massively, saw it was me, and gasped. He closed his phone slowly and indicated a direction with his eyes, for the briefest moment. He stared at me with an expression I was not sure I recognised.

The glance was not necessary. Though a small number of people were braving the overlapping crosshatched street, Bowden was instantly visible. That gait. Strange, impossible. Not properly describable, but to anyone used to the physical vernaculars of Besźel and Ul Qoma, it was rootless and untethered, purposeful and without a country. I saw him from behind. He did not drift but strode with pathological neutrality away from the cities' centres, ultimately to borders and the mountains and out to the rest of the continent.

353

In front of him a few curious locals were seeing him then with clear uncertainty half looking away, unsure where, in fact, to look. I pointed at them, each in turn, and made a *go* motion, and they went. Perhaps some watched from their windows, but that was deniable. I approached Bowden under the looming of Beszel and the intricate coiled gutters of Ul Qoma.

A few metres from him, Corwi watched me. She put her phone away and drew her weapon, but still would not look directly at Bowden, just in case he was not in Beszel. Perhaps we were watched by Breach, somewhere. Bowden had not yet transgressed for their attention: they could not touch him.

I held out my hand as I walked, and I did not slow down, but Corwi gripped it and we met each other's gaze a moment. Looking back I saw her and Dhatt, metres apart in different cities, staring at me. It was really dawn at last.

'BOWDEN.'

He turned. His face was set. Tense. He held something the shape of which I could not make out.

'Inspector Borlú. Fancy meeting you . . . here?' He tried to grin but it did not go well.

'Where's here?' I said. He shrugged. 'It's really impressive, what you're doing,' I said. He shrugged again, with a mannerism neither Besz nor Ul Qoman. It would take him a day or more of walking, but Beszel and Ul Qoma are small countries. He could do it, walk out. How expert a citizen, how consummate an urban dweller and observer, to mediate those million unnoticed mannerisms that marked out civic specificity, to refuse either aggregate of behaviours. He aimed with whatever it was he held.

'If you shoot me Breach'll be on you.'

354

'If they're watching,' he said. 'I think probably you're the only one here. There are centuries of borders to shore up, after tonight. And even if they are, it's a moot question. What kind of crime would it be? Where are *you*?'

'You tried to cut her face off.' That ragged under-chin slit. 'Did you . . . No, it was hers, it was her knife. You couldn't though. So you slathered on her makeup instead.' He blinked, said nothing. 'As if that would disguise her. What is that?' He showed the thing to me, a moment, before gripping and aiming it again. It was some verdigrised metal object, age-gnarled and ugly. It was clicking. It was patched with new metal bands.

'It broke. When I.' It did not sound as if he hesitated: his words simply stopped.

'. . . Jesus, that's what you hit her with. When you realised she knew it was lies.' Grabbed and flailed, a moment's rage. He could admit to anything now. So long as he remained in his superposition, whose law would take him? I saw that the thing's handle, that he held, that pointed towards him, ended in an ugly sharp spike. 'You grab it, smack her, she goes down.' I made stab motions. 'Heat of the moment,' I said. 'Right? Right?'

'So did you not know how to fire it, then? Are they true, then?' I said. 'All those 'strange physics' rumours? Is *that* one of the things Sear and Core were after? Sending one of their ranking visitors sightseeing, scuffing their heels in the park for? Just another tourist?'

'I wouldn't call it a gun,' he said. 'But . . . well, want to see what it can do?' He wagged it.

'Not tempted to sell it on yourself?' He looked offended. 'How do you know what it does?'

355

'I'm an archaeologist and an historian,' he said. 'And I'm incredibly good at it. And now I'm going.'

'Walking out of the city?' He inclined his head. 'Which city?' He wagged his weapon *no*.

'I didn't mean to, you know,' he said. 'She was . . .' That time his words dried up. He swallowed.

'She must have been angry. To realise how you'd been lying to her.'

'I always told the truth. You *heard* me, Inspector. I told you many times. There's no such place as Orciny.'

'Did you flatter her? Did you tell her she was the only one you could admit the truth to?'

'Borlú, I can kill you where you stand and, do you realise, no one will even know where we are. If you were in one place or the other they might come for me, but you're *not*. The thing is, and I know it wouldn't work this way and so do you but that's because *no one* in this place, and that includes Breach, obeys the rules, their own rules, and if they did it *would* work this way, the thing is that if you were to be killed by someone who no one was sure which city they were in and they weren't sure where *you* were either, your body would have to lie there, rotting, forever. People would have to step over you. Because no one breached. Neither Besźel nor Ul Qoma could risk clearing you up. You'd lie there stinking up both cities until you were just a stain. I am going, Borlú. You think Besźel will come for you if I shoot you? Ul Qoma?' Corwi and Dhatt must have heard him, even if they made to unhear. Bowden looked only at me and did not move.

'My, well, Breach, my partner, was right,' I said. 'Even if Buric could have thought this up, he didn't have the expertise or the patience to put it together so it would have fooled

Mahalia. She was smart. That took someone who knew the archives and the secrets and the Orciny rumours not just a bit but totally. Completely. You told the truth, like you say: there's no such place as Orciny. You said it again and again. That was the point, wasn't it?

'It wasn't Buric's idea, was it? After that conference where she made such a nuisance of herself? It certainly wasn't Sear and Core – they would have hired someone to smuggle more efficiently, a little nickel-and-dime operation like that, they just went along with an opportunity that was presented. Sure you needed Buric's resources to make it work, and he wasn't going to turn down a chance to steal from Ul Qoma, pimp Besźel out – how much investment was tied to this? – *and* make a mint for himself. But it was your idea, and it was never about the money.

'It was because you missed Orciny. A way to have it both ways. Yes, sure you were wrong about Orciny, but you could make it so you were right, too.'

Choice artefacts had been excavated, the details of which only the archaeologists could know – or those who had left them there, as poor Yolanda had thought. Supposed-Orciny sent their supposed-agent sudden instructions, not to be delayed, no time to think or rethink – only, quickly, liberate, hand over.

'You told Mahalia she was the only one you'd tell the truth. That when you turned your back on your book, that was just you playing politics? Or did you tell her it was cowardice? That would be pretty winning. I bet you did that.' I approached him. His expression shifted. '"It's my shame, Mahalia, the pressure was too much. You're braver than me, keep on; you're so close, you'll find it . . ." Your shit messed up your whole career, and you can't have that time back. So the next best thing, make it have been true all along. I'm sure the money was nice – can't tell me they didn't pay – and Buric had his reasons and Sear and Core had theirs, and the nats'll do for anyone with a way with words and a buck. But it was *Orciny* that was the point for you, right?

'But Mahalia figured out that it was nonsense, Doctor Bowden.'

How much more perfect that unhistory would be, second time around, when he could construct the evidence not only from fragments in archives, not from the cross-reference of mis-understood documents, but could add to those planted sources, suggest partisan texts, even create messages – to himself, too, for her benefit and later for ours, that all the while he could dismiss as the nothings they were – from the nonplace itself. But still she worked out the truth.

'That must have been unpleasant for you,' I said.

His eyes were unhitched from wherever we were. 'It got . . . That's why.' She told him her deliveries – so all secret payments – would end. That was not why his rage.

'Did she think you were fooled too? Or did she realise you were behind it?' It was amazing that such a detail should almost be epiphenomenal. 'I think she didn't know. It wasn't her character to taunt you. I think she thought she was *protecting* you. I think she arranged to meet you, to protect you. To tell you that you'd both been duped by someone. That you were both in danger.'

The rage of that attack. The task, that post-facto vindication of a dead project, destroyed. No point scoring, no competition. Just the pure fact that Mahalia had, without even knowing it, outsmarted him, realised that his invention was invention, despite his attempts to seal up the creation, to watertight it. She crushed him without guile or bile. The evidence destroyed his conception again, the improved version, Orciny 2.0, as it had the last time, when he had actually believed it. Mahalia died because she proved to Bowden that he had been a fool to believe the folktale he created.

'What is that thing? Did she . . .?' But she could not have got that out, and had she delivered it it would not be with him.

'I've had this for years,' he said. '*This* I found myself. When I was first digging. Security wasn't always like now.'

'Where did you meet her? A bullshit *dissensus*? Some old empty bollocks building you told her was where Orciny did their magic?' It did not matter. The murder site would just be some empty place.

'. . . Would you believe me if I told you I really don't remember the actual moment?' he said carefully.

'Yes.'

'Just this constant, this . . .' Reasoning, that broke his creation apart. He might have shown her the artefact as if it were evidence. *It s not Orciny!* she perhaps said. *We have to think! Who might want this stuff?* The fury at that.

'You broke it.'

'Not irreparably. It's tough. The artefacts are tough.' Despite being used to beat her to death.

'It was a good idea to take her through the checkpoint.'

'When I called him Buric wasn't happy sending the driver, but he understood. It's never been *militsya* or *policzai* that are the problem. We couldn't let Breach notice us.'

'But your maps are out of date. I saw it on your desk, that time. All that junk you or Yorj picked up – was that from where you killed her? – was useless.'

'When did they build that skate park?' For a moment he managed to make it sound as if he was genuinely humourous about it. 'That was supposed to be direct to the estuary.' Where the old iron would pull her down.

'Didn't Yorjavic know his way around? It's his city. Some soldier.'

'He never had reason to go to Pocost. I hadn't been over since the conference. I bought that map I gave him years ago, and it was right last time I was there.'

'But goddamn urban renewal, right? There he was, van all loaded up, and there's ramps and half-pipes between him and the water, and light's coming. When that went wrong, that was when Buric and you . . . fell out.'

'Not really. We had words, but we thought it had blown over. No, what got him troubled was when *you* came to Ul Qoma,' he said. 'That was when he realised there was trouble.'

'So . . . in a way I owe you an apology . . .' He tried to shrug. Even that motion was urbanly undecidable. He kept swallowing but his tics gave away nothing about where he was.

'If you like,' he said. 'That's when he set his True Citizens on hunt. Even tried to get you blaming Qoma First, with that bomb. And I think he thought *I* believed it, too.' Bowden looked disgusted. 'He must've heard about the time it happened before.'

'For real. All those notes you wrote in Precursor, threatening yourself to get us off you. Fake burglaries. Added to your Orciny.' How he looked at me, I stopped myself saying *Your bullshit*. 'What about Yolanda?'

'I'm . . . really sorry about her. Buric must have thought she and I were . . . that Mahalia or I'd told her something.'

'You hadn't, though. Nor did Mahalia – she protected her

360

from all that. In fact Yolanda was the only one who believed in Orciny all the way along. She was your biggest fan. Her and Aikam.' He stared, his face cold. He knew that neither of them were the smartest. I did not say anything for a minute.

'Christ you're a liar, Bowden,' I said. 'Even now, Jesus. Do you think I don't know it was you who told Buric Yolanda'd be there?' I spoke and I could hear his shaking breath. 'You sent them there in case of what she knew. Which as I say was nothing. You had her killed for nothing. But why did *you* come? You knew they'd try to kill you too.' We faced each other for a long silence.

'. . . You needed to be sure, didn't you?' I said. 'And so did they.'

They wouldn't send out Yorjavic and organise that extraordinary cross-border assassination for Yolanda alone. They did not even know for sure what if anything she knew. Bowden, though: they knew what he knew. Everything.

They thought I believed it too, he had said. 'You told them she'd be there, and that you were coming too because Qoma First were trying to kill you. Did they really think you'd believed it? . . . But they could check, couldn't they?' I answered myself. 'By if you turned up. You *had* to be there, or they'd know they were being played. If Yorjavic hadn't seen you he'd have known you were planning something. He had to have both targets there.' Bowden's strange gait and manner at the hall. 'So you had to turn up and try and keep someone in his way . . .' I stopped. 'Were there three targets?' I said. I was the reason it had gone wrong, after all. I shook my head.

'You knew they'd try to kill you, but it was worth the risk to get rid of her. Camouflage.' Who would suspect him of complicity, after Orciny tried to kill him?

He had a slowly souring face. 'Where is Buric?'

'Dead.'

'Good. Good . . .'

I stepped towards him. He pointed the artefact at me like some stubby Bronze Age wand.

'What do you care?' I said. 'What are you going to do? How long have you lived in the cities? Now what?

'It's over. Orciny's rubble.' Another step, he still aiming at me, mouth-breathing and eyes wide. 'You've got one option. You've been to Besźel. You've lived in Ul Qoma. There's one place left. Come on. You going to live anonymous in Istanbul? In Sebastopol? Make it to Paris? You think that's going to be enough?

'Orciny is bullshit. Do you want to see what's really in between?'

A second held. He hesitated long enough for some appearance.

Nasty broken man. The only thing more despicable than what he had done was the half-hidden eagerness with which he now took me up on my offer. It was not bravery on his part to come with me. He held out that heavy weapon thing to me and I took it. It rattled. The bulb full of gears, the old clockworks that had cut Mahalia's head when the metal burst.

He sagged, with some moan: apology, plea, relief. I was not listening and don't remember. I did not arrest him – I was not *policzai*, not then, and Breach do not arrest – but I had him, and exhaled, because it was over.

BOWDEN HAD STILL NOT COMMITTED to where he was. I said, 'Which city are you in?' Dhatt and Corwi were close, ready, and whichever shared a locus with him would come forward when he said.

362

'Either,' he said.

So I grabbed him by the scruff, turned him, marched him away. Under the authority I'd been granted, I dragged Breach with me, enveloped him in it, pulled him out of either town into neither, into the Breach. Corwi and Dhatt watched me take him out of either of their reaches. I nodded thanks to them across their borders. They would not look at each other, but both nodded to me.

It occurred as I led Bowden shuffling with me that the breach I had been empowered to pursue, that I was still investigating and of which he was evidence, was still my own.

CODA

BREACH

CHAPTER TWENTY-NINE

I DID NOT SEE THAT MACHINE AGAIN. It was funnelled into the bureaucracy of Breach. I never saw whatever it was it could do, whatever Sear and Core wanted, or if it could do anything.

Ul Qoma in the aftermath of Riot Night was buoyed up with tension. The *militsya*, even after the remaining unifs had been cleared out or arrested, or hidden their patches and disappeared, kept up high-profile, intrusive policing. Civil libertarians complained. Ul Qoma's government announced a new campaign, Vigilant Neighbours, neighbourliness referring both to the people next door (what were they doing?) and to the connected city (see how important borders are?).

In Besźel the night led to a kind of exaggerated mutedness. It became almost bad luck to mention it. The newspapers massively played it down. Politicians, if they said anything, made circuitous mention of *recent stresses* or similar. But there was a pall. The city was subdued. Its unif population was as depleted, the remnants as careful and out of sight, as in Ul Qoma.

Both cleanups were fast. The Breach closure lasted thirty-six hours and was not mentioned again. The night led to twenty-two deaths in Ul Qoma, thirteen in Besźel, not including the refugees who died after the initial accidents, nor the disappeared. Now there were more foreign journalists in both sets of streets, doing more and less subtle follow-up reports. They made regular attempts to arrange an interview – 'anonymous, of course' – with representatives of Breach.

'Has anyone from Breach ever broken ranks?' I said.

'Of course,' said Ashil. 'But then they're breaching, they're in-siles, and they're ours.' He walked carefully, and wore bandages below his clothes and his hidden armour.

The first day after the riots, when I returned to the office dragging a semicompliant Bowden with me, I was locked into my cell. But the door had been unlocked since then. I had spent three days with Ashil, since his release from whatever hidden hospital it was where Breach received care. Each day he spent in my company, we walked the cities, in the Breach. I was learning from him how to walk between them, first in one, then the other, or in either, but without the ostentation of Bowden's extraordinary motion – a more covert equivocation.

'How could he do it? Walk like that?'

'He's been a student of the cities,' Ashil said. 'Maybe it took an outsider to really see how citizens mark themselves, so as to walk between it.'

'Where is he?' I had asked Ashil this many times. He evaded answering in various ways. That time he said, as he had before, 'There are mechanisms. He's taken care of.'

It was overcast and dark, lightly raining. I turned up the collar of my coat. We were west of the river, by the cross-hatched rails, a short stretch of tracks used by the trains of both cities, the timetable agreed internationally.

'But the thing is, he never breached.' I had not voiced this anxiety to Ashil before. He turned to look at me, massaged his injury. 'Under what authority was he . . . How can we have him?'

Ashil walked us around the environs of the Bol Ye'an dig. I could hear the trains in Besźel, north of us, in Ul Qoma to the south. We would not go in, or even near enough to Bol Ye'an to be seen, but Ashil was walking through the various stages of the case, without saying so.

'I mean,' I said, 'I know Breach doesn't answer to anyone, but it . . . you have to present reports. Of all your cases. To the Oversight Committee.' He raised an eyebrow at that. 'I know, I know they've been discredited because of Buric, but their line's that that was the makeup of the members, right, not the committee itself. The checks and balances between the cities and Breach is still the same, right? They have a point, don't you think? So you'll have to justify taking Bowden.'

'No one cares about Bowden,' he said at last. 'Not Ul Qoma, not Besźel, not Canada, not Orciny. But yes, we'll present a form to them. Maybe, after he dumped Mahalia, he got back into Ul Qoma by Breach.'

'He didn't dump her; it was Yorj—' I said.

'Maybe that's how he did it,' Ashil continued. 'We'll see. Maybe we'll push him into Besźel and pull him back to Ul Qoma. If we say he breached, he breached.' I looked at him.

Mahalia was gone. Her body had at last gone home. Ashil told me on the day her parents held her funeral.

Sear and Core had not left Besźel. It would risk attention to pull out after the creeping, confused revelations of Buric's behaviour. The company and its tech arm had come up, but the chains of connection were vague. Buric's possible contact was a regrettable unknown, and mistakes had been made,

369

safeguards were being put in place. There were rumours that CorIntech would be sold.

Ashil and I went by tram, by Metro, by bus, by taxi, we walked. He threaded us like a suture in and out of Besźel and Ul Qoma.

'What about my breach?' I asked it at last. We had both been waiting for days. I did not ask *When do I get to go back home?* We took the funicular to the top of the park named for it, in Besźel at least.

'If he'd had an up-to-date map of Besźel you'd never have found her,' Ashil said. 'Orciny.' He shook his head.

'Do you see any children in the Breach?' he said. 'How would that work? If any were born—'

'They must be,' I interrupted, but he talked over me. '— how could they live here?' The clouds over the cities were dramatic, and I watched them, rather than him, and pictured children given up. 'You know how I was made Breach,' he suddenly said.

'When do I get to go home?' I said pointlessly. He even smiled at that.

'You did an excellent job. You've seen how we work. Nowhere else works like the cities,' he said. 'It's not just us keeping them apart. It's everyone in Besźel and everyone in Ul Qoma. Every minute, every day. We're only the last ditch: it's everyone in the cities who does most of the work. It works because you don't blink. That's why unseeing and unsensing are so vital. No one can admit it doesn't work. So if you don't admit it, it does. But if you breach, even if it's not your fault, for more than the shortest time . . . you can't come back from that.'

'Accidents. Road accidents, fires, inadvertent breaches . . .'

'Yes. Of course. If you race to get out again. If that's your response to the Breach, then maybe you've got a chance. But even then you're in trouble. And if it's any longer than a moment, you can't get out again. You'll never unsee again. Most people who breach, well, you'll find out about our sanctions soon. But there is another possibility, very occasionally.

'What do you know about the British Navy?' Ashil said. 'A few centuries ago?' I looked at him. 'I was recruited the same as everyone else in Breach. None of us were born here. We were all once in one place or the other. All of us breached once.'

There were many minutes of silence between us. 'There are people I'd like to call,' I said.

HE WAS RIGHT. I imagined myself in Besźel now, unseeing the Ul Qoma of the crosshatched terrain. Living in half of the space. Unseeing all the people and the architecture and vehicles and the everything in and among which I had lived. I could pretend, perhaps, at best, but something would happen, and Breach would know.

'It was a big case,' he said. 'The biggest ever. You'll never have so big a case again.'

'I'm a detective,' I said. 'Jesus. Do I have any choice?'

'Of course,' he said. 'You're here. There's Breach, and there's those who breach, those to whom we happen.' He did not look at me but out over the overlapping cities.

'Are any volunteers?'

'Volunteering's an early and strong indication that you're not suited,' he said.

We walked towards my old flat, my press-ganger and I.

'Can I say good-bye to anyone? There are people I want to—'

371

'No,' he said. We walked.

'I'm a detective,' I said again. 'Not a, whatever. I don't work like you do.'

'That's what we want. That's why we were so glad you breached. Times are changing.'

So the methods may not be so unfamiliar as I feared. There may be others who proceed the traditional Breach way, the levering of intimidation, that self-styling as a night-fear, while I – using the siphoned-off information we filch online, the bugged phone calls from both cities, the networks of inform-ants, the powers beyond any law, the centuries of fear, yes, too, sometimes, the intimations of other powers beyond us, of unknown shapes, that we are only avatars – was to investigate, as I have investigated for years. A new broom. Every office needs one. There's a humour to the situation.

'I want to see Sariska. You know who she is, I guess. And Biszaya. I want to talk to Corwi, and Dhatt. To say good-bye at least.'

He was quiet for a while. 'You can't talk to them. This is how we work. If we don't have that, we don't have anything. But you can see them. If you stay out of sight.'

We compromised. I wrote letters to my erstwhile lovers. Handwritten and delivered by hand, but not by my hand. I did not tell Sariska or Biszaya anything but that I would miss them. I was not just being kind.

My colleagues I came close to, and though I did not speak to them, both of them could see me. But Dhatt in Ul Qoma, and later Corwi in Besźel, could tell I was not, or not totally, or not only, in their city. They did not speak to me. They would not risk it.

Dhatt I saw as he emerged from his office. He stopped short

372

at the sight of me. I stood by a hoarding outside an Ul Qoman office, with my head down so he could tell it was me but not my expression. I raised my hand to him. He hesitated a long time then spread his fingers, a waveless wave. I backed into the shadows. He walked away first.

Corwi was at a café. She was in Besźel's Ul Qomatown. She made me smile. I watched her drinking her creamy Ul Qoman tea in the establishment I had shown her. I watched her from the shade of an alley for several seconds before I realised that she was looking right at me, that she knew I was there. It was she who said good-bye to me, with a raised cup, tipped in salute. I mouthed at her, though even she could not have seen it, thanks, and good-bye.

I have a great deal to learn, and no choice but to learn it, or to go rogue, and there is no one hunted like a Breach rene-gade. So, not ready for that or the revenge of my new community of bare, extra-city lives, I make my choice of those two nonchoices. My task is changed: not to uphold the law, or another law, but to maintain the skin that keeps law in place. Two laws in two places, in fact.

That is the end of the case of Orciny and the archaeolo-gists, the last case of Inspector Tyador Borlú of the Besźel Extreme Crime Squad. Inspector Tyador Borlú is gone. I sign off Tye, avatar of Breach, following my mentor on my proba-tion out of Besźel and out of Ul Qoma. We are all philosophers here where I am, and we debate among many other things the question of where it is that we live. On that issue I am a lib-eral. I live in the interstice yes, but I live in both the city and the city.